To
Chris

Just

One Day

SUMMER

Thanks for the quote
for the cover and
your friendship generally!
Love
Sooz

Susan Buchanan
x

Also by Susan Buchanan

Sign of the Times

The Dating Game

The Christmas Spirit

Return of the Christmas Spirit

Just One Day – Winter

Just One Day – Spring

Just One Day

SUMMER

SUSAN BUCHANAN

Copyright

First published in 2022 by Susan Buchanan

Copyright © 2022 Susan Buchanan
Print Edition

Susan Buchanan has asserted her right to be identified as the author
of this Work in accordance with the Copyright, Designs and Patents
Act 1988.

This novel is a work of fiction. Names and characters are the
product of the author's imagination and any resemblance to actual
persons, living or dead, is entirely coincidental.

All rights reserved. No part of this publication may be reproduced,
stored in a retrieval system, or transmitted in any form or by any
means, electronic, mechanical, photocopying, recording or
otherwise, without the prior permission of the copyright owner.

A CIP catalogue record of this title is available from the
British Library
Paperback – 978-1-915589-00-2

Dedication

For Auntie Cathy and Uncle Hughie, who represented everything that a family should be.

And for Gloria Maguire. Taken too soon, never forgotten. Gloria, if you're watching from up there, I hope you like Dolores.

Love always
Susan xxx

About the Author

Susan Buchanan lives in Scotland with her husband, their two young children and a crazy Labrador called Benji. She has been reading since the age of four and had to get an adult library card early as she had read the entire children's section by the age of ten. As a freelance book editor, she has books for breakfast, lunch and dinner and in her personal reading always has several books on the go at any one time.

If she's not reading, editing or writing, she's thinking about it. She loves romantic fiction, psychological thrillers, crime fiction and legal thrillers, but her favourite books feature books themselves.

In her past life, she worked in International Sales as she speaks five languages. She has travelled to 51 countries and her travel knowledge tends to pop up in her writing. Collecting books on her travels, even in languages she doesn't speak, became a bit of a hobby.

Susan writes contemporary fiction, often partly set in Scotland, usually featuring travel, food or Christmas. When not working, writing, or caring for her two delightful cherubs, Susan loves reading (obviously), the theatre, quiz shows and eating out – not necessarily in that order!

You can connect with Susan via her website www.susanbuchananauthor.com or on Facebook facebook.com/susan.buchanan.author Twitter @susan_buchanan and on Instagram @AuthorSusanBuchanan

Acknowledgements

Thanks go to

Antonia and Luke for losing valuable Mummy/girl and Mummy/boy time whilst I raced to meet this deadline

Wendy Janes for being generally awesome and stepping in to edit at short notice, due to unforeseen circumstances, and for always going above and beyond – www.wendyproof.co.uk

Claire at Jaboof Design Studio – no words needed. Look at the cover. My favourite of the Just One Day series so far – claire@jaboofdesignstudio.com

Trish Long for proofreading – trishlong3ok@gmail.com

Paul Salvette and his team at BBeBooks Thailand for formatting and having the speediest turnaround and most professional manner ever – www.bbebooksthailand.com

Catherine Ferguson, Wendy Janes and Barbara Wilkie for agreeing to be beta readers

My ever-expanding Advance Review team

Author Anita Faulkner for being such a fabulous cheerleader of my work and for providing the front cover quote for Spring

Authors Jo Thomas, Anne Booth, Anita Chapman and Clare Swatman for encouragement.

Christie Barlow for providing Summer's cover quote

Rachel's Random Resources for my fabulous cover reveals and blog tours for this series, and for engaging all the wonderful bloggers – thanks to them too

Margaret Haggerty, my wee sis, who will always tell me how it is, and for her help

And Dad, thanks so much for finally reading my work and devouring the Just One Day series so far. Now I just need to get you invested in the backlist!

Thanks to the following Facebook groups:

Lizzie's Book Group, run by the amazing Lizzie Chantree, for constant support

The Word Wranglers

The Friendly Book Community

Chick Lit and Prosecco, run by Anita Faulkner

Fiona Jenkins and Sue Baker for organising my launch day party

And thanks to all my readers for their wonderful comments about the series, and for investing in it. I hope you love Summer.

Chapter One

Wednesday 30 June

To-do list

Remember midwife appointment

Check if need to register with a new practice whilst we're living at Garfield Grange

Buy new sunglasses for Aria – others have split. Don't buy supermarket ones. They don't last.

'Mr and Mrs Halliday?'

I turn to Ronnie. 'That's right.'

'And how pregnant are we?'

'I'm about three to four weeks pregnant, I think. I did a test, and it came up three-plus weeks.'

'Excellent. That means you're actually about five weeks pregnant.' The midwife makes a note on her chart. 'And, I see this isn't your first rodeo.' She smiles.

'No, this is our fourth child.'

'So, it's five years since you were last pregnant.'

It seems to be a statement rather than a question, so I say nothing.

'As you'll be forty by the time you have the baby, we need to term you a geriatric mother.'

Normally, I wouldn't take umbrage at anything to do with my age, but it's difficult not to feel riled at being lumped into the past-it bracket, almost like I'm being put out to pasture.

'And what does that mean exactly?' An edge has crept into my voice, and Ronnie looks at me sharply.

'Well,' says the midwife, a little taken aback – clearly no one questions her normally '–it just means we'll have to keep a better track on how things are with Mum.'

'Ri-i-ight,' I say, drawing out the word. Hopefully, I've done enough to make it clear to her that she's clarified absolutely nothing and she needs to elaborate. However, she skips right over it and starts talking about diet and exercise and things to avoid – all the stuff I know, having gone through three pregnancies already.

Ronnie sits there as useful as a hammer when trying to eat a jar of Nutella. He's beginning to irritate me. I feel, unreasonably, that he should be asking questions. It's not all down to me. He should have jumped in there and said, 'Excuse me, no, I don't understand.' Instead, nothing.

She tells me a letter will be sent out, with my scan appointment around twelve weeks, but it could be between eleven and thirteen – nothing new there then. I thought what with me being a geriatric mother and all, they'd have to get me in for an earlier one. I'm not quite so annoyed with her now. She has left it on a high note, but I'm hoping she's a locum midwife and I'll have someone I know next time. I mean, c'mon, it's a village. How come I get the one person I don't know and who doesn't live here? Not that I intend to be unfair to her, but she needs to work on her bedside manner – patronising – and her ability to listen when people ask questions, and then answer, rather than simply parroting platitudes.

'Oh, and I almost forgot.' She inputs something into her system then announces, 'Due date of around the twenty-seventh of February.'

Great. Like it was an afterthought.

'That was useful, wasn't it?' Ronnie says. 'She was really nice.'

I hate that word. Nice. At school, my English teacher always told me to use any other adjective – positive, naturally – to replace nice. Nice was boring, bland and quite frankly, I have to agree.

The phrase 'geriatric mother' whirls around in my brain, and I wonder if my husband was in the same consultation as me. 'Hmm,' I say noncommittally, as he takes my hand whilst we walk back to our car, which we've parked on the other side of the village, the Hamwell end.

We parked there so we could walk past our house on the way to the doctor's surgery. It was eerie to see our house so, well, damaged, after a lorry crashed through it last month, injuring Nicky and her son Xander. Seeing all the boarding and scaffolding was really upsetting, but passing by the little shops we've come to know and love over the past decade or so made my heart soar, and really caused me to think about exactly how important this village is to us, to me.

Yes, we've been lucky enough to be put up in a swanky, five-star country hotel by my new business partner, for as long as we need substitute accommodation, but I miss the neighbourly feel of the village, popping into the butcher's and asking after his cousin I used to go to school with; taking the kids to the library; dropping into the Café on the Cobblestones – I was only just getting used to that, since it's relatively new, but I love it. There are so many things, not least having Martha as a fabulous neighbour, albeit a fabulous neighbour who's only there half the year, since she winters in Australia, visiting her son. And she was marvellous after the accident – took care of us all, letting us stay at her house in the immediate aftermath.

On our way back through the village, an overwhelming urge to stop for coffee and cake comes over me. 'Ronnie, you OK if we nip into the bookshop and then grab something at Café on the Cobblestones before we head back to Wendy's?'

My sister, Wendy, is watching the kids, who are on school holidays. We've not told the kids about the baby yet, so we spun them a little white lie about needing to sort out something with the house.

It's Wendy's birthday today. She's turning forty-three. We're having a garden party. She took a bit of a chance with that one as it's not a given that you'll have fine weather in Glasgow in June, but from the look of the cloudless blue sky at the moment, her bet has paid off.

We're big on family parties in our clan, and we're quite the clan. Nine children between the three of us. Soon to be ten. I can still barely believe it. Much of it hasn't sunk in yet, what with having to rehome us, deal with all the agencies and companies involved in putting our house back together again, ensuring the kids haven't been too traumatised by the accident and visiting Nicky in hospital most days. To have the pregnancy revelation thrown into the mix just about tipped me over the edge. And it didn't help that my thoughts haven't solely been on my husband the past few months.

I haven't registered that Ronnie has said yes, until I see him standing in front of me, peering into my eyes, a look of worry on his face. 'Lou, is anybody home?' He smiles.

I shake my head as if to reorganise my thoughts. 'Sorry, I was miles away. Thinking about this place.' I throw my hands out to encompass the village. True. Although that's not all I was thinking about…

Once I've spent a good twenty minutes browsing in the Book Nook, catching up on the new releases and admiring the new displays, as well as having a natter to the owner, who is keen to check we're OK after the accident, I choose a Richard & Judy book club choice for Wendy as an extra birthday present.

Ronnie and I chat whilst we tuck into our coffee and cake at the café. I know Wendy won't mind us taking a little longer, even though it's her birthday. She's been on at me to take some time for me to process everything that has happened. Plus, there are some huge changes happening to us, not only the baby and the rehousing. Ronnie, finally, after more than a decade offshore, at the Callan oil rig, has made the decision to move to an onshore position, even though it may mean less money. So, I get my husband back, which right now is more valuable to me than anything, given my unexpected pregnancy. Maybe now he's onshore, he can actually get the snip too, as there is definitely not going to be a baby number five. I'm a geriatric mother, remember?

Ferniehall Park is situated at the farthest end of the village from our house, near the cobbled lane of Iona Wynd. It's quite a big park considering the size of the village, but its focal point is the nineteenth-century bandstand, which I love. I even remember when marching bands and pipe bands still performed at it, although that's going back a while.

It has a lovely duck pond as well as some ornate seating, white cast-iron benches, a couple of picnic tables and a little free book box library at the front near the gate. And of course, the prerequisite swings, slide and roundabout for the kids and some nodding horses that the toddlers can ride on. I've often thought they're more likely to maim a child as the springs on them are so, well, springy, that once a kid really gets going on, they're quite likely to launch themselves into next week.

And it's quite simply a relaxing haven. Not that there's too much hustle and bustle in our village, more from the traffic passing through, which makes a lorry using our village as a through road on a Saturday night an unusual choice. We've since been told the police are investigating this. I sigh. I just want my house back. Most of the time it doesn't seem real.

Finally, after we've strolled round the park and circled the bandstand a couple of times, I concede we do have to head back, to relieve my sister and to stop clinging to every vestige of the village. I can't help it. I miss it so much. I find it hard to believe quite how much, but I do. Maybe this is what happens when you work from home: the people in your immediate community become your colleagues, and you miss them when you no longer see them on a daily basis. For once, Ronnie seems to understand how I'm feeling – good, I'm pregnant, and I'm finding it all a little overwhelming. I know I'll manage, I know I'll rise to the occasion, but knowing Ronnie is here will make it so much easier. He puts his arm around my shoulders, and I lean into him, grateful for his support. We have a lot going on. Time to embrace it.

Chapter Two

'Wow, you guys have been busy,' Ronnie says as Wendy opens the front door to us. A riot of colour greets us, and I feel certain there has been much decoration-making done in our absence. Wendy is probably secretly counting to ten as she'd told me she planned to decorate the house tastefully, in an attempt to have one adult day out of three hundred and sixty-five. However, it looks like Brandon, her husband, hasn't managed to keep the children from embellishing the décor with their own flavour. I smile, whilst I simultaneously feel for my sister.

'So, how did it go?' she asks, as she ushers us in. She has one eyelash painted a glittery pink, one a powder blue, and she could audition for a part in Extreme Cheerleaders, she's wearing so much make-up. I have a strong sense this isn't her doing. I'll put her out of her misery soon and let her go clean up and change. Clearly, the kids, hers and mine, thought she needed brightening up. The mark of the pre-schoolers – of which there are currently three here – is strong.

I give Wendy a hug of solidarity, careful not to cover my blue and white gingham dress in her 'tasteful' make-up. 'Happy birthday, sis.' I hand her the bag with the book in it.

'You already gave me my present. Is that baby brain kicking in so soon?'

'Ha ha. No, I just saw this and thought you'd like it.'

She takes it out of the Book Nook bag and opens it. 'Ooh, thank you.' She hugs me. 'I've been wanting this for ages. I love anything set abroad. A girl from work recommended this. Said she went to Dubrovnik last year and read it whilst she was there. Really stayed with her, reading it where it was set. I must try and do that more often.'

'Noted. Next time I'll buy you some Ian Rankin books. They're set in Edinburgh.'

'Ha ha, I do travel sometimes, you know.'

'Yeah, but not out of the country. Those days are gone.'

Wendy sighs. 'Not forever. Just until I can get past the horrific image of flight delays and managing to cope with four young children at an airport.' She shudders and shakes her head as if trying to erase the image.

'I know what you mean. We still haven't been abroad, and Gen's twelve. I'm beginning to feel a bit guilty. Perhaps we should all "holiday" in France. Drive there, book a campsite.'

Wendy stares at me in horror, as if I've suggested she run stark naked through George Square in Glasgow city centre.

'Mummy, you're back!' Aria flings herself around my legs as if I've been gone for a three-week vacation in Montana and not a morning in Ferniehall. I do love that part, in particular, about my children: they're all very affectionate. Plus, I know that as they grow up, and need, and want me less, I'll think wistfully upon these days.

Hugo's excited squeal as he plays the PlayStation with his cousin Logan, I presume, emanates from one of the upstairs bedrooms. It's good the boys are so close in age, Logan nine and Hugo turning nine in August, especially since Aria has the twins and Mollie to play with. She's already scarpered back to the playroom to be with them. Gen is notable by her absence, both physical and audible. No doubt she'll be ensconced in one of the bedrooms, texting her friends, or FaceTiming them. The trends for teenagers, and almost teenagers, changes so quickly these days, with new apps, it is virtually impossible to keep up. It hits me that in two weeks, my baby will be a teenager. Surreal.

Since the kids all seem busy, and Ronnie has sneaked off, presumably to be with Brandon, I take some time just to 'be'. Lord knows I need to draw breath with everything that's going on.

But today is Wendy's birthday, and super-efficient businesswoman and amazing mum that she is, I'm going to make sure she takes a break for once.

'Wendy, coffee? Something stronger?'

'Ooh, yes, please. I've been meaning to stop for the past hour, but I seem to have bought more food for this barbecue than I originally thought. So much so, I'm beginning to wonder if Brandon secreted some extra kebabs in the main fridge whilst I wasn't looking.'

Brandon likes his food, and annoyingly is stick-thin. I'm not a huge fan of my brother-in-law. To be honest, I think my sister could have done better, and I really wish he would pull his weight, especially with Wendy getting her promotion. I just hope she puts her foot down with him as much as she does with me sometimes and doesn't take any of his shit.

Travis, on the other hand, is the brother-in-law of my dreams, apart from the fact he knows about Caden. Honestly, who could have predicted that the hunky chef I kissed on my birthday weekend away would end up being hired by my brother-in-law? Not that Travis knew at the time… Oh, anyway, it's a moot point now, since he's been promoted to head chef at Travis and his business partner Ayren's new restaurant in the Highlands.

Even though Travis has his own restaurant, he and my sister Jo share everything almost straight down the middle: childcare, housework, chauffeur duties. They make it work. I wonder if Ronnie and I will make it work better now he'll be on the mainland. I really hope he gets this job at Petrocord. It's hard to know who's more nervous, him or me.

The doorbell ringing interrupts my reverie as the Nespresso maker pours coffee into a cup.

Jo.

Our sister wafts in on a cloud of Mugler Aura, various gift bags in clashing colours draped over one arm. 'Happy birthday, sis.' She enfolds Wendy in her embrace, then turns to me. 'I'll have a macchiato today, please, since you're making it, Lou.' Jo is unbelievable. She always arrives at exactly the right moment and always seems to get out of doing things as a result. At least she has the common decency to smile, and give me a hug. Probably the most annoying thing about my other sister is that it's impossible to be cross with her for long. She has this *way* about her, that makes you feel bad if you don't do what she asks. Still annoying though, when you take a step back.

My niece Aurora and nephew Jackson tumble into the

room. 'Happy birthday, Aunt Wendy,' they chorus. They're so cute. They envelop her in hugs and kisses, then it's my turn. I'm not sure what Aurora has been eating, but I'm all sticky now. Setting her down on the floor, having scooped her up for a kiss, I make a mental note to stop doing that. I'm in my first trimester and can't take any chances. Especially not as I'm a geriatric mother. I feel that phrase may stay with me for some time.

Once the final two children of the day have run off to see their cousins, Wendy and I draw breath again. 'Coffee, Travis? Your good lady wife has already put in her order.'

Travis grins. 'Yes, please. Americano, to go, if possible.' That grin again. No wonder he makes a fabulous restaurateur. He definitely has the gift of the gab, and he is rather charming. It's unsurprising he swept Jo off her feet all those years ago. I love the fact he's so charismatic, and he gets on equally well with men and women. Although the men in our family tend to congregate in one room when we're all together, Travis often gravitates back to us, once he's had his fill of guy talk. But he always leaves us time first to have our little sisterly chinwag. He's so thoughtful. And I find myself comparing Ronnie unfavourably to him. Not that I'm attracted to Travis or anything, God no, but it would be nice to have that balanced relationship he and Jo have. And now it's something I can aspire to, what with Ronnie moving onshore.

'Open your presents then,' commands Jo, almost as excited as if it were her birthday.

I hand her coffee to her as she watches Wendy avidly.

Wendy opens the envelope first. 'Wow! A spa day at Cameron House. Thanks, Jo.'

Jo beams at her. 'The one in the pink bag next.'

She really is bossy, but like I said, it's impossible to take umbrage at her behaviour or tone.

'Ooh, a Marc Jacobs purse. Thank you, thank you.' She kisses Jo. 'And my old one is just that, old. Right, out with the old, in with the new,' she says, extracting her current purse from her handbag, which is under one of the stools, and emptying it of its contents, children's library cards and Young Scot passes spilling out onto the counter. Glad to see it's not only my purse which is full of kids' cards.

'Blue one next,' Jo orders.

Honestly, she's wasted as an accountant. She should have gone into the army.

The blue bag hides a blue, white and gold chiffon scarf, with swirls that look almost Daliesque. It's gorgeous, and I can't help coveting it.

'That's beautiful. Where did you get it, if you don't mind me asking?'

'Monsoon,' Jo says, then turns to Wendy. 'No, let me fix it. It's best worn like this. Or rather, it looks more appealing on you if you wear it this way. See?'

And once again, annoyingly she's right!

'Anyway, you can open the rest with the others later. You know they like to see some of the presents before we open them.'

'You mean, they like to open them for us?' Wendy corrects.

'Yeah, that's precisely what I mean.' Jo turns to me. 'Anyway–' she ensures the door's closed '–how did it go at the midwife?'

Now Wendy turns to me. 'Yes. I haven't had a chance to ask you yet. It's been like Piccadilly Circus in here the past half hour.'

'Fine,' I reply.

'Fine?' Wendy raises an eyebrow. 'Fine?'

Jo shakes her head. 'Yeah, "fine" is never a good answer. It basically means "not fine at all".'

I blow out a breath. 'OK, if you must know, the midwife was really condescending and called me a geriatric mother. And although I don't usually bother about things like that, for some reason, it hit a nerve, and I was pissed off.'

'Hormones,' Jo says sagely.

'Bloody cheek.' Wendy's colour has heightened at her indignation on my behalf.

'I didn't think they were allowed to use that term any more. Highly disrespectful. Outdated,' Jo says, staring off into the middle distance as if trying to think of another term to call it.

'That's right,' Wendy chips in. 'Isn't it something equally as offensive, like "of advanced maternal age"?'

Jo slaps her hand down on the worktop. 'That's it. I knew they weren't supposed to use "geriatric mother". I mean, do they call all the seventy-something men having kids, geriatric? No, they do not. So why should they call a woman over thirty-five, geriatric? Just another example of gross inequality.'

And she's off on one. Give Jo a soapbox and she'll rise to the occasion every time.

I try to draw a line under it so we can move on. 'Apparently, I'm due on the twenty-seventh of February, and because I'm a mother of advanced years–' I give them a wry look '–they may want to monitor me more often. Like a VIP club. Got to be some advantage, right?'

My sisters still both look irked at the 'of advanced

years' comment. Indignant on my behalf, if you will, but they say nothing for a moment, then both agree simultaneously that it's great they're monitoring me more, for reassurance.

'Anyway, shall we get this party started?'

'Too right! Where's the wine? Travis is driving as it's your birthday, Wen, and I hope Brandon is staying sober for the kids, so you can at least have a glass or two on your birthday.'

At Jo's words, Wendy gives a slight nod, which doesn't convince me. Polar opposites my brothers-in-law. Travis would bend over backwards to do anything for Jo, whereas with Brandon, it's all about him. Clearly, I won't be drinking, so it will be interesting to see which bandwagon Brandon jumps on if Ronnie has a beer or cider. And it's such a lovely day, normally I couldn't blame them for wanting to have a few drinks, but it is, after all, Wendy's birthday, not his, and someone has to stay sober in case a visit to A & E ensues for any reason, or a call to NHS 24.

'I can smell barbecue,' I say. 'Dad will be gutted he and Mum missed this.'

'Mum says he asked if they could get out of going to the wedding, but that was a non-starter.'

'I should think so too. How often do they get to attend a wedding at Cameron House? Plus, they've known the Jacobs family for years. Back in a minute.' I follow my nose and take my cup with me towards the garden. The children are remarkably quiet, and when I get there, I see it's because their mouths are full of sausages and burgers. I say hi to Brandon, and he glances up from his phone momentarily to reply.

The kids are all sitting cross-legged on a tartan picnic

blanket – lends it more a sense of occasion than simply sitting on chairs, I guess – nibbling on, hopefully, cooked-all-the-way-through sausages and chomping on soft floury buns. A stray bun lies near the bottom of the garden, and I feel I missed an earlier food fight.

I lounge on one of the rattan chairs with floral padded cushion, and with a pang I remember we won't be able to use our garden this year. What's left of it. It will need to be relandscaped out front, although the back, hopefully, shouldn't require much attention. Unless the tradesmen need to work on the exterior of the house at the rear, in which case our lovely garden could be out of action for quite some time.

My thoughts wander to the hotel we're staying in, and luxurious though it is, as I watch the kids tear around the garden, sausages now forgotten, I realise they can't live in a hotel, for an extended period of time. It will be total carnage. We've already had a few incidents. And they will be bored out of their minds, especially the little ones, unless they start stalking the guests detective-style to find out all their secrets. OK, this pregnancy, in addition to making me have odd dreams, as happened with the others, is making me out and out ramble. However, for now, I decide to go with the flow and make the most of my sister's birthday barbecue. In the face of everything that has happened recently, and in light of everything still to come, I need to ground myself in the here and now, and enjoy the happy snippets life allows me.

Chapter Three

Thursday 1 July

To-do list

Contact Graziella Morricone – her cheque bounced

Talk to printer about latest pending jobs – double-check redelivery

Rearrange meeting with Anya Feltz

Ring insurance for an update

Find out if we are able to retrieve anything else from the house

Check Ronnie's car's MOT date – sure it's this month

Send Fiona Harkness directions to the Four Springs hotel for today's meeting

I really enjoyed my breakfast meeting this morning. I chose the Four Springs hotel in Hamwell, rather than having to traipse all the way into the city as I usually do. It saved the traffic for both of us, and it hasn't long opened. A fresh place to meet, or in my case, to use as a mobile office.

The only downside is it's hot. It's a beautiful day, and temperatures are forecast to be in the high twenties, and with the amount of glass in this building, I feel like a tomato in a greenhouse. I've stayed behind to make a few notes after the meeting and to have a cool drink – virgin mojito. It did cause the barman to raise his eyebrows, it is only ten o'clock, but it hits the spot.

I could've had Fiona come to Garfield Grange and meet me there, but it feels a bit underhanded somehow, conducting Wedded Bliss business in a property I'm living in rent-free out of the goodness of Fabien's heart.

And it's been a good start to the day as Fiona already enlisted my services. Sure, we still have the finer details to flesh out, I have samples to send her, but she has committed to engaging my services. I've never been to Kinnettles Castle, near Forfar. In fact, I'd never even heard of it until today, but she showed me some photos of it, and it's gorgeous. I love when the excitement shines out of the bride, and groom, although in this case he wasn't present.

It's eleven o'clock by the time I arrive back at Garfield Grange. I enter the foyer, and it seems like all hell has broken loose. Strange. This place is so ordered, it's almost as if it has OCD. I shake my head slightly and head upstairs, but I stop dead when I reach our corridor. What the hell? Piles of sheets and towels line the carpet, bottles of cleaning fluids, bin bags, miniature shampoo, body lotion and other assorted toiletries are dotted haphazardly almost as if they form part of a crime scene in a novel. *Death on the Perfume Express. Murder on the Second Floor. The Cleaner.*

Chaos would be putting it mildly, and I can't help wondering what's happened. As I head along the corridor, the manager steps out of the elevator with one of the maids. She's Eastern European, I think, from her accent, although I can't pin down from which part, and she's talking so fast, I barely catch what she says to him.

'Mess. Racing. Children. Cannot work like this. What to do.'

My blood runs cold. Children? I haven't seen any other children in the hotel, definitely not on this floor, except my own. But Ronnie's with them. I hurry along the corridor to our suite and open the door with my key card.

The moment I do, I know my children are the culprits. The pungent smell of cleaning fluid hits the back of my throat. Either the maid overdid it in here, or some small hands have been up to mischief.

'Aria! Hugo!' I call. No one is in the sitting area of the suite. Where is everyone? Where's Ronnie?

At that moment, Ronnie walks out of our bedroom, hair damp from the shower. Well, at least we have one body accounted for.

'Ah, you're back.' He smiles. 'Ugh, what's that smell?'

'I was hoping you could tell me.'

His eyebrows scrunch up. 'What do you mean?' He glances around and says, 'Where are Aria and Hugo? Gen was listening to music in her room when I went for a shower.'

I crook my finger at him and stride towards the suite door, then open it.

He frowns, but on my insistence, he crosses the room and looks outside. 'What the–?'

'My thoughts exactly. I have the feeling our youngest may have something to do with this. And I can tell you right now, the maid is furious, says she can't work like this, and the manager did not look pleased.'

Ronnie strides back across the room and throws open one of the bedroom doors. 'Aria, Hugo, get out here now.'

Oh dear. Ronnie doesn't often raise his voice, but when

he does, it instils fear into our brood no end.

Two little bodies clamber out from their hiding places, Aria from the wardrobe and Hugo from behind the floor-length curtain.

'What have you done?' Ronnie asks.

Silence.

'I said what have you done.' Slight increase in volume.

'I-I-I–' Hugo starts.

'You what? Did you leave the room whilst I was in the shower?' Ronnie thunders.

Hugo won't raise his head to meet Ronnie's eyes.

'Hugo.' Ronnie's voice is dangerously soft, but it doesn't mask the edge to it.

'Yes.' His voice comes out as a squeak.

'Right. So now we've established that, and we'll talk in a minute about why you are expressly forbidden from leaving the suite without either me or your mother, tell me, what did you do?'

'We were just having fun,' Aria pipes up.

Normally Daddy's little poppet, she isn't today. The glare Ronnie gives her would melt the polar ice caps.

'Hugo.'

Eyes downcast, Hugo says, 'Aria and I were playing with one of the cleaners' trolleys when they were in the room cleaning. We were trying to race it like we do with the shopping trolleys in the supermarket sometimes, but it's heavier than I thought, and it, well, crashed into the wall and lots of stuff fell off.'

The colour rises in Ronnie's face, and I can tell he's not a happy bunny. I'm not best pleased myself.

'And what did you do then?' I ask Hugo.

'We…well, we ran away,' he says sheepishly.

'You ran away?' Ronnie asks, disbelief evident in his tone. 'You didn't think to stay and clean it up or at the very least come and tell me so I could fix your mess before the hotel manager found out?'

'Sorry, Daddy,' says Aria. 'I thought you'd be cross.'

'I am cross, but I'm more cross because neither of you tried to fix the mess you made. Fabien, Mummy's...boss has been very kind letting us stay here, and you guys do this? I am so disappointed in you both.'

Silent tears run down Hugo's cheeks. He will hate having disappointed Ronnie. Although he's a mummy's boy, he's only a mummy's boy when Daddy's not around.

'And has Gen missed all of this?' Ronnie asks, shoving her door open.

She glances up and sees us all looking at her, then takes out her earbuds. 'What?'

'Come and see what your brother and sister have been up to whilst I've been in the shower.'

Gen stands up and follows him out into the hall. 'Oh my God, you guys are so busted.' She gives her siblings a look that is a mix of awe, respect and incredulity.

'Gen, next time Dad takes a shower, you're in charge,' I say pointedly. 'Now, can you supervise these two whilst Dad and I go try to build some bridges?'

Friday 2 July

They finally removed the cab today from our living room.

Monday 5 July

To-do list

*Provide Fabien with samples of the invitation suites for the
Hope, Jenner and Ferris weddings*
Order more cream organza card
Update my website with new prices
Bring invoices for all clients up to date
New swimming costume for Aria

'Mum, Aria won't give me the remote,' Hugo whines.

'Whose turn is it?' I ask, absentmindedly as I prepare some Wedded Bliss invoices, trying to work out the calculations in my head.

'Mine!' they both shout.

Great, it's going to be one of those mornings.

'Where's Dad?' I've come into our bedroom to get peace to work, but it's not, well, working so far.

'He's gone to talk to someone about some plums,' says Aria.

That gets my attention, and I look up. Aria is standing in the doorway, holding the remote. 'Plums?' I ask.

She nods, then repeats, 'Plums.'

'He has not, dummy,' says Hugo. 'He's gone to ask about a plumber, for the bathroom. The sink's blocked. The water won't drain away.'

'Oh? How did that happen?'

Aria slinks away as Hugo turns red.

'What happened, Hugo?' Then I call, 'Aria, get back here!'

Aria returns, eyes downcast. Great, they've been up to something. She glares at Hugo. I know she doesn't want him to tell me, but Hugo is a terrible liar, and feels bad telling lies, so tends not to, particularly if I tell him I want the truth.

He glances at Aria, who has folded her arms and is looking at him as if she'd like to chop his head off. The words pour out of him in a torrent. 'Aria was washing her dollies in the sink, and she left the water on, and it overflowed onto the floor, but then she tried to dry it up with a towel, and I helped her, but there was too much water, and some of it and the soap is over the carpet in the living room. And there's a lot of water on the bathroom floor. I think we may need more towels.'

I struggle to keep up with the speed he's speaking, but once I've taken it all in, I stand and head to the bathroom. There is water everywhere; it looks like a wet and wild theme park ride in there.

'What the–?' I begin. 'What blocked the sink?' I cross the bathroom, trying not to slip. This will need more than a few towels to clean up. In the sink is the soap dish, a heavy ceramic thing, not attached to the wall, as it was previously. It's covering the plughole. No wonder the water wasn't draining away. But as I remove the soap dish, I notice the plughole is covered in coloured goo. What the heck is that? I turn to Hugo, who shrugs.

'Aria?'

'I was making the dollies pretty. I wanted them to have rainbow skin, so I used my slime.'

'Slime? Where did you even get that?'

'Auntie Jo gave it to me the other day.'

I'm going to kill my sister. 'I don't think she meant you to take it home, Aria.'

She frowns. 'She didn't tell me not to.'

I sigh. 'So, you brought the dollies in here, put some slime on them, then what?'

'No, Mummy, I didn't put the slime on them in here, I did that in the bedroom.'

'The bedroom?' My heart sinks. I push past her and go into her bedroom. 'For the love of all that is holy,' I say sotto voce.

Her bedroom is covered in slime. Green for the pillowcase; the white duvet is now mainly yellow; the carpet has a blue tinge to it; and to round it off, the curtains are daubed pink. How on earth did she get slime on the curtains? Was she trying to redecorate the room? I thought she said she was playing with her dolls.

I turn round to berate her. Hugo has scarpered. Aria is standing there, no hint of regret showing. She almost looks pleased with her accomplishment. It doesn't happen often, but I'm lost for words. What a mess. What are we going to do? Does slime come out of soft furnishings? How will we fix this before Housekeeping see it?

I'm just about to rail at her when Ronnie's voice comes from the other room. He's obviously back from seeing about a plumber. I'm guessing he hasn't seen the state of this place, or I'd have heard him roar. But now I do hear him roar anyway.

'Aria! Come here!'

I shepherd Aria into the living area, where Ronnie looks as if he's about to have a coronary. He's bright red, and I don't remember the last time I saw him this angry. I frown.

'What is it?' I ask.

'Our darling daughter has only gone and flooded the ceiling below us with her water sports.'

I gasp. 'Oh no. You're kidding.' I turn to Aria. 'Do you want to tell Daddy, or shall I?'

She shakes her head and clamps her mouth shut.

I turn to Ronnie. 'You'd better take a look in her room. I'm going to have some apologising to do to Fabien, and God knows how much the cleaning bill will be.'

Ronnie passes me and strides towards Aria's room.

'No, Daddy, no! You can't go in there!' She pushes past him and tries to block the scene from his eyes by planting her body in the doorway. Not terribly well, given she's four feet tall and Ronnie's over six.

Ronnie's mouth falls open, then he rounds on Aria, his teeth gritted. 'Aria Halliday, you are in so much trouble.'

Tuesday 6 July

To-do list

Find something to occupy my little darlings that doesn't involve hotel management coming to the door

Download meditation app so I can block out the noise and refrain from murdering my LDs

Draw up a rota with Ronnie for taking the kids to do fun stuff as I'm struggling to work with all this noise

Find a quiet spot in the hotel where I can work for the foreseeable

Insurance company update

'No, I'm afraid there's no update to your case notes, Mrs Halliday.'

Thursday 8 July

'Your claims handler's off today, I'm afraid, and she hasn't left a note on the system about any further progress. Sorry.'

Friday 9 July

'We're waiting on some paperwork to arrive from the police.'

Monday 12 July

To-do list
Call insurance company and don't take no for an answer – have been fobbed off enough
Rightmove – start looking for a temporary house for us to live in
Do banking – home and business

I'm already downstairs in the hotel foyer, sipping a cup of English Breakfast tea when Fabien strolls towards me, looking more as if he's going to a wedding, in his pale grey three-piece suit, than managing a string of hotels.

'Morning, Fabien.' I rise to kiss him on the cheek. I have no idea if we do this because he has a French name, because he has always done this, because it's now socially the norm in the UK to do so, or, well, I've run out of reasons, but I know that in the past, it wasn't usual for men and women who were no relation to each other to kiss each other on the cheek, and I wonder when that changed. I think it's mostly for the better, though. Oh God, here we go, back with the rambling. Since I became pregnant, my brain seems to be zooming all over the place. Already it was overloaded, now it's off the chart.

I'm just off the phone to the insurance company, a call I specifically scheduled to tie in with my chat with Fabien, so I'd be better armed with information. It's not looking good. It's unlikely we'll have any settlement or return to the house in the next few months. I know I can't keep my family, my beloved brood, in a hotel room, no matter how sumptuous the surroundings, for any more than a week to ten days from now, tops. Already tempers are fraying, the lack of personal space is killing us all, and the clutter is driving every single one of us crazy. And despite being able to eat the best food in the hotel each night – I'm really enjoying that part, albeit quite a few things on the menu are off the menu for me, what with being pregnant – that doesn't fly for the kids.

Whilst it warms my heart that my beloved cherubs prefer my spag bol to the chef's, or that they're dismayed beyond belief when cannelloni isn't on the menu, and that I don't allow them to eat sausages each night – except Gen, our vegetarian-in-training – it does make it a tad difficult to feed everyone each night, and certainly not without a great deal of complaining.

The only saving grace in all this is that it's the summer holidays and they don't have to go to school each day. The downside is, much as I love my children to pieces, I have to entertain them each day, which in a confined space is rather difficult. And they don't live near their friends now, so can't simply walk to meet them.

No, today I've decided, together with Ronnie, that we really do need somewhere temporary to live. A house. Preferably a house. A flat would do, but with two dogs, currently with Mum and Dad, a flat isn't my first choice. I had a quick look on Rightmove and there are a couple of properties in Lymeburn – close to Wendy – and a few in Hamwell, but none, unsurprisingly in Ferniehall.

So, I want to thank Fabien for all his help during the

past few weeks. He has been unbelievable, but then I must make it clear that we'll be moving out not long after we find a place to stay. Hopefully there won't be any permanent damage to the room – felt-tip pen, dents in the walls, marks on the carpet – nope, I did not say those things existed, I'm merely thinking of potential issues – ahem!

'Louisa. So, have you had time to think about everything now? Are you ready to sign the contract?'

I am, but quite frankly I'd forgotten I hadn't already done so, so I play along and pretend that's what I wanted to talk about, smiling and making the right noises, hopefully in the right places.

'Sure. I'll do it now if you have it with you.'

Fabien produces a thick contract and a Mont Blanc pen. 'I'll come back in fifteen minutes. Give you time to read it at your leisure.'

'Thanks. I appreciate that.'

Fifteen minutes later, true to his word, Fabien returns. Now mollified that our business agreement is going ahead as planned, he relaxes back into his chair. I almost expect him to loosen his tie, he seems so chilled.

'Why do I have the feeling you have something else you'd like to discuss?'

Shrewd. Well, he wouldn't get very far in business, and certainly not to where he is now, without being able to read people.

'There is.' Nerves are tumbling around in my stomach like clothes in a washing machine. I put it down to the hormones, as why would I be nervous at telling him I want to move out? Surely being nervous at telling him I was moving in would make more sense.

'Ronnie and I—' yes, I'm putting Ronnie's name first so he gets the blame '—have talked about it, and whilst we're extremely grateful to you for putting us up, indefinitely—' I let the word hang there '—we feel it's time we looked for something house-like.'

When did I lose my ability to speak in proper sentences and using correct phraseology? House-like?

'I mean, we feel the kids need a home, particularly since it looks like it could be several months before we're back in ours, if we even do get back into ours. We still haven't had the decision on that yet.'

Fabien smiles at me. 'No problem, Louisa. You just take your time, find something you like, and you know you have the suite for as long as you need it. Obviously, I hope you find what you're looking for soon, for your sake, but don't feel under any pressure to move out. Honestly.'

'Thanks, Fabien. That means a lot.'

'Anyway, since I have you here, I was wondering if we could go over a few more details about the partnership.'

'Of course.' I nod at him like an overenthusiastic puppy waiting for the treats to be doled out.

Fabien stops a passing waitress and orders us tea and coffee. Half an hour later, I'm better versed in what Fabien's, or rather Cerulean's, expectations are of me and my company, Wedded Bliss, and what I should expect from them, and I must confess to being both exhilarated and a tiny bit intimidated. What if I can't pull this off?

From Fabien's explanation, it's clear I'll have some key clients to work with, both in the UK and in Europe, and there may be training to attend and to provide at various locations. I'm hoping he doesn't want me to go anywhere in the final trimester. I'm not exactly au fait with when it's no longer safe to fly, but there is definitely a period where the airline won't let you. The sooner I can tell him about the pregnancy the better.

I'll be both showing our range of products to clients and training some key staff on how to produce them the way Wedded Bliss does, for overseas clients only. Fabien doesn't want to take anything away from my current business. But then I mainly handle Scottish weddings anyway, as I like the in-person approach, and being able to meet my clients. This is all a bit new to me, and a far cry from the way I work with my own clients, but it sounds promising too.

From the way Fabien has explained matters, it makes sense for me to focus on the Cerulean stuff initially, then introduce all the elements to Mum later, so she can also become involved. Meanwhile, I'll talk to Mum about me passing her more Wedded Bliss stuff to do, and her taking a more central role in that. She'll love that. She has so enjoyed being involved since that first wedding fair she helped out at.

And then there's the baby. I haven't told Fabien yet. I can't, since I haven't even told my parents. Much though I love my mum, she cannot contain happy news. Half the village would know by the end of the day, and particularly with me being a mother 'of advanced years' I can't take the risk of putting the news out there and something going wrong. Funny how I hadn't thought of anything going wrong until the midwife labelled me a geriatric mother. I'm so going to have to get over that.

'So, how did he take it?' Ronnie asks me when I go back to

the suite.

'Really well. Not at all offended.'

He drops a kiss on my head. 'I told you he wouldn't be. That's a woman thing. You often imagine slights where none are intended.'

'Do you think?' I frown at him. I can feel my eyebrows retreating into my hairline.

'I know.' He hugs me to him. 'Right, what's on the agenda today?'

I give him a look as if to say 'Really?' and he has the grace to look shame-faced.

'Sorry, that sounded as if I hadn't been listening to a word, or taken in anything we've discussed.'

Amusement tugs the corners of my mouth upwards.

'I meant apart from looking for somewhere new to live, obviously.'

'Obviously.'

'Mum, are we moving?' Gen appears at my side. I swear that girl has bat ears.

'Well, yes, in the interim. Until the house is ready again.'

Her face lights up. 'So we'll definitely be moving back into our own house at some point. Yes!' She punches the air.

'Actually, we don't know yet,' Ronnie tells her, draping his arms around her shoulders, letting her lean back against him as they both rock from side to side as she has done with him ever since she was a toddler, particularly in times of stress or excitement.

'Don't know what?' Hugo plonks himself down on the sofa, Nintendo Switch in hand.

'If or when we can move back into our house,' Gen

says.

That 'if' catches Hugo's attention. 'What do you mean "if"? Is there a chance we won't be able to move back in?' His beseeching eyes find mine, and I can't lie to him.

'We don't have the definitive report back yet from the insurers. The men on site said there was a good chance, but nothing is final until the insurers give us the go-ahead.'

'So, we don't know,' Hugo finally says, sticking his bottom lip out under his top one then pushing it backwards and forwards, a nervous trait he has.

'Not yet, hon.'

His eyes fill with tears, and I'm reminded he's only eight. It's a lot to take in at that age. Heck, it's a lot to take in at my age.

'Listen, Dad and I were just talking about this last night, and, well, we've realised it's not as easy as we thought it would be, living in a hotel. So, we're going to look for somewhere temporary to live.'

Gen perks up. 'You mean a house? Where?'

'When? Now?' asks Hugo.

'Not right now.' I place a reassuring hand on Hugo's shoulder. 'Soon. Dad and I need to have a look to see what's available.' I turn to Gen. 'Yes, a house. It needs to be a house for us, so we can get Bear and Patch back.'

Aria joins us. 'I miss Patch, and Bear.' Her expression is so forlorn I don't know whether to smile or cover her in kisses to make all the negatives go away.

'I do too, sweetie. Right, let's get ourselves ready, and then we can go do something fun for the day.'

'I want to look at houses,' Hugo says.

'Me too.' Aria folds her arms across her front and eyes me mutinously. I haven't even said no yet.

'I meant like going to Flip Out, or roller skating, or the cinema...'

'Mum, we can do that any time.' Gen. Not Gen too. I feel as if they're ganging up on me. I need time to look at houses myself first, then share them with Ronnie, and maybe eventually show them to the kids once I've ascertained their suitability. Freudian slip – we've ascertained. Ronnie should have a say too. Maybe.

My eyes meet Ronnie's, and he shrugs. Fair enough. It would seem I've been outvoted, but if we're going to do this, we need to do it properly.

'Right, gang. Aria, get paper, Hugo, a pen, Gen, grab a laptop. We'll draw up a shortlist.'

A few minutes later, once Hugo has found a pen that works – never easy in this household, and particularly not when almost everything you own is crammed into a hotel room, even if it is a spacious suite – we settle down on the sofa to start making our list. Empowering the kids every so often isn't a bad thing, I tell myself, although perhaps not with something as monumental as choosing somewhere for us to live.

Under instruction, Gen navigates to Rightmove.

'OK, here's what we're looking for. Ferniehall.'

'It's asking for the search radius.' Gen eyes me, her fingers hovering over the mouse.

'Three miles.' I glance over her shoulder to see what the other criteria are. Price range. I have no idea. I don't remember the last time I rented anywhere. My eyes meet Ronnie's, and his lips turn downwards in an 'I have no clue either' expression.

'Mum, Mum,' Gen says, when I don't say anything.

'Eh, put in five hundred to a thousand pounds a

month, to give us a good range, and so we can see what we can get for our money. And put in three to four bedrooms.'

Ronnie looks like he's about to say something, but I know what it is: do we need four bedrooms? The answer is yes. Gen is almost thirteen, plus I can honestly see us not getting back into our own house for about six to eight months the way things are going. The thought makes my blood run cold. It almost feels like leaving the kids overnight with someone. That house, or home rather, is as much a part of me as the people in it are. People say 'it's just a house' when they decide to move, but I always think, 'No, it's not, or rather, it's not merely a house to me. Yours may be to you, but I'm very attached to mine.' I'm brought out of my reverie by Gen tapping out a beat impatiently on the laptop. 'Mum, did you hear what I said?'

'Sorry, and yes, say "any" to those last two – property type and when it was added to the site.'

Gen does so obediently, and we wait for the results to appear. The anticipation is almost that of waiting to find out how your horse has fared when riding in the Grand National.

It brings up nine results, and my heart sinks when I see the first one. Aria voices my thoughts before I get a chance to.

'Mummy, I don't like that first one. It's very grey and boring.'

'Yes, that's not for us, honey.' You had better believe it's not. It's in about the only bad area, in the surrounding, well, area. It's on the other side of Hamwell from us.

The second is relatively attractive, new build, driveway, top end of the budget though, and it's not in Ferniehall, it's in Lymeburn, but not too far from Wendy. Its driveway could do with a pressure wash, and two of the bedrooms are pretty small but doable, at a push. But is that really how much it costs for a very small four-bedroom detached house? Wow!

Thank goodness we bought ours twelve years ago then. I almost crumple as I recall the state it's in now.

The next one is more reasonably priced, but it's not furnished. That gets me thinking if I'd prefer it furnished or unfurnished. For ease of use, furnished, but from a 'using other people's stuff, and thinking of who lived or slept there before' perspective, maybe unfurnished. Although we're currently living in a hotel where presumably hundreds of guests have slept in the room before us. OK, best not to dwell on that, and I assume their cleaning staff are good at their job – excellent in fact. I digress. No, I think we need to bite the bullet and take something furnished. We have enough on our plate, plus we don't know how long we'll be there for. Best to have something furnished and in walk-in condition.

'Is there a way to look at only those that are furnished?' I ask.

Gen looks at me blankly, so I take over for a few seconds and type in a few keywords to narrow down the search, then expand it in other fields.

It's not looking promising, I have to say, and that fills me with dread. I thought there would be loads of properties available.

Ronnie guesses my thoughts. 'Maybe they simply haven't registered with Rightmove.'

'Unlikely. Isn't that who most people use?'

'A lot, but not everyone.'

Well, he has certainly kept himself more up to date on these matters than I have, as I haven't a clue.

So far, I've found one that's doable, one that is decent

enough but unfurnished, and I haven't seen either of the gardens yet. I also wonder how quickly we can move in.

'Why don't we drive round and see if there are any houses to rent?' says Gen.

I love my daughter's enthusiasm and initiative, but I'm about to dismiss this idea, when Ronnie says, 'Great idea, Gen.'

What? Is he kidding? I'm all for empowering the kids a little, but aimlessly driving round the streets to look for somewhere to live is not my idea of a fun day out. It's hard enough to keep them amused on car journeys, usually. And we don't exactly have a surplus of time at the moment.

Before I can utter my thoughts on the matter, Ronnie is bundling everyone through the door of the suite. 'Bring your jacket, Aria, in case it rains.' He turns to me as he holds the door. 'Well, what are you waiting for? Let the adventure begin.'

Two hours later, everyone is pretty frazzled and disconsolate. We've walked and driven all over Hamwell, Lymeburn and Ferniehall, trying to catch a glimpse of 'To Let' signs. We have come across a few that didn't show up on our internet searches, but to be honest, we'd have been better not uncovering them. The first one had an Alsatian next door that almost gave me a heart attack because I didn't see it crouched below the garden gate as I approached; the second was in a less than salubrious part of Hamwell, and had an old couch with the stuffing hanging out of it and a pram with rusty wheels sitting in the garden under the living room window; and the third was right next to a stream, which isn't ideal with young children. And I would never be able to relax.

'I'm tired, Mummy.' Aria leans into me as we walk, and I wrap an arm around her. Hugo assumes a similar position with Ronnie, and Gen bears a hangdog expression and slopes along beside us.

'Why don't we go see Nana and Papa?' The kids love my folks, and my parents are always delighted to see their grandchildren, plus Mum always has some gorgeous cake from M&S in her cake tin. I'm hoping it's carrot cake. I could do with a boost of energy. I think I'm more tired because the outcome of our search has been so depressing, rather than from actual physical weariness.

'Yay,' says Aria. 'My Furby is at Nana's.'

We still haven't been able to retrieve the kids' toys from the house yet, so something familiar for Aria to play with will mean a lot to her. Thank goodness she has Cornie. We would never have been able to get her to sleep without her unicorn. We have managed to pick up a few bits and pieces for them from the supermarkets, and their cousins have given them some toys, but it's not the same. And believe me, there are only so many times you can play I Spy or Hangman, before your patience runs out.

Gen scuffs her feet, and Hugo goes with the flow. We pile back into my car, and I huff out a breath. I could be doing with a guardian angel to come and sort all this out for me. Again, I wonder what we would have done if Fabien hadn't taken us under his wing, and I bless the day I met him. Otherwise, I think we may have ended up in some grotty roadside motel. I exaggerate, but not by much. Essentially, I mean somewhere not very nice at all, and where I would certainly not want us, and more specifically our children, to be living. Whilst living in the hotel isn't ideal, and has its challenges, there's no point jumping out of the frying pan into the fire. The search continues.

Chapter Four

Wednesday 14 July

To-do list

Speak to Mum about the Fountain wedding suite – they've gone out spelled Fontaine

Birthday cards and little presents for Gen's birthday

Pick up Gen's new mountain bike from cycle shop – ask Mum and Dad to store it

Collect cake from Icing on the Cake – remember candles and banner

Buy new sunglasses – sat on mine, again, and they're beyond repair this time.

Find somewhere that does factor 50 sun cream Sam was raving about. Text Sam to ask her name of it.

'I've been thinking, Gen. You know how you said you didn't want to make a big deal for your birthday, not wanting a party, especially with it being not long after Aunt Wendy's?'

Gen looks up from her iPad. 'Yeah?'

'Well, how about a pamper day, just you and me? I could ask Savannah at A Cut Above if she could fit you in and do something *amazing* with your hair, make you look and feel a million dollars.'

She smiles at that. 'Keep going.'

'And you could go and get your nails done, or a massage, or we could go for a swim and go in the jacuzzi. What do you think?'

When she doesn't immediately answer, I say, 'Or any ideas on what you'd like to do?'

She stares straight ahead for a second, the corners of her mouth turning down as she is wont to do when she's not sure about something or has questions. Then she says, 'Do you know what I'd really like?' I say nothing, hoping that urges her to continue. 'Yes, I'd like to have my hair done specially, but how about for my main birthday treat we all go to Terra Point Forest Park?'

I frown. 'Up north?'

'Yeah, Freya said it's near Inverness, but not as far up.'

'What made you think of that?' I ask.

She hesitates then says, 'I know my birthday is my important day, and yes, turning thirteen is a big thing, but I'd rather stay a big kid for a bit longer!'

I laugh. 'Tell me about it. I'd rather you did too.'

'And Hugo and Aria will love it.'

And there you have it, my lovely, sensitive, soon-to-be teenage daughter being totally selfless. I'm so proud of her, I could cry.

Chapter Five

Friday 16 July

To-do list

Decorate living area with banners for Gen

Take Gen to Mum and Dad's to see her main present – new bike

Have Aria sign Gen's card – she refused last night. She was a in a right strop

Pack bags for Ronnie for taking care of kids for the day since Gen and I are going to the salon

Order T-shirts for Hugo – not sure if laundry service is losing them, but he seems to only have about four, and they don't really fit him

'Gen, Gen, it's your birthday, wake up'. I hear Aria before I see her. I look at the clock. 5:57. Poor Gen. She's now a teenager, and her first experience is being woken up by her kid sister pre-6 a.m. Hopefully, this is not indicative of things to come.

Since Aria's shrieking has woken me, and Hugo, and Ronnie, we all get up, albeit Ronnie grudgingly. He tries to pull the covers over his head, but Aria is having none of it.

'Daddy, you have to get up so we can give Gen her

presents.'

Reluctantly, and after Aria jumping up and down on him four or five times, Ronnie gives up and gives in, sliding out of bed and yawning as he makes his way to the bathroom, where he splashes water on his face in an attempt to rouse himself.

Whilst Ronnie is attempting to wake up, I gather Gen's gifts and set them in a pile on the coffee table.

'Happy birthday!' I say as she shuffles into the room, face crumpled from sleep, or lack thereof.

'Thanks.'

I hug her to me. 'Can't believe you're a teenager. Please don't change overnight and start being horrible.'

I feel her grin against my cheek. 'I'll try, but no promises.'

'Gen, open your presents.' Aria is almost hopping up and down beside her. She looks like she may actually pop if Gen doesn't do as asked.

'I think you may need to humour her,' I murmur into Gen's ear. 'Or she'll wake all the guests. And I think we're already in enough trouble with the management.'

Gen duly opens her gifts: perfume from us, a plush from Aria, a couple of fantasy books from Hugo. And there are gifts from her relatives and even from the dogs.

'Your main gift from us is at Nana and Papa's,' I say. 'We'll go over there later, but first breakfast and the salon.'

'So, what would you like done?' Savannah asks.

Gen's sitting in a chair at A Cut Above as Savannah, the head stylist, gazes at her in the mirror, at the same time eyeing her long honey-coloured tresses and lifting sections of her hair this way and that. I've plopped myself on a seat beside her. Gen freezes a little, but then rallies. We've discussed this, looked at a few hairstyle magazines the past few days in preparation for her makeover.

'Well, I quite like this one.' She opens the magazine she has on her lap, to the page she had turned down. A model with long straight blonde hair and bangs peers out of it. 'Do you think you could make my hair look like that?' She gazes up at Savannah, hope in her eyes.

Savannah gives her a mock eye-roll. 'Ye-e-s. No problem. You have great hair. Strong. This style will really suit you. Right, let's get started.'

Whilst I watch Savannah snip away expertly at Gen's hair, I feel a warm glow suffuse me. This is what life is all about, these happy moments. Gen is chatting away effortlessly with Savannah about music and school and what it's like living in a 5-star hotel. And I relax back with the cup of tea Savannah's assistant has brought me and enjoy the experience.

When Savannah is done, and she shows Gen the back, Gen's smile speaks volumes. Her hair already looked good, but now she looks catwalk-ready, and I feel a pang of regret that she's growing up, and fast.

'You look amazing, sweetheart. Milan Fashion Week here we come.'

'Not quite. It's just a haircut, Mum.' She looks down at her cut-off T-shirt and jeans, then turns back to Savannah. 'Sorry, I don't mean it's *just* a haircut, which I love. I meant I wasn't a fashion icon.' She gestures to her clothes.

Savannah smiles. 'I know what you meant.'

'So that's why we're going into town to get you some new, what is it you call clothes these days, "threads"?'

Gen cringes. 'No, Mum. We call them "clothes".'

Ah, I'm showing my age now.

'Right,' I say, overbrightly. 'Let's get this show on the road.' I tip Savannah as I wink.

Several hours later, after a tour of virtually every clothes shop in Glasgow, and several dents to my credit card later, and after a quick trip to my folks' to view Gen's new mountain bike – which she loved – we're back at Garfield Grange with the rest of the gang, who've arrived home before us. We've barely closed the door behind us before Aria is asking, 'When can we have the cake, Mummy?'

I promise her it will be soon, have a quick chat with Ronnie, a hug from Hugo and then set to preparing the cake, asking Ronnie at the last minute to dim the lights.

'For she's a jolly good fellow, for she's a jolly good fellow…hip, hip, hooray!'

Gen blows out her candles, and I take the cake to the kitchen area and cut five slices. Aria is already hovering at my elbow. She adores sponge cake. I keep an eye on her to make sure she doesn't try to steal another piece and take a piece to the birthday girl and Hugo.

'Happy birthday, darling.'

'Thanks, Mum. This has been the best birthday ever.'

And that's all I needed to hear.

Saturday 17 July

To-do list
Buy sandwiches, include Lunchables for Hugo, dippers for Aria, cocktail sausages for Gen and pork pies for Ronnie.

Borrow cool box and picnic blanket from Mum – it will be so much easier when we can access all of our things again.

Remember sun cream – apply before we go. Aria's torture for running off the moment I open the car door so she doesn't need to wear it.

Call A Cut Above re Gen's hair appointment

Pick up a cheap lightweight football for playing with in the hotel grounds – something that won't break any windows.

Despite the long drive, and having had to get up two hours earlier than they usually would so we can make the most of the day, the kids have been remarkably well behaved. It's almost as if they sense they shouldn't play up, particularly when Gen has gifted them this day instead of having a day out with me on her own, or with her friends, although I'll make sure she and Freya have a little surprise for just the two of them at a slightly later date.

Aria and Hugo are both as high as the proverbial kite. Luckily, even though it's the school holidays, the queues aren't as bad as I'd anticipated, and there's soon much excitement over which ride to go on first. And Gen, once again, puts her brother and sister first, allowing them to make the first choices. Hugo opts for Dinosaur Land where the realistic dinsosaurs have Aria torn between awe and fear. I think she prefers the adrenaline rush Mowgli Madness provides, harnessed in high above the ground as they scramble across the rope bridges. I'm sure she'd go round again if she could.

Meanwhile, Gen takes it all in with a smile, and her siblings love her first choice: the wild water coaster. I breathe a sigh of relief when the operative measures Aria and deems her tall enough by a centimetre to go on it.

There would have been hell to pay if they'd refused to let her on.

We stop for a picnic lunch, bagging an outside table, despite the crowds. It is the summer holidays, after all. The stars seem to be aligning for us today, and I send thanks to whoever is pulling the strings up there in the sky. I'm happy everything is working out right for Gen on her special day, especially when she has been so thoughtful and magnanimous towards her siblings.

Even Ronnie and I are granted a choice. The butterfly house is lovely, and Ronnie decides upon Illusionarium, full of puzzles and optical illusions and stuff. It's truly a great day, and although the sun is casting its glow over us, it's not too hot at around twenty-one degrees. I'm so glad we don't witness the temperatures they have down south in the early thirties. I couldn't cope with that.

Ronnie's busy studying the map with Gen to see what we can visit next, whilst I dig in one of the backpacks looking for wet wipes as Hugo has managed to get chocolate ice cream all over his face, T-shirt and ear lobe, interestingly. Bingo. I dab at his T-shirt, wishing I'd brought a change of clothes for him, but he's no longer a toddler, why would I? A prickling sensation creeps up my neck, and I turn round, scanning the immediate area. No Aria.

'Ronnie,' I say, panic lacing my tone, despite me trying to remain calm. 'Where's Aria?'

He glances around then shields his eyes from the sun whilst looking around the park. Why does it seem busier suddenly? Were there really this many people around before?

I don't often see Ronnie rattled, but even he's blinking

more than usual, which is his tell.

'Is everything OK, Mum?' Gen asks, sensing something's not quite right.

'Aria's wandered off. Can you stay right here with Hugo? Don't move, in case Aria comes back. Dad and I are going to split up and look for her. And don't let Hugo out of your sight.'

Ronnie and I quickly confer regarding which side of the park we'll each search. I lope off to the right, Ronnie to the left, each of us calling, 'Aria!' multiple times. As I walk and search, I stop people randomly and say, 'Have you seen a little blonde girl. She's four. Blue eyes. She's wearing a pink top with a unicorn on it and matching shorts.'

But I'm met only with headshakes. My chest tightens, even though I'm telling myself she'll be fine, she'll have been distracted by something and wandered off. Yet a little voice enters my head and says, 'Or someone.'

No, no, no. I can't think like that. I redouble my efforts. 'Aria!' I stop every person I meet. Some even come and join in the search, for which I am truly grateful. How many minutes have passed? I call Gen. I didn't tell her to call me if Aria came back. I know she probably realises that, but I'm taking no chances.

'Has she come back?' I don't even trouble myself with niceties.

'No. We're both standing here, asking everyone who passes. I've got a photo up on my phone of her, but no one's seen her.'

Why didn't I think of that? 'You two OK? We'll find her, don't worry, but stay put.' I hang up and immediately my phone rings. Ronnie. Thank God.

'You got her!' I say.

'No, I was phoning to see if you had. Look, Lou, that's at least five minutes we've been searching. I'm getting a little concerned.'

Now I'm freaking out. Ronnie doesn't do concerned, he's so calm and measured usually, so for him to be worried it must be bad.

'I think we should report it to the staff, given her age, and to see if we can rope anyone in to help.'

'Right,' I say, nodding, then realising he can't see me. 'Let's get the kids, but keep asking people on the way back.'

'I will. Lou, try not to worry, we will find her.'

A lump lodges in my throat, and I swipe away the tears that are coursing down my face.

What if...? I can't even finish the thought. I can already feel myself crumpling at the very idea that someone has taken her.

I need to stay calm. I round the corner and Hugo and Aria's anxious faces greet me, just as Ronnie joins us.

We head for the nearest ride, where Ronnie, who is considerably more coherent at the moment, explains what has happened. The young boy calls it in, and we're told to go to the main building. Someone will meet us there. There haven't been any reported lost children. My heart sinks, and bile rises in my gut. Don't they say the first fifteen minutes are crucial in finding a missing child?

Both Hugo and Gen are openly crying now, and I check myself. My crying will have worried them. I wrap an arm around each of them and kiss the top of their heads. 'She'll be fine. We'll find her. You know what she's like. She'll be exploring.'

Hugo raises his eyes to mine, trusting, and he seems slightly mollified by my response, but Gen's thirteen now and doesn't just blindly believe what she's told any more, and with good reason. My heart is racing as we make for the main building, where a supervisor meets us and tells us what the protocol is.

'We've sent a red alert out to all the attractions, with her description. We have a photo of her now.' He points at Ronnie. 'Your husband helpfully gave one to my colleague. We're readying a team of staff to go out on bikes looking for her.'

'What's the best thing for us to do?' I ask, finally finding my tongue.

'I'd probably suggest staying here, or where you last saw her. We'll do the rest of the looking. We're also scanning all the CCTV within the park for any sightings of her.'

They have CCTV. That's a bonus, although I imagine in a park this big, it won't cover half the places she could be.

Gen and Hugo are clinging on to me as if they'll never let go. Out of the blue, it comes to me that this is so unfair on Gen's birthday, but I know that I'm just diverting for a second from the matter at hand.

We decide Gen and I should go back to where Aria was last seen, and Hugo should stay with Ronnie, who enfolds him in a bear hug the moment the decision is made.

Gen and I set off, silently at first, holding hands, then as we approach where we last saw her, Gen voices what I've barely allowed myself to.

'Mum, do you think someone might have taken her?' Then she bursts into agonising sobs, and people turn to look at us. God knows what they're thinking, but I don't have the energy or volition to engage with them right now. All that matters is finding Aria.

We reach the last place we saw her. And that's when I see him. Cornie. Her favourite unicorn. And then I am bawling. I pick Cornie up, and Gen and I hug each other. How didn't we see it before? It must have been all the people? The crowds. I dig my phone out, almost dropping it in my haste.

'Ronnie. We've found Cornie. Where we last saw her. No.' I glance around. 'Still no sign of her.' I listen to his end of the conversation, say 'Right' a few times, then hang up.

'She's not there?' Gen says.

'No, but Dad says the park have said they won't let anyone leave for the time being.'

'Mum, I'm scared.' Gen wipes her eyes with the tissue I pass her.

'Me too, hon, but everything is being done to find her. We have to stay positive. OK?'

She nods.

A thought occurs to me. 'Gen, if you were Aria, where would you go?'

She glances at me quizzically.

'She liked all of the rides and exhibits we've been to today, but which was her favourite? Could she have gone back there perhaps?'

Gen considers this for a sec then says, 'Definitely the rollercoaster. You know how much of a daredevil she is.'

I text Ronnie that info. 'Where else?'

'Well, she did like the butterfly house. Wait a minute–'

'What is it?' I ask.

'Remember the play area next to the butterfly house? She wanted to go to that, as it had a labyrinth, but Hugo needed the toilet, and we were about to do Dad's choice of the Illusionarium. Maybe she went there.'

'But how would she even know which way to go?'

Gen shrugs. 'Maybe she didn't, maybe she got lost.' When I remain silent, trying to digest this, Gen adds, 'It's got to be worth a look.'

I nod then call Ronnie. 'Ask them to have someone check the labyrinth near the butterfly house.'

'What?' Ronnie says.

'Please, there's no time to explain, just do it,' I beg him.

'OK. I'll call you back.'

Five minutes later, which feel like fifty, my phone rings.

'They've got her. I'm walking over there now.'

I burst into tears. I can't even speak. Then I see Gen's face, and I nod, so she knows it's OK.

When I can form words again, I say, 'Thank God. We'll be there as soon as we can.' I hang up and hug Gen to me. 'Well done, darling. You know your sister so well. That's where she was, playing quite the thing, not remotely worried we weren't with her. I swear I'm going to kill her when I get my hands on her.'

'Not if I get a hold of her first.' Gen manages a weak smile. 'That was horrible. She gave us a real fright.'

'I know. Thank goodness you never did anything like that.'

She grins. 'I was a model child.'

I can channel levity now I know Aria's safe. 'I wouldn't go that far,' I say as we walk hand in hand to the labyrinth to be with her sister.

'Aria!' I hug her to me as she tries to push me away. 'Mummy, I want to play. Come and see. This is how you get in–' she points to the entrance '–and this is how you get out.' She points round the corner and away to the far side of the field.

'Aria, don't you ever, ever wander off like that again. Mummy and Daddy were very worried.'

'And me,' says Gen.

'Me too.' Hugo is still wiping away tears.

'Well, you should have let me go when I asked,' she says, bold as brass.

I swear if I wasn't so relieved to find her safe and sound, I'd strangle her.

'Right, troops. It's been a bit of a day. Let's get back to the car. It's a long drive home,' Ronnie says.

I don't argue, and we all traipse after him. As we approach the car, Hugo says, 'Do we have any snacks left in the bag?' And just like that normality resumes, but I won't forget the side order of fear that crept in today. Never.

Chapter Six

Monday 19 July

To-do list

Take extra battery for laptop

Buy £10 Robux for Hugo – reset password to something I remember

Discuss Hugo and Aria's pocket money with Ronnie

Book haircuts for going back to school for Hugo and Aria– can never get an appointment nearer the time

'Guys, can you keep your voices down? The whole floor will be able to hear you.'

'But he won't give me the iPad charger,' Gen moans, 'and I'm at two per cent.'

'It's my charger. And I'm just about to get to level forty-seven, and I'm almost out of charge,' Hugo says, without even looking up from the screen.

I've had enough of this. Since we've been staying here, inevitably the kids have been on their devices more, what with us being so busy trying to sort everything out, but also because they're off school and we don't have a garden they can pop into to play in.

We really are getting on top of each other here, and until things are running normally, and that includes us having a house to live in, I don't see anything improving.

'Mummy, can we go and see Bear and Patch this morning?'

I'm trying to apply mascara in the bathroom, as I have a meeting with Fabien and one of his clients later. It coincided, of course, with Ronnie's interview at Petrocord, which is at nine thirty today. He was nervous as hell, not having been for an interview for over a decade, except within his own company, plus he knows how much is riding on this. I didn't want to add undue pressure on him, but we really need him, I really need him, to get the job. The very thought of having to manage the kids on my own, from a hotel room, for the summer, whilst our house is rebuilt, and we have our best friend in hospital still, doesn't bear thinking about. Oh, and I almost forgot the baby there, too. As that meerkat off the TV ad would say, 'Simples!' Not.

Focusing on Aria, and bending down to her level, I say, 'Not today, honey. You're going to Valentin's, remember?'

Valentin offered to watch them, when he found out at the hospital the other night what a bind I'm in over this first Cerulean meeting and Ronnie's interview clashing. In fact, he's been brilliant, offering me business advice on subjects I hadn't even considered when moving into a partnership.

'But I miss Patch, and Bear.' Aria's eyes fill with tears, and I know she's not just being difficult, it's really affecting her, being without them.

I hug her to me, as I block out the argument ensuing in the background between Gen and Hugo. I swear I'm about to put them on a device ban. They're both old enough to realise how important today is, well, Gen is at least, but Hugo should also know better. He's almost nine.

'We'll see them soon. Maybe I can take you this afternoon or tomorrow.' I dry her tears away and kiss her head. This is killing me that it's so hard for the kids. Usually, I'd pick Aria up to comfort her too, but I'm aware I can't do that, as I'm pregnant. We've already had a couple of instances where the kids have been a little rough and tumble with me, playing or in Aria's case, wanting me to carry her to bed when she's tired, and I've had to fake a sore back. I hate lying to them, but we're not ready to tell them about the baby yet. We can't. Even without everything else going on, I'm nervous about telling them, and don't want to jinx anything. I couldn't bear it if we told them about the baby and something went wrong, so we're waiting until after the twelve-week scan. It can't come soon enough.

Eventually, whilst I'm comforting Aria, Gen and Hugo sort their own problem out, thank goodness. I have to drop everyone at Valentin's in half an hour, so I remind them – the irony not lost on me – to take their chargers, a light jacket and their patience and good manners, before we head off.

Fortunately, Valentin lives close to the Cerulean hotel where my meeting is taking place. As I drive, I simultaneously think about the meeting and try to calm the nerves in my fluttering stomach. Am I really good enough to do this? Especially given the current mess I'm in. I also fear letting Fabien down, given how much he has helped us. What if his client doesn't like my designs? Fabien told me not to stress about it, he'd love them, but a lot is riding on this. Fabien's partnership offer allowed Ronnie to consider a role onshore, as the extra money from the Cerulean deal cancels out Ronnie's expected pay cut. And I'm never more mindful of this than as I drive to this meeting, in the knowledge that Ronnie is currently in

Aberdeen, at an interview with Petrocord which could change our family dynamic, life and marriage forever. No pressure then! For either of us.

Fortunately, the kids are better behaved in the car. Gen's on her phone, Hugo's on his iPad and Aria is literally counting sheep, although I hate to tell her we're about to run out of sheep to count as we head towards the city.

'Mummy, look a horse! Two horses!' Aria cries in delight.

I glance across to see, just off the motorway, a pair of horses in a field. They're usually there when we pass, but it's often evening and Aria has fallen asleep. It warms my heart to see her so happy over such a small thing, and it buoys my spirits.

'Thanks, Valentin. I really appreciate it. Sorry to rush off, but the traffic on the bridge was torture, and now I'm a little later than I'd hoped to be.'

Valentin flashes me his trademark smile. 'Don't worry, Louisa. We have it all in hand. Who wants to have a go with my new VR headset?'

Cheers of 'Me, me' go up from both Gen and Hugo. Aria looks at me. 'Mummy, what's a VR headset?'

Valentin sees me about to be waylaid again and starts to explain to her. 'I don't think I'm big enough for that,' she declares. 'Do you have any My Little Ponies?'

The way she asks, as if she's in a café ordering off the menu, makes me smile.

'I'm afraid I don't have,' says Valentin, 'but I think I have something even better. Why don't you come and see?'

She takes his hand, blows me a kiss and I mouth a silent thank you to Valentin, who grins and turns Aria by the shoulders in the other direction to the front door, through which I then exit.

'Louisa, there you are.' Fabien rises from his seat in the meeting room at the Glaston Spa Resort and Hotel. He shakes my hand, and the man to his side follows suit.

'Louisa, meet Charles Pickford. Charles, Louisa Halliday.'

Introductions made, we sit down, and the barista comes in with a tray of tea, coffee, and some delicious-looking scones and muffins. I'm dying to have the lemon one, as with all the drama this morning and the kids breakfasting downstairs with Ronnie whilst I had a shower, I haven't actually eaten yet. I know this is bad, and especially for the baby's sake, I need to look after myself, but I simply didn't have time. I thought I'd be able to grab a muffin from the little patisserie they have downstairs in the foyer, but it was closed. So now I'm practically salivating at the sight of the muffins, and oh no, not that.

'I'm sorry. Could you excuse me one second? Where are the bathrooms?'

Fabien eyes me curiously. I know how rude it is to leave before we've even started, but if I don't reach the toilet quickly, there's going to be an accident.

A few minutes later I throw up into the toilet bowl, then lay my cheek against the cool wall of the toilet. I know it's not the most sanitary, but it is a posh hotel, and it's either that or start stripping off layers of clothes as I feel so warm, as if I'm about to combust.

The aroma of the coffee set me off. I can handle Nescafe and Douwe Egberts, but place a freshly brewed cup of coffee in my vicinity, and there's a good chance I'll be sick. God, how could I have forgotten how easily this happens? Aria's only four, so five years ago, I was living through the same nightmare, although I wasn't trying to actively impress a client, or rather a partner's client.

How do I explain my rudeness? I don't want to come across as flaky, or ill – he'll want to sit as far away from me as possible – or incompetent, and I can't yet tell Fabien, never mind Charles, that I'm pregnant. Argh! I have no idea how to explain my actions.

By the time I've composed myself, and feel slightly better, I've decided the only thing I can do is say the kids are coming down with something, and I must be too. I can't exactly say I must have eaten something that disagreed with me, since I'm dining at Garfield Grange each day. I don't want Fabien haranguing the chef, making him think he'd given one of the guests food poisoning. What a mess. The sooner I can come clean about my pregnancy, the better.

'Sorry about that. I wasn't feeling great in the car on the way in. My daughter's coming down with something, and I think I may have caught whatever it is.'

Charles shifts almost imperceptibly in his seat as if distancing himself from me, but he has nowhere really he can go.

'Sorry to hear that, Louisa,' Fabien says. 'Well, we'll not prolong the meeting then, in case you feel unwell again.' I can't help but notice a slight barb in his words, but I'm unsure if I'm being oversensitive or not. Pregnancy does that too, I recall. 'Let's crack on.'

As Fabien talks, discussing how our relationship would work and what my contribution would be, I take the time to assess Charles. He looks monied. I mean, seriously monied. Even to my untrained eye, he's wearing an expensive grey pinstripe suit. No off the rack for him. I don't imagine this came from Slater's either, more like Armani. He looks well in it. Single-breasted, two button. And I don't know what aftershave he's wearing, but it is pungent. My eyes are almost watering. In fact, the woodsy scent is so strong, I gag, then have to disguise it with a cough.

I'd say he's in his late fifties, but he looks younger. And I'm sure his teeth weren't originally that colour. They're so white I almost have to look away for fear of being blinded. And his posture is so relaxed, one foot crossed over the other leg, his elbow resting on the sofa, two fingers against his cheek as he takes in what Fabien is saying, he must be powerful. I can't help drawing a parallel with how poor Ronnie might be feeling or behaving right now in his interview. He was a bag of nerves last night and this morning, and he wore the suit I bought him for Ayren and Eloise's wedding, which we'd been able to snaffle from the house, via our trusty policeman friend.

I'm aware of the nausea creeping back in, and I try surreptitiously to inhale a couple of breaths, but Fabien draws me a look, and I figure I've probably come across as impatient or bored, when nothing is further from the truth. I wish the staff would remove the coffee pot as the smell is making me want to heave. It's also making it hard for me to concentrate as I'm so busy focusing on not being sick.

I'm lucky if I've caught half of what Fabien has said, and I only hope it's enough to see me through and I can fill in the blanks by quizzing him later.

'So essentially, Charles would like you to lead a training session in Madrid, next month, to show his staff your designs and talk them through the practices of British weddings. His company has a lot of destination weddings in Spain and other parts of the Mediterranean, and he's looking to upsell to offer complete wedding packages, from the stationery suites, to the favours, hotel rooms to the flights.'

'Sounds incredibly organised, and it would certainly make it easier for the bride and groom, and their families,' I say, privately thinking that it's almost taking the soul out of the wedding. Brides and their families, for the most part, enjoy the planning stage, the seeing everything coming together.

The meeting can't end soon enough. It has taken all my inner strength not to vomit all over Charles Pickford's no doubt two-thousand-pound Church shoes. I only recognise them as one of my brides was telling me how her husband had shelled out for these exorbitant shoes for the wedding, when it would have covered the price of the honeymoon. But he wanted their wedding to be classy, apparently. Pity it only lasted seven months. At least he has his lovely shoes made in Northampton to cuddle at night. I digress. I'm still willing myself to get through this meeting without hurling, or making more of a tit of myself than I have already. At best, Charles must think me disinterested, at worst, incompetent. Guilt clings to me at letting Fabien down.

'So, I'll be in touch to arrange the training in Madrid,' says Charles, holding out his hand for me to shake. I'm surprised he's being so civil. I've been almost totally monosyllabic the whole time. I have never portrayed myself, or my company, or anyone else's company, for that matter, as badly as I have in this meeting. I want to weep, and I don't think it's just the hormones this time.

Fabien escorts Charles out and returns five minutes later, his eyes part flashing with anger, part laced with concern. I wasn't even aware that was possible.

'Louisa, do you want to tell me what is going on?'

Chapter Seven

Monday 19 July

'So, how did it go?' Valentin is all smiles as my children descend upon me. If we were still of the generation where mothers wore underskirts – they do? – Aria would be literally clinging to mine – Hugo too for that matter.

'Don't ask.'

Valentin frowns. 'You are rather pale. Would you like something to eat? Maybe a coffee.'

I bolt for the bathroom. Thank God I know where it is.

When I return, the kids are waiting, staring at me, their eyes wide.

'Mummy, are you OK? Were they mean to you? Did they make you cry?' Aria, my little warrior asks me. No one had better get on the wrong side of her – she's very defensive of her family.

Gen rubs my arm. 'Mum, you look awful.' My face must fall as she says, 'That came out wrong. I mean, you don't look well. Are you sure you're OK? What happened?'

I hate lying to the kids, but Ronnie and I agreed we would wait until after the scan before telling the kids, so I grit my teeth and say, 'I think it must be something I ate.'

'At the hotel?' Hugo looks outraged. 'Isn't it six stars or something?'

'Five,' I gasp. Now I'm really not feeling well.

Valentin seems to sense this. 'Louisa, why don't you go for a lie-down in the guest room. We can play here a bit longer. In fact, Sebastian's collecting Xander soon. They can all play together, but we'll try to keep the noise down, won't we, guys?'

'Yes, Mummy. We'll be on our best behaviour. Won't we?' Aria eyes her brother and sister as if daring them to contradict her.

'Yes, Aria,' they say in the tone you'd use if you were addressing your sergeant major in the army.

'That's settled then. Why don't I bring you some ginger tea in the guest room? Maybe that will settle your stomach too,' Valentin says.

Belatedly, I recall I haven't eaten anything. My blood sugar is probably dangerously low.

'Thanks. That would be great, Valentin.'

The kids fuss over me until I prop myself up with pillows in the guest room, mind awhirl with thoughts of Valentin and Sebastian being in the same room. That's not awkward at all. Hopefully, I'll miss that, if I stay in here long enough.

I'm amazed, and gratified, if they've come to some agreement over how to help Nicky and manage Xander whilst Nicky's in hospital, and I wonder if Sebastian knows Nicky and Xander are moving in here. I certainly won't be the one to tell Sebastian, who has a very unorthodox attitude towards his ex dating anyone, despite him living with, and having already impregnated, someone else, and now being a new dad to another child.

I roll back on the bed, thoughts of the nightmarish meeting with Charles and Fabien running through my mind. Hopefully, I managed to talk my way out of things with Fabien, apologising profusely and convincing him I simply didn't feel well and I'd go to the doctor. I knew he'd be straight on the phone to Charles after we spoke to apologise on my behalf. Normally, I'd be irked by that, but quite frankly I could have damaged a client relationship, so he can apologise away. Or maybe he already did when he saw him out. I'll just close my eyes for a little bit, and hopefully this feeling will pass.

I wake to the sound of Hugo shouting 'Xan!' Clearly, he has forgotten he was supposed to keep quiet. How long have I been asleep? I glance at the clock on the bedside table. Crikey – I've been sleeping for more than two hours. Where did my day go? My phone is on the table too, and I see I have a few missed calls. Ronnie. Well, I slept through those. No message. Hmm.

I go into the en suite to wash my face and spruce myself up a little before facing the masses again. I'm keen to see how Xander is doing, even though it's only a few days since I last saw him. Although he's staying with his father, I feel as if I should unofficially be keeping an eye on him for Nicky. She doesn't exactly rate Sebastian as a parent, but needs must. No one could have foreseen her lengthy stay in hospital.

When I venture out into the living area, it seems I'm only just in time as the doorbell rings and Sebastian soon fills the doorway.

'He's been no trouble,' Valentin says. Sebastian hasn't seen me yet. 'Xander, that's your dad. Can you go get your stuff and say your goodbyes?'

'Sebastian,' I say. 'How's he doing?' I've gravitated towards the outer living room, nearer the front door, where Valentin is talking with Sebastian. Clearly, Valentin has limits – he doesn't want Sebastian poking about his house, or maybe my brain's going haywire, imagining scenarios that don't exist.

'Oh, hi, Louisa. Yeah–' he looks to where Xander is playing the VR game with Hugo '–I think he's doing all right.'

'That's good.'

'Yeah.' He taps his hand against his legs, beating out a rhythm. He's obviously finding this as awkward as I am.

'Xander, Dad's here,' Valentin calls again.

'I can't believe you get to live here,' I hear Hugo say.

'Well, he has worked hard, Hugo.' I smile at Valentin. 'If you work hard, maybe you'll have a lovely house like Valentin one day.'

'Mum! I don't mean Valentin. I know he lives here, I meant Xander, when he and Nicky move in with him.'

Oh shit. How does he know that?

Never mind cutting the atmosphere with a knife, how about a ruddy, big stinking hacksaw. My eyes close involuntarily as if to will away the scene unfolding in front of me.

'What's that, Hugo?' Sebastian says, his voice dangerously soft.

'Oh, hi, Sebastian. I was just saying how cool it'll be for Xan when he moves in here when Nicky gets out of hospital.'

'Are we, Valentin? Are we really moving in here?' Xander's eyes are shining.

Oh God, I'm guessing Nicky hasn't discussed it with

either of them. I didn't think she would have. I thought she would have waited until she was out of hospital, and from the blood draining from Valentin's face, and the blood rising in Sebastian's, I'm right.

Time to intervene. 'Valentin, thanks so much for looking after them for me and for letting me use your guest room. I'm much better now.' My eyes don't meet Sebastian's, but I can feel them boring into the top of my head. 'Guys, thank Valentin, and let's get your things.'

But that tactic doesn't work.

Valentin is too dumbstruck to answer. His brain will no doubt still be stuck trying to figure out how this situation has come about, and how Hugo knows, something I'd quite like to know too.

'Come on, Xan. We'll discuss it later, with your mum.' Again, his voice is dangerously soft. I'll need to pre-warn Nicky. The last thing I want is Sebastian stomping into the hospital with his size twelves, shouting the odds and scuppering Nicky's recovery.

I throw Valentin a helpless look, but when I turn back towards the door, Sebastian's eyes are locked on Valentin, and if looks could kill…

'Well, that was uncomfortable.' Valentin blows out a breath, almost a sigh of relief at Sebastian and Xander's departure.

The kids have taken my stalling as reason to resume playing the VR, or in Aria's case watching on the cinema screen TV.

'I'm so sorry, Valentin. I don't know how Hugo knows, as we haven't told the kids. The only thing I can think of is he overheard me and Ronnie talking about it, but we're always so careful around the kids with stuff they shouldn't know.' I think of my pregnancy.

He sighs, audibly this time. 'Don't worry. He would have found out eventually. I'll let Nicky know tonight when I go in.'

I shake my head. Can this day get any worse?

As I draw into the car park at the hotel, I suddenly remember the missed calls from Ronnie. Ronnie. Damn, the interview. Well, there's no point calling him back now, we're 'home'. I can ask him in a minute, but first, as we exit the car, I take Hugo aside, ushering the girls on ahead of us.

'Hugo, who told you Nicky and Xander were moving into Valentin's?'

He has the good grace to hang his head a little. 'I-I-I heard you and Dad talking about it. Sorry, I didn't realise it was a secret. Why *is* it a secret?' His eyebrows furrow in puzzlement.

'Don't worry. It's just because Nicky is still in hospital and hasn't had a chance to discuss it with Sebastian. I think she wanted to wait until she came out, and I imagine Sebastian is a bit sad as he is Xander's daddy.'

Hugo frowns. 'But Sebastian doesn't live with Nicky any more. He hasn't for absolutely ages.' He draws out these last two words, and I stifle a smile. He can be so grown-up sometimes. 'Sebastian lives with Brittany now, and they have a new baby. Sabena. She's so cute, Mummy. Can we go and see her again?'

Although I'd assumed Brittany would have made herself scarce with the baby when Xander returned home from hospital, she'd returned later before the children and Ronnie's visit was over, so they had met the new baby, Sabena, and loved her.

'I'm not sure when that will be possible, sweetheart,' I say as a way of avoiding having this conversation. I think we, as a family, have put our foot in it enough for one day, with the Valentin and Nicky moving in together revelation, without adding to the tension by visiting Nicky's ex's baby.

Ronnie's car is parked a few spaces away from mine. Good, he's back. I'm keen to see how he fared at his interview. It's hard to know who was more nervous about it. I shepherd the kids into the hotel, and after shrieks of 'Daddy', the kids soon peel off to their different areas and rooms whilst Ronnie and I settle down on the sofa.

I scan his face for clues of how it went, but it gives nothing away. Then he puts his hand on my arm and says, 'Listen, I'm really sorry, I know you hoped this might be the answer, but…it went really well!' he shouts.

'You're horrible! You had me going there!' Relief swamps me as he takes me into his arms and giggles against my neck. Despite my heart initially sinking at the announcement I expected him to make, I appreciate the light-hearted moment he created. Particularly after the day I've had. If we could only fix everything else so easily.

'Well, this deserves a celebration. I think we have a bottle of Shloer in the fridge.'

Ronnie grins. 'I was thinking more of the real thing, but perhaps we can wait until tonight for that.'

I glance at my watch. It's two o'clock. 'Yes, let's put that idea on ice.'

Ronnie groans. 'Sometimes I think you're a man, your jokes are so bad.'

'Oh really? You think I'm a man?'

He glances down my body, thankfully no children are present, then he tugs me towards him and says, 'Not your body, just your mind.' Then he kisses me until I break away and remind him that the kids are in the adjoining rooms and that when you're pregnant, it makes you horny as hell.

He laughs. 'Good. Hopefully that will keep until later too.'

I bat him away and bring two glasses and the bottle of Shloer, which I do indeed have in the fridge. 'To possibilities!'

Ronnie raises his glass to mine, and we clink them together. 'To possibilities.'

'Now, tell me exactly what happened at the interview.'

Ronnie proceeds to tell me the ins and outs. I try not to zone out at the technical bits, as my intention is to support him fully, and he's so animated, it's lovely to see that shine back in him. It has been sadly lacking of late. By the time he's finished regaling me with the interview questions and how he thinks he answered each one, and the vibe he had from the interview panel, I have to say they'd be crazy not to give him the job. Things are looking up, and it can't come soon enough.

Chapter Eight

Friday 30 July

To-do list

Call insurance – purely because I feel they'll miss me if I don't, not because I think they're actually trying to find a solution for us

Take ring to jeweller to get resized

Place materials order for Wedded Bliss

Buy Ronnie a couple of Craghoppers tops – what he prefers when off duty on rigs

'I thought I'd have heard something by now.' Ronnie paces the floor until I fear it will soon be threadbare.

'These things take time,' I say, but he doesn't appreciate my platitude.

'In this day and age, with email, there's no reason for everything to take so long.'

'Ronnie, you're worrying unnecessarily. You know how much red tape there is with the oil industry.'

He stops pacing for a second. 'You're right. Well, I need something to take my mind off things for now.'

I think for a second, then say, 'Well, you could apply for other jobs in the meantime. Nothing to say you have to put all your eggs in one oil company.'

He glares at me, unimpressed by my attempt at levity. 'This is no joke, Louisa.'

Louisa. I hate when he calls me Louisa. It's like when Mum used to call me it when I was naughty. Where Ronnie's concerned, it means he's unhappy with me.

'I know it isn't, but getting uptight about it won't help anything.' *Or anyone.* 'Seriously, why don't we sit down together and see if any new jobs have come up in the past few days?'

Ronnie sits down sulkily. Honestly, he's worse than a child sometimes, and I have three of those – soon to be four – and the last thing I need is him morphing into one entirely.

I understand he's disappointed not to have heard from Petrocord yet, but the interview went well, so he's overanalysing the delay. Worrying about nothing.

But he won't be placated. He obviously has something else on his mind.

'Ronnie, out with it? What's really bothering you?'

'The job *is* bothering me.'

'I'm not saying it isn't–'

'But it's everything. It would have been hard enough adjusting to moving back to the mainland, but to do it and live in a hotel room, which is amazing, but the kids are falling over each other, we're falling over each other, we're all sniping at each other, and we can't find a bloody house to rent. And those loss adjusters are dragging their feet, I know they are. I can't see how we'll be back in the house this year.' He draws breath, and I nod and am about to say something, when he continues. 'And you're pregnant, and instead of working less, you're working more. A new partnership. And I feel redundant.'

'Ronnie, you do still work at Callan. You could go back if you wanted to.'

'What? To Azerbaijan?'

'Temporarily if need be,' I say, trying to hide the weight of disappointment descending on my chest.

He looks at me as though searching for the right answer.

A silence stretches between us.

I have to help him, support him. 'I know it's not what we want, but if you're feeling this dejected, and if the job doesn't pan out, or materialise, then you have that option.'

'I'm supposed to go back soon or take unpaid leave. I took all my holidays at once because of the crash.'

The set of his jaw and the way he is holding his shoulders rigid show me just how uptight he is about it all.

I massage his shoulder with one hand. 'Ronnie, we're not at that stage yet. I know it's frustrating being unable to find a temporary house, and we'll keep looking–' there's nothing out there '–but you had a good feeling about the interview, so let's not allow the other stuff to put you on a downer. We can address that, together, OK?' I gaze into his eyes until he nods.

He sighs. 'You're right. I'm sorry to be on such a massive downer. It's just all getting to me. I thought it'd be easier than this to return onshore.'

'Ronnie, we're not in a usual situation.' I throw my arm out around the suite. 'Did you ever envisage this?'

He grins. 'Yes, but not to live in, and not with the kids.'

I smile. 'Yeah, it's not as easy as I thought, living in a luxury hotel suite.'

Ronnie bounces to his feet. 'Right, let's get this show on the road. We're not doing CVs right now, that can wait, but since Wendy has the kids, we're going for lunch.'

'What? Not in the hotel?'

'Nope, we're going back to Ferniehall. I really liked the Café on the Cobblestones.'

'I'll get my bag.' *Before you change your mind.*

We have a lovely lunch at Café on the Cobblestones, even though I do covet Ronnie's shellfish cappuccino starter – I'm definitely coming back for that when I'm no longer pregnant. Fortunately, my aged beef meatball is equally as delicious as Ronnie proclaims his seafood to be.

I'm surprisingly starving for someone who is still in the first trimester. So, my main course of North Sea hake with baby leeks and parsley butter hits the spot. Ronnie opts for the salt-aged pork with sticky sausages. That sounds good too. I'm pretty sure they've changed the menu since I was in last, but in any case, they can keep doing what they're doing, as the food is amazing.

I order a peppermint tea whilst Ronnie – bottomless pit – has rhubarb with honeycomb semifreddo.

'Babe, isn't peppermint tea bad for you in the first trimester?' he says before the waitress walks away.

'It is?' I try to remember but draw a blank. 'Can you give me a second, sorry, just to check?' I ask the waitress.

'Of course. Take your time.'

I quickly google it and discover Ronnie is right, so I decide to have hot chocolate with marshmallows and cream. I already couldn't have the goats' cheese starter, I think it's only fair I have some sort of treat.

Whilst we wait for the waitress to bring my drink and Ronnie's dessert, I recall the last time I was here was when Sam told me she was pregnant, and I worked out I probably was too. I tell Ronnie this and he smiles at me, fondly, then down at my as-yet non-existent bump. I always feel like a fraud until I have a bump, as if people won't believe me.

Belatedly, I realise we probably shouldn't have mentioned in front of the waitress about the peppermint tea being bad for pregnant women. I still haven't told my parents yet, and here we are mentioning it in front of a stranger. But then, who's she going to tell?

The bill is somewhat steeper than we'd usually pay, but the menu does seem to have morphed into some gastronomic delight, so I decide it's OK to live a little. Let's face it, everything else is being paid for, back at the hotel, and I wonder once again how I'll ever repay Fabien. Right now, I'm wondering how I'll ever face him again after the debacle last week. I still turn tomato red when I think of it.

Since we're on our own, and out and about anyway, we stroll along Main Street, retracing the steps we took the day we saw the midwife. It's been a few days since we visited the house to check on the progress, and we really should pop our heads in to see Martha too, see how she's doing.

We're about to pass our local bakery, Icing on the Cake, when I grab Ronnie's sleeve. 'We can't go home without some cakes for the kids.'

'Lou, we're living in a 5-star hotel, all expenses paid. What more could they possibly want to eat?'

'I know Hugo. And nothing will make him happier than a special gingerbread man from here. Aria, too, for that matter. And I dare say Gen won't say no to one of their chocolate éclairs.'

'OK, but you mollycoddle them.'

'Maybe. But if you can't treat your own kids, who can you?'

Ronnie stands to the side once we enter as I choose cakes for the kids and then add a selection including a cream cornet and an apple turnover.

'Louisa, Ronnie, how are you both doing?' Cynthia asks, her voice dropping to a whisper as if she's attending a funeral.

'We're good, thanks,' I say. 'And I think the family will be even better once they have some of your cakes.'

'Oh, so kind of you to say so.' She turns to Ronnie. 'Or is she trying to butter me up?' She winks at him, and Ronnie looks away, uncomfortable. She's seventy-five if she's a day, Cynthia, but she can still appreciate a good-looking man it seems. I stifle a laugh. Ronnie's terrible at dealing with people flirting with him. When we were first together, it used to happen all the time. He never did learn how to brush it off with a laugh.

Once I've given Cynthia our order, and she's packing it into little paper bags, she says, 'So, terrible business about your house.'

Understatement of the century. 'Yes, although we're just lucky no one was killed.'

She shakes her head sagely. 'You're so right, and that's absolutely the attitude to have. Many people would have gone to pieces if it happened to them, but look at you both. Strong. Ready to face the world.'

I don't know about that.

'We do what we can–' I shrug '–but we can't wait for it to be ready to move back into.'

'That won't be for a while, though,' Ronnie mutters under his breath as he lounges against the wall, scrolling through his phone, barely paying attention.

'Oh? Have they told you when yet then?' Cynthia asks, curiosity getting the better of her.

'No, but they have indicated it's likely to be a good few months, maybe more.'

'That's terrible. Poor you. How are the kids coping?'

Ronnie snorts, and Cynthia nods her head towards him. 'That good then?'

'They're just finding it very difficult to be so confined. I mean, I know how lucky we are to be staying in a fancy hotel, but kids don't really see that after the first few days.'

She grimaces. 'I suppose not, poor dears.'

Since she seems to care, I go on: 'We were trying to rent somewhere, but the places we saw online were – how can I put this? – horrific.'

'Oh dear. You don't want that. Tell you what, why don't you advertise, in here? In the library, the bookshop, anywhere and everywhere that has a noticeboard?'

My eyes widen. 'Really? I hadn't thought of that. Thanks, Cynthia. It's got to be worth a try. Hasn't it, Ronnie?'

'Hasn't what?' Ronnie glances up from his phone, and Cynthia and I share a look. Men.

'Never mind. Cynthia, I'll let you know how we get on.'

We pay a visit to the bookshop to purchase some plain postcards and funky-coloured pens so we can write our ads. It doesn't take us long to cobble something decent together.

Soon after, we're walking through the village leaving ads on every community board we can, indoor and outdoor: at the park, the church, in Jumping Bean, the library, the hairdresser, even in the Tesco Express.

By the time we've put a pin in the last ad, I have quite the spring in my step.

'Kids?' Ronnie asks.

'Suppose we'd better. Wendy will be needing the break.' We head back to the car, arm in arm, positive vibes radiating from us. And I can't help thinking I wish we could be together like this more often.

Chapter Nine

Saturday 31 July

To-do list
Eat humble pie with Nicky
Buy Nicky Monty Bojangles – only thing that might make her forgive our lapse
Fall at Nicky's feet and beg for forgiveness

'I'm so sorry, Nicky. I had no idea he was nearby when we were talking about it.'

I sit down on one of the uncomfortable beige plastic chairs that seem to be de rigueur for visitors in hospital wards and do my best to find a position that isn't positively excruciating.

Nicky's still in pain. I can see from the wince she gives as she tries to lever herself higher up on the bed.

'Here, let me.' I go to prop a pillow behind her to make life easier for her, but she waves me away.

'I've got to learn to manage all this by myself, or they'll never let me out of here.' Her voice cracks, and I can tell the longevity of her stay is getting to her. Plus, she's still in plaster. I can only imagine how she feels, although I know that I too would struggle to be in hospital for any length of time. We might fool ourselves as busy mums that we'd like to go in for a bit of a rest, but the stark overhead lights on all the time, the constant noise, the beeps, the occasional scream – depends which hospital you're in, and in which department – don't make for a pleasant experience. And don't get me started on the food. Café on the Cobblestones it is not. Fleetingly, I think of how I'll be in hospital again in the not-too-distant future, giving birth. Hopefully, I'll be in and out in one to two days, though, since I'm no stranger to childbirth.

'Sorry, I didn't mean to be sharp, it's just…Sebastian.'

My heart sinks. I knew Hugo blabbing about the move would be a problem, but the very last thing Nicky needs right now is anything else piled onto her plate, and certainly not from her ungracious ex.

'What happened?' I pour myself and Nicky some water from the jug on her bedside locker, hand her one glass, and take a sip of my own. My throat has gone as dry as the Gobi Desert.

'Well, you know Sebastian's not one to mince his words, so after the text he sent the other day with an ambiguous "We need to talk", he came in here, eyes flashing, nostrils flaring, talking in that dangerously soft way he used to when he was angry with me. I swear to God, if I hadn't been in a hospital bed, I think he might've hit me.' Her voice cracks. 'He certainly looked like he wanted to.'

'Oh God, Nicky, I'm so sorry.'

'I don't know why I let him get to me. He's not in control of my life now, we only link via Xander, but he still acts as if he is.'

Nausea rises in my stomach. Oh, please, no. Not now.

And I don't think the nausea is pregnancy-related. I know Sebastian never hit Nicky, well, as long as she was truthful with me, but he was often verbally abusive, and he chipped away at her self-esteem until she felt worthless. How dare he try this crap on her again? Where does he get off? I feel like punching him myself. And doubly how dare he, when she's lying here in a hospital bed, shattered, after a serious accident. Yes, my original opinion of him is upheld, and it's not something I'm happy to be right about.

'Listen,' I say, 'don't worry about him. He's all bluster, and anyway, you have Valentin now. You did tell him, didn't you, about Sebastian's behaviour?'

Nicky doesn't meet my eyes.

'Nic, you have to tell him. How much does he know about Sebastian?'

'Not much. Just that we don't get on, and it ended badly between us.'

I shake my head. 'Nic, you need to tell him more than that. I understand why you wouldn't have told him earlier, it's hardly something you want to throw into a fledgling relationship, after all, but Valentin needs to know how much Sebastian got inside your head.'

She sighs and fights back tears. 'Why is nothing ever easy?'

I copy her sigh. 'Unfortunately, that's life. But once Valentin knows the full story, he won't put up with Sebastian trying to take the moral high ground and browbeating you with the fact you're moving his son in with another man.' I pause and she nods. 'And, apart from Sebastian's supreme sense of being in the right about everything, no one in their right mind would think it OK to rant and rave like he has done, when he shacked up with someone else and got them pregnant.'

Nicky winces again, and I temper my next words. 'My point is, he has no right, as we know, to act all high and mighty. He left you, and he left you in the lurch, and didn't see Xander for several years. And if he really becomes a problem, or starts shouting the odds again, you can always threaten him with a restraining order.'

Nicky blanches. 'I couldn't do that.'

Fury boils up from deep in my gut. I hate that Sebastian has reduced Nicky to this meek, quivering mess again. All it took was one conversation. If I get my hands on him, I'll break his neck myself. He seems to forget Nicky isn't alone, she has friends, some of whom are six foot, broad and unlikely to cave or quail at his verbal assaults. Perhaps he needs reminding of that. But before I get too carried away with 'sorting Sebastian out', I hug Nicky to me and say, 'You could, and you will if he persists.'

'He said he might not let Xander come back to the hospital to see me.' Tears flow freely down her face now.

That's it. I'm not having this. Sebastian needs reminding of his past misdeeds and that he's in no position to put the frighteners on my friend. He's messed with the wrong person one time too many.

'That's not going to happen, so don't worry about it. Ronnie and I will go see him later.'

'Would you?' Her face visibly relaxes: hours, days of tension undoing themselves in a split second.

'Just you leave it to me.'

'He did what?' Ronnie asks.

'Told her he would stop Xander going to visit.'

'I never did like him, but I didn't know he was that much of a–'

'Yep, I often find it difficult to find the right name for him too.' I wrap my arms around Ronnie's neck. 'You'll come with me, won't you?'

'I'll definitely go see him, but I'm not sure I want you going, especially in your condition.'

'I'll be fine. And I won't do anything stupid. Plus, it's not as if he'll get violent. His blows are all verbal.'

'OK then. As long as you're sure about that.'

'I am.' I kiss him, long and hard. How I love this man, and as I think it, I realise just how true it is.

'You're not really going round to Sebastian's, are you?' Sam says when I call her to see how she's doing.

Once we'd caught up on each other's news, I'd filled her in on the latest with Nicky, and told her of Sebastian's latest stunt and threat.

'Yes, Ronnie and I are going together. I can't let Sebastian get away with stressing Nicky out like this. It can't be good for her, and surely as a parent he must realise how it will negatively impact on Xander. Plus, what happens if she's so stressed out the doctors delay her release from hospital? Xander would be gutted.'

'Yeah, but Sebastian always was all about himself.'

'I won't disagree with you there, Sam.'

'I can't believe he would think he can stop her seeing Xander whilst she's in hospital. That would never hold up in court.'

'I know, but people like Sebastian don't believe the

rules apply to them. Anyway, hopefully, Ronnie and I can set him straight sooner rather than later.'

'Let me know how you get on as soon as you're back, please. I'll only worry otherwise.'

'I will, and I know you will, but please don't. There's no need. Anyway, did I tell you we put up notices in the village and in Hamwell and Lymeburn too, advertising for a house to rent?'

'No, you did not. I think we've both had so much going on, it's like playing dot-to-dot with some of the numbers missing.'

'I can relate to that. Well, anyway, we were in Icing on the Cake, when Cynthia suggested we put up an ad in the bakery window, and then it kind of mushroomed from there, and we placed them all over.'

'Have you had any bites yet?'

'Sadly not, but I'm hopeful something will turn up soon. It's got to. I have everything crossed, plus I think if we have to spend another month cooped up in a luxury hotel suite, we may kill each other.'

'I'm guessing you're saying that tongue in cheek.'

'Yes. It's the lack of outdoor space, places to escape to within the room as opposed to our house, that kind of thing. And it's the fact we have no idea when we can move back into the house. We still don't know for sure we can. This uncertainty is killing us. Everything takes so long. No wonder everyone hates insurance companies.'

'Yes, they don't do anything quickly, do they? Oh, Lou, I'm sorry, I've got to go. I'm bursting for the loo. Has that happened to you again recently – the needing the toilet all the time? I'd forgotten about that.'

'No, not yet, although since I had Aria I've needed the

loo about twenty times a day. Must have forgotten to do my pelvic floor exercises or something.'

'Love you, good luck!' is her parting shot, and I smile as I imagine her dashing to the bathroom.

Some things never change.

'You ready to go?' I ask Ronnie, who looks anything but. He's reclined on the sofa with Aria almost under one arm, Gen in a onesie cuddled into his side, and Hugo lying at his feet, on his elbows, hair sticking up in every direction, watching some David Attenborough nature programme.

'Hmm?'

'I hate to interrupt this scene of familial bliss–' and I do '–but Jo texted to say she'll be five minutes.'

'Ah, no worries. I'll just freshen up.'

'For His Nibs?' I say.

'No–' he shakes his head in exasperation '–for all the women I'll pass as I leave the foyer.'

'You're not funny.' I give him a mock slap to the head and tell him, 'Four minutes.'

'OK, OK, I'm getting ready.'

When Jo arrives, for once she's serious. Usually, she'd like the idea that she's covering for a clandestine operation, but even she recognises the severity of Sebastian's behaviour, not to mention how totally uncool he is being. I'm being polite, obviously.

We whisper in the entrance of the suite so the kids don't overhear, and I tell her I've had confirmation from Nicky that Sebastian didn't bring Xander to visit tonight. I knew he wouldn't, but he's not getting away with it. He thinks Nicky will simply roll over and let him do what he likes, especially given her current situation – helpless in hospital. He couldn't be more wrong, not with us at her side.

Soon the kids notice their aunt's presence, and she's besieged by her nieces and nephew. They don't often get one-on-one time with her and they're clearly going to make the most of it.

Ronnie cuts the engine just outside Sebastian's and turns to me. 'You don't need to do this. I can do it on my own.'

I lean over and kiss him. 'I know you can, but Nicky's my friend, and if Xander's around, he would wonder why you were there without me.'

Reluctantly, Ronnie accepts the truth in this. We stand in front of Sebastian's house. I take a deep breath and knock on the door.

But it's not Sebastian who answers, it's Brittany. We've only met a few times, and her eyes widen as if wondering why we're gracing her doorstep at this hour.

'Hi, Brittany, I'm looking for Sebastian.'

'Who is it, love?' Sebastian calls from inside.

Love. Wish he knew the meaning of the word. Or perhaps he does, with Brittany, but he certainly didn't, and doesn't, with Nicky.

'Can we come in?' I ask Brittany, already ushering her backwards into her house.

Belatedly she says, 'Sure.'

'Hi, Sebastian,' I say, taking in the scene of domesticity in front of me as Sebastian changes the baby's nappy on the changing mat on the living room floor. Looks a dab hand at it too. Glad he's good at something apart from being a total shit to my best friend.

'Louisa?' He pales, then a myriad of emotions cross his face: unease, anger, arrogance, until he spots Ronnie, and he turns even paler. Yes, Sebastian's quite the big man, until he's confronted by, well, a big man. And Ronnie at six foot one fits the bill perfectly.

'Can I have a word, Sebastian?' I say in a tone that would have earned me a job in a police drama. I know my fake confidence is my way of deflecting from the severity of the situation, but it's my coping mechanism, and I embrace it. I will not have this man hurt my friend.

'Eh, yeah, sure. Just let me put this away and wash my hands.'

I bet he's stalling for time so he can come up with something, or do a runner out the back. Like I said, Ronnie's a big man, and Sebastian doesn't know him well enough to realise he wouldn't thump a fly.

Xander, mercifully, is notable by his absence, although it does make me wonder where he is. As if reading my mind, Brittany says, 'Xander's at his gran's. Give us a bit of peace…time on our own.'

'Right,' I say, eyeing Sebastian, who has returned but is studiously ignoring me, instead finding a frayed piece of terracotta-coloured rug unbelievably scintillating.

'So, Sebastian, want to tell me why Xander didn't visit his mum tonight?'

His eyes meet mine, and he juts his chin out. Too late, I realise I've just given him his excuse. 'Like Brit said, he's at his gran's. Couldn't ask her to take him to hospital for us, could we?'

'No, I suppose not,' I say calmly, 'but his gran was at

the hospital for visiting tonight, so you must have dropped him off as soon as she got back.'

Caught out in the lie, Sebastian squirms. 'Look, Louisa, I know you mean well, but this isn't really anything to do with you.'

'That's where you're wrong, Sebastian. You're not going to keep Xander from Nicky, and that's the end of it. Otherwise, I swear to God, I'll personally see to it that she takes you to court. You were missing from his life for so many years when she had to bring Xander up on her own, whilst you–' I indicate Brittany '–cavorted around behind her back.'

I pause to stop myself losing it with him. 'Now, you may be making a better job of fatherhood this time around, and certainly I didn't see you once change Xander's nappy, but that doesn't give you the right to give Nicky shit for meeting and moving in with someone else.'

He goes to interrupt, but I hold up a hand. 'Let's face it, you were beyond awful to Nicky, and I hope for Brittany's sake, and your daughter's, that the leopard really has changed his spots, but you have no right to try to stop Nicky from seeing Xander, or indeed be pissed off at her moving in with Valentin. No right. Do you understand?'

He stares at me, but I clock him keeping an eye on Ronnie out of the corner of his eye.

'I know you, Sebastian, and I know you can't bear the thought of Nicky living the high life with Valentin, and Valentin being able to provide everything for her and Xander. On some level, I can understand why that upsets your ego, but you never wanted to give Nicky that. You chose someone else. You have absolutely no justification to withhold her right to see her son.'

He has the decency to look a little shame-faced at this

point, but still he remains silent. Ronnie takes my hand discreetly in his.

'And lastly, how is this benefitting Xander? He's already been through so much. So, sorry for my bluntness, but do you think that for once in your life, you could put someone else first? Even if you can't bring yourself to do it for Nicky, do it for your son.'

He finally seems to find his voice and he visibly stretches up to his full height. 'Thanks for your concern, Louisa, but I think it's time you left.'

'Sebastian, I saw a chink of goodness in you the night Nicky nearly died, a humanity I've never seen before. I almost liked that person. Do the right thing.'

I turn to Brittany and apologise for interrupting her evening.

'You've nothing to apologise for,' she says firmly as she sees me out. 'But I know someone who does. I can't believe he tried to stop Nicky seeing Xander. Don't worry, I'll be having words with him myself.'

I'm having to concentrate on ensuring my jaw doesn't drop. Brittany is onside. And whilst I don't consider her an ally, she has certainly shown me a different side of her today. Had I known she'd be so helpful and accommodating, I'd have asked her to reason with Sebastian, instead of going in all guns blazing. Oh well, you live and learn.

It's only when she goes back inside that I realise Ronnie isn't with me. I wait, eyebrows furrowing, wondering what he's up to, what he's saying, until a few minutes later, he appears.

'You want me to drive?' he asks.

As we approach the car, I say, 'No, but I do want to know what the hell you said to him.'

Chapter Ten

Sunday 1 August

To-do list
Order remaining uniforms when get back from Jo's
Call blazer company and see if they can do me a special order for a new blazer for Hugo
Get Gen a new jacket from Next – one I approve of
Chase up trainers delivery. Doesn't appear to have arrived – check with reception or call vendor

Jo, Wendy and I have taken the kids to Loch Lomond for the day. The sun is a yellow disc high in the cloudless sky, it's blistering hot, and everyone is slathered in sun cream. Floppy hats, sunglasses and swimming costumes and arm bands, as well as snorkels, flippers, masks, goggles, a picnic hamper and a cool box have been loaded into the cars, as well as about a trillion things in carrier bags. Ronnie would go spare if he saw it all.

After we got back last night, and explained to Jo what had occurred at Sebastian's, she had the brainwave of us all coming up to hers, so we could then go to Loch Lomond next day as the next day's forecast was for a heatwave. We don't get many heatwaves in Scotland, so when we do, we make the most of it. And, with Jo living in the Trossachs, if we stayed overnight with her, not only would it be fun for all the cousins, and us, it would mean we wouldn't have to sit in the ungodly summer holiday queues of traffic that snake all the way along the route to the popular beauty spot.

Aria had already fallen asleep, but it didn't take much to bundle her and the others into the car, and we followed Jo back to hers. A quick text to Wendy and she was apprised of the plan too.

'I can't believe you went head-to-head with Sebastian like that, Lou,' Wendy says as she opens bottles of juice and pours drinks for the kids. 'Weren't you shaking? I know I would have been.'

'I was, but it was too important. I just hope it has done some good.'

'And tell her what Ronnie said to him,' Jo says, smoothing down the picnic blanket for the little ones to sit on.

Wendy looks at me quizzically and I say, 'Ronnie didn't immediately follow me out of Sebastian's. He was in for a good couple of minutes, and he basically told him to do as I said, and do the right thing, or he'd have a word in the ear of a friend who specialises in family law, and have them help Nicky fight for sole custody, if that's what she wanted, and given the way he was behaving towards her, not letting her see her son, kicking a dog when it's down, she'd probably go for that.'

'He did not!' Wendy's mouth falls open.

'Oh yes he did.' Jo is quick to try out the pantomime

lines.

Wendy's jaw drops. 'But neither of you had checked with Nicky if that's what she wanted.'

'No time. And desperate times require desperate measures.' I give her a sad smile. 'And Sebastian has driven us to that.'

'And has she heard anything from him?'

'Not that I know of. She hasn't texted me yet.' I pick up one of the drinks and take a sip. Only now do I realise how parched my throat feels, and I hope it's only with the heat of the day and not at the prospect that we may have overstepped the mark.

'Fingers crossed. Carrot stick, anyone?' Jo holds them out, and gratefully, I clutch at straws, or in this case, carrot sticks.

We're having a lovely time watching the kids play together, on the sand, paddling in the water, with a ball at piggy in the middle, basking in the sun. Even Gen seems to be really getting into the spirit of things, and I smile as I see her rugby-tackle Hugo to get the ball – it reminds me of when they were younger. They're growing up too fast. Staying in the hotel is probably hitting Gen the hardest as she has less privacy than usual, and I know she's missing Rain. She hasn't seen him since the beginning of the holidays, as his family went to Switzerland for a month. I must try and arrange some Mummy/girl time with her in the very near future. We need that one on one.

I quickly scan the immediate vicinity to ensure the kids are all where they should be. I'm lucky Gen is happy to monitor Hugo whilst paddling and that she and Aria are inseparable on days like today. They really are so close, and I hope they always will be. Being so close to my own sisters makes me want that for my kids. I know someone always has my back and I always have someone to turn to.

My phone rings, startling me out of my reverie. It's a mobile number I don't recognise.

'Hello?'

'Is that Louisa Halliday?' comes a tinny voice. It sounds like the person is driving through a tunnel.

'That's right.' Perhaps it's a Wedded Bliss call.

'My name's Benedict Lamington. I saw your ad for a house, in the library.'

My heart leaps. Please, please, please be a real possibility. 'Yes? Do you have something?'

'Actually, I think I do. My parents left me a house there last year, and I've been coming and going, modernising it, a bit at a time. I live in Aberdeen, you see, but I'm moving to the States for six months and won't be visiting it at all, or using it, during that time.'

He goes on to tell me about the house: how many bedrooms, the layout, the condition, the location. It all sounds perfect, and although I try not to let excitement overwhelm me, it's hard. This could be exactly what we're looking for. And he's happy for us to bring the dogs. Result!

'What's happened?' Jo asks. 'You look like the cat that got the cream. Spill.'

Once I've divulged the contents of the call, in between us fielding requests to 'play with me, Mummy', 'Mummy, I'm hungry', 'Mummy, I've got sand in my eyes' and 'Mummy, Jackson's being mean to me', Jo asks, 'Where is the house exactly?'

'It's the street behind the park. You know, the one on the way to Lymeburn, before you leave the village?' Wendy says.

Jo shakes her head. She was a city-dweller until she became an almost Earth Mother, so although she knows where we live – where we usually live – and the cafés in the village, she's not so au fait with the rest of the village.

'I'll give you the address. You can do a drive-by. Anyway, I've provisionally booked for us to go see it tomorrow.'

'Aw, I really hope this is suitable for you all.' Wendy hugs me. 'You must be due some luck. Brilliant that they'll let you take the dogs.'

Wistfully, I think of my mornings with my coffee, Bear at my feet, Patch on my lap, as I check my emails on my phone. Yep, we're missing out. It's so unfair. I pray the property can accommodate our needs, and I'm so glad we're going to see it tomorrow. I fire off a quick text to tell Ronnie, and settle back to build sandcastles with Aria, Hallie and Kayla, as Wendy tells us about her new job, which she starts tomorrow.

'I can't believe you're starting already. It feels like you just told me yesterday.' I take a bite of caramelised onion quiche. Delicious.

'I know. It has all come round really quickly, after me waiting years for the promotion,' Wendy says. 'Hopefully, that's a good omen.'

'It'll be fine. You know the job inside out. You should have been doing it years ago – you know it, we know it, and they know it.'

A smile passes between my two sisters, and I think how blessed I am. I have no idea what I'd do without them.

'So, what's your exact title again?' I ask.

Wendy launches off into a detailed description of her

job title and remit, and whilst much of it is too technical for me to understand, I listen, because it's great to see her so animated. She deserves this.

My mind flits back to the house we want. Thank goodness we're allowed to take the dogs with us. I couldn't ask Mum and Dad to hold on to them for much longer, especially as Mum is already practically keeping my existing business afloat, whilst I deal with the kids over the school holidays and try to sort out the aftermath of the crash, and to some extent negotiate my new business life with Fabien. That reminds me – not long until my Madrid training trip. I'm starting to get nervous. Fortunately, I checked, and my passport is still valid – just – it has a year left on it. This is not the time of year to apply for a new passport as it takes months to come through, with the massive backlogs they always have.

I need to remember to buy Wendy a good luck in your new job card, since she starts soon. It's fallen through the cracks with everything else I've had to deal with these past few weeks.

'Are you looking forward to starting school, Aria?' Jo asks her as they put the finishing touches on their sand palace. It's a thing of beauty, and I study the earlier effort Aria and I made together. I'm not as creative as Jo, or perhaps just not at imagining sand palaces. Hers has turrets and battlements and looks like something that Dreamworks designed. Mine looks more something a trainee builder made on their first day on the job.

Aria nods vigorously at Jo's question. 'Yes, and I'm getting a Shimmer and Shine schoolbag and pencil case, and pencils with my name on them, and it's going to be amazing.'

As I have often thought in the past, I hope Ferniehall Primary School is ready for my littlest darling. She's a very single-minded, confident individual.

The smell of waffles fills the air. There's a little van just up from the patch of sandy beach we're on. Ah, wonder if that's a craving. I haven't had any cravings yet. The burr of a jet ski has me turn my head to watch as the rider arcs through the water, skilfully. I used to love going out on the jet ski. Always thought I'd do it with the kids, and often, but life has got in the way. We need to make more time, like today, to do these kinds of things.

Now I'm smelling fish and chips. How can I detect all this? I'm like a sniffer dog. And it's making my mouth water, yet we have a lovely picnic right in front of us. Clearly, my body is craving greasy and sugary treats.

A drone passes overhead.

'What's a drone doing over here?' I ask Jo.

She waves a hand in dismissal. 'Oh, they're here constantly. It's probably from the Lodge on Loch Lomond or something. People arrange drone footage of their weddings now, so they can film the stunning scenery.' She sounds like she's quoting from a drone brochure.

'Oh, right.'

'You all ready for school starting?' Jo asks me.

'Mentally, yes,' I say.

With a jolt, I realise I haven't ordered any of the uniforms yet. Where would I put them? A hotel suite may seem large, palatial even, but not when you're trying to fit all your essential belongings into it. The wardrobes are already crammed full, but I'll need to buy their uniforms. I remember one year Hugo had to wear blue shirts instead of white for the first two weeks as I could not get them anywhere for love nor money. And it wasn't that I hadn't been organised and bought them, I had, but I had assumed, wrongly, that those I had bought would fit him. Nope. They hung like a bag of rags on him. I could easily have fitted two of him into the shirts. So, after that, slim fit only for my boy.

I close my eyes and silently pray for a moment that this house in the village will meet our needs. At least Aria has a tie. (Note to self – buy school shoes.) The school gave her one at her final settling-in day. In fact, she has two – the nursery gave the kids one at graduation too. Not that she can go to school solely wearing a tie, but it's a start.

A day at the beach with nine children is exhausting but so much fun. We had two rounds of ice cream, a twenty-minute trip to the aquarium – the kids participated in the interactive rockpool experience, where they got to handle a crab – and we had dinner in one of the restaurants at Loch Lomond Shores. I even managed a little time with the kids out on a duck-yellow pedalo, and discovered it's a lot more taxing than you'd think. I'm sure my muscles will pay for it tomorrow. Plus, I slathered us, again, in so much sun cream – I'm uber aware of how we can burn easier on the water – that we ran out, but at least we'll return home without being burnt to a crisp. It has been such a great day, and I vow that despite everything going on with the house, the hotel, the search for somewhere temporary to live, we will do more of this.

Originally, Jo had said we could stay another night, but now with the offer to view this house in our village, I've taken a rain check, and we'll do it some other time, but soon.

Even Gen can barely keep her eyes open on the drive back to the hotel. Aria is asleep before we leave the car park, and Hugo's eyes droop as he drifts off on the drive down the A82 towards Glasgow.

What a perfect day.

For mile after mile, I listen to Classic FM and enjoy the view of the countryside flowing past. I'm in no hurry. Don't need to be anywhere anytime soon, and for once, I enjoy driving, without all the stress of having to be anywhere on time. Even the heavier than usual traffic doesn't irk me, and I arrive at the hotel, thoroughly relaxed and in a great mood. A great mood that is only enhanced by picking up a voicemail from Nicky when I stop, in which she tells me Xander was in to see her tonight, with Valentin. I smile, happy that the world appears to be back on its axis again.

Hugo wakes up with the car engine turning off. Gen rubs her eyes and yawns. Aria is fast asleep, and I ask her siblings to carry our belongings inside as I scoop Aria out of her car seat, and her little face immediately finds that spot between my chin and my neck where kids always gravitate to when they're tired, or asleep.

Ronnie is lying on the sofa watching TV when we come in. Distractedly, I note the bags under his eyes. Maybe he was asleep earlier. God knows if I could catch up on sleep, I would. And I think he needed this day to himself, so everything worked out well with Jo suggesting we go and stay with them last night.

I kiss him and say, 'Valentin and Xander went to see Nicky tonight. Thank you.'

His eyes light up, and I know I've said the right thing.

'I'll just put Aria in her PJs, and then I'll be back. Could you maybe get Hugo something to drink before bed? Gen, you staying up or going to bed?'

'Bed.' She yawns again and settles in beside her dad for a hug first. It warms my heart to see them like that – it's so sweet. Hugo slumps down on the other side of his dad. Bless him, he looks like he's about to keel over from exhaustion. Fresh air really is the best medicine.

I think I'll sleep well too, tonight. I can already feel a yawn coming on.

Finally, with the kids in bed, I'll be able to sit down and talk to Ronnie about the house and about how hopeful I am that it might be the answer to our prayers.

I snuggle into him, after getting myself a glass of fizzy grape juice. From the absence of a beer bottle or wine glass, I see Ronnie hasn't had a drink at all. Unusual. You'd think with him having all that peace to himself he'd have booked in for a massage at the hotel, or watched the big screen in his boxer shorts – in the privacy of our room naturally, not the one in the lounge bar – and had a couple of beers, but nope. Strange.

'So, how's your day been?'

'Fine.'

'Just fine?'

'Yep, just fine.'

I sense an undercurrent of something, but my husband's not being remotely forthcoming.

'Right, well, do you want to hear about this house?'

''Course.'

I scrunch my eyebrows. I thought he'd be a little more interested.

'Ronnie, what's wrong? You're showing about as much interest in this house as you do in crocheting.'

He turns to me, and now I see. He has tears in his eyes. 'I'm sorry, Lou. I didn't get the job.'

Then my lovely rock of a husband bursts into tears.

Chapter Eleven

Sunday 1 August

'Ronnie, Ronnie, it's OK.'

'I'm sorry, Lou. I'm usually so together, you know I am, but I just…everything is getting on top of me.'

I let him lean his head on my chest as tears continue to spill over. He sighs and takes shuddering breaths as he tries to bring his emotions back under control.

His eyes are red and puffy from crying when he resurfaces to face me. 'Tears and a snot-fest. Attractive.'

I smile at his attempt to make light of his distress.

'Tell me what happened. Did they call you?'

He shakes his head, then grabs a tissue from the coffee table and blows his nose noisily, then shoves the tissue into the pocket of his pyjama bottoms. 'No, they sent me a letter. Can you believe it? In this day and age, with us living in a hotel. Rather than email me or call me, they kept me waiting longer than was necessary to let me know I'd been unsuccessful.' He shakes his head again as if he can't quite believe it.

'So, what did they say exactly?'

He points to a piece of paper sticking out from under a couple of the kids' books on the coffee table. He has ripped off the bottom quarter of the page, and shredded it into little pieces, something he does when he's nervous or angry. I used to hate when we'd go to pubs pre-kids and they had those cardboard beer mats – I always felt as if I was surrounded by piles of torn-to-pieces ones, courtesy of my beloved.

I reach for the letter and scan its contents. Standard rejection letter. No feedback. Poor Ronnie. I remember how tough it was finding out you hadn't been chosen for a job you'd really wanted, or in Ronnie's case, applied for as a means to get him onshore. My heart sinks as I know we're both aware this will probably mean him returning to Baku and having to be away from us for longer each stint. That's the last thing we, this marriage and our family need right now.

'Remember the time I was verbally offered that purchasing job and then I didn't get the contract through and kept ringing them to see what the hold-up was and it turned out at the last minute they'd had a candidate whose credentials matched their remit one hundred per cent?'

'What's your point?' Ronnie asks, raising his eyes to meet mine.

'Sometimes things just aren't meant to be. And if I hadn't pressed the point with them, I wouldn't have found out why I didn't get the job in the end.' Ronnie shrugs. 'I think you should call them and ask them for feedback.'

He shakes his head again, vehemently this time. 'No, I'm not doing that. They've already made a mockery of me, by letting me think I had a good chance, and then I didn't even get a second interview? I mean, I'm not saying the job was in the bag, but I honestly thought I had a good chance. Am I so out of touch with applying for jobs that I believe I'm better than I am?' His brow furrows.

'Ronnie, you're great at your job, you know you are. I

don't know why they've turned you down for this particular post. It could be any number of reasons. The boss' nephew has a friend who needs a job; this is their way of saying they can't afford you; someone else fit the bill one hundred per cent as happened to me. Honestly, you could drive yourself crazy rehashing this, but the only way you're going to know for sure is if you ask them.'

'Nope, not doing it.'

God, my husband can be so stubborn sometimes. 'Fine, don't ask for feedback, but let's get some rest, and I'm sure things will look different in the morning.'

'I wouldn't count on it,' Ronnie mutters.

Monday 2 August

To-do list
Nail this bloody presentation
Upgrade Netflix subscription
Distribute cards re looking for a house to libraries, hairdressers, general stores in Ferniehall and surrounding areas
Send Fabien the figures he asked for, as well as the costs per stationery time
Prepare list of materials suppliers for Fabien to negotiate discounts with

Two o'clock, three o'clock, three forty-five, four thirty, five thirty. Six. Yeah, that was a great sleep. Keep your sarcasm monitor turned on. I was so shattered, I did eventually drop off for half an hour or so, but since then I've been awake, not even dozing, just marking the minutes. I'd so hoped today would be a great day as we might find a new temporary home, but now I'm exhausted and it's time to start the day. Mum has been covering a lot of Wedded Bliss' business for me since the crash, and because the kids are off for seven weeks – give me strength – but she can't do everything, nor should she have to.

Once I've slogged through my emails, many from Mum, trying to keep abreast of weddings I'd dealt with myself, prior to hiring Mum to help, I turn my attention to the presentation I need to prepare for the event in Madrid. I'm aware it's not far away now. Ronnie and I had already discussed how we'd cover this trip, from a childcare perspective, but now, with him not getting the UK-based job, it's looking likely he'll have to return to Azerbaijan, and that kind of scuppers those carefully laid plans.

I sigh. Something else for the to-do list.

So far, my presentation consists of six slides. I'm definitely out of my comfort zone. I'm most at home showing brides, grooms and their families what I'm capable of preparing for them, but somehow when no one connected with the wedding will be present, the task seems a bit soulless and therefore more difficult. The words won't come. And how to show someone how to design stationery on InDesign? Will they already be designers? Surely, they don't expect me to show people who are totally new to this craft? Maybe it will be beginners who've only dabbled with Canva. But no, Fabien said his family used to have a stationery business. He'll know what their capabilities need to be. It'll probably be easier to do hands-on demonstrations, but the fact I can't figure out how to convey this on a Powerpoint is freaking me out. It'll be fine. I just need to relax and inspiration will strike. Best to have a break from it in the meantime, let the ideas percolate.

I race through a raft of tasks: ordering school uniforms,

top up the kids' ParentPay accounts – I'll never remember nearer the time – order Aria's schoolbag and pencil case. I'm in luck. When she told Jo yesterday about the schoolbag she'd chosen, I almost had a heart attack as I had forgotten all about it, and I was worried they might be out of stock, but I found one at some obscure retailer, so it should arrive in a few weeks, albeit it looks as if it probably has to come all the way from China. I try not to think too hard about its carbon footprint.

I'm on my second cup of tea and flicking through onshore oil and gas jobs on a site I haven't looked at recently, when Gen gets up.

'Morning, sweetheart. How are you this morning?'

'I think I'm dead.' She groans and flops down beside me on the sofa.

'Ah, so not an ounce of melodrama in your body then.'

She grabs Ronnie's fleece, which is hanging over the back of the sofa, and pops it on. When I raise an eyebrow, she says, 'What? I'm cold. It's summer. I have shortie pyjamas on, but in the morning, it's freezing. Daddy's fleece is snuggly.'

It's not freezing, it's positively tropical, but I hold my hands up in submission.

'Tea?' I ask, dropping a kiss on her head as I pass.

'Yes, please. Can I put the TV on, or are you working?'

'Sure, but keep it down low so we don't wake the others. Movie?'

She purses her lips then says, 'Pitch Perfect?'

'Done, but which one?'

She muses over this a few seconds, creasing the side of her lip. 'Let's go for the third one. I know it's your favourite.'

We settle down with our teas, and Gen snuggles into

me as we watch *Pitch Perfect 3* at a low volume, covering our mouths to stifle our giggles at Rebel Wilson and the rest of the cast's antics.

I try to just 'be', to live in the moment with Gen, but although it's lovely relaxing with her, part of me seems to be perpetually switched to supersonic speed, debating all the things I have to tick off my to-do list. Once we've been for the viewing today, somehow, without palming the kids off on someone else, again, we have to find time to take stock. We've been firefighting, no pun intended, so much recently, it's been impossible to take a step back and look at everything with an objective eye.

Gen and I manage to watch half the movie – I even fit in another cup of tea for us both – before signs of life emanate from the other rooms. Aria breezes in, Cornie at her side, her unicorn dressing gown in her other hand. It's not as white as I think it should be. I'll need to pop it in a laundry bag. I have to say, there are many benefits to living in a luxury hotel, but the one I love most – apart from having shelter over my head – is the laundry service. As Fabien decreed, all expenses paid, and without a washing machine, what else was I meant to do?

That said, I'd prefer to be able to shove a load of washing in my own washing machine and return to my tea and emails in my own home with Bear and Patch at my feet. I don't know who misses them most, me or the kids. Hugo was even talking in his sleep about Patch the other day, and Aria burst into tears thinking the breeder might take him back as we couldn't look after him properly, without a house.

'Mummy, if we like the house, can we sleep there tonight?' Aria asks as I lean forward and wipe the sandman from her eyes.

'Not tonight, but soon.'

'How soon?' She's tenacious is Aria.

'A few days perhaps, a week? But remember, it might not be right for us, OK, so we have to wait and see.'

She purses her lips like a woman in her seventies or eighties, showing her disapproval of my comment. If I could read minds, I'm sure she'd be saying, 'We'll see about that.'

Aria also loves the music in *Pitch Perfect 3*, albeit it's too adult for her, but she snuggles into Gen, and I decide we have far greater things to worry about than whether the movie has the occasional minor swear word in it. She's bonding with her big sister, and that's more important.

I glance at the clock. I'll have to wake the others soon. We're viewing the house at ten, and everyone needs to be showered before then and have had breakfast, and breakfast finishes at ten anyway. It's so hard to live in a hotel and be able to have full Scottish breakfasts every day if you want them, particularly when you're pregnant, as I don't care what anyone says, I've always been hungrier from the first trimester, not the third when the baby is meant to need it. I could easily scoff an entire full cooked breakfast every day. That said, I don't gorge myself, but I am partial to a potato scone or a square slice sausage in a roll. Being unable to have a soft fried egg is killing me, and there are some cheeses I can't eat, but all in all, I think we manage a pretty decent breakfast each day. The kids have certainly eaten well. They might not think it, but they'll miss it when we move into a house.

A message alert beeps. Mum. *Can you pop round later?*

Me: *Morning! I was going to anyway. Didn't have a chance to tell you last night, but someone contacted* *us about a house in Staffa Place, the one behind the park.*

Mum: *Oh yes? Some lovely big houses round there.*

Me: *Really?*

Mum: *Yes, big detached sandstone ones. Hilary Mann used to have one years ago, before she sold it and moved to Spain.*

Mum cracks me up. I have no idea who Hilary Mann is, but as with every person my mother has ever encountered in her life, she expects us all to know who they are and their backstories and life histories to the extent she does.

Me: *Right. Excellent. Hopefully it's a goer then. See you later x*

Mum: *Bear and Patch are missing you all x*

And us them. Please let this house be right for us.

'I like it, Mummy!' Aria declares as we crunch up the drive. We've left our car on the driveway, where a Mazda is already parked up – Benedict's, I guess – and I peer up at the blonde sandstone frontage. It's lovely, with huge bay windows and decorative detail on the outside. Semi-detached. I glance into the next-door neighbour's garden, surreptitiously. It's well-maintained, a riot of colourful blooms grace its borders, and I imagine a retired schoolteacher pruning his rose bushes of an afternoon, kneeler, gardening gloves and secateurs at the ready. What am I like? Focus on the task in hand, girl, task in hand!

The front garden is a little overgrown, but some large

trees shield us from the road, giving us plenty of privacy. More than we get from our own house, which is right on a road, or rather the convergence of two. The street itself is a quiet cul-de-sac with perhaps ten houses like this, the rear of the park taking up the rest of the street. The only sounds I can hear are the occasional bark of a dog or shriek of glee of a child as they play in the park behind. And that would be ideal for the kids. I can't see a path from the park to the interior of the cul-de-sac – looks like you have to go all the way round – but that's no bad thing in my book. We'd have no through traffic, and no teenagers passing through causing havoc at the weekend. Whilst I hate to be negative, I'm also pragmatic. I'm also glad Gen isn't at that stage yet. Yes, her years of teenage drinking are hopefully a long way in the future.

'Morning. Benedict.' He stands in the doorway, one hand in a pocket. A few years younger than us, I'd wager, he almost has a Jay Gatsby look from *The Great Gatsby*, minus the tux. His charming smile immediately disarms us, and he leads us into the house. 'Lovely to meet you, Louisa.' He shakes my hand then turns to Ronnie and does the same.

'And you. Wow, this is beautiful,' I say, and it is. All walnut woodwork, period details, Charles Rennie Mackintosh stained glass in the doors.

The living room is enormous, and those gorgeous bay windows let in so much light, and one of them has a window seat in it. Perfect for curling up with a good book. I know Gen is a fan of doing that, too, and I could envisage us chilling at the weekend, rain pouring down, or sunlight streaming in, as we relax on the window seat with our latest read, although Gen's may well be on her phone. I prefer a good paperback myself.

The fireplace, a mix of walnut and marble, has columns, for goodness' sake. Columns! That's how big it is. I do have a slight reservation about having an open fire, but Benedict seems to sense my hesitation and says, 'We have a very strong fire guard for it. It takes two adults to move it, once it's in place.'

My heart soars again. I like what I see so far.

'Mummy, where's my bedroom?' says Aria. She really doesn't give up, does she?

'In a minute, sweetie. We need to view the downstairs first.'

She sticks out her bottom lip, and I almost think she's going to stamp her foot, such is her petulance, but one warning look from me, and she backs down, and slips her hand into mine.

The kitchen is right at the end of the hall, with steps leading down to it, and again it's a generous space with French doors out to the garden, and what a garden. OK, it clearly hasn't been a family garden for a while, it's a gardener's delight, all mature trees and shrubs, with not a swing nor a slide in sight, but it's huge. You could play tag there for days without catching the other person, and there are myriad places to hide too. The kids are equally enthralled by it.

'Mummy, can we go outside to explore?' I hesitate. 'Please, Mummy.' Hugo folds his hands together prayerlike. Nothing like hamming it up.

I turn to Benedict, and he nods so vigorously I fear he'll make himself dizzy.

'Gen, can you supervise, whilst Dad and I have a look around?'

'Sure. Let's go, guys.'

'Yay!' Aria bolts into the garden like a Commonwealth

Games one-hundred-metre gold medallist approaching the finish line. Hugo races after her, and Gen smiles at me over her shoulder and follows her siblings.

The dining room is generous, plenty of room for the table and eight chairs, with a dresser, and a bookcase, and bags of space all around. It even has a log burner. I do love a log burner, and that's on top of the living room having an actual real fire. I know fossil fuels are bad and everything, but nothing beats a coal fire. Mum and Dad had a coal fire when we were young, until central heating came along and they had it removed. A shame really.

So far, I like what I see, and when I sneak a look at Ronnie, he's nodding to Benedict, absorbed in what he's saying. 'Turn of the century', 'mouldings', 'centrepieces', 'period features'.

I haven't zoned out, but I'm too busy picturing us in this house, with our things, and our daily life. And I can see it, I really can, but just before Ronnie and I talk it over, I need to see the rest. The only niggle for me so far is the kitchen, I don't particularly like the layout, but it does have a double oven, which gains it two extra points. I've always wanted a double oven.

It's the master bedroom that wins me over, though, not that I'll spend much time in it. It's the biggest bedroom I've ever seen. Sleigh bed, high ceilings, but it's the view of the park from the bay window which blows me away – acres of lush greenery, flower beds, and the bandstand. It's so serene. I could be doing with some serenity.

The furniture throughout is an unusual mix of modern and items that wouldn't be out of place on the *Antiques Roadshow*. In fact, there's an armoire in the master bedroom that probably predates those I've seen on it.

'Hey, Ronnie. Check out the *armoire*.'

'It's a wardrobe, love.'

'Don't be silly. It's an *armoire*, my sweet.'

He rolls his eyes at my attempt at humour. 'Can you put clothes in it?'

'Yes.'

'Well, it's a bloody wardrobe then, isn't it!'

How many rooms does this place have? We take in another two double bedrooms, one with a log burner, the other with a sofa in it, then another smaller bedroom, an office, a playroom, a huge family bathroom, and a shower room.

It's probably similar in size to our house, but everything is distributed differently.

'Let's go see the garden,' I say, stalling for time. It's only now as we descend to the split-level landing that it hits me – this place must cost a fortune. I have no idea how much rents are for this type of place, and because we haven't needed to use our insurance's temporary accommodation clause yet, I don't know if what they will give us will be enough to cover the cost to live here. Why didn't I think to ask the cost yesterday? I was so excited at the possibility of there being somewhere in the village where we could live. Why didn't Ronnie ask me? Scratch that, Ronnie's mind was elsewhere yesterday.

My gut twists as we stroll out into the garden, where the children are already making themselves at home, playing hide and seek. The sound of Hugo's laughter, the sight of a Red Admiral landing on a nearby buttercup and the perfumes of the various flowers in bloom make my decision for me: I want us to live here.

Ronnie gives a slight smile and raises a questioning eyebrow, and I nod. 'So, Benedict, I think we like what we see. What's the rent and the terms?'

'Two thousand five hundred a month, a month's deposit in advance.'

I can't help it. I gasp. Two and a half grand a month? Holy moo. Who the heck can afford that?

But Ronnie, unperturbed, keeps listening to Benedict, interjecting now and again with a question.

'We'll be in touch,' Ronnie says. 'Just need to talk to the insurance company first.'

'Yes, I saw on the news. Terrible business about your house. Sorry to hear that.'

'Still doesn't feel real, if I'm honest,' Ronnie replies with a sad smile. 'But, hopefully we can take you up on your offer here. We should know more tomorrow.'

'Good luck.'

We're almost out the door when I realise Aria isn't with us. 'Gen, where's Aria?'

'I don't know. She came in looking for you ages ago.'

My heart pounds in my chest, as I worry she may have left via the front door, but when I glance at it, the lock is too high up for her to reach.

'Aria. Aria,' I call.

'Sorry about this,' Ronnie says. 'Little scamp. She likes hiding, and she's very good at it. Do you mind if we have another look around and find her at the same time?'

Benedict waves away his concern. 'Not at all. I'll be in the living room when you're ready.'

'Aria,' I call up the stairs. Where is she? We move from room to room, opening doors, looking under beds, in cupboards, wardrobes and armoires, until we finally find her, in the smallest bedroom, flaked out, fast asleep. Cornie beside her.

Ronnie smiles at me as he goes to scoop her up. 'Well, it looks like she has chosen her bedroom already.'

Chapter Twelve

Monday 2 August

'Nana, Papa!' Aria runs across the grass towards my parents then detours quickly to the dogs, but Hugo beats her to it, with Gen not far behind.

'You've been usurped by a canine,' I say.

'At least it's not by their gran and grampa,' Mum says.

'Now, now.' Mum is aware I don't meet my mother-in-law's exacting standards, and although she's always polite to them both, Annabelle isn't someone Mum would like to spend a spa day together with, something we discovered at my hen weekend.

'How is everything?' I bend down to pat Bear as he makes a beeline for me, clearly having received enough cuddles from the children. Yeah, he's still my dog.

'There's my boy.' I press my nose to his. Gee. He needs a dental stick, or better still, his teeth brushed.

I glance over to see Patch rolling on his back, adoring having his tummy tickled. He's getting so big. A pang of loss flits through me at everything we've lost since this stupid crash. Guiltily, I pull myself up. I've lost nothing in comparison to Nicky. She's lost her confidence, almost her son, and her mobility, for now. And she was lucky not to lose her clients. Fortunately, Fabien was also able to step in there as they have a bank of photographers, and rather than the bride and groom have no photographer for their wedding, Fabien found someone to fill in, something that was a great relief to Nicky, and I imagine the bridal parties and their families.

'They're both fine.' Dad strokes Bear's ears, also my favourite thing to do, as Mum breaks away to deal with Patch having become a little overexcited.

'Ugh, Mummy, Nana, Patch pooed,' Aria screams.

'Of course he pooed, Aria. So do you.'

'But not in the street,' she practically yells.

'No, not in the street, but dogs don't use indoor toilets like us.'

She folds her arms and scowls. 'Why not? Everyone always says dogs are clever.'

'Not that clever,' Dad murmurs.

I catch his eye, and we chuckle. 'Nana's getting a poo bag, don't worry.'

'I'm not worrying, but it's yucky.'

Give me strength. 'Aria, leave it alone, Nana will sort it, and Patch will be back to his non-pooping self in a few minutes.'

'Humph!'

I don't think I've convinced her.

'So, how are you feeling, Lou?'

Dad is watching me, rather than just looking at me. Weird.

'I'm…fine?'

'Just "fine"?' Dad leans forward, clasps his hands in front of him, legs slightly apart, elbows resting on his knees.

Now we've tipped over from weird to bizarre. 'Yes, just…fine. Good days and bad days, you know.'

'Nothing to tell me?' Dad pauses, clearly waiting for me to jump in, so I do.

'Oh, sorry, yes, I forgot to say, the house looks fantastic, but it's so much money. In fact, Ronnie is away home – well, to the hotel – to check with the insurers to see if they will cover the monthly cost. It's astronomical, but apparently that's how much rental properties are now.'

Ronnie checked whilst I drove him back to the hotel earlier, to drop him off before coming here. I also urged him to call Petrocord for feedback, and maybe make a few calls, put some feelers out, see if there was anything else available. You have to check the job sites every day.

'Right,' Dad says, clasping and unclasping his hands, a sign of agitation.

I frown. 'Oh, and Ronnie didn't get the job.'

Dad's face falls. 'But he was so sure he'd done well.'

I sigh. 'I know. But sometimes no matter if you have the best interview in the world, it makes no difference. And you don't always find out why, although I have strongly suggested he ask.'

'Too right.' Dad's vehemence catches me by surprise. 'Especially now.'

What? Especially now what? I'm obviously missing something.

'Dad, is there something you'd like to say?'

I feel a hand on my shoulder. 'No, but I'd like to say something.'

I stare up into Mum's eyes. 'What?'

'When exactly were you going to tell me you were pregnant?'

An awkward pause ensues, when I can't quite believe what I'm hearing. Mum knows? How does Mum know?

My sisters would never break that confidence. Did Ronnie cave? If he did, I'll kill him. No, that would leave the baby, and our other children, without a father.

Mum is staring at me so hard I wouldn't be surprised to discover she has seared a hole in my head all the way through to the other side.

'How did you know?' I ask, deciding there's no point hiding the truth now.

'Can you imagine the embarrassment when Ariadne Fellowes congratulated me, and then realised I had no idea what she was talking about?'

Ariadne Fellowes. The woman who does tai chi with Mum, pretends to be her friend, but secretly talks about her behind her back?

When I say nothing, Mum continues, 'You don't google 'can pregnant women drink peppermint tea?' in the vicinity of the barista, who for the record is Ariadne's niece. She mentioned to her yesterday when she was visiting, and Ariadne took great delight in having a piece of private info to share. She simply didn't realise how private it was.'

I inhale noisily. 'OK, yes, I'm pregnant, but I didn't tell you, because…'

Why didn't I tell them again? I know it will sound feeble once I utter the words, but I really didn't want to raise their hopes only to dash them if anything…happened. I look at Mum, beseeching her to understand, but all I see is hurt emblazoned across her face.

'So, I'm trustworthy enough to manage your company for you in your absence, but not this?'

She's beginning to turn an unspecified shade of purple. Barney the dinosaur? Aubergine? The latter would certainly match her black mood.

'Mum, it's not like that. Ronnie and I decided not to tell anyone until after the scan.'

'But you should always tell us. You know you can tell us anything.'

What Mum means is 'everything'. Whilst it's great having a wonderful family, sometimes everyone knowing your business can be a bad thing. What if something does go wrong? Ronnie and I are only trying to protect the grandparents from worrying about us. They're getting on. It's our turn to worry about them now.

'They said I was a geriatric mother.' My voice has clearly risen as the children pause from playing with Patch, and Bear, who has slunk back to them in the meantime, and stare at us, their brows furrowed at the change in pitch.

'Geriatric mother!' My mother's outrage matches mine the moment the nurse said it.

'I know! And I didn't want to tell you in case…' The words remain unspoken between us, but my parents understand what I'm referring to. 'I'm sorry.' My eyes meet Mum's.

'So, how pregnant are you?' Mum asks as she casts a glance over her shoulder towards the kids to ensure little ears aren't listening in.

'Nine weeks, ten weeks? They're not one hundred per cent sure.'

Dad rises from his chair and hugs me to him. 'Congratulations, darling. I'm so happy for you both. What does Ronnie say?'

I mull this over for a second. 'Well, he's delighted about the baby, not so much about the timing, or the circumstances, what with the house, the job scenario.'

Belatedly, it occurs to me that we didn't tell my parents

the full details of the job Ronnie was going for, or how important it was to us.

'That's a real pity.' Dad purses his lips. 'But he's a talented man, he'll get another job soon. I have every confidence.'

If only it were that easy.

'Yes, yes.' Mum waves away the job topic as if it's no more than a bluebottle irritating her. 'Now, tell me more about this baby. Names? Can I start knitting?'

I give my mum a deadpan look. 'I take it you were being ironic.' Mum no more knits than I do.

'I was.' She smirks. 'Did you think you were getting baby blankets and cardies and so forth from me?'

'Well, it will be a winter baby, so if you're not knitting them, you can start stocking up on them,' I shoot back.

'Touché. Right, so, names!'

She never gives up. Now I know where my tenacity came from.

The kids decided they wanted to stay with their grandparents for a bit to discuss possibilities for Hugo's birthday. Since we're currently in a hotel, my parents thought it would be a good idea – and it was – to host the party at their house as they have a large enough garden. The very thought of eight primary four boys in our hotel room just about has me reaching for gas and air.

I'd told Hugo he could have a few friends to Laser Quest or paintball, but he said he wanted a birthday party outside. One of his friends had apparently had a football party recently, and he convinced Hugo outdoor was the way to go – pity he doesn't listen to me when I suggest he goes outdoors.

Out of that germ of an idea was born the beach party with beach-themed party games and a net put up so they can play beach volleyball. Mum and Dad have cleared it with their neighbours about a little additional noise as the plan is to have an outdoor disco too. Nothing too rowdy, but certainly at a decibel level far higher than usually experienced by the residents of the leafy street Mum and Dad live in.

Anyway, Mum says she has everything in hand, which I'm immensely grateful about, although I'm worried I'm leaning on her far too much at the moment. I realise our lives have been turned upside down, shredded and stamped upon, but she's not getting any younger, and as she said earlier, she's already keeping things ticking over for me at Wedded Bliss.

And I miss all the preparation for the party. I mean, I'll be here on the day, obviously, but I really look forward to the big events for the kids, the milestones, although they do seem to come around quicker every year. How can Hugo be nine? It doesn't seem that long since he was five and about to start school. Now Aria's starting school. I feel like screaming at the speed with which everything is happening, or perhaps I could invent a time machine and go back and make them babies again. No, that wouldn't work. I was about to say, the new baby period was such hard work, thank God I'm over that, when I remember I'm pregnant. I can really tell I'm pregnant too, as for a moment my brain seemed to forget.

All of this is spinning through my head as I drive back to the hotel, but first I need to stop off in Hamwell to pick up Hugo's main birthday present. He'd asked for a hoverboard, and although I was a bit reticent about them – who hasn't googled how many people have been hospitalised with a hoverboard-related accident? – I've come round. He's clumsy, but sensible. My heart will still beat a thousand times faster each time he uses it, but I can't be a helicopter mum – well, at least, not all the time.

His friend Jonah has one. Santa brought it… Santa has a lot to answer for. And they're not cheap. If there's one sure way to tell you're getting old, it's when you starting noticing how much everything costs and your jaw drops, and your stock response is 'It was how much?' before you pass out with shock. I had originally thought about getting him a new bike, as he's reaching the top end of the size of his current one, and I figured a couple of hundred quid would seal the deal easily. Holy moo. How wrong was I? So, the hoverboard was a godsend in some ways. Five hundred quid for a kids' mountain bike. Think we'll just keep him on the flat and avoid mountains if that's the cost of it.

Oh, I'm in Hamwell already. I've subconsciously driven to the toy store from where I'm picking up the hoverboard. They emailed yesterday to say my order had arrived, so since I have a little time on my own, this is the perfect opportunity to pick it up, without inquisitive eyes vying to see what's in the box.

Wow, it's hot. As I step out of the car, I've never been more thankful of my air conditioning. This isn't normal. I glance at the dashboard. Twenty-seven degrees. Do I feel hotter because I'm pregnant or am I not pregnant enough for that yet? Who decides when you're pregnant enough?

'I'm back,' I call, pushing the suite door closed with my foot.

'Hey,' Ronnie replies, then turns the corner to where I'm taking off my shoes. 'Where are the kids?'

'They wanted to stay at Mum and Dad's for a bit. Hugo has a list of things to discuss with Mum about the party.'

Ronnie rolls his eyes. 'Rather her than me.'

I smirk. 'Not your strong point.'

He bats me on the arm and feigns outrage. 'Are you trying to say I couldn't handle ten eight-year-olds?'

My lips curve into a smile. 'Nope. I'm telling you, you can't manage nine nine-year-olds.'

He frowns.

'Hugo's going to be nine, and he has invited eight friends, plus him. Nine. Simple.'

He rolls his eyes again. 'Fair enough. So, do you want the good news or the not quite so good news?'

Now it's my turn to frown. 'The not quite so good news?' I'm going out on a limb here, hoping it's not terrible. I'm also concerned as, as far as I knew, Ronnie's task was to call the insurance company.

He sits on the sofa then says, 'Sit.'

Who am I? Bear? Patch?

I can tell the frown lines on my face are multiplying. He's drawing this out more than I'd like. 'Ronnie, get a move on, and just spit it out.'

He bites the inside of his mouth so the indent is visible from the outside. I hate when he does that, but that's his thinking pose. 'I phoned the insurers.'

I lean forward, 'And?'

'It's not a no, but it's not brilliant, especially if it's over any length of time.'

I scrunch up my eyebrows. 'What does that mean exactly? Stop with the quiz and tell me!' I'd forgotten how short-tempered I become when pregnant. Some people turn into mellow Earth Mothers. Not me, not bloody likely. I already don't suffer fools, not that Ronnie's a fool, but I hate people taking forever to get to the point.

'They will pay some of it, but we need to make up the difference.'

My face falls. 'How much are we talking?'

'A grand a month, give or take.'

'What? You've got to be kidding. You hear of people getting two grand a week for a three-bedroom private landlord house, and we can't even get that for a month for a four-bedroom. Did you tell them I was pregnant?' Heat rises in my cheeks, and I do my best to remain calm, but it isn't easy.

'Look, I know it might seem a lot, but maybe we can do it.'

'Ronnie, we could be out of our own house for the rest of the year, maybe more, maybe forever. We can't drain our savings like that, and more to the point, why should we?'

'I know.' He leans his hands heavily on his thighs then rubs them up and down as if this helps his thought processes, all the while looking at the floor as if the mysteries of the universe can be solved there, or perhaps at the very least our housing woes. Who knows? Maybe it can.

He doesn't look inclined to add anything, so I say softly, 'Ronnie.' No answer. A little louder. 'Ronnie.'

'Hmm?'

'We can't afford it. We'll need to go back to the drawing board, but I'm not giving up without a fight.' My hackles rise thinking of how unfair the insurer's decision is. We haven't even asked them for any money up until now, having been lucky enough to have a friend – Fabien – who has helped us out on that front. Actually, I'm going to use that and write a strongly worded letter if I have to. I'm good at a strongly worded letter.

'I would expect nothing less.' Ronnie manages a slight smile.

I spread out on the sofa. 'What was the good news? Please make it be something totally awesome, after that. I feel totally deflated.'

'Me too. I could see us living there.'

'The master bedroom was gorgeous and the period details and the garden and–'

'I got a second interview at Petrocord,' Ronnie says.

I blink, once, twice. 'What?'

'You heard right. A second interview, next week.'

'Oh my God, that's amazing.' I hug him to me. 'Oh, Ronnie, but how–?'

'One of the candidates dropped out. Accepted another job offer, so they had a space after all.'

'That's fantastic, well, for all concerned, but especially you, us.' I kiss him on the lips, and he responds.

'Fingers crossed this time. Not sure what I did wrong last time, but I won't mess it up this time.'

I bolt upright. 'Ronnie, you did not do anything wrong, I know you didn't, and we already talked about how sometimes it can just be Lady Luck. So, get any thoughts that you did something wrong out of your head. Simply go, be yourself, believe in yourself, and do your best. That's all anyone can ask.'

Ronnie smiles down at me. 'I do love you, you know.'

'I should bloody well think so. I've been married to you for thirteen years, nearly fourteen, borne you three children, and–' I point to my still non-existent bump '–I'm busy cooking a fourth in here.'

Ronnie pushes my hair back from my face. 'I just want you to know. And Lou, thanks for all your support. I don't know what I'd do without you.'

With a smirk, I jump up from the sofa and say, 'Neither do I. So, what shall we do until it's time to get the kids?'

'Quick swim? Full use of the spa facilities?'

'Aah, sounds bliss. Let's do it.'

He kisses me hard on the mouth, then we dig out our swimming costumes and throw some toiletries into a bag and head down to the leisure suite. We may as well make the most of it whilst we're still living here, because tomorrow I'm taking that insurance company to task.

Chapter Thirteen

Tuesday 3 August

To-do list

Pay bills

Renew science centre memberships

Increase taekwondo direct debit – again?

Finalise everything for Hugo's birthday tomorrow – I want it
to be perfect – liaise with Mum

*Contact Fionnuala Matheson to let her know her invitations
will be going out tomorrow via UPS*

*Ask Mum to start looking into booths for winter wedding fairs
and boutique venues. Need to see if we're going to exhibit this
year and costs.*

Next day, on returning from a client meeting, I enter the
foyer and Fabien is standing chatting to the receptionist.
'Fabien, how are you?'

'Louisa, the very woman. I was hoping to grab you to
speak to you about the Madrid gig, but I've not had a
chance to call yet.'

I smile. His confidence and enthusiasm are always so
infectious. He really does light up every room he walks
into. It's hard to imagine him being pissed-off. Ah, no, it's

not, I remember, as an image of our meeting with Charles Pickford comes to mind.

'Oh? I've not quite finished the presentation yet.' That's a lie. I've barely started it.

'It's nothing major, but there has been a change of date, I'm afraid. Several of those attending are now required at a major event in Huelva.'

He says this as if I should know where Huelva is. I don't, but I'm assuming it's in Spain.

'So, when's the new date?' I ask, hoping it's not once the kids go back to school as that could be tricky.

'It's Tuesday.'

'OK. I'll need to see if I can change my flight.'

'Don't worry about that. I'll have the office do it.' He bestows his beaming smile upon me again.

I'd forgotten he has 'people' to manage these things for him.

'That's great. Well, if there's nothing else…' I really do need to get on.

'No, that's it, although I'd like us to sit down sometime beforehand and go over your presentation together.'

Oh, no. Then he'll see what a non-presentation it is. How am I going to glitz it up so it looks substantial? I know my business, but putting it in presentation form isn't proving the easiest of tasks, particularly with everything else going on.

'Sure. A couple of days before,' I parrot back to him, my eyes not meeting his. Glad it's not now.

'Oh, I meant to ask, how is the house-hunting going?'

My face falls. 'Not great. Well, we found somewhere but our insurance company don't want to pay anywhere near the full amount, so it's back to the search unless I can convince them to stop being so stingy.'

Fabien's outrage breaks through his usually unruffled exterior. 'They can't do that, surely?'

I sigh. 'You know what insurance companies are like.'

'Unfortunately, and perhaps, fortunately, I do all too well. They should be offering you something like up to twenty per cent of the sum insured. Don't quote me on that, as it will vary from insurer to insurer, obviously, and I'm talking about business insurance, but I'm sure it's similar with home insurance. Can't hurt to check it out.'

'I fully intend to.' Part of me is glad he's defending me, whilst the other part is irked he thought I'd just back down and roll over. Perhaps I'm being unfair, and overly sensitive after Ronnie and his 'little woman' attitude with regards to the tradesmen when we replaced our kitchen earlier this year.

'Mrs Halliday.' The receptionist interrupts us. 'You have some mail.' She hands me the letters.

'Thank you.' I turn to Fabien. 'See you later. I'm taking the kids to the science centre. There will be hell to pay if I don't get a move on.'

Again with the dazzling smile. 'No problem, Louisa. I'll have my assistant send you the revised schedule.'

I dip my head in acknowledgement.

I trudge up the stairs to our suite, in an attempt to stay fit. By the time I get halfway, I'm wishing I hadn't. How did I forget pregnancy was so tiring?

I leaf through the mail as I go: junk, more junk, Mastercard bill, and finally a white NHS envelope. I rip it open and devour the contents. My scan has been arranged for Tuesday, the tenth of August. Then it tells me all the usual stuff I need to know. Oh, wow! It's starting to feel rather real, all of a sudden. I'm going to have four children by early next year. I don't know whether to be jubilant or panic, but I do know one thing: I'm looking forward to meeting my baby.

The kids are in various states of undress when I walk into the suite. Well, Ronnie did promise them a pyjama morning whilst I had my breakfast meeting with a client in Stirling. She'd wanted to meet in person, and had insisted it be me, not Mum. Suffice to say, Mum was none too thrilled at that response. Fortunately, Mum also seems to have overcome being upset with me over not initially telling her I was pregnant, and has been sending me lots of excited texts. You'd think it was her first grandchild the way she's going on.

'We're never going to get to the science centre at a decent time, guys, if you don't go and get dressed,' I say as I enter.

'Mummy!' Aria launches herself at me and buries her chocolate-smeared face into my Karen Millen blouse. That will need to be dry-cleaned now. They've clearly ordered breakfast to the room, as the remains of the tray's contents are strewn liberally across the coffee table, flakes of pastry everywhere. I go to berate Ronnie for allowing such a mess, but draw myself up, recognising not everyone is as tidy as me, and the scan news is too good to blot by moaning at him. Although I am still a little annoyed at it, because it's me who'll have to clean it up in a minute.

'Mum, have you seen my iPad?' Hugo approaches and allows a hug under one arm, as I squish him to me.

'No, Hugo, I'm just in the door. Did you think to ask

Dad?'

Hugo eyes me as if this is a trick question. 'No? Anyway, have you? I was designing posters for the beach party, and I can't find it now, nor the pen.'

Ah, we're in whiny mode today. 'Tell you what, why don't you get dressed, tidy up – you too, Gen, and Aria – and then we may actually be able to find it?'

Hugo regards me as if I'm something unpleasant he's stepped in.

'But, but can't you find it, Mum, please?'

'Hugo–' my voice is suddenly a tad sharper '–I probably could, but I'm not going to before you look for it yourself. I've just arrived home, from *work*, and the first thing you do even before saying hi, is ask me to find your iPad that you've had all morning to look for. Is that about the size of it?' I refrain from putting my hands on my hips and glowering down at him, but I'm close.

His shoulders slump. 'Yes, Mum. I'll look for it first.' He drags himself away, feet shuffling in the most pathetic fashion ever.

'Excellent.' I beam broadly around the room. 'So, go, go go, all three of you. Meet back here in ten minutes.'

That'll give me just enough time to talk to Ronnie about the scan, the fact my parents now know I'm pregnant – something I didn't have time to tell him last night – and to advise him that my meeting in Madrid is now on a different date.

'Hey.' Ronnie reaches up from the sofa to plant a kiss on my lips. As he returns to the slumped position, he notes the letters. 'Anything for me?'

'Nope, but there is something for us.' I wave the NHS letter at him.

His eyes widen. 'Is that what I think it is?'

'Yep!'

'Fantastic. I'll get to see this one.'

I knew missing Aria's scan had affected him more than he let on at the time. He doesn't even realise he has let that slip.

'I'll ask Mum and Dad to look after the kids. It's Tuesday. The kids won't be back at school yet. They're not back until the following week.'

Ronnie rubs the back of his neck. 'Tuesday coming?'

'Yes. That's not a problem, is it?'

He shakes his head in frustration then huffs out a breath. 'That's the day of my interview.'

What? Really? Oh, shit, so it is. 'Oh, Ronnie.' I hesitate, trying to figure out what to do for the best. 'I'll call and ask to reschedule.'

'No, you can't, Lou. It's important.' He gives a rueful smile. 'You're a geriatric mother, remember?'

I give him a Paddington-esque hard stare. 'As my mother would say, "Do you want to live to see your next birthday?"'

He laughs and the tension breaks momentarily. He can't miss another scan. And this will definitely be the last baby, even though it's not the last scan.

'Look, let's get the kids ready for the science centre, and we'll see what we can do later.'

I nod. The other two pieces of information will have to wait. Now is not the time.

The kids enjoy themselves immensely at the science centre, Gen just as much as the other two. Hugo proclaims himself too old for Little Explorer (under sevens), and heads off for the STEM section with Ronnie, whilst Aria and Gen go into the Little Explorer section whilst I find a seat opposite and try to ring the insurance company. Fortunately, everyone is happily playing as I'm on hold for over twenty minutes, during which time Gen has come out to tell me she needs to take Aria to the toilet, Hugo has come down with Ronnie to ask when we can have something to eat and Gen has returned drenched, and without a change of clothes – at twelve years old, she's not someone I pack a change of clothes for any more – after Aria soaked her, in the water play area.

Finally, I get through, and although this person empathises with me, they can't give the OK to a higher amount without the approval of a supervisor, who isn't in this morning. Give me strength. Why should the world stop because someone is off work? Shouldn't they have thought of that and had someone else in the same or a similar role covering? Why does this seem common sense to me, but huge corporations don't seem to get it? The woman promises me a callback from her supervisor when she gets in, and the call ends with me feeling even more annoyed than before.

Gen returns from the toilets a little drier than she was when she left. I'm guessing she stood under the hand dryer, waving her T-shirt from left to right until she dried off a bit.

I embrace the day out with the family, and we rattle through a whole host of activities: running on a hamster wheel, jumping off a board and landing to see how heavy you are; putting back the pieces of the skeleton puzzle to recreate the human body – that makes for an interesting vision. We then tackle the craziness that is dining out with our family in a tourist attraction café.

'Mummy, I don't like sandwiches,' Aria cries.

'Yes, you do, Aria,' I say firmly, leading her towards a table, kids' lunch box in hand.

'Mum, this is too babyish for me. I don't eat Munch Bunch yoghurts any more.' Hugo.

Ronnie must see the steam about to erupt from my ears as he says, 'Come on, little man, I still eat them. In fact, if you don't want yours, give it here. I'll have it.' Ronnie plonks himself down at a booth, and the younger ones follow.

I would have killed to be taken out to a café when I was younger, but nobody really did that back then, unless it was a special treat, twice a year, often to buy school shoes, or for those who went to Catholic schools, a Holy Communion dress.

Ah, Gen. She'll be easier, surely. Her face falls, and my non-pregnancy brain returns. No, she's not going to be easier. I'd forgotten that this week she wants to be vegetarian/vegan/fruitarian, or something. Who the heck knows?

At least she doesn't whine about it. Much. 'Mum, they don't have a very varied vegetarian offering.'

'Oh?' I say, my tone insouciant.

'Well, they have a Mediterranean vegetable pot, but that's it.'

'OK. Does it have anything in it that your current lifestyle diet doesn't allow?' I raise my eyebrows as if to clarify my point.

She frowns. 'No, but…it's not exactly exciting.'

We're not in a five-star vegan restaurant, I want to say.

You can't expect cauliflower Caesar salad with broad beans and tahini. Or a hoisin mushroom noodle bowl with gomashio. But instead I say, 'Why don't you eat that and maybe we can find a dessert that's a little more appetising?'

All I really want to do is sit down before I fall down. Tiredness has taken hold of me and quickly. Damn being pregnant. I'd forgotten how sometimes it catches you unawares like this, and I can't even explain it to my daughter as we haven't told them yet that I'm pregnant. At least in a week I'll be able to do so, after the scan.

We take our seats, and the kids eat their food with various levels of reluctance. I catch Ronnie narrowing his eyes at me as I check my messages with one hand whilst I eat with the other. It's not my preference, but quite frankly I'm short on time at the minute. If I don't multi-task in this way, nothing will ever get done.

Ah, I have the new flight details for my Madrid trip. I cough, then splutter, then choke.

'You OK, Mum?' Gen eyes me with concern, hand poised behind my back ready to give me a pat if needed.

I nod, as I can't speak. I'm trying to get my breathing to return to normal, but I feel as if I've inhaled icing sugar or something, like when you inhale it off a tart in a posh restaurant and it goes down the wrong way. Exactly like that. I'm busy concentrating on not turning blue.

Eventually, I calm, and my heart rate returns to normal, by which point my family are deep in conversation with each other, or on tablets or phones. Thanks, guys, for your concern. At least Gen showed some, even if it was only for a nanosecond.

I reread the email, this time not daring to take a morsel of food in case I choke again. *Dear Louisa, Fabien has asked me to send you your updated flight and meeting details…*

F-f-f–lip! No, no, no, this can't be happening. The flight out has only been changed to the same day as my scan, which is also the same day as Ronnie's interview. I glance at the ceiling. Someone up there most definitely does not like me. I haven't even told Fabien yet that I'm pregnant. What am I going to do now?

'Guys, if you've finished lunch, do you want to go out and play in the little area outside?'

'Yay! Hugo, let's go. Gen, c'mon,' Aria says, ready to hare it out the door.

'Gen.' We exchange a look. She knows the drill. She needs to keep a good eye on them. Aria can be unpredictable.

Ronnie senses something's up. 'I thought we were heading back to the hotel after.'

'Thought we'd give them some fresh air, plus, there's a few things I need to talk to you about.'

The two of us watch as Gen shepherds her siblings towards the side exit. I turn to Ronnie, sigh and say, 'We have a problem.'

He frowns, then listens as I relay the contents of the email I've received.

'Oh, Lou, you're kidding.'

'I'm not.' I show him the email.

'Well, you'll have to tell Fabien it's not possible.'

'I can't do that, we've only just started working together.'

'Yeah, and you need to start the way you mean to go on.'

My mind flits to the meeting with Charles Pickford. Not bloody likely, I don't.

'I can't mess him about after everything he's done for us, Ronnie.'

'Lou, I appreciate all he's done too, more than you, or he, will ever know, but this is our baby.'

I tip my head back and stare at the ceiling. 'I know, but you can't make the scan either, so I would already have rather rearranged it, and now I'm supposed to be somewhere else too, on the day.'

Ronnie ruminates for a second then says, 'Are you sure you haven't taken on more than you can handle?'

I'm about to snap 'of course not', but then I soften – he's only looking out for me, and the baby. Us. Our family. 'Honestly, I don't know. But would you have turned down the opportunity to work with a huge, well-respected organisation like Cerulean if you were me?'

He lowers his eyes.

'I didn't think so.' I sigh. 'I just feel as if we're constantly being thrown curveballs, and that's not even taking into consideration a lorry crashing into our house.'

'Yeah, that's one giant curveball, all right. Look, why don't you phone the number on the letter, explain what's happened and see if it's possible to make it the day before or after.'

I nod.

'How long are you in Madrid for?' He bites his lip in concentration.

'Two days, but it's the best part of a day travelling there and back too.'

'Well, whatever the case, we need someone to look after the kids. Do you think your mum and dad could watch them? If not, I'll ask mine. They haven't seen them much since the crash, what with there being nowhere for them to stay when they come over.'

Thank God. Ronnie's mum is best taken in small doses, microscopic, in fact. And apparently, she's too good to meet us at our hotel. She has an aversion to meeting us in what she terms our 'bedroom'.

'I'm sure they will, and you'll be around apart from for the interview, right?'

He nods. 'More's the pity.'

I give him a sharp look.

'No, not like that. I love spending time with the kids, and you, but I really want to get a job. I…' he visibly deflates '…I had a message from Callan. They're pressuring me about a return date.'

'Oh, Ronnie, no. Geez, would someone please give us a break? I'm getting fed up with this.'

I blow out a breath.

'Look, why don't we drop by your folks on the way back and we can ask them then?'

I nod, glumly, then rise to go tell the kids to come back in. I stop and return to my seat.

Ronnie furrows his brow. 'What is it?'

'I didn't get a chance to tell you last night, or so far today. Mum and Dad know I'm pregnant.'

'What?' Ronnie pinches his lips together. 'And how did that come about?'

'Well, I didn't tell them, if that's what you're thinking.'

'Really?' He doesn't look convinced.

'Really, Ronnie. God, we discussed this. We said we'd keep it quiet until after the scan and we'd only tell Wendy and Jo. I had to tell Wendy, remember, as I needed to tell her the reason she had to come watch the kids. And, as you know, there's no show without Punch.' Punch, in this case, is Jo. I can't tell one sister without telling the other. Pretty much anything.

Heat rises up my neck, and I resent that he doesn't appear to believe me.

'So, they just guessed, did they?'

'Actually, no.' I then tell him how she found out.

'For God's sake, is nothing sacred round here? You can't even have a private conversation without someone blabbing.'

At least he's no longer blaming me.

'Anyway, I thought you should know since we're going there now.'

The mood has changed. Ronnie looks totally hacked-off. Well, it's not my fault.

'So, what are we going to do? Tell my folks? Rhys? Sandra? Your whole family knows, why shouldn't mine?'

'It's not a damned competition,' I hiss, finding it hard to keep my cool. 'And it's not as if your brother and Sandra live nearby. Or your parents for that matter.'

'But it's always your family who finds everything out first,' he bats back at me.

'And? Is it a failing on our part that we're so involved in each other's lives?'

His silence says it all. Bad move, Ronnie. Don't ever diss my family. I'm so on the cusp of telling him perhaps his parents would know more and be more involved if his mother wasn't so self-absorbed, but I rein it in at the last minute. Going there won't help anyone.

'Let's go. We can't sit about here all day achieving nothing.' I turn towards the door, not caring that Ronnie is probably staring at my back gawping. How can he honestly think that the frostiness his cold-fish of a mother exudes is better than the warmth of my family?

Chapter Fourteen

Tuesday 3 August

The positively glacial silence between Ronnie and me coats the interior of the car as we drive to my parents'. Aria and Hugo don't seem to notice, but Gen is switched-on. I know she realises something's up. Although we're only a week away from the scan, maybe, I'm still not ready for us to tell her about the baby. Despite me not anticipating any problems, I'm pragmatic enough to know it is possible to miscarry, particularly if you're an 'older woman'.

We pull into my parents' driveway with us barely having exchanged a word. A ping on his phone alerts Ronnie to a message. Since I'm driving, he reads it, curses almost wordlessly under his breath and falls silent again. Wonder what that's all about. I have the feeling if we were on talking terms, he'd have mouthed off to me about it, but since we're at the stony silence stage, there's little chance of that.

The kids spill out of the car and immediately go in search of the dogs, who aren't long in bounding towards them, tails wagging, barks reaching a new pitch only previously heard by, well, other dogs.

'Tea?' Mum says as soon as she spots us. She says it even before she says hi. We must look like crap. That's a new record even for her.

'Yeah, I'll help you make it.'

'Oh, it's all right, it's all in hand,' she says as I walk into the kitchen straight into the chest of my brother-in-law Travis, who startles and sloshes tea over the floor.

'Wow! Hey, sis. Didn't know you guys were coming over.' Outwardly Travis seems friendly enough, but ever since he spotted me and Caden together a couple of times a few months back, he has been guarded around me, and we haven't had quite the same easy-going relationship.

As Travis cleans up the floor with a kitchen towel, I make the tea. 'How you doing? Jo didn't say you were coming by today.'

'She asked me to drop something off for Hugo's birthday party.'

'Ah.' I'm curious to know what, but somehow I can't make myself ask him.

'Travis has brought over their giant paddling pool,' Mum says.

I glance at my brother-in-law, who smiles slightly.

'Yes, he was down in Glasgow to interview replacements for Caden. Such a nice boy. We'll miss him when he goes.'

'He's already gone,' Travis says.

I can't help it. My head snaps up, and Travis clocks my expression just as Ronnie walks in.

'Any tea going?' he asks Mum.

''Course there is, Ronnie.'

He's always been Mum's favourite. Could charm the skin off a snake's back, that one.

'All right, Travis?'

'Yeah, good, you?' He studiously avoids meeting my

eyes, so I slink out of the room with my tea, glad to have dodged a potentially unpalatable situation.

Dad's in the garden, sitting in his wooden deckchair, watching the world go by. Nothing fazes Dad much. Sometimes, I think it's because he's seen it all. With our family he probably has.

There's no need to babble or make small talk with Dad – he's happy to sit in my company, silently. I raise my face to the sun and close my eyes for a second, taking in what I heard in the kitchen. Caden's gone. Gone. It's so final. And suddenly, whether it's because of my and Ronnie's spat in the car, or some other reason, I don't want Caden to be gone, erased from our lives as if he was never there.

Eventually Dad says, 'Something on your mind, love?'

I sigh. Where to start? 'I'm sure the cosmos will sort it out at some point, Dad, or maybe Mum will.'

We both laugh. Mum's a force to be reckoned with.

'Actually, we do have a bit of a dilemma.'

'Dilemma?' Mum says as she reappears and settles herself beside us.

I swear that woman is a vampire. She hovers or levitates, she doesn't walk. She's always materialising when you least expect it.

'Yes. You know how I'm going to Madrid on a course, well, to give a course.'

Mum leans forward. 'Uh-huh.'

'Well, it turns out Ronnie does have a second interview after all, and it's the same day.'

'Oh, no. That's so unlucky. Of course we'll help out.'

'Thanks. That's not all, though.'

Mum's eyebrows nearly disappear into her hairline as

she waits to find out what else. 'My scan is scheduled for the same day. I'll need to change it.'

'Oh, you can't. The baby has to come first.'

I grit my teeth. 'Yes, I'm aware of that, Mum.'

'Liv, leave her be. It must be hard enough having these three things at the same time without you poking your nose in,' Dad says.

Thanks, I mouth to Dad when Mum rounds on him.

'I'm just saying she has to look after herself, her body and the baby, above all else.'

'Well, my mental health will be affected, Mum, if I don't sort these three things out, and Ronnie has to go for that interview. It's the only way he can stay onshore.'

Too late I realise what I've said. Something else I haven't shared…until now.

'What do you mean?' Mum's nostrils are almost flaring. She senses a secret, and right now she resembles Ronnie's mum more than mine. She's a veritable dragon is Annabelle. Thinks the sun shines out of Ronnie's derriere and that I'm some backward oik or something. She seems to forget we went to the same uni, and that I got a better degree than he did, a 2:1 to his 2:2.

The glare she gives me leaves no room to backtrack. 'Ronnie needs this job. Callan are moving his role to Azerbaijan, permanently, and it will mean longer stints away from home.'

Mum's jaw drops. Finally, she says, 'In the middle of all this chaos, with the house, now the baby, your new role with Cerulean?'

I jut my chin out. 'It's not like we have much choice in the matter. They've been trying to get him to go for ages, years even. Now you go where you're sent, or you leave.' I lower my eyes and tap the arm of the chair, then glance back up. 'That's why it's even more important he gets this job at Petrocord.'

The man himself appears at that moment with Travis, and I excuse myself to go see to the children. I don't want any more uncomfortable moments with Travis. It's as if in the past few months he has discovered a way to see directly into my soul, and it unnerves me more than I can say.

My thoughts tumble around inside my head, creating pressure there that I could do without. Caden. Madrid. Baby. Petrocord. Callan. Fabien. Insurance company. I don't make it to the children. Instead, I turn and rush for the bathroom where I release the contents of my stomach, and again, I'm not sure whether it's morning sickness or something else.

I can't face seeing Travis again just now, especially given the state of me. Mum will immediately know I've been sick. She seems to know everything, and I don't want her letting slip in front of Travis that I'm pregnant. I'm not ready for it yet, not after the way he looked at me when Mum caught me unprepared with her comment about Caden.

I slip out to the garden and observe the children playing with Bear and Patch. Oh, how I've missed their dear little faces – the dogs', that is.

Bear notices me and lopes up to me, tongue hanging out, tail wagging so much he looks like he could take off. 'Hi, boy. Did you miss me?' I crouch on my hunkers and stroke his muzzle, then under his chin, which he loves, and his tail increases its pace further. I hug him to me. Somehow when things are tough, Bear always makes me feel better, but lately I've not had him by my side, and until

I saw him again, I hadn't realised how much being away from him had affected me.

I stroke his floppy ears and a sense of calm descends over me. Bear. My rock. It should be Ronnie, my rock, but no, it's Bear. That's not the way it should be though, is it? Although Ronnie and I have been muddling along a lot better the past few weeks, there's no quick fix to our relationship, and the baby isn't the answer. The distraction of the baby is just a sticking plaster. Sooner or later, once all the other problems resolve themselves, we'll be back facing each other, facing the same old problems, wondering if we're going to make it. Or, at least, I will.

All it took was one mention of Caden to throw everything into disarray. I should be thinking about my presentation, how I'm going to bluff it or fluff it; the temporary home we need to find; school clothes I need to order for the kids; making the remainder of the school holidays as fun for the kids as possible; checking in on Nicky to see how she's doing at the hospital; ensuring Sam is doing OK, not thinking about Caden. But I am.

As Patch joins Bear and yips around me, I smile and give him my attention. Bear doesn't mind – he's clearly used to it. Second-best to the new pup, with most, but not me. He understands me in a way I'm not sure any human ever will.

I take deep breaths in an effort to maintain the calm Bear has helped me find, however temporary.

What I need right now is a break – how sad is it that a break for me is a visit to hospital to see my friend? I've been going into hospital every second night to see Nicky, even if just for half an hour. I pray for her sake they release her soon. She does seem to finally be on the mend, although it will clearly take a long time before she's back to normal. And I'm so glad she's moving in with Valentin, not only because anyone can see they're deeply in love, but because I dread to think how she would have managed financially with no job and no way of working for the foreseeable. I'm not sure she had illness cover. I know we don't. Something we should probably rectify.

An hour later, we're back in the car, having discussed at great length the details for Hugo's birthday party tomorrow. It sounds marvellous, I have to say. In fact, I'm feeling a bit put-out that Mum and Dad didn't do this for me! OK, I know it was different times, but…

Anyway, Hugo will have a fantastic time, and so will all his friends. Gen and Aria will be there too, and they're allowed to bring one friend each, but apart from that, it's the nine boys. I pray the weather's good for it. The last thing we need is a washed-out beach party.

Ronnie drives this time. We still haven't spoken. And I barely said a word to Travis today, which makes me sad, as I miss the easy banter between me and my brother-in-law that we used to enjoy. Everything's a mess, and not even Aria's excited jabbering away about the beach party, and Hugo agreeing with Gen for once, can lift me from my slump.

I need my friends, and my sisters.

We arrive back at the hotel, and I decide to stay down in one of the quiet areas off the foyer to make some calls for work, but also to the insurance company.

'Gen, can you take the guys up?' says Ronnie. 'I'm

going to speak to Mum for a second.'

Great. This should be fun. When they've disappeared up the stairs, I gesture to Ronnie to sit down in front of me, but he remains standing and says, 'It won't take long.'

I'm taken aback by his tone, and tears come unbidden to my eyes – bloody hormones.

'Go on then.' If he wants to be spiky, let him be, but he'll receive the same in spades. No more Mrs Nice Guy from me. I'm fed up with being the good guy all the time. It doesn't appear to be getting me anywhere.

'I got a text from Benedict. There's another party interested, and he's fobbed them off for a few days, but he needs to know by Saturday, or he'll have no choice but to rent the house to them.'

Now the tears fall thick and fast, and I don't care that I'm in the foyer for all to see, I don't care if it's hormones or not, I just care that nothing seems to be going our way right now, and I'm heartsick at it.

'It was kind of him at least to delay them,' I say through a haze of tears, my voice cracking with emotion. I'm so confused right now. Whenever we fix something, another thing breaks, and I don't know how much longer I can do this for. I'm not sure how much longer I can honestly be expected to do it for.

'Yeah.' Ronnie nods his agreement. 'Lou–'

I cut him off. I don't want his platitudes right now. 'I'm going to call the insurers. I'll let you know what they say.'

Ronnie recoils as if I've struck him, my dismissal is so firm. 'Right. I'll go up and see to the kids.'

'Fine,' I say, my tone clipped. I'm not letting him off for being so mean to me earlier. He can earn my forgiveness.

Thirty-five minutes I'm on hold to the insurance company, and once I finally get through, I have to wait at least another five minutes to be put through to the supervisor I've requested to speak to.

'Mrs Halliday?'

'Yes, this is she,' I say, sounding like a member of the aristocracy, my accent modified to match my vocabulary too.

'I'm Harmony Evergood, supervisor here.'

I can't help it. I snigger. Harmony. Evergood. In a complaints department. It's too good, pun intended, to be true.

'Is everything OK?' she asks.

I can sense even down the phone that she's bristling, so I decide to come clean. 'I'm sure it's not the first time someone has pointed out how soothing your name is for those calling a complaints department.'

'Well, I don't only deal with complaints, but yes, it has been mentioned once or twice.' Her abruptness indicates the end of the discussion. 'I believe you were calling about the amount agreed for your replacement accommodation.'

'That's right. It's nowhere near enough, and I have it on good authority, from my boss, no less, who deals with accommodation claims on a regular basis–' white lie '–that the paltry sum you have offered is far below the average for this type of claim.'

'Well, there were extenuating circumstances, plus you didn't claim within the initial period…'

I do listen to everything she says, but all I really hear is blah, excuse, blah, blah, blah.

'Look, I'm sure you saw us in the newspapers and on TV. None of this is our fault. Go after the lorry driver if you must, do whatever insurance companies do, but there is no other suitable accommodation in our area, and it's nowhere near the price point I've been led to believe is the high end of what our cover should provide. All I'm asking is that you match the amount the landlord has asked for so I don't have to bring my children up in a hotel whilst our house is rebuilt.'

I'm suddenly aware that my tone has risen slightly. Well, whose wouldn't?

'We take verbally abusing our staff very seriously, Mrs Halliday. I think it's better if we email you your offer.'

'No, no. Verbally abusing? I raised my voice a smidge. I've paid insurance to your company for at least a decade, and the one time I need it, you won't uphold your end of the bargain. It's not good enough!' OK, I'll admit I am shouting now.

'Like I said, Mrs Halliday, we don't appreciate anyone abusing our staff. I'll send the email out.'

'I'm not abusing you,' I whisper, in a stark attempt to get her to remain on the phone. 'I just want what's right, a home for my family. I'm pregnant!'

'Congratulations. Please remember to update your policy when the baby arrives so we have the right number of people in your household listed.'

One, two, three, four. 'You haven't heard the last of this.' I end the call, furious that I don't have the satisfaction of slamming down the phone.

I sit, fizzing, wiping away the tears that are coursing down my face. Why can't I have some bloody luck?

A barista comes over, and I'm not sure if it's to take my order or surreptitiously to check if I'm OK. I must look a right red blotchy, snotty mess. I can't even say 'It's hormones, I'm pregnant' as hardly anyone knows, and it has to stay that way for a little while yet.

'I'll have a sparkling mineral water, please.'

Whilst I wait, I message Sam, Wendy, Jo, Nicky, all the women who are important in my life. It occurs to me I haven't told Ronnie that Sam and Nicky know, but what he doesn't know won't hurt him.

How's Junior? x

How did your first couple of days go? x

Just met Travis at Mum and Dad's. Didn't realise he was coming down this way today to interview for Caden's replacement. x

Can I come in a bit earlier tonight? x

Not that I can talk to Nicky about the whole Caden situation, but perhaps if I focus on two people who are so obviously right for each other, it will take my mind off me and Caden.

I take a deep breath and call the hospital, about my scan this time. I explain the situation, and unbelievably, they've had a cancellation and can see us on the Monday, the day before I go to Madrid, and the day before Ronnie's interview. Oh, thank you, thank you, thank you. I think I say that to myself, but I'm not sure as there's a bemused silence on the other end of the phone.

Only six more days until I'll see my baby. I wonder how it will have grown. Hopefully, we'll be able to get clear images. My three always outfoxed the sonographer. Well, not Gen, as she was the first, but then she became my benchmark and the other two were completely different, lying different ways. We couldn't even find Aria to begin with. She was hiding.

I exhale in a whoosh, almost as if that positive news has lightened my load.

But just as quickly, reality kicks in, and I recall that I still have the problem of securing us somewhere to live. I'm not asking the earth after all, only what we're due. I'm not looking for the equivalent of a Fifth Avenue apartment overlooking Central Park, but a four-bedroom house, which granted overlooks a village park.

And in the back of my head is always the concern that the problems with the kids living here: their acting out, their belligerence, their boredom and the ensuing events caused by it, may make Fabien change his mind about allowing us to live here. I know it would make me think twice if I were in his position. Only Ronnie having a quite word with the guest in the room two down from ours, stopped a major incident, after the misunderstanding with Aria and the jewellery. The least said about that the better. That girl needs locked up, and if she continues to pop into people's bedrooms when their doors are inadvertently left open and try on their jewellery, admiring herself in the mirror, and then get caught by the maid, she may well end up in prison down the line.

Now the clock is against us too; Benedict has another interested party. I close my eyes and will myself to think positive thoughts as the enormity of my task threatens to overwhelm me, and stress isn't good for the baby either.

After taking a few sips of my mineral water, I'm about to head upstairs to rejoin the others when the same barista who brought my water passes, dropping the *Times*, the *Daily Record* and the *Ferniehall Echo* on the table. Wait a minute. An idea forms, then percolates in my brain, gathering momentum. I wonder…

Chapter Fifteen

Tuesday 3 August

I'm going to call the *Ferniehall Echo*.

When the crash happened, we were all in too much of a daze, but the phone kept ringing with reporters wanting to speak to us. Even if I had been able to process what was going on, I wouldn't have spoken to those bottom-feeders, however, perhaps now I can use that to my advantage. Surely, they'll be interested in a feature on the family made homeless by the crash and the heartless insurance company who won't pay what they're due? Everyone hates insurance companies, even the people who work for them. I should know, I worked in insurance before I was a purchaser, aeons ago.

'Hello, my name's Louisa Halliday. I'd like to speak to Justin Barnes.'

The operator asks, 'What's it regarding?'

'It's about the lorry that crashed through the house in Ferniehall two months ago. It was my house.'

'One moment, please.'

'You did what?' Ronnie's face is so red, I fear for his health. I hope I don't have to call him an ambulance.

'I thought it too good a chance to turn down. We need

help, they'd contacted us before, made sense.' To me. At the time. Not so much now.

'Jesus, Lou, I left you for less than an hour, and in that time, the havoc you've caused is off the chart.'

'Look, calm down, we won't even have to see the guy. He's just going to lift a photo from the night of the accident, throw together some copy based on what I told him, and hopefully we'll get enough coverage that the insurance company will have to back down. He was off to phone them for their comment.'

'And how's Nicky going to feel about that?' fumes Ronnie. 'If anyone should be going to the papers for help, it should be her. She's the one lying in a hospital bed, immobile, away from her family, her work life crumbling around her.'

I hang my head. 'I didn't think of that.'

Ronnie is apoplectic now. 'No, Lou, that's your problem, you never do, you steamroll in there and bulldoze everything to the ground.'

I inhale sharply. 'That's not fair, Ronnie.' Nor is it accurate. 'And if Nicky wants to go to the papers, our article won't prevent her from doing so.'

'Life's not fair, Lou. Do you at least have approval on the photos and text?'

I gulp. I haven't, but perhaps I can get it retrospectively. 'Of course I have.'

Ronnie shakes his head. 'I'm going for a walk.' He picks up his wallet from the table and strolls out of the suite, leaving Gen gaping after him as she walks into the living area.

'Is everything OK? Dad sounded angry.'

'It's nothing, honey. Dad just wasn't very happy with a

decision I made.' That's putting it mildly.

She wraps herself around me in a hug, and I'm reminded she's only twelve. It's not healthy for her to hear Ronnie and me argue. I smile ruefully at my next thought: we need a house not a hotel suite so we can at least have privacy for our disagreements.

'Tea?' I ask as I hold her away from me, then drop a kiss on her head.

'I'll make it.'

'Thanks. I'll pour the water though.'

'I know.' She rolls her eyes at me. I'm still too protective to let her pour boiling water from a kettle into the cups. So shoot me! I can't help if I always want to protect my kids.

Gen and I sit drinking our tea, a quiz show on in the background. She informs me her brother and sister are playing Guess Who in the bedroom. We'll leave them to it for now. A quality catch-up with my eldest is long overdue.

'So, how you feeling about going back to school?'

She nods. 'Yeah, it will be good to see all my friends again.'

A pang of guilt invades me again. It hasn't been as easy for the kids to see their friends this summer, and they haven't had the freedom to go out on their bikes and take off as they'd usually do, Gen in particular. I'm still a little reticent over Hugo near main roads, but if Gen's with him, that's OK, as long as it's in the village, but with the current situation, it's simply not feasible. My thoughts turn to the journalist I spoke with. He was pretty confident he could run the story the day after tomorrow. Just as well. With Hugo's birthday tomorrow, I can't risk anything shanghaiing that.

'And is there one person in particular you can't wait to see?' I tease, as I smooth down her hair.

'Mu-u-um!' Colour rises in her face, and I grin. 'Stop winding me up.' She bats me in the arm.

My phone beeps. Sam.

Sam: *Junior's fine. Feel as if I haven't seen you for ages.*

That's because she hasn't. Guilt envelops me again.

Sam: *Any chance of a decaff coffee or ginger tea at Cobblestones anytime soon?*

I love how she has given the café a nickname. Can I fit in a coffee date before I go to Madrid? God, this is getting ridiculous. We're still house-hunting, it's Hugo's birthday party tomorrow, I'm off on a business trip and I've had to reorganise a scan, as well as all the other things. Why does life always get in the way? I realise my circumstances are more than a little unusual at the moment, but it shouldn't get in the way of friendship.

Me: *Tell you what, why don't we meet on Thursday? Once Hugo's party is out of the way?*

Sam: *Excellent. I can give you Hugo's present then too. How are you feeling?*

Me: *Sick and busy and fed up. You?*

Sam: *Just sick. Missing you, and Nic.*

Me: *Me too. See you about 11? I'll ask Ronnie to watch the kids. Hugs to everyone x*

Sam: *And yours x*

I sit back feeling a bit more cheered. Seeing friends always helps, particularly in a crisis.

Aria and Hugo burst out of the bedroom as if they're being chased by a lion.

'Hey, what's the hurry?' I stand up to stop them in their tracks. At this rate, they'll smack straight into one of the walls.

'Mummy, we heard the ice-cream van. Can we go get some ice creams?'

Ice-cream van? At a luxury hotel? 'Guys, I don't think you did, or at least, if it was an ice-cream van, it must have sounded closer than it is. There's no way it can be close to the hotel. Think of the size of the grounds.'

'Please, Mummy, can we go and look?' Aria latches onto me, making her best puppy eyes. God, she's good.

'By the time we get there, wherever there is, the van will have gone.'

'Don't care,' Aria says, defiance flashing in her eyes, hands on her hips.

'Gen?'

'I'd quite like an ice cream too, if the van's around,' she admits.

'Hugo?'

'Yes, yes, of course. Can we go, please?' He's already opening the suite door, his tongue lolling out of his mouth like that of an oversized Great Dane.

We don't find the ice-cream van, but the kids' disappointment is such that I bundle them into the car and we head into Ferniehall to Ricci's.

'Louisa, Hugo, Aria, Genevieve, my favourite customers.' Aldo beams at us from behind the counter. 'We miss you. When are you moving home again? I think I'm going bankrupt, Louisa,' he says, pretending to hide his words behind a hand.

The kids lap it up, and I smile with them. Aldo represents everything that's right about this village – camaraderie, community and friendship. And I don't know about the kids, but I'm missing being a part of all of this.

We chit-chat with Aldo as we choose our ice creams: vanilla for Hugo, strawberry for Aria, chocolate for Gen, and salted caramel for me. Mmm. Aldo's ice cream really is amongst the best I've ever tasted. We need to make trips back to the village simply to sample it.

Once we've said our goodbyes, we stroll along the main street. I stop the children from visiting our house. It's too demoralising seeing how little has been done since we were forced to move out.

We take a peek in the bookshop, and Aria comes to the counter with six books, Hugo with two and a puzzle, and Gen with three.

'Aria, choose three, and we'll come back for the other three another time.'

Initially, this is met with some resistance, but in the end, she replaces three on the shelf, but not before debating her choices for a good ten minutes.

Beep. Message. Wendy. *I feel sick. Beginning to think promotion wasn't a great idea. What if I'm not ready? What if it's too much?*

Me: *Aw, stop it. You're more than ready. You deserve this, you need this and you've earned this. You've got this! x*

'Mum, can we go to the park?' Aria asks, tugging me towards it. How can I say no?

The kids play in the park, climbing on the climbing wall, swinging on the swings, and sliding down the slide. Gen pushes Hugo and Aria on the roundabout, hops on herself, then waves me over.

'No, I'm good,' I say.

She raises her eyebrows in a 'Don't mess with me, and be a fun mum' expression, and I cave.

Soon I'm flying round on the roundabout, giggling and snorting with laughter with them, forgetting all my worries for a few moments.

When we leave the park, Hugo says, 'Mum, can we go see the house we visited the other day?'

'Hugo.' I'm tired, in every sense, and I just want to go back to the hotel. I'd quite like to go back to the hotel as a guest, not a lodger. An hour-long massage, a minifacial and a sauna is what I need most right now. I'm also feeling a little green after the roundabout. Too late did I remember I was pregnant. Odd how it creeps up on you; even stranger that I sometimes forget until it smacks me in the face. I suppose it's down to having a to-do list that a wedding planner could be proud of. In fact, maybe I should have been a wedding planner, not a wedding stationer.

Actually, no, the very idea petrifies me. It's hard enough being responsible for the kids and the family, never mind being in charge of someone's big day. Goosebumps prickle up on my skin at the thought.

'I'd quite like to see it again, too, Mum,' Gen says, and in an instant my resolve fades to nothing. Gen doesn't ask for much, and I don't have the heart to tell them it's unlikely we'll be able to live there.

The three children chatter excitedly about how close to the park we'll be once we move in, although Gen's more interested in how close she'll be to her friends, and Hugo is as interested in the ice-cream parlour and the bakery. Always thinking of his stomach, that boy.

The tree-lined cul-de-sac has a lot to offer, and unlike our own house, it's secluded, not next to a road. Each of the eight houses in the street are enormous, and the cars in their driveways include Range Rovers, Teslas and Maseratis. Who knew Ferniehall was such a monied area? I've lived here twelve years, and I'm only learning this now.

Everyone's chattering as we pile back into the car, and I revel in the fact the impromptu trip has done us all some good.

When we arrive back at the hotel, Ronnie has returned and is sitting in the foyer, nursing a beer.

'Hi,' I say, as Hugo and Aria clamber on top of him, whilst Gen sits beside him and accepts a kiss on the cheek.

'Hi,' he says gruffly, his eyes not leaving mine.

My phone beeps. Jeez, will this thing ever stop? Nicky. Oh, yes, I sent a few messages earlier – baby brain has already kicked in, I see.

> **Nicky:** *Don't come visit me tonight.* Huh? *I'm getting out!!! Valentin is picking me up. Come see me tomorrow if you can.*
>
> **Me:** *That's fantastic! What a relief. Woo hoo! It's Hugo's birthday tomorrow, but we'll pop by after the party. Welcome home! Well, you know what I mean. I'm so glad you're on the mend. Sending hugs. Love to Valentin and Xander too x*

Now I know what all the cliches mean: floating on air, feeling as if you're on cloud nine, smiling like a Cheshire cat. That's me right at this moment. Finally, Nicky is getting home, and finally we can start putting this whole mess behind us. It can't come soon enough.

Chapter Sixteen

Wednesday 4 August

To-do list
Wake Hugo half an hour earlier than the others, so we can have Mummy/boy time
Ensure Hugo has best birthday ever
Check partygoers' allergies – before Mum serves them Nutella sandwiches

'Happy birthday to you, happy birthday to you, happy birthday, dear Hugo, happy birthday to you. Hip, hip, hooray!'

Hugo blows out his candles, and we all clap and cheer. He and his friends have had an amazing time today. Mum, Dad, Wendy and Jo have gone all out to ensure he has a birthday to remember.

Gen and Aria enjoyed their roles as helpers, as well as the opportunity to join in some of the activities. They loved paddling pool pass the parcel, and water musical bumps – which was hysterical as the boys kept cannonballing. I don't think there was a single adult on the sidelines who wasn't completely drenched. Gen even helped make up the numbers for the beach volleyball – Mum put down a special mat for the occasion, then she and Dad poured sand on top of it, for an authentic experience. I didn't like to tell her that her grass will probably never recover. She'll find that out in due course.

Jo made Hawaiian leis with help from Aurora. The eight boy party guests loved them, and Mum gave them all Hawaiian shirts the moment they walked through her gate, so they could 'get into character'. It was like an episode of *Miami Vice* but with Lilliputians.

Meanwhile, to add to the surrealism, Hugo experimented with his new hoverboard, and although he's no Marty McFly from *Back to the Future*, I have to admit, it did look kinda cool, but I'm way too clumsy to allow myself to be railroaded into participating. Ronnie wasn't so lucky and soon got roped in. Ha ha, well, that's what dads are for.

And I had to intervene as Xander, still with his cast on, wanted a go on the hoverboard. I felt bad telling him no, but the last thing I need is him injuring himself further. Fortunately, it was easy enough to distract him with something else, I roped in Gen to help with that, and he was soon enjoying himself, all thoughts of the hoverboard forgotten, for now. It wouldn't surprise me though if he goes home and asks Nicky if he can have one.

Mum made all the kids mocktails and scooped out the inside of coconuts for them to use as glasses. In fact, if you took a snapshot, you'd be forgiven for thinking the photos were taken in the Bahamas or Maui, instead of a sedate housing estate in suburbia.

The kids were slathered in sun cream. They ate lots of tropical fruit – allergies were checked beforehand – and of course consumed their own body weight in hot dogs, hamburgers and French fries, except Will, who has a gluten allergy.

By the time the party is over at five o'clock, the parents are collecting children who look like they will go straight to bed. They're all exhausted, and that includes mine, thank goodness.

And Ronnie and I shared a few moments together, particularly bonding over memories of a younger Hugo, and all the scrapes he has got himself into in the past. It's also been lovely having the family here, everyone together, even though Mum and Dad's house has been bulging with the sheer volume of people filling the inside and outside of it.

Fortunately, the neighbours seemed more curious than annoyed. It's probably the highlight of their week.

We help Mum and Dad tidy up, and I stay behind in the kitchen catching up a little more with Wendy and Jo. Jo, like me, has been telling Wendy she was born for this promotion and to stop dithering about it – she's ready, and it's too late now anyway, she got the job. You can always count on Jo not to mince her words.

My phone rings. Unknown number. I excuse myself and take the call outside.

'Hello?'

'Mrs Halliday? It's Justin Barnes from the *Ferniehall Echo*.'

'Oh, hi. How did you get on?'

'Well, you see, the thing is, my boss only wants us to run the story if we can have a photo of you and your family together, now.'

'Now? It's my son's birthday.'

'Oh, sorry, happy birthday. No, I didn't mean, now,

now, I meant, as your life is now.'

'But how will that help? We're living in a luxury hotel.'

'Yeah, don't you worry about that. I can put spin on it. So, can I come over tomorrow?'

'Tomorrow? I'm…I've got an appointment tomorrow morning.'

'Afternoon then, or even better, first thing in the morning, that way we can get it to press. I've already written the copy.'

'Oh good. So, I can see it?'

Am I imagining it, or did he hesitate?

'Yeah, that's fine. I'll show you the rough draft tomorrow. Nine too early?'

I blow out a breath. For a moment, I consider calling the whole thing off, but then I steel myself. Eyes on the prize, literally. We deserve somewhere decent to live. We've paid our dues. We need to get out of the hotel before it ruins holidaying in hotels for me forever, or the kids get sent to a secure unit for constantly creating mayhem. 'Nine will be fine.' I just need to get the kids up and presentable. No easy task. But if it gets us our 'dream home', it will be worth it.

'You ready?' Ronnie comes up behind me a second after I end the call.

'Sure.'

He looks at the kids, who are stumbling down the drive towards us, in various states of tiredness. 'I don't think this lot will last long tonight.'

'I think you're right.' I turn to Hugo. 'Right, birthday boy, you still got room for another slice of cake?'

'Mum. Go away, don't mention the C word ever again.'

Ha! I didn't think I'd ever hear Hugo tell me he was full up. He does look a little green, though. I wonder exactly how many hot dogs he ate, and slices of cake.

In the car, Aria regales us with a few of the hilarious anecdotes from the party which we missed, including when the volleyball sailed up into the air, launched by one of Hugo's ultra-competitive friends, into the neighbour's garden and got stuck in one of their apple trees. Two of the boys then scaled the wall, sneaked into the garden, shinned up the tree and retrieved the volleyball, without the old man, who was weeding, spotting them.

Hugo had told them he was a crotchety old man, like in the Peter Rabbit films, so they'd been terrified, when unbeknownst to them, Hugo was pulling their leg, and Mr Marsh was a sweetheart and would have happily allowed them into the garden to retrieve the ball.

In any case, the kids all enjoyed themselves, and that's what matters.

As Ronnie is shepherding the kids into the hotel, on our return, I roll down the window and beckon him over. 'I won't be long at Nicky's. Oh, one other thing, that reporter called. He does actually need a current family pic, post-accident, so I told him tomorrow around nine. See you later. Love you.' I blow him a kiss and reverse at top speed out of the car park. He's going to kill me, but right now, he doesn't have the chance. I'll pay for it later, of course, once I get back, as I'll have to listen to him rant and rave about my irresponsibility, short-sightedness, being taken advantage of. The latter grates the most. Clearly, I'm still some 'little woman' who doesn't know what she's doing.

I pull up at Nicky's, euphoric to have her back and on familiar territory, albeit she's at Valentin's, but it's not a hospital, and that can only be a good thing.

'Pleased to be home?' I hug Nicky to me. She feels as if she's made of skin and bone. Despite the three-course meals in hospital, she's lost a considerable amount of weight, weight she could ill-afford to lose.

Valentin is studying her with a rapturous expression on his face, which Nicky is oblivious to.

'So, did Xander enjoy the party?'

'Oh, he was full of it when Mum brought him back. You'd think I'd never been gone. It was all 'coconut cups' and 'volleyball', 'sand', and 'water party games'. I barely understood a word he said, he was talking so fast. I almost felt like escaping back to hospital for a rest.

I smile. 'But not quite.'

Her eyes meet Valentin's, and she smiles. 'No, not quite.'

'This is the life.' I point to how Valentin is waiting on her like some butler in a stately home.

'Ha! Don't you worry, Louisa. This is just her welcome home, to our home, for the first time. Tomorrow, I'll start cracking the whip!'

The three of us laugh, and it feels so good, so right, after all this time, to have some semblance of normality.

'How are you feeling?' I ask, taking in what's visible of her injuries.

'Like I've been hit by a bus.'

I roll my eyes. 'Well, it was a lorry, but no need to split hairs.'

Her smirk shows she appreciates my attempt at levity. She exhales noisily. 'I simply want to get back to normal –

whatever that is – as fast as I can.'

'I know. I'm meeting Sam for a coffee tomorrow.'

Nicky raises her eyebrows.

'Decaff, obviously.'

She grins, but there's a tightness to her expression that could be jealousy, although it may well have been a twinge of pain.

'How is she?' Nicky asks.

'Good. Well, I say good, I have no idea really. I've barely seen her, hence the catch-up tomorrow. Tell you what, if you feel up to it, will we drop round for half an hour once we're done? Don't want to overtire you. Your butler will give me grief.'

'No, no, no!' Valentin shakes a finger. 'Housekeeper.'

'So, how are you feeling?' She points to my stomach.

'Oh, you know, OK. Sick. Tired. The usual. To be honest, I've been so busy I can barely catch my breath. I'm off to Madrid on Tuesday.'

'Check you. My passport's not even up to date. It ran out when I was in hospital. Not that I'll be going anywhere anytime soon.' She looks down ruefully at her body.

'That's enough of that. Between me and the physio, we'll have you back to your old self in no time.' Valentin's clearly determined she should remain upbeat.

'Oh. I suppose it is a male physio.' She winks at me.

Valentin reddens and rubs a hand on the back of his neck. 'Right. Anyway, tea?'

'How was Nicky?' Ronnie asks when I return. He follows my glance. 'They're all in bed. Wiped out.'

'Ah, good. Nicky's putting a brave face on. I'm just so

glad she has Valentin.'

'Me too.' He turns his body towards me as I sit on the sofa. 'So, what do Nicky and Valentin think of your latest stunt?' Ronnie's eyes flash, and I recoil from the anger in them.

'Wh-a-a-t?'

'You heard me. What do they think about you going public about the accident?'

Shit. I was so focused on Nicky and her recovery and her settling into Valentin's and how much I hoped Xander had enjoyed the party, I completely forgot to mention it. Aargh!

I draw air into my lungs. Despite Mum taking over the majority of the work at Wedded Bliss and Jo and Wendy helping out with the kids as needed, and Mum and Dad too, I'm still trudging through treacle. I just can't seem to get going. My to-do lists are having babies of their own, and I'm scoring off what feels like precisely nothing, and whether it's related to the accident or baby brain, I can't remember stuff. Stuff I need to remember. My brain cells seem to be floating in the middle of a big bowl of jelly. Everything is foggy and fuzzy. I keep adding four and four and making nine.

'I forgot to tell them,' I admit.

'How convenient,' Ronnie snaps, and it feels like he has sucker-punched me. I understand he's none too impressed about the family photo tomorrow morning, but that's no excuse for being downright nasty.

'Actually, it's not. I'll simply tell her tomorrow,' I say breezily as if it's of no consequence. It bloody is, but I'm not letting Ronnie realise that. He's obviously been fizzing about this whilst I've been gone. Let him stew. It will only do him good.

Shortly afterwards, as I'm heading for bed, Ronnie says, 'By the way, this farce of a family photo shoot tomorrow?'

When I don't deign that with a response, he goes on. 'You're on your own. I'm not doing it, and I won't allow the kids to be part of it.'

I draw myself up to my full five feet five. 'Excuse me? You won't *allow* it? Last time I checked they had two parents, and this one wants to get them the house they want, and this is the only way I could see to do that. So, unless you're going to be helpful, perhaps it's better you're not there.'

Colour rises in Ronnie's face. I don't think I've ever seen him so angry. 'And you think you're making the better choice here? You think it's OK for you to decide this about our family, our children, without consulting me?' Flecks of spittle land on my top.

I look down at them. 'Hmm, attractive, Ronnie. Try not to spit when you speak.'

He rises then and for a second, I think he's going to hit me, and I take a step back instinctively. But I should have known better – Ronnie would never hit me or any other woman, but to say he's incandescent would be putting it mildly. He opens the suite door and lets it bang shut behind him.

That went well.

Chapter Seventeen

Thursday 5 August

To-do list

Buy summer slippers

Message everyone to let them know about the newspaper article

Contact Benedict and tell him we're still working on a solution, but hope to be able to take the house.

Ask Sam if she fancies starting an aquanatal class

I toss and turn most of the night, and it's not even baby-related. I hate arguing with Ronnie, and even worse, I hate going to bed on an unresolved argument. It's impossible to sleep well in those situations. I reach out with one hand to caress Ronnie's back, his arm, anything, just to show I'm sorry about our fight, but his side of the bed is empty. Empty? Ronnie never gets up early. Or perhaps he didn't come to bed at all. That's more like it – he'll have holed up in the living room, some action movie on with the volume down low, or he'll have headphones in.

I stretch and shove my feet into my fluffy sheep slippers, then pad through to the living area. He's not there either. Oh well, a bit of peace and quiet for me then. Maybe I'll try to read a book for a bit before everyone gets up, although I'll have to watch the time as the reporter's due at nine, and I want us all to look semi-presentable. Presentable would be asking too much.

I pop the kettle on, then go back through and pick up my phone. Holy crap. It's half eight. How is that possible, and where is Ronnie? Screw the tea, I'll have to jump in the shower, or at the least do something with this bird's nest that passes for my hair. Frantically, I cast around in the bedroom for some clean clothes, something that says 'poor woman who has had her life and home torn from her in tragic accident' without me looking too scummy. I do have to hold my head up at school in a few weeks. As do the kids. They probably care more.

The lack of activity from the other rooms has me frowning. Usually, Aria or Hugo, or both, are out of their rooms like greyhounds out of their traps the minute they hear even a sniffle from me, or a throat clearing or God forbid the turning of a page of a book.

Still frowning, I approach their doors. We really did tire them out yesterday at the party. Maybe we should have one monthly.

But when I open the doors, silence greets me, as does the lack of bodies in their beds or rooms. What the…?

My phone pings. Dazed, I head back into the living room where I've left it.

> **Ronnie:** *Like I said, you're not making our kids part of this circus you've arranged. By all means have your photo taken, make a fool of yourself, but we're away out for the day. R*

No kiss. Christ. The one time the man takes initiative and it's to scupper my plans. Thanks a bloody bunch,

Ronnie. Now it's my turn to seethe. I'm doing this for us, for all of us. Can't he see that?

'Morning, Mrs Halliday. So, I'd like a few shots of you and the family here, next to the sign for Garfield Grange. And another in the lobby near the baristas, and we'll lift a shot of your own house and drop it in beside the rest.'

'Actually–' I wave a hand at him as he has already bent to sort his camera out '–it's just me. The children and my husband aren't here.'

He straightens up. 'Sorry?' He's not very good at hiding how hacked-off he is. 'We agreed–'

'We may have agreed, however, my husband didn't, and wasn't very happy about the children being in the newspaper, so he and they won't be taking part in the interview, or photo.'

'Well, I don't know what my boss will say about this?' He shakes his head, clearly disgruntled.

I'm at the end of my patience with the whole situation. 'He shouldn't have a problem, as, if you recall, when we first talked about running a story, there wasn't to be any family photo.'

He huffs out a breath and takes the camera from its shoulder holster. 'I'll see what I can do. But no promises.'

God, you'd think he was doing me a favour and had nothing to gain from this. I bet if he wasn't here, he'd be at some eccentric's house discussing pet psychics and how they'd managed to communicate with their dead cat, or perhaps conversing with a ninety-five-year-old who'd won the bingo for the first time, despite playing it for the past sixty years.

He takes the shot, where I try to look dutifully woebegone, but by this time, I'm more than a little narked, at, well, everyone. I just want us to be able to afford the house, so we can move in. Is that too much to ask? I'm not sure if it's the hormones changing my mood, or the run of bad luck we've had that has me finally reaching the end of my tether, but I'm practically ushering the reporter out of the hotel so I can get ready to see Sam for our coffee date.

I dare say some of my hostility stems from Ronnie 'abducting' our kids this morning so they couldn't participate in the photo. They might quite like to have taken part in a photo shoot. OK, I get it's not exactly a London studio, having their hair and make-up done, whilst being fed an array of dainty sandwiches and cakes, but most kids surely would be happy to be in the newspaper, whatever the reason. Unless, of course, it was a parent going to jail, or being revealed as a serial killer.

Ah, I'd forgotten pregnancy waffling. I'm back in the suite, finally having managed to rid myself of the reporter when I realise I didn't ask to see the copy. Grrr. I hate pregnancy brain. I talk to my bump. 'I hope you know all the hassle you're causing me. You're eating my brain cells. But Mummy still loves you,' I hastily add.

I'm sure the copy will be fine. It won't matter, but one thing's for sure, I'll show Ronnie. I'll show him, and the insurance company, not to mess with this 'little woman'.

'You look amazing.' I kiss Sam on the cheek then slide in opposite her. And she does. Pregnancy clearly agrees with her.

'You must have caught me on a good day. I can't stop

feeling sick.'

'Oh?' I scrunch my eyebrows. 'You having much morning sickness?'

'Constantly.' She sighs. 'I managed to get an emergency appointment for the doctor yesterday, and he says I have hyperemesis gravidarum.'

'Oh no, really? Isn't that what the Duchess of Cambridge had?'

'The very same, and I can tell you, it's no fun.' The corners of her mouth turn down, and my heart goes out to her. You want to enjoy being pregnant, plus she still has the girls to look after. Constant nausea and parenting do not make good bedfellows.

'Poor you. Are you able to keep any food down?'

One side of her mouth lifts, slightly. 'A bit. Not a great deal, though.'

'And you wanted to come out for drinks?' I raise an eyebrow.

'Well, I still need to eat, and increase my food and drink uptake, since half of it either comes up, or wants to.'

'Lovely.' I grimace.

'Well, you did ask!'

'Oh, I know. So, what do you think you can eat that will stay down? Muffin? Bagel?'

'Maybe a lightly toasted bagel.'

Once we've ordered, we get right down to the business of catching up, although it feels weird for us to meet without Nicky, albeit we're heading there afterwards. Oh no, not again.

'Sam, I'm really sorry.' I throw my hands up in the air. 'I meant to message you and ask if you wanted to come see Nicky with me after here. Are you busy or can you manage?'

'I'm meant to be meeting Eric and the girls, but I can ask him to push it back an hour or so.'

'Sorry. I don't remember being this absent-minded last time I was pregnant.'

'Ha, sometimes it just hits you in different ways. Plus, I didn't have severe morning sickness with Ava or Emily. This is new, thank God. Otherwise, I might not have got pregnant again.'

'Really?' My mouth falls open. 'It's that bad?'

'Yes, it is, and I probably would still have gone ahead with it, had I known, but I won't be having a fourth, let's put it that way.'

I grin. 'Yeah, three's the lucky number. Look at me. No, don't. I've just remembered I'm having a fourth. Oh my goodness, this is ridiculous. I feel like I've had a lobotomy.'

'Yeah, I know that feeling.'

I message Nicky. *We'll see you in about an hour.*

We head for Valentin's in separate cars as Sam will have to leave earlier to meet Eric and the kids. I check my messages for a few minutes as I clearly drive faster than Sam and have arrived first.

Ronnie has sent through a couple of photos of the kids at the park in Hamwell. They love it there, although they don't go there so often since we have a lovely park in Ferniehall. It's good for them to have a change. Usually, we spend so much of the summer holidays either away, or visiting tourist attractions within a fifty-mile radius, that we forget some of the simpler, and most enjoyable, things are on our doorstep. However, I think ruefully, we don't have our own doorstep at the minute.

Looks like they're having fun anyway. Gen is swinging on the asymmetric bars, Hugo is zooming along the zip line and Aria is hanging onto a climbing wall as if she's clinging to the Jungfrau.

I'm smiling at the images when Sam taps on the window and I jump.

'Oh, you're here. Let's go.'

Valentin answers the door. 'Sam, lovely to see you.' He bends to kiss her on both cheeks. 'Louisa.' He ushers us through. I frown. What? No kiss? I know he's my mate's boyfriend, but he kissed Sam, and his aftershave is divine, and I have absolutely no interest in him romantically, but I do love how good he smells.

Nicky is reclining on the sofa. Her eyes light up when Sam bends down for a hug and a kiss.

'I brought you these.' Sam places a bouquet of roses, sunflowers, and three other different types of flowers I don't know the names of, but which look ferny, foxglove-like (but without the digitalis hopefully) and pretty on the coffee table in front of Nicky.

'Aw, they're beautiful. So colourful. Thanks, Sam. She beams at her. So, what have you been up to?'

I glance up and see Valentin watching me, thoughtfully.

'I'll put these in some water whilst you guys catch up,' I say. 'Valentin, do you have a vase?'

'Of course.' His clipped tone startles me, and puzzlement creeps over me. What was all that about? Then I dismiss it. He probably has a lot on with work, given he has a multi-million-pound restaurant business to run, and now he has Nicky, and Xander, to take care of, too. I'd offer to help, but I have enough to sort out with our house, or rather lack of one.

I chatter away to him, but his monosyllabic replies only serve to perturb me further, and I return to the girls to see what they're nattering about. I can't help being upset at Valentin's behaviour towards me, it's so uncharacteristic. He's always been so welcoming to me, including when I was here less than twenty-four hours ago.

Nicky stops speaking when I enter the room, and I swear she glowers at me. Glowers. I mean, who glowers? Apart from bare-chested moody men on the covers of romance novels. I've no idea what's in the water in this penthouse today, but I won't be drinking any of it. It's like my friends have transformed into demons overnight.

With that in mind, when Valentin offers us drinks, I politely refuse, although not because I think anything is actually in the water. God, I'm being so literal here. What is going on in my brain? What is going on with my friends?

We muddle through the next forty-five minutes, with Sam leading most of the conversation, which is weird, as Sam is usually the quieter of the three. Nicky has barely glanced in my direction, even though I'm sitting just off to her right.

Valentin shows Sam out then says, 'I have some work to do. I'll leave you to it,' and disappears into his study. At least, I think it's a study. This place is huge.

I turn to Nicky. 'So–'

She glares at me. 'So, do you want to tell me why a reporter called me this morning, telling me you're running a story about the accident?'

Oh shit.

Chapter Eighteen

Friday 6 August

To-do list
Nothing. I can't face it today. Or possibly ever again.

I lie in bed and pull the covers over me, trying to block everything out. I've never seen Nicky so furious before. She was almost unhinged. When I tried to explain that I was doing the story to secure us the house behind the park, she screamed at me, asking if I didn't think she might want to forget all about the bloody accident and get on with her life, not be constantly reminded of it, never mind dragged through the tabloids, or have reporters call her. 'And what about Xander?' she'd asked.

I didn't know where to look. Honestly, I wasn't trying to be selfish. I guess this is what Ronnie feared might happen. I wish he'd been less subtle. If I'd known Nicky would react in such a way, I probably wouldn't have agreed to do the story, never mind do it and forget to tell her.

The sun is shining through the thick velour curtains, testament to exactly how bright the day is, but my mood doesn't reflect that at all.

Ronnie is up and out of bed again. I didn't sleep well, fits and starts. It's becoming a bit of a pattern now. There's no sound coming from the other parts of the suite, but there's nothing for it, I'm going to have to face it all. I wrench myself out of bed and sit on the side, then grapple for my phone which I threw into a corner of the duvet last night, after I'd sent Nicky a conciliatory message for the nth time. She won't speak to me. I thought she'd get it, but she doesn't. I wonder if she would if she were in my position. Sure, I can see why she's annoyed, but she really flipped out. I know she's suffered, and how, but it's not as if my family have come out of this whole scenario unscathed, is it? In so many ways...

I turn my phone on and type in the address for the newspaper. I scroll down and quickly find the article. It's on page three, so not quite front-page news, but not far off. Good, hopefully the article will give the insurers the kick up the backside they need to do the decent thing.

As I start to read, my elation turns to horror.

Crash victim mum locks horns with insurers

Mum-of-three Louisa Halliday, 39, gained our sympathy last month when a lorry crashed through her living room, destroying a good part of her home and seriously injuring two of her friends, Nicky and Xander Tonner.

Local businessman, Fabien Price, with whom Mrs Halliday has recently started a business relationship was philanthropic enough to instal Mrs Halliday and her family in the 5-star Garfield Grange. Many would thank their lucky stars for living for an unspecified period of time in a luxury hotel – myself included – however, Mrs Halliday told us how eating out every night and having laundry service isn't all it's cracked up to be. 'Sometimes the kids just want to be able to have beans and toast at nine o'clock, and they can't run around the garden like they used to. Plus, they have to try to be quiet all the time out of respect for the other guests. And if they don't have a room each again soon, they're liable to kill each other, or me them.'

Oh my God, how could he take my comments out of context? That was an off-the-record joke, not intended for the article.

Mrs Halliday met with me yesterday, minus her family. Has the crash and its aftermath caused friction in her marriage? Mr Halliday, an oil worker, was notable by his absence.

Oh, no!

Mrs Halliday has crossed swords with her insurers, who are refusing to pay the rent she has requested, which, according to Mrs Halliday's financial sources is well below the amount stipulated on her policy. 'They're trying any old excuse to duck out of what's rightfully ours. What do we pay insurance for if not to be covered in our hour of need? And believe me, we're in our hour of need now. We've been very lucky that Cerulean Hotels has put us up, but that's out of the kindness of their heart, and now the insurance company won't pay for somewhere decent to live for my family, and it could be many months before we can return to our home, if ever. We still haven't had clarification if our home will be habitable again, and that's over a month already. This is what we pay insurance for. All I want is for my children and my family to have as normal a life as possible following an extremely traumatic period for us all.'

A spokesman for Prendergast Insurance said they couldn't comment on individual cases, but would be in touch with Mrs Halliday shortly to further discuss her claim.

Well, that second part of the article didn't paint me or us in too bad a light, but what the hell is the reporter playing at? Ronnie is going to go apeshit. And I don't blame him.

When I finally creak open the door to the living area, the three kids are lounging on the sofa with Ronnie watching Disney+.

Interestingly, Ronnie doesn't look rattled: no tense jaw, no glower, no clenching of fists. Clearly, he hasn't seen the article yet. He's probably forgotten it'll go online too. No doubt he's thinking we'll pick up a copy from the newsagent's when we go out. I'll have to show him the article, but first, a cuppa, for courage.

'Morning,' I say breezily as I wrap my silk robe around me.

'Hi.' Ronnie gives a rueful smile.

Well, that's progress from being so angry he's spitting, so perhaps there's hope of reconciliation today. I weight my phone in my hand, absent-mindedly, then recall the contents of the article. Maybe not.

'How are you guys?' I ask the trio in their PJs, curled up like commas around their dad and each other. It's such a touching family tableau, it makes me want to weep, especially today.

'Good. Mummy, do you remember this bit?' Aria asks me, as she grabs my hand, trying to tug me down beside her.

I peer at the screen. Thank goodness it's large as I'm really having to focus. Oh well, I am nearly forty.

'I don't think so, honey.'

'Oh, Mummy.' Aria rolls her eyes in exasperation. 'You do. It's the bit where they overtake the bad guy, Ercole, and then they do all sorts of dangerous things on their bikes, but have lots of fun.'

That's specific. I look again. Ah, it's *Luca*. I should have guessed.

'Yes, yes, you're right, darling.'

Aria eyes me mutinously. 'Mummy, I don't think you mean that. I think you're telling lies.'

'Aria!' I'm shocked she's found me out and uttered it out loud. Good grief, now I'm being berated by a four-year-old.

'Tea?' I ask Ronnie.

He points to the discarded cup on the table. 'I'm fine, thanks.'

Feeling suitably superfluous, I try to marshal my thoughts as I pop the Teapigs teabag in the cup. I've gone for something a bit stronger, hoping it will give me the energy to get through the day.

I need to check with Mum about the problem she had with the Finches' wedding invitation quantities; the printer has sent 50 evening invitations and 150 day invitations, but it's supposed to be the other way around. And I have to contact Fabien about my upcoming trip to Madrid. We haven't had a chance to go through my presentation, which is just as well as I've barely had time to add to the slides, but I can't think about that right now.

With everything that's happened, I haven't had a chance to let my family know what's happening. Jo. Wendy. Mum and Dad. I didn't even tell Sam yesterday, as I was so focused on discussing Nicky and our pregnancies. What a mess! I thought I was fixing a problem, but I seem to have made things a thousand times worse.

The irony is, there's no guarantee the insurers will back down, and quite frankly after that article, if I worked in the claims department, I probably wouldn't change my mind.

I sit down with my tea, and Ronnie, uncharacteristically of late, moves closer to me, freeing himself of a child. Hopefully, it's a sign he wants to mend our rift and not simply that he fancied getting shot of one of our children, or relieving himself of a dead arm.

My phone pings. I haven't even taken my first sip. Then again. Sam. Mum. Wendy.

Are you OK? Sam.

Why are you in the paper today? And why are they saying all these things about you and Ronnie? Mum. Her confusion and anguish are nuanced but present. She probably can't believe what she's reading.

Never trust reporters. Wendy. *Call me.*

I'm about to do just that when another message pings in. Jo. *Wtaf?*

Dread pools in my gut, and the nausea I'm experiencing isn't down to morning sickness. I can't look at Ronnie, although I feel his penetrating stare on my neck.

Has he read it? He was so angry before, yet now he's as cool as half a cucumber from the chilled section at Tesco.

Damn the reporter. Damn the newspaper. Damn the

bloody insurance company. If they'd only been reasonable in the first place, none of this would have happened. It's just as well school hasn't started back. I don't imagine Gen would thank me for portraying her and her siblings as spoiled brats. That's not how I meant it, I was referring to their well-being and to helping them get over the crash, but that's not how it looks in print.

I massage my forehead with one hand. A headache is brewing right below the surface. Can't I catch a break? All I want is a home for my family until ours is repaired. Is that really too much to ask? I don't want to be lambasted in the newspaper, jeered at for coming across as some posh princess who's too good for even a luxury hotel, but that's exactly the picture the reporter has painted. Wait until I get a hold of him.

'Ronnie, I need to make some calls in private.' I gesture to our bedroom.

He nods, but says nothing. I still have no idea if he has seen the article. Why don't I just ask him? Is it because he's with the kids, or am I too much of a coward to admit I might have got this wrong? That perhaps my decision to ask the press for help with this particular facet of our lives wasn't the best of my life?

The first person I call is Wendy.

'What the hell, sis?'

But she doesn't get the chance to say anything further. The pressure in my head, the futility, the unfairness of it, the rage at the reporter 'handling' me are too overwhelming, and I burst into noisy, snot-inducing sobs.

Once I've calmed enough and I'm past the hiccup-sobs, out pours the whole sorry tale.

'Oh, Lou, why didn't you tell me? Why didn't you

come to me for advice?'

'Because I thought I could deal with it on my own, and you've got your new job to keep you busy, and four kids, and I just seized the moment as I was so angry with the insurance company for being so jobsworth, and well, in the wrong.' I sniff then blow my nose into a tissue. I sound like a bloody circus elephant trumpeting its disapproval.

'But you can always come to me, you know that, and Jo, and Mum and Dad. You don't need to do things alone. That's what families are for.'

Not my family. Ronnie's comments about neither him nor the kids participating in the interview spring to mind, and I thank the Lord they weren't present for it.

'I know. I feel so bloody useless. I thought I was doing a good thing, and now it's a nightmare. Oh, and I forgot to tell you, Nicky's furious with me, as the reporter called her yesterday. She doesn't, obviously, want the accident dredging up, but how was I to know he would call her?'

'You don't always take time to stop and think, Lou. It's your greatest failing.' I go to interrupt, but she stops me. 'Listen, I'm not getting at you, I'm just saying. We love you as you are, but sometimes a bit of reflection would help you, before you go in all guns blazing.'

She's right. I know she is. And that's exactly what I did do – go in, all guns blazing. But I was furious, and it was as if the world was doing its business on me from a great height.

I sniff again. 'I don't know how to fix it. I need to talk to Mum, Sam, Jo, I haven't even spoken to Ronnie, and Nicky, again, if she'll take my call.'

'Baby steps. I'll talk to the family, tell them what you told me. So don't worry about that.'

I exhale a huge sigh. She has no idea of the weight she has lifted from me. Having to repeat the pathetic story over and over may have undone me completely. 'Thanks, Wen.'

'Any time.' I can hear the grin in her voice. 'But don't make a habit of it.'

Now I'm half smiling.

'What do you think I should do about the reporter?'

'Honestly, nothing. It's done. You could ask for a retraction, but the story's already out there. You could threaten to talk to his boss about it, but it's probably his boss who has put him under pressure to give the story a more "interesting" slant.'

'Hmm,' I mutter, sighing again.

'I'd concentrate on building that bridge with Nicky, let Sam know, and talk things through with Ronnie.'

'OK,' I squeak, my voice still not having returned to normal post-cry.

'And sis, most importantly, try to calm down and let it go. This will not do you or the baby any good.'

She's right there.

'I love you, Wen.'

'I love you, too. Now, go and talk to Ronnie.'

We take the kids to the park in Ambleworth. It's different to those in Hamwell and Ferniehall, in that it's more a trim trail for the kids, a skate park, a mini-golf and lots of neatly manicured lawns with floral arrangements bursting with summer blooms and carved wooden benches placed at strategic points to allow those less mobile, pregnant mums, nursing mums and the elderly to rest. Having eyed up the current patrons, I decide that no one falls into those categories, so I flump down on a bench to watch the kids. Ronnie joins me.

'I'm sorry we fought.' He leans forward, his legs wide, his hands clasped together in a praying pose.

I'm so startled that he has apologised first that initially I don't know what to say. 'Me too.' Lame, but it's all I can come up with.

'I'm also sorry the reporter took advantage.'

My hackles start to raise. We're not going to revisit the 'little woman' talk again, are we? OK, he may have a point, but that's not the, well, point.

'Yeah, he did. I'm sorry. I didn't say some of that stuff. He twisted my words.'

'Unfortunately, that's all too common.' Ronnie winces.

'Are we going to be OK?' I ask, needing the reassurance.

He looks at me long and hard before answering. 'I hope so, Lou. We have a lot to deal with at the moment.'

I'm not sure he understood my question properly. I meant him and me, not the family, but he seems to have interpreted it as encompassing all of us.

'Has anyone…you know, contacted you?'

After a pause, he says, 'Like who? My folks? Rhys? My boss? My colleagues?'

I nod. 'All of those.'

'Some have, but fortunately I don't think Mum and Dad read the gutter press.'

'No, I can't see that somehow.' Thank God. They'd be horrified at us ostensibly airing our dirty laundry, even though it was the reporter who sullied my words.

Ronnie sits back and watches the kids, and I follow his example. Chat over. Would that the rest were so straightforward.

I take in the scene in front of me – the kids, playing happily in a park, their parents with them. This is what's important. Not stuff. All we need is each other. Sometimes it's hard to remember that, though, particularly when times are hard, or things between Ronnie and me are difficult.

I sit and try to be in the now. Live in the moment, isn't that what they say, whoever 'they' are. I calm my mind by recalling the meditation exercises I used to do when first pregnant with Hugo.

Sometime later, I open my eyes. Ronnie is still staring at the kids, but hasn't uttered a word. The chatter of children, the twitter of birdsong, the thud of a football, the whoosh of a skateboard going back and forth, the putter putter of a sprinkler rotating over the grass, each of these things come more sharply into focus. I feel as if I'm seeing, really seeing, and hearing, and feeling and smelling for the first time in a very long time. As if I've come out of hibernation after a long winter. The scent of the sweet nectar coming from the flowers nearby assaults my senses, and I breathe it in. Someone's barbecuing nearby. I turn my head and see that the park backs onto a residential area. A jogger stops beside us to catch his breath, and as he moves off, I note the pungent odour of his sweat.

All these things are real. All these things matter. What is divulged, erroneously, in a newspaper isn't what matters, but how you deal with it is.

'Valentin, I'm not leaving until I've seen her. You, or she, can throw me out after, but I've come to say my piece, and make peace.'

He meets my gaze then says, 'You'd better come in.'

When Nicky spots me, she scowls. 'Seriously? Are you back to do more damage?' Turning to Valentin, she says, 'Why did you even let her in?'

Valentin shrugs. 'She comes in peace.'

I give a half smile at that, and say, 'Nicky. I'm sorry. I got it wrong. I feel I may be apologising a lot over the next few days, but I'm most sorry about how I didn't consider how this would affect you, your mental health, and you just out of hospital.'

Her lips form a thin line.

'Nicky, I'll beg if I have to. I am so, so, so times a thousand sorry. Tell me what I have to do. I hate that I've let you down. I wasn't trying to. You're the last person I'd want to hurt.'

Nothing.

Desperately, I say, 'I was protecting my cubs!'

She frowns.

'You know, like in the wildlife programmes. I'd do anything for the kids. All I want is to offer them a stable, loving home, and an actual physical home to live in. One that isn't riddled with damp, doesn't have rat-chewed electrical cables and doesn't pong of cannabis.'

At the latter, she raises an eyebrow.

'And that was the good ones,' I say, my lips curving upwards slightly.

Nicky mirrors my smile. 'Lou, you've got to think before you act.'

Whilst this line is reminiscent of what Mum used to say when I was growing up, somehow, I don't take umbrage at this comment, possibly because it's become apparent it's painfully true.

'I know. I'm so sorry, really I am.' Belatedly, I realise Xander isn't around.

'And you've got to thank Wendy.'

'Wendy? Why?'

'Because she called and pleaded your case. If it hadn't been for her, Valentin wouldn't even have answered the door.'

'What did she say?' I ask, interested and impressed at my sister's ingenuity.

'Much as you've just done, although she did say you were a tit for doing it.'

I give a measured nod. 'Sounds like something Wendy would say.'

'And I'm not letting you off scot-free. There will be penance to pay.'

'I'd expect nothing less,' I say solemnly.

'Good, get a pen and paper. I have a list of demands.' She's not kidding. She turns to Valentin. 'Can we have some tea, please, hon?'

'Of course, darling. He kisses her cheek and as he passes me, he pats my shoulder and says, 'Good to have you out of the doghouse.'

I grin. I kick off my shoes and fold my legs underneath myself as I sit on the huge armchair. That's better.

Chapter Nineteen

Saturday 7 August

To-do list

Return uniform items I previously bought that have no chance of fitting anyone. Was I buying for toddlers?

Individual sun cream for carrying in school bags – roll-on so Aria can do it herself

Put money for milk on Aria's Parentpay account

Pick up Hugo's gaming magazine from supermarket

How did it go with Nicky? Wendy.

> **Me:** *We're good, thankfully.*

> **Wendy:** *I'm glad. Have you heard anything from, well, anyone?*

> **Me:** *Nope. I'm going to start looking for somewhere else to live once I get back from Madrid. And once this is all over, we're changing insurance company.*

> **Wendy:** *Good plan. Kids excited about going back to school?*

> **Me:** *I wouldn't say Gen's excited, but Hugo can't wait to see his friends, and Aria would go now if you let her. Have you got all the uniforms? I've managed to order a few bits and pieces online and have them sent to*

Mum's. It was getting too confusing trying to explain we were living in a hotel. Think they thought we were scammers.

Wendy: *Ha, I can imagine. Mollie's bursting at the seams to go back, Logan too, I suppose.*

To be honest, I'm bursting at the seams for them to start. Feel as if we haven't had a holiday, well, we haven't, but you know what I mean.

Me: *I do. Don't worry, we'll go in October instead.*

Wendy: *That would be great. Can't wait to see your scan photo.*

Me: *Me neither. Love you x*

Wendy: *Love you too x*

I'm finishing up my presentation as best I can when my phone rings. Nicky.

'Hi, Nic. Everything OK?'

'Yeah, I'm just bored. I can relate to you finding too much beauty in an apartment stultifying.'

'Stultifying? Good word choice. But I didn't say I found it stultifying, only that it was easier for the kids when they had a room each, a playroom and a garden. Quite frankly, if I didn't have kids, I'd be living it up, well, living here. What's not to like?'

'I hear you, but I need more stimulation.'

'There's a joke in there, but I won't go there.' I smirk.

'No, please don't lower yourself to cheap puns.'

'I think I've already sunk as low as I can go this week.'

'Oh well, look on the bright side.'

I wait for Nicky to elaborate but she doesn't. 'Which is?'

'The only way is up.'

I groan. 'Nicky, coin a cliché, why don't you? Tell you what, if you're so bored, FaceTime me back and you can help me with my presentation.

Nicky visibly straightens. 'Ooh, something useful. Hurrah.'

'No offence, but that's sad.'

'I know. Right, I'm going so I can phone back.'

'Missing you already.'

As we draw into the swimming pool car park later, I'm thankful for the fact their swimming lessons weren't off during the school holidays. In all the uncertainty around them, this weekly event has provided some structure. Gen is too old for lessons as she's good enough to swim for the school team, but she opted to concentrate on gymnastics as a sport, so she swims solely for pleasure. She'll also watch the little ones for me whilst I do a breadth, if we're only in for a play, but I'm still too reticent to leave her alone with her brother and sister for too long, despite their wearing water wings.

But today Daddy is also present, so Gen does some lengths, Ronnie and I take it in turns to do some actual swimming whilst the kids are in lessons, and when they're done, we have a play with the inflatable toys scattered around the edge of the pool. We play water basketball, then throw the hoop on each other's head and our own brand of water polo with the adults being the horses, and it's the best fun we've had together as a family in ages.

We're in the changing rooms, drying Hugo and Aria, when Ronnie's mobile goes. He lets it go to voicemail. Then mine rings, at which point I panic. Dad's had a heart attack, Mum's fallen down the stairs, the remainder of our house has collapsed. I rifle in my bag for my phone. 'Hello?' I say breathlessly. I probably sound as if I've been disturbed getting down to business as opposed to drying my children post-swimming.

'Is that Mrs Halliday?'

'Yes.' I dry the inside of my ear with a towel so I can hear better, shushing Hugo, who is about to interrupt, with a glare that would freeze oceans.

'This is Edith from Prendergast Insurance claims department.'

That gets my attention. 'Yes?'

'I've been instructed, following a further review of your claim to offer you the original monthly sum requested to cover the rent of the property you were hoping to move into, until such time as your own home is habitable again, or a decision is made about whether you need to be rehoused permanently.'

Tears fill my eyes. It was worth it. It was all worth it. All the angst, the tears, even the snot. Even the falling-out with Nicky, temporarily, and the initial big freeze from Ronnie.

'Thank you so much. Can you send me that in writing, please? By email, if possible, so I can act upon it today.'

'The email will go out as soon as I hang up the phone.'

'Thank you again.' It's hard not to gush. I'm in a real gushy mood now.

'Who was that?' Ronnie jerks his chin at the phone.

'That, beloved husband, was the insurance company. They're giving us the money!'

Ronnie's jaw drops. 'You're joking!'

'No. I'm not.' I do a victory dance, which is rather difficult in a swimming pool changing cubicle, even a family one. I stop when Hugo yelps as I've trodden on his foot.

Next door, Gen, who needs her privacy, says, 'Did I hear right? Are the insurance company giving us the money for that house behind the park?'

'Yes, Dumbo ears. You heard right,' I say, happier than I could possibly explain.

'Woo hoo!' says Hugo, and Aria picks up on his enthusiasm, and the two of them try to run round the changing cubicle, which curtails our movements considerably.

'Right, c'mere you,' I say to Aria, grabbing her and tickling her under the arms. She's nearly dry, so she squirms and giggles. 'Let's finish getting ready so we can go celebrate. Who's up for Ricci's for ice cream?'

A chorus of 'Me' goes up, led by Ronnie, surprisingly. Our eyes meet, and I can't help but think, and pray, that perhaps everything will be all right.

'Yes, Benedict, that's right. Yes, I was in the paper. Yes, it was to do with renting the house. And yes, finally, for once the little guy has prevailed and we've beaten the nasty, money-grabbing insurance company.'

'Well done. I'm so glad it's you and your family who are moving in. I really feel you're right for the house, and I think the kids thought so too.'

'Oh, they did. They're champing at the bit. They want to move today.'

'Well, I can't manage today, but we could have it ready

for you to move in within a few days.'

'Perfect, I can't thank you enough. Do you have a contract or anything to email over?'

'Give me your email, and I'll send it across now.'

I float to the car, a huge smile on my face. Ronnie drives, allowing me to luxuriate in the concept of us living in that house. I can't believe we're really going to move into it. If I'm honest, it's even nicer than our own, and I love our house.

We drive along the main street past Jumping Beans – I've not been there for ages. We've been favouring the new Café on the Cobblestones of late. We pass Blooming Marvellous, which has a riot of summer flowers hanging from baskets outside and in buckets on the pavement. I must pick up some flowers for Wendy for starting her new job, and Mum for keeping Bear and Patch for so long. Oh, how wonderful it'll be to be reunited with them after so long. I can't wait to have them sit at my feet whilst I'm drinking my coffee each morning, browsing my emails. Never again will I moan at having to take them out to do their business in torrential rain. I'll just be glad to have their wee warm bodies beside me on the sofa, saving on my heating bill.

'Mummy, can we go to the library after ice cream?' Aria asks as we tumble out of the car, after parking outside Ricci's. We were lucky someone drove away when we approached, as the village is unusually busy today.

'Sure. You can do anything you want.'

'Yay, we're having a yes day,' shouts Hugo.

'A what?' I ask, frowning at him.

'A yes day. Where the mums and dads have to allow the kids to do anything, as long as it doesn't involve killing anyone, going further than fifty miles away or is any more expensive than thirty pounds per activity.'

'You seem reliably well informed,' I say.

'M-u-u-m, how is it possible you don't know what a yes day is? Didn't you have them back when you were a kid?'

Ronnie and I exchange a bemused glance.

'No, there were no yes days, back then, only go out and find something to do days,' says Ronnie, smiling.

'So, can we have a yes day, Daddy?' Aria asks, eyes pleading, bottom lip jutting out.

'I think we already got our yes day, guys, by getting this amazing house that we're going to move into,' I remind them.

'True.' Hugo shakes his head. 'Anyway, are we going for ice cream or what?'

'Hugo.' My warning tone comes out. 'No cheek, please.'

'So-rry,' he replies in his best not-sorry-at-all voice.

'Can we have a yes day another day, Mummy?' Aria pleads, tugging at my T-shirt.

Exasperated and unable to form words right now, I say, 'We'll see.'

'M-u-um. Everyone knows "we'll see" means no,' Hugo complains.

'Not necessarily, but right now we have quite a lot of other things going on. Why don't you wait until after you're back at school, then perhaps we can discuss it for a weekend day? What do you think, Dad?'

'Hmm?' Ronnie, in a wee world of his own, has missed all this.

'Yes day,' I practically growl at him. 'In the future. A

possibility. But not now. Busy.'

'Oh, yeah, right. Sure.'

Sometimes it's best to break it all down into almost caveman or cavewoman-like words and ways of expressing myself. He pays more attention then. Takes more in.

'I'm starving.' Hugo.

'Right, right, we're just coming.'

Aldo has won me over, insisting I try his new ice cream flavour. 'Just out this week, Louisa.' Lavender. I was dubious, at first, but it's lovely. Creamy, sweet, a teensy taste of soap, but mainly floral, kinda like Parma Violets. Ronnie has opted for extra hazelnut, and Gen has been brave and chosen something unusual too – butter pecan. Her siblings stick to tried and tested favourites, too afraid to choose something else in case they don't like it.

Once we all have our cones and tubs of ice cream from Ricci's, we walk along Main Street savouring them as we head towards the florist's.

'I need to nip in and buy some flowers, Ronnie. Can you take Aria to the library?'

'Yay!' Aria says.

'Hugo, you coming?' Ronnie asks.

Hugo hurries after them. He really misses his dad when he's away on the rig. He's like his shadow when he's home.

I also want to book them in for their haircuts at A Cut Above next door but one to the library. I've been meaning to for weeks. I can do that whilst Ronnie has the younger ones. Gen has decided she fancies looking at the flowers. I thought she'd have jumped at the chance to go to the library, but I'm delighted to have her company, and to be able to ask her opinion.

'So, what are we getting, Mum?' she asks, raising her glance from where she has been tapping out a message on her phone.

'A bouquet for Aunt Wendy to wish her well in her new job and say well done. And a thank you to Nana for watching the dogs for us, and looking after my business for me.'

'Yeah, everything kind of happened at once, didn't it? In some ways, it would have been better if it hadn't happened immediately before the school holidays started.' Gen shows wisdom beyond her years, and I feel a twinge of pride.

'Hi, Louisa, Genevieve, how are you both?'

Susan, the florist, comes out to the front shop just then, clearly having been preparing bouquets in the back as she's still carrying ribbon and a pair of scissors.

'We're great, thanks. Had some much-needed good news, actually.'

'Oh?' she asks.

'Well, you may as well know, we're going to be moving into one of the houses behind the park next week. You know, the big sandstone ones?'

'Oh, those are lovely. That's great news. Welcome back!'

'Yeah, we're really pleased. It has been a long time coming, sorting this mess out.'

'You've certainly had your work cut out. Any news on your own house?'

I shake my head. 'No. You get to the stage where you no longer expect the phone call. We'll just need to wait and see. At least now we have a house, with a garden, for the kids to spend time in.'

'Absolutely. So important when they're little. Not so much for Gen, but Hugo and Aria should be haring around on scooters, bikes, jumping on trampolines.'

'I still like going on trampolines,' Gen declares, eager not to be left out.

'Oh, I didn't say you didn't, love. I just meant, well, you have other interests now. Teenagers aren't going to be playing with their dollies in the garden now, are they?'

Gen agreed that was unlikely.

'So, what are you looking for today?'

I explain that we're looking for special gifts for Mum and Wendy, and Susan asks Gen if she'd like to learn how to make up the bouquets since she has time.

Interestingly, Gen's eyes light up. I call Ronnie and tell him we'll be a little longer, as I watch Gen choose the flowers for the bouquets, whilst Susan explains which flowers complement each other well. Another rush of pride for Gen overcomes me. Two in one day. Steady on, Gen. I'll expect this all the time.

'Good eye you have there, Genevieve. Maybe I could get you in as a Saturday girl in the future, when you're old enough.'

Gen flushes at the praise, but I can tell she's pleased.

When we arrive back at the hotel, Fabien is standing in reception holding court with a few employees. With the help Nicky gave me earlier with my presentation, the sight of him doesn't have me running for the hills. And his timing is good. I can tell him we have a moving-out date.

'Louisa, how are you?'

'Not bad, Fabien. You?'

'I was hoping we could go over your presentation.'

'Now?'

'Only if you have time,' he says in such a way that I know I need to make the time.

I hope things aren't going to be off with Fabien and me again, after what happened with Charles Pickford. We've not really had much chance to meet in person since then. Mostly, I've been bringing myself up to speed on Cerulean's clients, terms and conditions, best business practices and expectations by email. And I've been talking to a few of the staff by phone or contacting them via email, which has suited me, given the upheaval we've had.

'If you give me fifteen minutes, I'll grab my laptop and come down.'

'Excellent.'

As I trudge upstairs, my balloon bursts. I've been so happy today, but now I need to face the music. I don't know if I've made a terrible mistake taking on this role. Maybe I could have managed it if a lorry hadn't crashed into my house, I hadn't spent the summer living out of a hotel – albeit a luxury suite – and I wasn't pregnant, but I sense a discontent in Fabien that wasn't there before, and it concerns me. Am I up to the job, and if I'm not, how can I let him down after everything he has done for me?

Chapter Twenty

Saturday 7 August

Moths circle in my stomach, not butterflies, those would be too pretty. These are malevolent. I still haven't finished the presentation, but as I shepherd the kids and Ronnie through the suite door, I say, 'Can you deal with the kids? Fabien wants to go over my presentation, but I'm not sure if it's OK. Nicky helped me, but now I'm panicking again.'

Ronnie looks at me, long and hard. 'Kids, go shove a movie on. I need ten minutes with Mummy.'

Gen throws us a look of disgust. She clearly thinks we have other things on the agenda. Nope, look where that got us last time. And yeah, sometimes it has been only ten minutes, but to give my husband his due, he's more of a half-hour man.

'We need to go over my presentation for Fabien, so can you be nice and quiet, whilst Daddy gives me some advice.'

Realisation flits across Gen's face, and she has the good grace to grin.

Yes, my girl, you got it wrong.

I boot up my laptop, bring up the presentation and turn it round to Ronnie, who reads, scrolls, reads, scrolls. When he's finished, he glances up at me. 'Right?'

'Right, what?'

'Right, what's the problem?'

'Doesn't it seem a bit basic to you?'

'Well, without knowing the intricate details of the wedding stationery business, I'd say this comes across as a professional, knowledgeable, yet succinct presentation by someone who knows their stuff.'

You see, sometimes I really, really love my husband. That's exactly what I needed to hear right now. I take a deep breath. 'OK. I'm ready. Wish me luck.'

'Luck!' He bends down and kisses me. 'Stop being so nervous. It's just Fabien, he's not going to bite. And like I said, the presentation is fine.'

I pull up short. 'Fine?'

'Oh, no, don't do that,' Ronnie says, waving a finger.

'Do what?' I frown.

'Manufacture slights where there are none. To a man "fine" means "good". To a woman, especially your wife, it means "a step up from trash". I meant "fine" from a man's perspective. Obviously.'

'OK,' I say, suitably mollified.

'Stop procrastinating and get your backside down there and show him what you're made of.'

Ronnie and Nicky were right. I had no reason to be concerned about the presentation. It was all in my head. Fabien and I have just gone over the whole presentation, the itinerary for the days I'll be in Madrid, and I'm about to wish him a good evening when he stops me.

'One more thing, Louisa.'

'Yes?'

'I'd really rather you kept Cerulean out of the papers and your business and private lives separate, at least the parts regarding Cerulean. All of our employees, and business partners, need to do everything in their power to ensure they don't show the brand in a negative light. And whilst I realise that your mention of Cerulean in the article was probably innocently done, and in fact, mainly showed us in a good light, we want to avoid being mentioned in the tabloids. Broadsheet reviews, fabulous. Hard-luck stories in the tabloids, a no-no.'

My colour heightens, and I wish I could hide under the table. The only saving grace is that our meeting was already drawing to a close.

'I'm really sorry, Fabien.'

'It's done now. The important thing is the future.'

I note he doesn't say 'never mind' or 'don't worry about it'. Hmm. He really wasn't happy, was he?

I'm annoyed that my usually impeccable work record is taking a pounding, for various reasons, and I resolve to restore it to its former glory forthwith. By forthwith, I mean Madrid. I need to scintillate there, impress the Spanish contingent.

I return to Ronnie and the kids and try to reignite my glowing ember of happiness that filled me during the day, but it's no good.

'C'mon, out of your funk.' Ronnie snuggles into me, and it's nice. I pull a length of sheepskin throw off my children, to shouts of 'Oi', 'Hey', 'Mu-u-um!' and settle down to watch the rest of their game of Monopoly. Aria already has the Mayfair set. It doesn't bode well for the others.

Monday 9 August

To-do list
Don't forget hospital letter and double-check and triple-check time and date

Leave plenty of time for parking – it's always a nightmare
Order Hugo personalised pencils – he saw Aria's and wants some now
Sketch pads – buy A4

Sleeps until Aria starts school – 7. She made me add this to my list.

Today's the day. Scan day. I'll get to see how my baby has grown. I know I've done this several times before, with several different babies, but that doesn't stop it being tremendously special. Nothing, but nothing had better put me in a bad mood today. I can be in a thunderous mood tomorrow, but today, I aim to channel serenity. I'm seeing my baby, and I want it to sense tranquil thoughts from its mama.

Jo and Travis are taking the kids to the forest trail up near them. They arrived an hour ago, whisked them off forthwith – it was a surprise – and Ronnie and I have been able to relax a little, pack some of our stuff for the move, I've thrown what I require for my trip into one of our trusty suitcases. Privately, I'm thinking if I start travelling for work, I need a much better quality suitcase. I'm not channelling Louis Vuitton, but I'd really rather have a Tripp or Samsonite one than a generic black one from the supermarket. You can never find them on baggage carousels either. Every time the belt starts, you think 'oh, there it is', but it never is. You have to tie coloured string, or have a souvenir luggage label or something on it to identify it, and those cases are the ones that arrive, having been thrown down a chute, with a missing zip, a torn corner, or a missing wheel. False economy. Anyway, bottom line, I want a better suitcase.

Ronnie's running through his interview technique and considering questions they may throw at him tomorrow. I can tell he's beginning to get nervous. He's pacing about like a mother hen, or a caged polar bear, difficult to tell which.

Finally, before he wears out a section of the carpet, I convince him it's time to leave for the hospital. Ronnie drives and I sit back, relax and watch the countryside whizz past as we head into the city.

'Well, that was painless,' Ronnie says as he unfolds his rangy frame from the car.

'Yeah, I thought we'd take ages to get parked.''

'Today's our lucky day,' Ronnie says, clicking the car shut and taking my hand. His hand is warm, and he smooths his fingers over my knuckles. It's oddly erotic. God, pregnancy hormones. I forgot how horny they make you.

We enter the ultrasound department. Two other couples are already seated. A sign on the door to the ultrasound room reads 'Do not knock. Please wait. The sonographer will see you at your appointed time.'

So, we sit. And we wait. And we wait. And one of the couples goes in. Another couple arrives. We flash each other smiles. The first couple comes out, all smiles. The sonographer calls the second couple's name. I frown.

'What time is it, Ronnie?'

'Twenty to.'

'Our appointment was at half past.'

'Don't start. They're probably just running late.'

Another couple arrives and takes a seat. The small waiting room is busying up.

The sonographer shows out the second people and calls

out, 'Callahan.' The first couple who came in after us stand and make their way towards her.

'What time is it now?'

'Twelve.'

'Our appointment was half an hour ago.'

'There'll be a good reason. Don't bust a blood vessel. It's not good for you, or the baby,' Ronnie says pointedly.

Fair enough. I do a lot of sighing over the next fifteen minutes. The couple come out, the sonographer too, and when she calls, 'Medici,' I can't help it, I stand and say, 'Excuse me. Can I ask if we've been missed? Our appointment was forty minutes ago.'

She frowns. 'All my appointments are running to time today. A miracle. Can I see your card?'

'Sure.' I dig in my bag and pull out my card, then hand it to her. 'Here you go.'

She glances at it then says, 'I see the problem. You're meant to be at the Queen Elizabeth Hospital.'

'What?' I take the card back from her. 'Oh, you have got to be kidding me? Why on earth have I to go to the Queen Elizabeth? I've never gone there before. I've always come to the Royal.'

She shakes her head and splays her hands as if to say 'beats me'. 'I don't know, but you're definitely not on my list, and it states quite clearly here that you've to go to the Queen Elizabeth.'

I burst into tears. I've missed it, not because I got the wrong day as I did with Aria, but because I've got the wrong bloody hospital. I don't believe this. Just when I thought the stars might finally be aligning for us.

Ronnie puts an arm around me and hugs me to him, and I heave great sobs into his shoulder. 'Thanks,' I hear him say.

A few minutes later, when I've calmed a little, he says,

'Let's go back to the car, and I'll call the hospital and tell them what's happened.'

Luckily, Ronnie gets through, and we're soon on our way to the Queen Elizabeth Hospital.

When we arrive, Ronnie approaches the desk and speaks with the girl he talked to on the phone.

'That's fine. You'll have to wait either until there's a gap or the end of the day, but we'll slot you in. The sonographer says she'll stay late if she has to, just to do your scan.'

'Thank you,' Ronnie says as I sit a few metres away, trying to stem the flow of tears – this time tears of relief.

Two hours later, we finally see our baby, and it was so worth the wait. Whilst I waited, I had to go to the toilet several times, because, pregnancy, and then refill my bladder when it became clear they couldn't see anything on the scan as I hadn't drunk enough fluid.

I watch my baby, who seems to be lying upside down. I see the curve of their back, their head, clear as day, which is about half the size of their body. A little arm, a little leg. I'd forgotten the legs don't seem in proportion at the beginning of a pregnancy.

'Is he hiccupping?' Ronnie asks.

The midwife smiles. 'Yes, it's quite common.'

Ronnie stares in wonder at the screen, whilst I reflect on his use of 'he'. Does he want a boy? Then he glances at me, and we share a knowing smile. Baby number four. I never thought I'd be here again, but I'm glad I am. And it doesn't matter to me which it is, boy or girl, this baby will receive all the love I can give it. All the love we can give it.

Ronnie takes my hand, and I sigh. Everything feels right.

'Everything looks good. Based on this, my measurements suggest a due date of the seventeenth of February.'

Earlier than originally thought then. I smile so much the part behind my ears that hurts when I laugh too much is in danger of activating.

Jo brings the kids back around six. Ronnie and I spend the remainder of the afternoon tidying the suite, then chilling in front of the TV, and it's bliss. The kids barrel in, Gen on her phone relaying her day to a friend. She gives me a wave and a smile. Hugo and Aria vie for pole position on the explaining every detail of their day to me. Eventually, Hugo gives up – Aria is the outright winner in talking over people, not a trait we should encourage – and he tails Ronnie to the kitchen, where he has gone to make coffee for Jo.

'Mummy, we went to the forest on our bikes and Hugo hit a tree trunk and fell off and hurt his arm.'

'Tree root,' Hugo calls from the other side of the room.

'Root,' Aria affirms.

'You OK, Hugo?' I ask.

'I'm fine. It was awesome. I somersaulted through the air, I thought I was a goner, but I'm alive!' he declares, rather unnecessarily.

'Right, king of melodrama,' I say.

'Hey!' It was really sore, and my back still hurts and look, I have a bruise which looks a bit like an island.' He holds his arm up for us to inspect it.

'It does a bit, but which island, Dad? You're a bit better at geography than me.'

Ronnie plays along, examining it at length, his fingers stroking his chin as he studies it. 'Hmm, it's a tough one.

Perhaps Sardinia.'

'Sardinia? I thought it looked more like Madagascar,' I scoff.

'Well, you're both wrong. It looks like Arran, see. There's the top of the island near Lochranza Castle. There's Brodick ferry terminal–' he points to a part of the bruise around the four o'clock spot '–and there's the String Road.' He indicates a scratch running through the middle of the bruise.

'So it is,' I say, putting on my best poker face.

When the kids have disappeared to their rooms, Jo hugs me and asks how it all went.

'We went to the wrong hospital.'

'What? How come?'

'Because despite having gone to Aria's scan on the wrong day in the past, it didn't occur to me that I'd be sent to a different hospital this time.'

'It could only–' starts Jo.

'I know, "happen to me". Don't think I haven't already had that thought. Ronnie too, I'm sure.' My eyes meet Ronnie's and we share a smile.

'But all was well with the baby?' Jo asks, her sisterly anxiety evident in the creases at the corner of her eyes.

'Baby looks great.' I beam. 'And I have a firmer due date. Seventeenth of February. Ten days earlier than the midwife said.'

She comes over and gives me a hug. 'That's great. I always thought it was much more real once you had the dating scan and knew when to expect Junior in your life.'

I grin. 'Me too.'

'So, when are you telling the troops?' She inclines her head towards the bedroom doors.

'Well–' I glance at Ronnie '–we were going to tell them

tonight, since I'm away first thing to Madrid, but they seem too wired. They'll never sleep. I think we should wait until I get back on Thursday morning. We're moving on Friday, so they probably won't sleep on Thursday anyway, from the excitement over the move.'

Jo nods her agreement. 'Makes sense. Before I go, do you have a scan pic to show me?'

'Oh, I almost forgot, of course.' I fish it out of my handbag and pass it to her.

'Hey, Ronnie, the baby has your nose,' she says.

Ronnie rolls his eyes.

'Can you see that?' I ask incredulously.

Jo shakes her head, equally incredulously. 'Don't be daft, I'm just kidding him on.'

I shove her slightly in the arm. 'Don't mess with me. My brain cells are depleted.'

'There's more of that to come. No luck, Ronnie,' Jo says with a grin.

'Enough, you. Whose side are you on, anyway?' I ask in mock outrage.

'Don't worry. I'm going. Don't want to be too late in case Travis can't get the kids down.'

I pull Jo into a hug. 'Thanks, sis.'

'Anytime.'

I walk her to the door of the suite, where she hands me back the scan pic which she's still carrying. 'I think the baby has your nose.'

'Get out! Call you when I get back.'

'Have fun.' She kisses me on the cheek. 'Love you.'

'I love you too.'

As I return to my place on the sofa, I can't help but be thankful for how much love this baby will have in its life.

Chapter Twenty-one

Tuesday 10 August

To-do list
Buy Teapigs teabags – running low
Buy insulated cup
Take white top back to shop. Frayed at edge after first wear.

Sleeps until Aria starts school – 6

I shade my eyes from the sun as I sit at the coffee shop, sipping my decaff latte, people-watching. Standing in the queue, I realised the aroma of the coffee no longer made me want to gag, so I took a risk and ordered a coffee.

The book I've brought along is out on the table, but I'm honestly too tired to focus on it. I set my alarm for four thirty so I had enough time to wake up, get ready, drive through a sleeping city – which was the only benefit – only to arrive and discover bag drop isn't open yet. Normally, I'd be delighted at a little extra time by myself, but I didn't sleep well, excitement over yesterday's scan then apprehension over today's trip, I imagine, so quite frankly, I'd rather have had an extra hour in bed. Three hours before the airline said to be here, and they're not even open. Grr.

Glasgow Airport is relatively quiet at this time in the morning. Later, everyone will be scurrying here and there, backwards and forwards like ants on a tight schedule.

I've pored over my presentation so many times, I could recite it in my sleep. It will be fine. I just need to project confidence. I'm going to stop trying to reinvent the wheel and allow myself to enjoy the trip. C'mon, how often do I get two days away, in Madrid, *sans* children?

Deciding I should really have a look at the guidebook app for Madrid, so if I have any free time, I can go to the Retiro park, or the Paseo del Prado and do a little shopping, I apply myself to my task. Soon I have a list of about ten places, including the famous El Escorial monastery, and apparently commonly considered the eighth wonder of the world – who knew? – and the Royal Palace.

Yeah, I feel I may need a second trip to cover the absolute minimum of the attractions on my list. I glance at my watch, conscious that after arriving so early, I don't want to be late for checking my bag and navigating the horrendous security queues by losing track of time.

'Lou.'

Oh my God. I look up to see Caden standing over me.

For a good few seconds, my throat is so dry, I can't speak. At all. Finally, 'Caden' emerges from my lips.

'I thought it was you. How are you?'

His initial enthusiasm has changed to slightly guarded, perhaps at my hesitance, or maybe because it wasn't so long ago we were wrapped around each other at a friend's wedding in the gardens in the dead of night. If it hadn't been for Travis turning up, I can honestly say I'm not sure what would have happened.

I'm not proud of it, but it's a moment I'll never forget as long as I live.

I shake my head as if to dispel thoughts of that night. Caden tilts his head. Oh crap, I shook my head, didn't I? I pull myself together. 'I'm good, thanks.'

His gaze holds mine, and I sense him asking me if that's really true. Then I realise how rude I'm being. 'How are you?'

'Great. The new job is everything I wanted, and more. I can't believe how lucky I've been to be offered two such amazing jobs in such a short space of time.'

I nod. Yes, lucky, but perhaps fate had a hand in it too. Or Travis. I'm still not sure what exactly Travis knows about Caden and me, but he definitely had his suspicions.

He smiles, his enthusiasm for his new role evident in every word he speaks. He's so animated, it's infectious, and for a moment I'm able to think of us as we used to be, two acquaintances who were friendly with each other.

I nod again, unsure what to say. What do you say to the man who was just as attracted to you as you were to him? The man you would happily have slept with, have constantly dreamt about, all the while being married to someone you didn't think saw you as a person and who appears to have no idea who you are nowadays?

'Do you mind if I sit down? I was going to grab a coffee too.'

How can I say no? I don't want to say no. Despite these feelings that are still raw, and even though my emotions, and hormones, are raging all over the place because of my pregnancy, I still want this connection with this man. I still need this connection. I crave it. God, I hope I didn't say that out loud.

Caden is standing there looking at me expectantly. Oh crap, I didn't answer him.

'Eh, sure.'

Yeah, that sounded really positive, really welcoming. Well done. Although perhaps that's no bad thing, since we definitely need boundaries between us. That said, it's only coffee, in an airport, in broad daylight, and he'll soon be going his way, and I'll be going mine, two separate flights taking off for different parts of the world, or at least Europe. Or maybe he's going to London? Oh, for goodness' sake, it doesn't matter. The point is, it's not like we're absconding to Madrid together. Which is just as well, as he would be a terrible distraction. I gulp, thinking of the last time he distracted me, and to what extent.

'Great, I'll get a coffee. He looks at the scum at the bottom of my cup. 'Would you like another?'

'Thanks.'

'Latte, right?'

I nod and he says, 'Be right back.'

'Decaff,' I call after him.

He raises an eyebrow, possibly wondering why I prefer decaff at this ungodly hour of the morning, but I'm not about to enlighten him.

'So, I hear you're staying in a hotel,' he says when he sits down beside me a few minutes later. The few minutes did nothing to calm the swirling in my gut. There's a veritable Magic Mountain of rollercoasters making themselves felt in my stomach right now.

'Yes. We were very lucky.'

'In all senses.' His dark, brooding gaze holds mine.

'Yes. We were, although Nicky and Xander not so much.'

'I heard. I saw Jo a few times after at the restaurant. I can't begin to imagine what the past two months have been like for you. How you've coped. You're an incredible woman, Lou…Louisa, but what you had to deal with was unbelievable, fantastical even. It was like something out of a Hollywood disaster movie.'

I get he's trying to be empathetic, but I'm doing my best to forget all this stuff, not relive it.

'Yeah, well, it is what it is. We're finally moving to a house, later this week.'

He gives a wide smile. 'Oh, that's brilliant news, Lou. After everything you've gone through, you deserve some luck.'

He's got that right. But was it lucky to meet him here today or not? I wonder.

In an attempt to divert him from gleaning any more information about my life, currently, I ask him more about the new Highland restaurant, the Salty Squid, I think it was called.

'So, there's a staff of about fifteen at the minute…'

I listen as he tells me about the new venture, the fittings, the kitchen, the menu, anecdotes about the staff. He gesticulates with his hands when he's passionate about something. Passionate. God, will I ever get the double-entendres out of my head? Will I ever get the images of Caden and me out of my head? Will I ever stop wondering what would have happened at the wedding if Travis hadn't interrupted us?

I can't help it. I'm focusing on his lips, remembering them softly kissing mine, then more urgently, then, oh my goodness, I need a cold shower. Heat rises up my neck and suffuses my face. I don't think it's healthy or appropriate for us to be together, no matter how innocent. I understand he's unlikely to suggest we sneak off to the disabled toilet and have a quickie, but the fact that thought implanted itself in my mind is telling enough. I can't spend time with him. It's not a good idea. In fact, it's a very bad idea.

I've been so manic with everything that has needed to be dealt with since the crash that I've had no headspace for the whole Caden debacle, but now the aftermath of the crash is starting to reach some resolution – despite our house still not being habitable – I may have a little room in my head, in my thoughts for him, and that's a dangerous place. A terrifying concept. Particularly now that I'm three months pregnant.

'I'd better go.' I glance at my watch. It feels weird to me, as I never wear a watch at home, preferring to use my mobile phone to check the time, or my laptop or iPad. But when I travel abroad, I somehow feel better knowing I have the time on my wrist. And no, it's not just another pregnancy foible.

'Final call for passengers Halliday, McMahon, Smith and Garety travelling to London Gatwick. Your flight is now fully boarded and awaiting departure.'

'What? Oh no, no, no, no!' What time is it? I look at my watch, but in my confusion the dial blurs. I glance at Caden in panic.

'Shit,' says Caden, checking his ticket. 'Are you on the flight to London?'

I nod.

'Sorry, I wasn't saying "shit" because you're on the flight, but because it means we're going to miss it. C'mon.' He takes my hand like it's the most natural gesture in the world.

My jaw drops. 'You're going to London?'

'Well, Madrid, but via London.'

I take a millisecond to process the fates taking the mick then say, 'Caden, I'm going to Madrid, too, but I haven't even checked my bag. The bag drop wasn't open.'

'What?' he says, turning back.

'I haven't checked my bag. I won't be allowed on with this.'

He eyes the bag, then my laptop bag and my handbag, then glances at his own small backpack. It's almost as small as the Paw Patrol one Aria has for nursery. What on earth could he possibly fit in there? A pair of boxers, two pairs of socks, a toothbrush and some aftershave? There's not a great deal of space for much else.

'Look, I can take your laptop as a personal item, and you can take your trolley case and your handbag.'

I process this. 'That could work.'

'Right, but let's think as we run. C'mon.' He takes my trolley case and his backpack, and we race to the security gates. I'm just glad I'm only a few months pregnant as it'd be harder to channel my inner Usain Bolt if I was any heavier. As it is, I think my Fitbit is lying to me, because unlike Caden, for whom it's a breeze, I'm huffing and puffing like an octogenarian after dancing a particularly frenetic ceilidh dance.

Caden, unlike me, has the charm and charisma, as well as the balls, to politely ask people if we can go ahead of them in order to catch our flight. Either that or we have the politest, least stressed out and affable security queue in the history of airports. If I'd asked, they'd have told me I should have arrived earlier. Caden asks and the Red Sea parts.

Fortunately, all I have to do is run as Caden seems to know exactly which gate we're heading to, where it is on the concourse and how long it should, normally, take us to get there, so despite me being stopped by security and wanded, due to the metallic stars on my T-shirt – will I never learn? Note to self, check metal content of my clothing before leaving for airport. Or better still check it the night before. Usually, it's the underwire in my bra, but thankfully that wasn't the case today. That would have been too close for comfort with Caden standing right next to me. Other memories of my bra...for the love of God, please, thoughts, get out of my head. I have a flight to catch.

Or not. 'I'm afraid I can't let you on the plane. We're about to close up,' says the ground staff attendant.

'Look,' I pant. 'Please, please, please, let us on the plane. This is my first presentation for my new job, I've run so far and so fast that I think I'm going to have a panic attack any minute, and–' I pant heavily, trying and failing to catch my breath '–I'm three months pregnant.' I burst into tears just as another flight attendant pitches up, confers in hushed whispers with her colleague, then says, 'Give me your boarding passes, but please, on your return journey, make sure you leave more time.'

If only they knew.

'Thank you, thank you.' I could kiss them, both of them. They each take a step back, as if they know what I'm thinking.

They open the door to the corridor that leads to the plane. 'Be quick,' says the woman who was originally dealing with us. 'Congratulations, and try not to stress.'

I nod and give a tight smile, and as Caden and I run down towards the plane entrance, he says, 'Are you really pregnant?'

The flight flies past. God, even my jokes are terrible today. Fortunately, or unfortunately, depending on your viewpoint, Caden and I are sitting at opposite ends of the plane. Cerulean have me in an extended leg room seat at the front, and Caden is somewhere at the back. He's so far back, I can't even see him. And that's not a bad thing, as I need some time to process what has happened this morning. It has been quite the morning.

The array of emotions flitting across his face as he asked me if I was really pregnant could be catalogued as follows: surprise, shock, hurt, frustration, and I'm sure we could throw a few more into the mix, but that seems plenty to be getting on with for now. He did, however, seem to age about ten years in as many seconds. Fine lines appeared at the corners of his eyes. I was sure they weren't there when we were having coffee earlier.

I haven't really had time to digest that he's going to Madrid at the same time as me. I mean, what are the chances? He doesn't even live in the Glasgow area any more. I haven't even had a chance to ask him where he was going, although I suppose with Inverness as his nearest airport, his travel choices from there would have been considerably limited. That said, he could have flown from Aberdeen. Anyway, he didn't, he flew from Glasgow, and serendipity decided to insert itself into our day and have us not only travelling from the same airport, but to the same destination. I wonder what he's going to do there that he's travelling so light. I take a bigger bag on the school run.

At Gatwick we have just over an hour to kill once we reach the gate before the next flight. Since he was in the seat across the aisle from me and two rows back, we leave the plane at almost exactly the same time.

'I can't believe you're going to Madrid too,' Caden says.

'That makes two of us.'

He puts his hands in his pockets and smiles at me. 'So, when's the baby due?'

'February.'

We stare at each other for a long moment, then I change the subject before we veer off into territory best avoided.

'Sorry, I'll carry my laptop bag. I shouldn't have lumbered you with it.'

'It's no problem, and you'd just have to give it back to me for boarding the next flight.' He grins, and it's infectious.

'Fair enough. Thank you.'

We walk companionably to the gate, where Caden is called to board almost immediately, whilst I have to wait until almost final call before my zone is called to board.

The two hours plus flight passes quickly, as I doze most of it. I wake to the sound of the pilot saying,

We're now starting our descent into Madrid–Barajas, where the temperature is a comfortable twenty-eight degrees...

The stewardess opens the door, and I file out, one of the first, given my position at the front of the plane. I glance behind me. Doesn't look like they have two sets of stairs for this flight, so Caden will have to wait his turn in row two hundred or whatever he's in. I know there aren't two hundred rows, but there may as well be, given the distance between us. Do I wait for him? What's the protocol? Do I ditch him and see him next time we all meet up at the restaurant? Unlikely, given he's moved to the one in the

Highlands now. Oh, and he has my laptop bag, so that's not a possibility. Aargh! Where's the rule book when you need one?

I'm overthinking this. Like a sheep, I follow everyone else, until I realise they're heading to baggage claim. Since I don't have a suitcase to collect, there's little point in me going there, so I rummage in my handbag for my phone: perfect delaying tactic. My thoughts fast-forward to my plans for the day. My clients are meeting me for dinner before tomorrow's presentation, but the remainder of the afternoon I have free. I'm staying at the Hotel Mayor, one of Cerulean's European flagship hotels. I'm quite excited about my stay there. I'll be starfishing in the bed, that's for sure. Two nights, stretched out in a bed the size of my home office, hopefully, with no one to disturb me. No snoring. No 'Mum'. No barking. No 'I need the toilet, but there's no toilet paper.' Hugo. No 'Mummy, I had a bad dream, and now I can't find Cornie.' Aria. No 'Mum, can't you do something about Dad? His snoring's so bad I can't even get to sleep with earplugs in.' Gen.

I'm so absorbed in thinking about how much peace I'll have in my room or suite, whatever it is, I don't notice Caden approach. I fiddle with my handbag. 'Oh God, I'm so sorry, you still have my laptop. I should have waited for you so I could carry it. Sorry.'

He waves a hand at me. 'Don't be silly. I have a spare hand anyway.'

Then we both burst out laughing.

'Obviously, I don't have a spare hand, that would mean I have three, I mean, I have a free hand.'

'I knew what you meant, but it was still a funny image.'

He grins. 'It was. Glad to be the source of your

amusement.'

I look into his eyes, the flecks of gold darkening when I don't look away. He's also the source of my ardour. My heart's beating faster, my face is flushing – I can feel heat rising in me, and not just in my face – and I'm sweating. How attractive.

Somehow, we've inched closer a little, somehow his face is closer to mine, as if he's about to tell me a secret, somehow, I'm incontrovertibly drawn to this man. Somehow…

'*Amor!*'

Like magnets repelling, Caden and I are 'torn' apart. When I look up, a twenty-something Spanish girl with long honey tresses and Gucci sunglasses perched atop her head has her arms wrapped around Caden and is pouting her Hollywood starlet lips at him.

'I-I-I didn't know you were coming to the airport,' Caden stammers.

'Pah! I haven't seen you in four months. I wasn't going to wait a second longer.' She's about to lower her lips to his when she catches sight of me, and possibly my expression.

'*Amor*, aren't you going to introduce me to your friend?'

Caden looks like he has swallowed something that disagreed with his constitution. I hope it's at the situation and not how he feels at my being 'his friend'.

He glances between the girl and me, then back at her. 'Dolores, this is Louisa. I work for her brother-in-law.' Then he returns his gaze to me. 'Lou-isa, this is Dolores. My girlfriend.'

Chapter Twenty-two

Tuesday 10 August

Caden has a girlfriend. He never mentioned a girlfriend.
OK, I have a husband, but he always knew I was married.
That sounds worse than it is. I know I'm being irrational,
but somehow finding out I've been screwing myself over
and tying myself in knots emotionally over someone who
has a girlfriend, one who hasn't seen him for four months,
makes both my heart sink and blood boil in equal measure.

'Louisa, how nice to meet you.' She kisses me on both
cheeks. 'Where are you staying?'

Her smile is so wide and disarming, I half expect her to
invite me to stay with them.

'Oh, I'm at the Hotel Mayor.'

'Ah, we're going that way. Is someone coming to collect
you?' She adjusts her sunglasses on her head.

'No, I'm just going to get a cab.'

She waves this idea away and shakes her head. 'No, not
at all. I will drive you. I know the hotel well. My brother
used to work there.'

We chit-chat on the way, Dolores playing the part of
amenable Spanish host to both of us, eager to find out what
we've been up to and why I'm in Madrid. When she learns
of the crash, she says '*Dios mio*, was anyone hurt? I hope

you and your family were OK.'

'My friend and her son were injured, my friend in particular pretty badly, but she's out of hospital now.'

'I will pray for her,' Dolores says solemnly, and I smile in thanks and at the thought of this hip girl saying this and meaning it. Things are very different in Spain to back in the UK.

'So, how long are you staying?' she asks.

'I'm just here today and tomorrow, then I fly home on Thursday. We have quite a few things going on at the minute.'

'Oh?'

'Yes, my husband–' I note Caden flinch slightly at the word '–has a second interview for a job today. He works in the oil industry, and is looking to move to a job onshore.'

'Oh, that is very important. I hope he gets it,' Dolores says, seeming to understand. 'Being away from your beloved for a long time is not so easy.'

My throat dries, and I can't look at Caden. I change subject to avoid any further uncomfortable silence. 'Yes, and we're moving house on Friday.'

'*Madre mia*, you really are having a busy week.'

'Well, hopefully next week, once the schools go back, it will be a bit easier.'

Dolores frowns. 'But it's only the middle of August.' She looks at Caden. 'I thought the schools went back at the start of September.'

Caden explains. 'In England they do, but in Scotland it's about three weeks earlier.'

Dolores' jaw drops. 'Poor babies. They have fewer holidays. Less time to be with family.'

'Oh, no, to clarify, Dolores, they get plenty of holidays, believe me! In Scotland, the children finish school three weeks earlier too, in June instead of July.'

She holds her hand to her chest. '*Ai*, I was asking myself how this was fair. That makes sense now.'

A comfortable silence reigns this time, until Caden says, 'Oh, and Louisa has another big piece of news. Huge, in fact.' Dolores doesn't know our history, so she wouldn't detect the undercurrent in those words, but I do. Caden is pissed off, and he's having a dig. What's he got to be pissed off for? I'm married. I already have three children. We're not together. But then, who am I to talk? I was narked at him having a girlfriend. Maybe we should be together – we're a right pair.

'Oh? What is your big news, Louisa?' Her smile is so dazzling and her persona so radiant she's like an angel sent from heaven. Absent-mindedly, I wonder if there is a Saint Dolores. I'll need to ask Alexa later. Oh, I can't, I'm in a hotel. I'll google it.

'I'm…three months pregnant.'

'*Felicitaciones!* That is wonderful news.'

'Thank you. I'm pretty excited.' Again, I can't look at Caden.

Finally, we arrive at the hotel. I almost sigh with relief. As Caden takes my luggage out of the boot, neither of us looking at each other, Dolores says, 'Hey, why don't we catch up for dinner tonight?'

His back goes rigid, and horror flashes across his face as he turns before he can mask it. Dolores is facing in the other direction, but I don't miss it. I almost wish I didn't have a work thing just so I could prolong Caden's agony here, since clearly the idea of us having dinner together is so abhorrent. OK, I get that it's not ideal circumstances, far from, but even so. His reaction hurts.

'Oh, that's a lovely idea, but I have dinner meetings whilst I'm here, but thanks ever so much.'

Dolores tuts in exasperation. 'That's a pity, but tell you what, we can do drinks after. It will also give you the perfect excuse to leave if they are boring to you.'

'*Gracias.*' I tip the porter – it's that sort of hotel – and take in my room. Palatial is not the word I'd use. Obscenely opulent is more accurate. Three floor-to-ceiling windows look out over the Retiro park. I hadn't realised the park was so big. It's enormous. The lake dominates, and I can see why it belonged to the royal family and even more so why UNESCO granted it World Heritage Site status a decade or so ago. I did read the guide book a little.

The bed is even better than I'd hoped. I actually have to google what it might be called as I'm sure it's bigger than a super king. So it's either a Caesar or an Emperor, apparently. Never heard of them. Don't care. I'm going to roll around in that, taking up every available inch, and enjoy it to the max.

After I starfish and basically try out every comfortable position possible – my body is so used to small children crawling all over me whilst I'm trying to sleep, I have to unlearn those sleep positions – I lie for a while simply taking in the surroundings. The chaise longue. Nope. Let's not go there. Yep, too late, I think of the chaise longue where I was sitting in the holiday home my sisters and I had rented for my birthday, in the Lake District, where we first met Caden, who was our chef. Caden, the chef, who I kissed after he forgot his phone and returned after midnight to find me sipping tea on the chaise longue, as you do.

Aargh! Why do so many memories link back to him? Even everyday objects. OK, well, granted, a chaise longue isn't an everyday object. You don't see many of those in our friends' homes, nor in high-rise flats in the city, but my point is…actually, what is my point? Oh yeah, everyday objects. I mean, I could understand if memories were triggered by a piece of music that had been playing during our kiss – there wasn't one, but that's immaterial – but a chaise longue!

The furnishings generally in the room are fussier than I'd like if I was choosing them for my own house: armchairs with fringes hanging beneath the seat cushions; chandeliers; gilt-edged headboards; a huge centrepiece of a cloud that is like something out of the Sistine Chapel. I fully expect angels and perhaps Cupid to pop into the scene any minute. I'm almost concerned about going to bed in case my behaviour is found wanting. I thank my lucky stars that Caden isn't here, as the behaviour would definitely be questionable, although it would be wanton not wanting.

The carpet is more like an elaborate tapestry, and seems to bear a royal emblem. I'm no expert but it could be. And there are more swags and tails and pelmets in here than in a fabric shop.

My phone rings. Ronnie.

'Hi. How are you?'

'Good. How was your flight?'

My throat constricts, and again I find it difficult to speak. 'F-ine,' I squeak.

'You OK. You've either got a terrible connection or you're coming down with something.'

'It's only tiredness. Early start, you know.'

'Yeah.' I sense him nodding. 'How's the hotel?'

I describe it in great detail, at the end of which he says, 'I miss you, Lou. I wish I could be there with you.'

'Me too,' I say, although that's stretching the truth. It'd be too weird after Caden and Dolores having dropped me off at the hotel. But up until last night, I would have been grateful for a few days away on our own, just me and Ronnie, to bond, or whatever couples do when they're trying to save their marriage or improve elements of it. But, as usual, seeing Caden has wrong-footed me.

'And have you met your clients yet?'

'No, I'm meeting them for dinner. I'm about to go soak in the free-standing bath.'

'In August? Won't you be boiling?'

'Fair point. Perhaps, I'll have a cool shower in the rainforest.'

'Right, stop rubbing it in. Oh, I almost forgot to tell you.' He pauses.

'OK, what is it?' I ask, impatience asserting itself when he doesn't continue for at least five seconds.

'I got the job.'

Oh God, I didn't even remember about the interview. I'm a terrible, terrible wife. I over-egg my enthusiasm to make up for it. 'You didn't! Woo hoo! Yay! I can't believe it! How many more joyful phrases can I use? Sorry, I've run out,' I say.

'Ha ha. Isn't it great? The interview went like a dream, so much so, they called me an hour later and offered me the job.'

'I'm grinning, Ronnie. I know you can't see me, but I'm like the Cheshire cat.'

'I can imagine.'

'And I know you're grinning too.'

'I am.'

'A man of few words.'

'That too.'

'Congratulations, darling. You deserve it.'

'Thanks for being there, Lou. I really appreciate it.'

'Oh well, what are wives for?'

Ronnie goes on to explain the terms and conditions of his contract, his start date, and I already sense a huge change in him – and it's for the better. Things are looking up.

'Louisa?' asks a man, who appears to be around sixty with salt and pepper hair and matching facial hair.

I'm standing against the entrance to the hotel, having called the kids as I walked back from the Retiro park, which is literally on my doorstep.

'Yes?'

'I'm Jorge. I'm the coordinator for the course.'

'Ah, Jorge, lovely to meet you. Are you early, or have I lost track of time?' I glance at my watch.

'Oh, no, you're not late. I just like to come here to relax, walk through the park, before dinner.'

'I just came from the park. It's lovely.'

'It's my favourite park in Madrid.'

I smile. 'Well, it's the only park I've visited in Madrid, but it's beautiful. And I only saw a tiny piece of it.'

He blinks and flashes me a smile. 'We'll have to see if we can rectify that tomorrow.'

'Would you like to have a drink first before dinner? Matías and Alejandro are running late, and Pilar says she is already in a bar around the corner having an aperitif.'

'Sounds great. Shall we go?'

Dinner is a relaxed affair, and the food is incredible, the company too. I feel so at home with this lovely group of people, and I am honestly sad to have to leave, but I sense that if I don't contact Dolores, she will hound me. She's lovely, but insistent. And I've already spent three hours over dinner with the team, so I'm not neglecting them. It's all too easy to lose track of time when eating the Spanish way: a leisurely meal with lashings of great conversation.

However, eventually, I do the deed and text her, saying I'm ready to be picked up. If I wait much longer, it will be after midnight before we go for a drink, and then I will be absolutely useless in the morning. And I need to portray myself in a good light, not have Fabien and Charles think I got pissed and wasn't up to the job, particularly as nothing could be further from the truth, on both counts.

With regret, I say goodbye to my new friends and tell them I'll see them tomorrow. I wait in the doorway of the restaurant, and a few minutes later, Dolores' SEAT skids to a halt beside me. I still find it unnerving how fast Spanish people drive. All of them.

Dolores greets me with a huge grin. 'Full up? Eating dinner so late is an art form. Get in.'

Five minutes later, Dolores pulls up outside a nondescript building out of which come the faint sounds of salsa music.

'It's a salsa club. My sister owns it. Come.' She ushers me inside, Caden, I assume bringing up the rear.

Once inside, Dolores leads us to a relatively quiet spot, away from the makeshift dance floor. Caden goes to the bar to get us some drinks, and Dolores explains to me a little about the origins of salsa, and how it originated in Cuba, but that there a great following in Spain, although Barcelona has the edge over Madrid with regards to the salsa movement. Nonetheless, she says Madrid has followed suit, and this club, *Bailar*, to dance, is the most successful in Madrid.

As she talks, I watch the men and women dancing the salsa steps. Caden returns and clocks me watching the dancers. I avert my eyes. I wonder if he's thinking what I am – how erotic salsa is. Maybe he's as uncomfortable as me, watching this type of dance, knowing our shared history, particularly when his girlfriend is sitting opposite.

It makes it so much worse that Dolores is lovely. She's so bubbly and vivacious and quintessentially Spanish, that it would be difficult not to like her. She's so full of joie de vivre and has such a zest for life that you feel an instant bond with her. She's truly a lovely person, and I feel like a terrible one, as I unwittingly snogged and indulged in a bit more with her boyfriend, albeit I didn't know he had a girlfriend, and I'm married.

How ironic that I had qualms about my trip to Madrid, and yet now I'm here, they have nothing to do with my presentation. I'm fearful of letting anything slip about my involvement with Caden, particularly after Dolores asks how we first met exactly, and we both start off saying different things. Awkward.

'So, how long have you and Caden been together?' I ask, picking the proverbial scab.

'Oh…' she glances at Caden '–two and a half years.'

I draw in a breath as surreptitiously as possible. So, it's serious.

'That's a long time,' I say.

She laughs. 'Sometimes it seems long–' she smiles at Caden '–like when we're apart for so long as with this job in Scotland, and before that in England. But other times, it's like it has also passed in a flash.'

I can't help noticing how good her English is, and I tell

her so.

She laughs. 'Thank you. I've had much practice, with Caden.'

I bet you have, I think, wryly, and I'm not talking about speaking English.

The next couple of hours pass in a mix of uncomfortable moments, sweet ones, and my wishing Dolores could be my best friend and that she wasn't Caden's girlfriend, because I feel horribly guilty. And I feel even worse sitting here, pretending Caden is nothing more than my brother-in-law's chef when not long ago we were almost tearing each other's clothes off, devouring each other's kisses.

God, I need to stop this. I'm about to make my excuse to leave, when Dolores says, 'Watch what I taught him.'

I gasp, wondering what she's referring to, but she leads him by the hand onto the dance floor, and they each move perfectly in synch with one other. It's torture to watch, but equally I'm fascinated, as I had no idea, and why would I, that Caden could salsa dance. It's hypnotic. I can't tear my gaze away, no matter how hard I try.

I'm counting down the seconds until the dance is over, when they come back to the table and Dolores says, 'Your turn.'

'Wh-a-a-t? N-n-n-no. I can't.'

She smiles. 'You can. You have Caden. He knows what to do. Caden, show her.'

Caden looks as if he would rather be anywhere than on this dance floor with me right now. The feeling's mutual, and it isn't helped by the fact the dance floor has emptied and we're all alone on it. Oh my goodness, the humiliation.

But Dolores is right, Caden does know what he's doing. And I partly enjoy, partly loathe myself for enjoying the dance, particularly as Caden is much closer to me than I'm comfortable with, the music is sensual as hell and I am so turned-on. Did I mention his beautiful girlfriend Dolores was watching? Yes, I did, didn't I? And now I feel like the female version of a cad.

It's exquisite torture. I can't decide whether I need it to end now, or whether I need it to be prolonged, but fortunately the music comes to an end, making that decision for us.

We walk back to Dolores, who is now clapping. 'Well done. See, you are a natural. A salsa dancer in the making. And now you can tell everyone you have been salsa dancing in Spain.'

I smile. 'Yes, that was great.' I turn to Caden. 'Thanks for being such a good teacher.'

When Dolores reaches into her bag for something, Caden takes the opportunity to mouth, 'I'm sorry.'

I give him a sad smile then yawn and say aloud. 'I'm sorry. I really better get going.'

'But of course,' Dolores says, fishing her key out of her bag. 'We have kept you up longer than expected. I'm sorry, I lied. I just wanted you to have a great time in Madrid. I am very passionate about my city, and I want other people to be too. I hope you enjoyed the salsa.'

'Oh, I did, very much,' I tell her. Well, it's partly true.

Dolores drives me to the hotel and gets out when I do. 'Well, Louisa, it was my pleasure to meet you. I hope your trip goes well, your husband gets his job, you like your new house and all goes OK with the baby.'

'Thanks so much, Dolores. The pleasure was mine.' I try not to dwell on the double-entendre there. The pleasure of having her boyfriend, or almost having, my inner devil says.

'See you, Caden. Enjoy your stay.'

Dolores curls a slender multi-braceleted arm around his shoulder and says, 'Yes, I have him for a whole week. Lucky me. Enjoy Madrid.' She blows me a kiss before getting back in the car and driving off.

I stand there for a few moments, watching the SEAT eat dust, then turn and trudge into the hotel. What a day!

I lie in my room thinking of what a tumultuous day I've had. Caden. Ronnie. Work. I don't know what I was worried about with my clients. Although we were having dinner and barely discussed work – apparently, that's not how things are done here – they put me totally at ease. It feels like I've known them forever. I drift off to sleep despite the constant honking of horns, the pealing of bells and the gentle burr of the air conditioning unit to combat the heat and humidity of the Spanish night, thinking only that life is definitely going in the right direction now.

At three months, the baby is approximately the size of a lime. 'Good night, little lime,' I say. It's as good an analogy as any.

Wednesday 11 August

To-do list

Look up guidebook so I can throw in some knowledgeable remarks about Madrid

Revise phrases I learned to show I'm making an effort with the language too. Hola, adiós, gracias, buenas tardes, suerte (good luck), salud (cheers)…

Learn Spanish – in case I get sent here again

Buy presents for kids and Ronnie

Do NOT screw up presentation

Remember flash drive
Drink water
Breathe
Do not tell anyone I'm pregnant

Sleeps until Aria starts school — 5

'So, in conclusion, I'd like to take any questions.' I beam round the room as twenty faces stare back at me. My drinking and foodie buddies from the night before smile back at me, but don't ask any questions.

'Come on, don't be shy, I don't bite.' That was brave of me. I wonder if the humour translates.

'Bite what?' Alejandra.

I guess it doesn't.

'Just kidding. I know what you mean.' Minx. I like her. She's funny.

All in all, the presentation seems to have gone well. Although there aren't any questions, there has been plenty of furious scribbling throughout the day. They could well be drawing stick men, or giant penises or playing Hangman or even writing their list to Santa for all I know, but they do appear to have enjoyed it. I've been glad, though, of the breather when it has been someone else's turn to present.

And I have no idea what I was worried about. Once I started talking, everything seemed to fall into place. Plus, they each had laptops with InDesign on, so I could show them easily enough with practical examples what to do. Some of them were learning a totally new skill, and were delighted to have the possibility to learn from someone who has been doing this role as long as I have; others were curious about the methods used and interested in learning how they could incorporate it into their day-to-day work, with their own clients.

Plus, Charles and Fabien had arranged some of the equipment I work with be brought up, for those jobs that we can do in-house. So, we experimented with laser-cut invitations and making foil ones. And Matías explained that they wouldn't just be using the skills they'd learned to make wedding invitations, but also for invitations for saints days, First Communion and other special events in Spain. The possibilities, he said, were endless.

'Louisa, good job. Very interesting and informative,' says Santiago, an intense-looking forty-something with glasses that don't quite fit him. I found it very distracting last night at dinner when he readjusted them on his nose about forty times. Today, during a full-length course, for my sanity, I didn't count.

And as I listen to Santiago and Matías discuss the presentation and what they've learned today and how they intend to implement it, I realise that I've really enjoyed myself: the presentation, the people, the culture change, the businesswoman-about-town part. And it hits me: I want more of this, although I do wonder how I'll juggle presenting abroad with an expanded family once the baby comes. Why is nothing ever simple?

'Now, after-work drinks,' says Matías.

Oh, no. Already I had to make excuses yesterday about why I wasn't drinking. Since I haven't yet told Fabien that I'm pregnant, the last thing I want is to let it slip to the staff here.

Fabien messages me whilst I'm at the bar with the clients. *Well done, I hear you nailed it. Will I see you before you move out?*

Me: *You can count on it. See you tomorrow.*

Chapter Twenty-three

Thursday 12 August

To-do list
Tell the kids we're having a baby

Sleeps until Aria starts school – 4

'Mama!' Aria sprints towards me the minute I swipe my room key and open the door to the suite. It's almost like she's been sitting waiting on me.

'I've been waiting for you.' Now, that's a tad freaky. 'Daddy told me you said you'd be home in forty minutes.'

'Hello, sweetheart. I missed you.' I hug her little warm body to me, taking in the mismatched shorts and T-shirt combo Daddy has clearly allowed her to wear today. Black and white stripes and yellow, pink and green spots. Nice. Fortunately, my darling girl is gorgeous, so she can carry it off…just.

'Hey, Mum.' Hugo enfolds me in a sandwich with Aria as we try to ascertain who has the greatest huggability factor. 'It's a draw,' I proclaim, desperate to draw breath.

'How was your trip, Mum?' Gen asks as she walks into the living area carrying a box of her stuff to go to the house, I'm guessing.

'Great. Presentation went well. Can't complain.' I omit any reference, obviously, to meeting Caden. Some things are best left unsaid.

'Can we all gather round, please? Ronnie, you too.'

He kisses me as he sits with the kids on the sofa.

'There are two reasons why I want you all together. First, I have some pressies.'

A collective cheer goes up, led by Ronnie.

I open my bag. 'Starting with the youngest, Aria, this is for you.' She comes forward and takes her parcel. Then I repeat the process for the other two.

'OK, open.'

Surprisingly, it's Hugo who needs help to open his, Aria leaving him in her wake.

'A new unicorn. Thanks. Mama.' She hugs my knees.

'Wow, Mum, this is so cool.' Hugo holds up a black T-shirt that reads 'I paused my game to be here' complete with various icons and some controllers in neon green text. 'Thank you.' He goes for the full Hollywood movie star kiss on the lips. Soon that won't be cool enough for him. He'll be walking three paces ahead of me or behind me, so I make the most of it, hint of Freddo taste and all.

Gen uncovers her tan leather purse with 'chica' emblazoned on it and flashes me a smile. 'I love it, but did you remember Nana's rule?'

I smile at her. 'Of course I did.'

She opens it and out falls a pound coin.

She grins. 'Just checking.'

'And last but not least…Daddy.' I hand Ronnie a gift-wrapped parcel. He opens it to reveal a black wallet of the softest leather. I could sit and stroke it all night. Now whether that's because I'm pregnant and behaving oddly, it's difficult to tell.

'Thanks, Mummy.'

'Can I have your old one, Daddy?' Hugo asks.

'It's kinda kicked, H,' Ronnie says.

'Don't care.' Hugo smiles up at his dad.

'Fair enough, little man. He removes the notes and cards from his old wallet and hands it to Hugo. Then he stops midway. Hugo frowns. Ronnie digs in a pocket, opens the coin section of the wallet, pops in a two-pound coin and passes it to Hugo.

'Can't have Nana giving us into trouble, now, can we?'

Hugo grins, and Gen says, 'Hey, I only got...' but I silence her with a look.

'Anyway,' I say, 'I'm not sure that rule works for wallets. But, you know, if you boys wanna copy us, far be it from me to stop you.'

'You said there were two things, Mummy,' Hugo says.

'Oh, I did, didn't I?' I pause for effect.

'Well?' Gen says.

'Well–' Ronnie comes and sits beside me '–the thing is, we're going to have an eighth member of the family.'

'Wow! Mummy, Mummy, are we getting a kitten?' Aria squeals.

'Or the hamster I asked for a while back. Please be the hamster, not the kitten. No offence, Aria,' says Hugo.

Aria's scowl, however, shows that offence may well have been taken.

'Guys,' Gen says, softly. 'I don't think we're getting a kitten or a hamster.' She's eyeing me very carefully, in particular Ronnie's hand on my stomach.

'We're getting a baby brother or sister, right?' Her face lights up when I nod.

'We're getting a baby! We're getting a baby! Yay!' Gen runs round the room, vaults over a table and then a chair, and continues on her lap of celebration.

'A baby? But I want a kitten!' Aria stamps her foot and runs to her room.

'I'd have quite liked a hamster, but I suppose a baby could be fun,' says Hugo, mulling it over. 'When it grows up.'

'Congratulations, Mum and Dad.' Gen stops her assault-course antics and holds her arms out wide. 'Group hug.'

The three of us hug, then Hugo joins us.

'Aria,' I shout. 'You're missing out on the best group hug ever. Get in here.'

The door opens and a sulky face appears, face blotchy.

'I won't be the youngest any more,' she says.

'C'mere.' I hold out an arm to her, and she rushes forward. 'You won't the youngest, but you'll be a big sister. Just ask Gen how amazing that is.' I drop a kiss on her head.

'Aria, you'll be the most wonderful big sister,' Gen says, wrapping her other arm around Aria. 'You'll learn from the best. Lesson one – bring it in.' And they stand and hug for a solid two minutes, long after the rest of us have broken apart.

It's these moments I need to hold onto. Today has been a good day. No, scratch that, it has been a fantastic day.

Friday 13 August

To-do list
Move house!

Check in all drawers, wardrobes and high places that we haven't left anything behind

Ensure all key cards are returned to reception

Leave tips for all members of staff who've dealt with us during our stay

Present for Fabien – leave in his office

Clean pen mark off wall in girls' bedroom where Aria got creative

Sleeps until Aria starts school – 3

It's the big move. Well, I say big, it's not as if we have furniture or anything to take with us. Thank goodness. It's bad enough packing up everything we've left around this hotel suite the past few months. And I'm glad Ronnie picked up the keys from Benedict the other day, as it's one less thing to worry about this morning.

Excitement is radiating off all three kids in equal measure. I'm sure Gen can't wait to have some privacy to FaceTime her friends again, or do what almost teenagers do. Aria just wants more space to play, so she'll love the playroom, and we've bought her a princess tent for her room, so she can go use it as a hideout within her room. Something special to remind her of moving into her new temporary home. We bought Gen one too. A different one, granted, but it's all floaty fabrics, and ditzy cushions, as well as a dash of sparkle and glamour. We may not be able to redecorate, but they will have their own little oasis within each of their rooms.

Not to be left out, Hugo has a Marvel-themed one. I think he's going to love it. In any case, the kids will adore having their own rooms, the playroom, the garden, more space. I can't wait. It's hard to tell who's more excited.

This morning before we started gearing ourselves up properly for leaving, Aria came and sat beside me on the sofa. 'Mummy, do you think the baby will like me?' she asked, face scrunched up in consternation.

'Yes, I do,' I said, solemnly.

She nodded her head, then pulled Cornie from behind her back. 'Do you think the baby will like Cornie?'

Hmm, trick question. Did she want to give the baby Cornie, or did she want to ensure the baby wasn't going to steal Cornie off her?

'What's not to like, Aria? Cornie's lovely, but the baby, when it comes, will have its own toys. In fact, you and I will go, specially, and choose the baby a teddy when it's born.'

'Really?' Her eyes lit up. Then she fell silent for a second. 'You know, Mummy, it would make sense for me and the baby to have matching teddies.' She raised an eyebrow as a challenge. 'Maybe Cornie needs a baby brother or sister too.'

I tried not to laugh at the blatant manipulation and instead agreed very seriously that she and the baby very probably did require matching teddies.

The last bag is packed into the car for the first trip. Ronnie took some stuff over the day I was doing my presentation in Madrid, but there are still a few things that won't make it possible to have only one journey.

Now I'm just champing at the bit to get started. To begin this new era of our life. Our new home. For a bit, anyway. Some stability. I heave a sigh. We could definitely be doing with some of that.

As I glance one final time at the suite, having already

ushered everyone ahead of me through the door, my mobile rings. Caden. Oh fuck! What does he want now?

I stab at my phone to turn it off and notice today's Friday the thirteenth. I'm not traditionally superstitious, but I wouldn't fly on a Friday on that date if I could help it. And I certainly wouldn't place any bets or walk down a dark alleyway – to be fair, I wouldn't do that last one anyway.

I shake my head to dismiss thoughts of Caden. No time for that now. It'll have to wait. Much to do this morning.

At reception, I ask if I can leave something for Fabien.

'Oh, he's actually just come in. You can give it to him yourself if you like.'

I go to protest. Now is not the time, what with the family about to leave for our new home, but I text Ronnie to tell him I will be five minutes as I need to speak to Fabien, and await his arrival.

'Louisa.' Fabien gives me a warm smile as he comes out of his office. 'You didn't think I'd let you leave without being here to wish you well in your new home, did you?'

I return his smile. 'Thanks, Fabien.'

'And very well done in Madrid. Charles and his team have been singing your praises. In fact, I have another project to discuss with you...'

He must see my anxious expression, as he says, 'But that can wait.' He glances at my bags. 'Are you leaving right now?'

I nod. 'Ronnie and the kids are in the car.'

'Oh, well, I won't keep you. We can catch up in a day or so.'

'Actually, Fabien, could we speak in private for a moment?'

He looks taken aback for a second then says, 'Sure.' He ushers me into his office, and I follow.

It takes me a second or so to find my voice, then I say, 'I just thought you should know, I'm pregnant.'

His eyebrows disappear into his hairline, and he looks wrong-footed for a moment before his composure returns and he says, 'Well, I wasn't expecting you to say that, but congratulations.'

I breathe a sigh of relief.

'So, how pregnant are you?'

'I've just had my twelve-week scan, well, at eleven weeks, but we didn't want to tell anyone, not even our families, until we'd had the scan.'

'No.' He nods. 'I can understand that.'

'I also wanted to tell you that's why I was so weird the day I first met Charles.'

He frowns as if trying to recall.

'I had severe morning sickness, and was feeling dizzy, but I couldn't tell you that's why I was being so flaky. The smell of coffee when the girl brought the pot made me feel ill.'

Realisation dawns. 'Ah, that explains a lot.'

'Yeah, sorry. I'm actually not incompetent.'

Fabien grins. 'I didn't think that for a second.'

I'm sure he's simply being polite, but I'll take him at face value.

I arrive at the car as Ronnie is closing the boot, which he opens to allow me to pop in the two light bags I'm carrying – I'm not 'allowed' to carry anything heavy now I'm pregnant. It's sweet of him to worry, but if I listened to him, I wouldn't even be lifting a packet of toilet rolls. I could see the point if it was a twenty-four pack of lager, but, well, then I'd probably have a different problem.

We wind our way back towards Ferniehall, leaving the delights of Garfield Grange behind. My heart lifts as we return to our little village, with its sleepy ambience and its overenthusiastic but concerned shopkeepers, nosy librarian and skilled baker. I've missed it all. I know we've been back to visit a few times, but it's not the same thing at all. I want to be able to walk the streets – no, that's not the image I was trying to create – stroll along the pavements of Ferniehall, stopping to chat to neighbours, looking in on Martha.

I know, eventually, the kids' curiosity will get the better of them, and Hugo and Gen will want to go and see what's happening with our own house, but for now, until the news is better, I'd rather not dwell on it, or even suggest they visit it.

At least for now, we have this fabulous house to move into, and make our own, for as long as we need it. The relief I feel at that realisation is indescribable.

Ronnie parks in the sweeping driveway. This time it's our driveway, and we're no longer visitors. The kids pile out of the car, and I simultaneously wince and smile – difficult to do. Have you tried? I'm hoping the neighbours in this ultra-sleepy cul-de-sac of Ferniehall will grant us a grace period. Kids will be excited, of course, on moving day.

Talking of kids, I don't see any out in the street. I didn't think to ask Benedict if there were any young families here, but then he probably wouldn't have known. He didn't live here.

Not that that will matter to my squad. They're chattering away like a troop of monkeys. From the way

Hugo is scratching himself and Gen is removing something from Aria's hair, you could be forgiven for thinking that evolution hadn't actually occurred.

The kids run ahead, straight upstairs to their rooms, I presume, to make them their own. They already half bagsied them when we came to view the house. Excellent. A bit of peace. I'll do my tour later. For now, I just want to unpack the car and sit down with Ronnie in our new front room and gaze out over the park from our lofty vantage point. The bay windows and the period features in the living room are as gorgeous as I remembered.

When we've hefted the final box into the house, Ronnie and I have that cuppa.

'The first in our new home,' he says. 'Ah, that's a good cup of tea. All the tea I used to get on the rig was like builder's tea – too sweet and too strong.'

I sip my tea and enjoy the relative silence. It's so big, this house. It's almost cavernous. I hadn't realised just how much bigger it is than our own home. And it's not as if that's particularly small.

'I can't believe Aria's starting school on Monday,' I say.

Ronnie blinks and shakes his head. 'That makes two of us. Seems like yesterday that she was…well, in there–' he points at my stomach '–and now she's a proper little person, off to school. And Gen, going into second year. How did that happen?'

'Mum, I can't get the wi-fi to work,' Gen calls down.

'Ah, nothing changes,' Ronnie says.

'Yeah, too lazy to come downstairs to tell us.'

Ronnie grins. 'Well, we'll need to pretend not to hear then, and I don't want you going up and down the stairs pandering to them. Not in your condition. Make them come to you if they want something, not the other way around.'

He's right, I know he is, but it's easier said than done. If I had to rely on the kids doing as asked first time around, or second time I called or shouted, I'd still be waiting now.

I nod in agreement just as my phone pings. Wendy.

Wendy: *Are we good to come over after I get back from work? I'm dying to see the place. What did the kids say about the baby?*

Me: *Of course you can come over. Jo's coming at five thirty. We'll get some Chinese in, or something, as I haven't been to the shops yet. It'll take a while to get back into the swing of things, I think.*

Wendy: *Sounds like a plan. I'll bring wine. And Brandon says he'll drive back. Result!*

Me: *Indeed! Although, clearly I won't be drinking. P.S. Aria wanted a kitten, Hugo a hamster, but they all seem fine now about the baby. Let's hope so as I can't send it back!*

The doorbell goes. Ooh, our first visitors.

'You stay there, Lou,' says Ronnie, heading for the door.

I hear him talking and a moment later, my mum and dad enter the living room. 'It's only us. Thought we'd pop round and give you a housewarming card and gift.'

'Aw, Mum, you didn't need to do that.' I hug her and accept the ficus plant she gives me. Please let me not kill it. I'm not brilliant with plants. But plants are good for homes, aren't they?

'Actually, that's not your real present,' Dad says, a huge grin splitting his face.

'Oh?'

He opens the door, and Patch and Bear bound in, almost knocking me off my feet. Wow, Patch has grown. And if possible, he seems to have got faster. He's snaking in and out of my legs at an alarming rate, alarming because I can't tell where his legs start, his tail ends and which bit's the middle. He's just a blur.

'Oh my God, my boys!' Never mind Patch being a blur, tears blur my vision as I put my hand out to pet them, then fold them into my arms. God, I've missed them so much. It hits me hard that Patch has grown so fast. He's a whirlwind of activity. He simply doesn't know how to act or what to do with himself. He knows me, but he doesn't. I'm his mistress, well, technically Gen, but really me. I pick him up. He's still small enough to put on my lap. The more sedate Bear comes to join us, and after pirouetting to find his perfect position, he audibly slumps at my feet. He has found his new home, within his new home.

'Thanks, Dad.'

He smiles and a look passes between us, and nothing else needs to be said. The debt of my gratitude to him couldn't be put into words anyway, but Dad knows how much I appreciate everything he's done for us, particularly with regards to these two very important family members.

'Are Ronnie's parents coming over soon, now that they don't need to come visit you in your bedroom?' She tries to suppress a laugh but isn't terribly successful.

'Mum, what have I told you about taking the mick? Ronnie's only next door,' I hiss.

'Well, I can't help it. What a ridiculous reason for not seeing your son or grandchildren. Couldn't she have met you in the foyer if it was too beneath her or unsavoury to meet you in your "bedroom", even though it was a suite? I mean, you were staying in a five-star luxury hotel, not a flea-ridden youth hostel!' She chortles, actually chortles at her own joke.

I glare at her. 'Annabelle isn't on my top hundred favourite people list, but if you don't quit it, you'll be joining her,' I say. 'Now, behave, and I can show you the rest of the house.'

Gen pops her had in. 'Nana!' She envelops her nana in a hug then says, 'Mum, did you just tell Nana to behave?' When I nod and roll my eyes, she turns to her nana and says, 'What did you do that upset Mum?'

'Never you mind,' I say before my rent-a-gob mother makes matters a thousand times worse. Gen loves her nana, but for some reason, she also loves her gran. Oh well, I suppose Annabelle is kind to the children at least. Probably because they have her full pedigree lineage, and because they're her heirs. To what, I'm not sure.

'Mum, can I show Nana the rest of the house? I'd love to do the tour.'

I smile. 'Of course you can. Now take her away before she gets on my goat any more.'

Mum sticks her tongue out at me, and Dad and I laugh.

'You can show me after, Louisa. Now, how about a cup of tea?' Dad says.

'Come on. I'll show you the kitchen.' I stand, much to Bear and Patch's dismay and walk towards the kitchen, the dogs trailing in my wake.

Chapter Twenty-four

Sunday 15 August

To-do list

Make packed lunches for everyone

Pack Aria and Hugo's bags

Buy more snacks for playtime – I'm sure Hugo and Aria have been siphoning them off

Buy lock for snack cupboard – ask Benedict if OK to adhere to surface

Ensure Gen has her bag packed

Recheck labels on all new clothes

Renew Gen's bus pass – too cool for Mummy to take her now. Let's see how that pans out when it's pouring.

Sleeps until Aria starts school – 1

Hours until I bawl my eyes out that my baby is starting school – 24 give or take

Hours until I bawl my eyes out that the freedom I expected when she went to school has now been revoked by imminent arrival of another baby – 25

'But I'm not tired, Mummy.' Aria is standing in the living room, for possibly the eightieth time this evening, repeating how 'not tired' she is, whilst looking like the sandman has sprinkled her with a sleeping potion. She's yawning, she's rubbing her eyes, and when she's not rubbing her eyes, her ears, all sure-fire signs she's exhausted.

'Aria, you can't start school until after you go to bed and go to sleep, just like with Santa,' I reason.

She frowns. 'But the school doesn't have to come to our house, Mummy. The building's still going to be there tomorrow. Santa has to come visit us.'

She's such a wee negotiator. And the fact she's deciphered all this is impressive, but also damned annoying.

'Aria, Hugo is in bed. Mummy is going to bed in ten minutes, so you need to go to bed and to sleep.'

'But I'm not tired.'

Oh my God, I'm so sick listening to that phrase. My eyes meet Ronnie's, willing him to throw me a lifeline here, but clever man that he is, he's staying out of it. He knows how strong-willed she is, and I was the sucker who engaged with her in the first place. More fool me.

And with Aria, there's no point grounding her; she's only four. There's no sense in reducing her TV time, or taking away a favourite toy, as she doesn't respond to that. So, I do the only thing I can do, I promise to go lie beside her in five minutes, so she can fall asleep with me. Ronnie's already read her four stories. We haven't even had dinner yet.

I nip into the kitchen and wolf down three biscuits. That may be the sum total of my dinner. It's highly likely I'll pass out before Aria. She's absolutely hyper, and that was with us being ultra-careful not to give her any treats after two o'clock today as we knew how wired she'd be.

I lie in bed beside Aria, her Shimmer and Shine bedcover
barely covering me. Although it's August, the nights are
cool, and I wish I'd put my pyjamas on. The shorts I'm
wearing feel skimpy now, and I shiver.

'Mummy, you know if you're cold, you can cuddle
me,' Aria says.

I'm already cuddling her. We'd have to merge into one
entity for me to be any physically closer to her. I love my
daughter dearly, but right now, I'd love her even more if
she'd go to sleep. It has been a long day, and I'm exhausted.
Belatedly, I realise I didn't even bring my phone upstairs
with me so I could keep track of time. Note to self: buy a
clock for Aria's room.

'Mummy, will school be like it was when we went to
visit?'

I sigh. She has asked me this question a thousand times
over the summer, as well as asking me to relive each of her
settle days, particularly those Ronnie took her to, as she
didn't want me to miss out.

'Yes.'

A pause. Great. Maybe that's her satisfied for the night
and we can get some sleep.

'Mu-u-ummy…'

Not bloody likely.

'Yes, Aria?'

'Won't it be very boring if we do the same thing every
day?'

Good luck with that, you'll be there for the next twelve
or thirteen years. Deal with it.

'Not at all, honey. The teachers find different activities
for you to do each day.'

A pause. I hold my breath.

'But what if I'm not very good at them?'

This is new. Aria doesn't worry about anything. She has the confidence of a seasoned politician. She could go up against Boris Johnson or Donald Trump any day of the week, and she'd win, at four.

'That won't happen. The teacher practises it with you all until you're sure what to do.' I readjust the pillow, my eyes getting heavier, my throat scratchier, and I yawn.

'But what if I don't get it?'

'You will, sweetie. C'mere.' I entwine my arms around her and nuzzle my face into her neck, giving her a kiss on the cheek.

'You'll be just fine.'

'I love you, Mummy.' She snuffles and clutches Cornie.

'I love you, too, Aria.'

'I think I'll love the baby too.'

'That's good. It will love you too.'

She pulls back from me slightly as if to view me properly. 'Mummy, will the baby be a boy or a girl?'

'We don't know yet. We have to wait and see.'

'Why?'

'Because it has to grow some more first.'

'And then we'll find out?' She eyes me suspiciously, like I'm lying.

'Yes.'

'OK, Mummy. Night night.'

'Night, Aria.'

I'm just drifting off when Aria bolts upright. Has she managed to have a bad dream in that time? Does she need the toilet? Is she feeling sick?

She turns to me and gazes into my eyes. 'Mummy, will you still love me when the baby comes?'

Not this again. 'Yes.'

'Will you love me more than the baby?'

I sigh. 'Aria, as I've told you before, I love all of you the same. You, Hugo, Gen, and it will be the same with the baby.'

She exhales noisily. 'Fine. Night, Mummy. Love you.'

'Love you too, sweetie.'

I wake up, and it's silent and dark, the table lamp off and only the night light shining pink from the socket. What time is it? Ugh, my head hurts. Oh, that's right, there's no clock in here. I ease myself out of bed and pad along the landing to my own room. As I approach, Ronnie's presence is guaranteed from the snoring emanating from within.

I open the door, and the digital clock reads three thirty-two. For God's sake. No wonder I'm always stiff and feel about ninety. I never seem to spend a full night in my own bed. And it's such a shame, as this is a fabulous bed, even better than the one we have at home. I crawl between the sheets, after setting the alarm on the clock. I can't be bothered going to the living room to retrieve my mobile, and I don't want to disturb the dogs. The last thing I need at this hour is to set off a cacophony of barking due to my unexpected entrance downstairs.

Roll on tomorrow. It's a big day for us all. Or rather, today. I'm looking forward to getting some time back to myself. And with that thought, I yawn and spoon into Ronnie.

Monday 16 August

To-do list

Ensure bodies are at correct school at correct time
Packed lunches, snacks, pencil cases, trainers for PE – we don't
know which days they are yet
Buy new rain jackets – damn it, I always forget something

'Mummy, I'm going to school today. Yay!' Aria is jumping
on our bed, although it feels like she's pounding my head
with bricks. I'm glad someone's bright-eyed and bushy-
tailed this morning, because I'm not.

Fixing on my best smile, I rise onto one elbow, plant a
kiss on Aria's proffered cheek and swing my legs over the
side of the bed. Time to face the day.

Unsurprisingly, Aria is first dressed, the first to have
breakfast and the first to be anxious to leave for school.
Hugo, meanwhile, has to be coaxed out of bed.

'I'll go later, Mummy. I'm tired.'

Tired. He doesn't know the definition of tired, clearly.
Try sleeping in a single bed for half the night as an adult
with your sister. That's tired. Oh, did I mention I was
pregnant with my *fourth* child? I swear if Aria kicks off
tonight, it's Ronnie who's fulfilling that task. I'm going to
hole up in my lovely big bed in my fabulous new bedroom
with a novel. And headphones, or at the very least ear plugs.

'Aria, it's not time for school yet. It's half past seven.'
You should only just be getting up now, I want to tell her.
'And remember you start later today. Nine forty-five,
because it's your first day.'

She stamps her foot. 'But I want to go with Hugo.' She
turns on Hugo. 'Hugo, you promised me we'd walk to
school together.'

Hugo, who's munching his own body weight in Rice Krispies replies, as soon as his mouth is empty, 'I will, Aria, but I didn't mean today.' He dips his spoon in again and soon resumes keeping Kellogg's in business.

Gen yawns and sits down at the breakfast table, hair damp from the shower. I smile at her. 'Morning, darling. How you feeling about starting second year?'

She shrugs. 'Fine.'

Oh no. And just like that we're back to school. It must be the scholastic influence that encourages monosyllabic responses in teenagers.

'Looking forward to seeing your friends?'

She nods. 'Yeah.'

Riveting. I hope the English essays she submits are more interesting than those responses, or she won't get far.

'So, does everyone know what's happening today?' I ask.

Everyone looks at me blankly. I exhale heavily and say, 'Gen, you're taking the bus with your friends. The bus leaves at eight fifteen.' I turn to Hugo. 'Hugo, school starts for you at five to nine. Dad will walk you to school today as Aria and I have to come in a bit later.'

Hugo nods, his mouth still full of cereal.

'At home time, I'll pick both you and Aria up, Hugo. I collect Aria from inside the playground, but I have to wait for you outside the outer gate, so if you aren't out sharp, I'll probably already be out at the gate. I'm guessing they'll let the primary ones out a few minutes early.' The last part I say partly to myself.

'Gen, you're getting the bus back, but you must be home before half past four. It's fine if you want to spend a little time with your friends after school, but half past four is your deadline. Take your phone with you, ensure it's charged, but don't use it in class.'

She rolls her eyes at me as if to say 'as if'.

'Good, we're clear. Progress. Daddy, what are you doing today?'

Ronnie has just tumbled into the room, wearing only pyjama bottoms, hair all mussed and standing on end, like Hugo's. When he looks at his son, it must be like looking in a mirror.

'I'm going to enjoy my last few days of freedom before I start my new job.'

'Daddy!' I use my special don't-mess-with-me, we-have-stuff-to-do, focus tone.

'Oh yeah, I'm taking Hugo to school, then going to see Gran and Grampa.'

'Excellent. So, we all know what we're doing. Toast, Ronnie?'

'Yes, please.'

'Patch, drop that. Drop it right now.' Patch is dragging Aria's Shimmer and Shine lunch box through the hall, a sheen of drool covering the handle. Patch ignores me.

'Ugh, Patch. Stop that.' Aria stands over him, and his ears go back. His puppy eyes droop, and he drops the offending article. Aria wags her finger at him. 'Don't do that again, naughty boy.' Patch lies down and covers one eye with a paw.

Great, now not even the dogs listen to me, and in fact, Aria is Patch's mistress, not me? Gee whizz.

'Now, do we have everything?' I ask. I'm using the royal we, as I'm addressing Gen and Hugo. Gen needs to leave, I estimate, five minutes ago, and Hugo and Ronnie, since they're walking, as was our vow for this year – to walk to school as much as possible and cut down on emissions – need to leave in five minutes.

'Water bottle?' I count the items off on my fingers.

'Check,' Hugo says.

'Pencil case?'

'Check.'

'Snacks?'

'I added a few more. Check.'

I scrunch up my eyebrows. 'Why did you add a few more?'

Hugo turns a fetching shade of tomato, all the way to the tips of his ears. 'I ate some last night after you packed the bags.'

'Hugo!' I rail at him. 'That's the point of packing the bags the night before.'

'I know, but I was hungry, and I didn't want to go into the kitchen…'

'Why not? Were you afraid of the kitchen monster or something?' I'm aiming for levity in the face of being supremely exasperated. Best-laid plans and all that.

'No, but you can hear me rustling in the kitchen.'

'Hugo! We'll deal with this later. In fact–' I turn to Ronnie '–you and Daddy can have a nice chat about it on the walk to school.'

Ronnie goes to protest, but I silence him with a warning glare. Time to step up, Daddy. Onshore Parenting 101 starts here. And since he still hasn't started his new job, he can fulfil the role this week. It's about time I got back to my job, and, well my new partnership with Fabien and Cerulean.

'Bye, Mummy, see you at three o'clock.' Aria kisses me on the cheek and wraps her arms around me in a hug, then walks away without a backwards glance. Well, that's me surplus to requirements now. I walk through the assembly hall door as the children are escorted by the classroom assistant up to their classroom to meet their teacher and their peers.

On my way through the playground to the exit, I look back up at the school and see Hugo waving at me from a second-floor window. Ah, so that's which classroom he's in this year. Different to Gen's primary four class then. She was round the other side, overlooking the sports field.

When I reach the gate, several mums and one dad are standing chatting, tissues on display, red eyes also. I don't know all of them, but I stop when one asks me how Aria settled.

'Fine, she'll be just fine.'

'Our Daisy was a wreck. They'd to pull her off me as she was holding onto me like a limpet. It was awful. I don't know who was the most upset.' From the looks of it, her mother was.

'Jessica wouldn't stop talking, she was so excited, and the teacher had to ask her to stop talking so she could speak. She doesn't know what she's let herself in for. My daughter could talk for Scotland. Good luck to her. She'll need it,' another mum says.

The only man says, 'My sons were both fine, but then as twins they have each other. They were just a little upset my husband couldn't be here to see them start school, but he's at a conference in Dubai.'

The light goes out of one woman's eyes. I guess she'd already pegged him as a yummy daddy then. And he is, but unfortunately for her, he's very much taken.

'Best get on. Must make the most of when they're in. See you all later.'

'Yeah, see ya,' they say.

I wait until I'm round the corner, where no one can see me, then I burst into noisy tears. Hormones.

I've almost reached home when I decide to have a stroll through the park. It's so peaceful now that the kids are at school. Only toddlers with their parents, retired people and the occasional nanny – yes, we do have some nannies in Ferniehall – frequent the park when school's in session. I walk round snapping a few shots, of flowers, the bandstand, the little duck pond, where a mother duck is leading her ducklings past some lily pads. I burst into tears again. For goodness' sake. She's only gone to school. I'll see her in less than six hours. Think of all the things I can do in the meantime. Like enjoying the park. And it's lovely, so relaxing.

I sit on one of the wrought-iron benches and turn my face upwards to the sun, letting it bathe me in its warm glow. This is the life. I know I need to return to my new reality soon, but right now, I'm living in the moment.

I close my eyes and listen to the birds twittering in the trees. Absent-mindedly, I wonder what type of birds we have here. Swallows? Swifts? Chaffinches? Sparrows? Quite frankly, I know the fast ones are swifts and maybe swallows, but unless it's a parrot, a toucan or a robin, I honestly have no idea. Where was I when they were giving nature lessons at school? My knowledge of birds, plants and flowers is abysmal, although I'd do quite well on a wildlife quiz, as long as it didn't feature birds.

Their twittering is so soothing. My eyes droop. I'm so tired. I hope Aria doesn't play up tonight at bedtime. I'm shattered. I'll just rest here for a little minute. I'm aware of my breathing slowing, and I relax.

'All the Single Ladies' blasts out of my phone. God, what a fright I got! I'll kill Gen. She's been messing with my ringtone again. Why, I'll never know, as she has her own phone. I think she does it to see if I can figure out how to change it back. With my brain cell loss since pregnancy, that's debatable.

Ferniehall Primary School? Surely Aria hasn't got herself in trouble already? I have visions of Aria refusing a child entry to the sand pit because they used her rubber or took a book she wanted to read. There are so many options. I knew that girl would be trouble the moment she bawled her lungs out for the first time.

'Hello?' I say.

'Mrs Halliday, it's Christine here at the school. There's been a bit of an accident…'

Chapter Twenty-five

Monday 16 August

I make Ronnie drive slowly into the car park, even though it's tempting to approach like a boy racer. I ran all the way from the park to the house, calling Ronnie on the way. He'd reversed the car down the drive by the time I got there, and I jumped in the car, and we hared it over to the school, within the speed limit, of course. As he drives, I notice it's ten forty-five. I must have fallen asleep on that bench. I probably had drool attractively dripping from my chin. I know concentrating on minutiae is just my way of coping, but it's working for now.

Apparently, Aria fell off the climbing frame at playtime. She's hurt her arm, and they think she needs an X-ray. Are they being cautious or do they suspect it's broken? First day, for goodness' sake. I knew she'd be trouble, just not this soon.

When we arrive at the office, one of the staff buzzes us through, and we immediately see Aria sitting outside the school office with her classroom assistant, tears running down her dear little face. She's a brave girl. If she has been crying, it's sore. I nod to the classroom assistant, who is holding an ice pack to her arm.

'Aria, we're here, sweetheart,' I say.

'Mummy, it hurts. It hurts a lot,' she says, before

bursting into noisy, snotty sobs.

'Hi, honey, we're going to take you to the hospital to let the doctor see you, OK?' Ronnie says, hunkering down so he's level with her, and dropping a kiss on her head.

'I'm trained in first-aid,' Ronnie says to the classroom assistant. 'Let me see.'

She takes the ice pack away, and Ronnie sucks air in through his teeth. I don't need him to tell me it's broken. The angle her arm is at is so unnatural, and I can see bone almost poking through the skin. She must be in terrible pain. Ronnie exchanges a look with me.

'Let's just put her in the car,' I say.

'We can't give her anything for the pain,' he whispers, before he picks her up, careful to protect the side of her clearly broken arm. 'She may need to go into surgery, and if she's had pain relief, that may delay it or mean they can't give her something stronger.'

It's her right arm, naturally. Had to be. She's right-handed. Why is nothing ever straightforward?

We thank the staff and carry her to the car, where I sit in the back with her, whilst Ronnie drives. I do my best to soothe her, and wish I'd thought to ask the school for a book or something, a toy, to distract her whilst we drive, and for when we reach the hospital, particularly given hospital waiting times.

Ronnie reaches into the passenger seat. 'Give her this,' and he produces Cornie.

Thank God. When it mattered, he came up trumps. Cornie is the one thing that might help her right now, although I'm sure she'd far prefer an arm with no bones sticking out.

The hospital's not so far away, about fifteen minutes or so, and since rush hour is over, we reach it quite quickly.

We're lucky enough that it's not a Saturday night and

there are no boozed-up or drugged-up individuals filling the waiting room. It hits me as we enter that it's not long since I was last in A & E with Nicky and Xander, and bile rises in my throat. Articulated lorry, Xander under the cab, Nicky pinned against the wall. Wow, I wasn't prepared for that. My head spins, and I hold out a hand.

'You OK?' Ronnie's voice is full of concern.

'I'm fine. Flashback,' I mutter. Nausea swirls in my stomach, and I bolt for the visitor toilet.

When I return, Ronnie is eyeing me carefully. 'You don't look fine. Here, sit down. They've said they shouldn't be too long in triaging Aria.'

I sigh with relief. 'Thank goodness for that.' I turn to her. 'How are you, sweetie?'

Tears run down her face, but she's being so brave. I want to take her in my arms, but I sense she's better in her daddy's at the minute. He seems to have found a position for her that's the least painful she can expect at the minute.

'It still hurts,' she croaks and then snuffles into Cornie.

I stroke her hair in an attempt to provide her with some sort of comfort. It's hard to know whether to chat to her about what they did at school before playtime or to let her be quiet. In fact, it's usually more worrying when kids are quiet. How I long for her to be noisy now. That way I'd know she was OK. Poor wee thing. On her first day too. What was she doing on the climbing frame? I thought only primary three and upwards were allowed on it for this exact reason. Don't they have playground monitors? I know I haven't been to the most recent PTA meetings, but I thought the younger children were segregated at playtime from the main areas, to protect them, in case the bigger ones, being a bit more rough and tumble, fell on them.

All of this is going round and round in my head, until I hear, 'Aria Halliday?'

I sigh audibly, and we stand up and follow the triage nurse.

'Hi, Aria, I'm Layla, one of the nurses here. I'm just going to ask you a few questions, is that all right?'

Aria nods, tears still flowing down her face. Wee soul.

After Aria's been triaged, the wait seems interminable but is probably only twenty minutes to half an hour, but when your child's in excruciating pain, a minute is an hour, an hour is ten.

Whilst we wait, I text Mum and Dad and ask if they can pick Hugo up from school later and wait at home with Gen and Hugo if we're not back. Once again, I think of how much of an advantage it is having my parents so close.

'Hi. I'm Dr Chopra. Is it OK if I have a look at Aria's arm?'

Ronnie and I nod.

'Aria, I'm a doctor, and I'd like to have a look to see what's going on with your arm. Is that OK?'

She nods but holds on to me with her left arm.

The doctor presses gently on her arm and surveys it from all sides, trying to move it as little as possible, then seeing if he can move it without causing too much pain.

'Well done, Aria. What a brave girl.'

He turns to us. 'So, she's going to need surgery as she has snapped her radius.' He points to the bone which is almost protruding through the skin. I knew it was bad, but snapped? I feel sick. Surgery. She's so tiny.

'When will she go to surgery?' I croak.

'We'll get her admitted shortly. I think there are some beds available.' He glances at the nurse behind him, who nods. 'We'll get her some pain relief, and we'll see when we can slot her on the theatre list.'

Roll on disaster movie, part two. Seriously? After all the crap we've been through recently, this is what's thrown at us now? Surely, we've had our fair share of bad luck.

'How long will she be in for?' Ronnie asks.

'Depends how the surgery goes. And also, when she goes to surgery. I'm hopeful she can go today, but if we have an emergency, it may be tomorrow. And as it'll be a general anaesthetic, she'll have a recovery period too.'

I feel sick again. A general. I hadn't thought about that. Of course that's what she'll have. The idea of my baby being put to sleep makes me want to throw up again.

'Will I be able to stay with her?' I ask. 'She's only four.'

'Four. And first day at school, I see.' The doctor smiles at her. 'Well, you certainly made an impression, didn't you?'

Aria gives a weak smile.

'I'll leave you with the nurse for now. She'll explain what'll happen next.'

'Thanks, doctor,' Ronnie and I say.

Within the hour, Aria is in the children's ward, and I'm installed in the chair beside her. Apparently, I'll be allowed to sleep there with her overnight. Ronnie has gone home to get some clothes for Aria and me and to pop in and see my folks to update them. He also cancelled the trip to see his parents but filled them in about Aria.

Aria, fortunately, manages to drift off to sleep for a little bit. I take the time to let Fabien know as we were meant to be having a meeting tomorrow morning and I won't be able to do that since I'll be staying in hospital overnight.

What a start to school life. I log in to the Wedded Bliss account and see a few things outstanding. Poor Mum. She has all this to handle, and has had to deal with most of it, whilst I've been with the kids and the whole apocalyptic situation we found ourselves in after the crash. Just when I thought we were getting back on our feet, and I could take over the reins again, this happens.

And it will fall to me, naturally, as Ronnie starts his new job next week. Petrocord don't hang about, plus they wanted him to be able to attend a group training Monday to Friday in Aberdeen. So, he won't be home until Friday night. What a mess.

I gaze down at Aria. Life is so unfair. A general anaesthetic, aged four.

Images of Aria's arm not healing properly flit through my mind, and I wish I'd asked the doctor if it would heal one hundred per cent. She's really young, though. Aren't their bones soft and malleable when they're young? That should be a good sign then, hopefully.

Ronnie appears with her Shimmer and Shine backpack and my black one with some clothes and snacks. I guess those are for me. I'm not sure if they'll feed me when I'm in here, although I recall when Aria was ill a few months ago, I did quite well out of it.

'No news yet on when she'll go to theatre?'

I shake my head. 'Not yet. I'm just glad she's so exhausted, she's flaked out. At least she can't feel the pain then.'

'I know. Look, why don't you get some rest at home, and I'll stay? If you're staying overnight, you'll be exhausted from sleeping on a chair all night.'

'Thanks, but I'm not leaving her.'

Ronnie smiles slightly. 'I understand. No worries. Just know that the offer stands.' He lifts a chair over and sits down.

We're lucky, in one way. Currently, Aria is in a four-bedded room and no one else is here. I'm sure it won't last long, but I'll take the wins where we can get them, especially at the moment. I lie back as far as I can on the recliner and close my eyes.

My eyes fly open when a nurse comes in some time later and says, 'We're going to prep her for theatre.'

My heart sinks, and I reach for Ronnie's hand. When I glance up at him, he's deathly pale. How have I not noticed this before? I squeeze his fingers. He's evidently more concerned about Aria than he projects.

Hours pass, but they seem like decades. Ronnie and I sat in relative silence, only the faint hum of the overhead strip lighting for company, until they wheeled Aria's bed back in. Since then, we've still barely exchanged a word. It's hard to tell whether it's weariness or worry that drives this.

Ronnie's phone bursts to life.

'It's Gen.' He holds the phone out towards me and puts it on speakerphone. 'Hi, darling. You OK?'

'How's Aria?' She's crying.

'Hey, it's OK. I know it's worse because you can't see her, but I'm right in front of her, and she's sleeping now. The doctor says the operation went well. Hopefully, she'll be home the day after tomorrow.'

'Is she really OK? You're not just saying that to make me feel better?'

Ronnie leans towards the phone a little. 'Princess, she's definitely OK. Mum and I both promise you. Can you look after Hugo for us, help him get his stuff ready for school, show Nana and Papa what he likes for snack, that kind of thing?'

'Yes, Daddy, no problem.'

'She'll be home soon, Princess. I promise. Night.'

'Night, Dad. Night, Mum.'

'Love you, Gen. Tell Hugo we love him and Daddy will be home soon.'

'Will do.' She hangs up.

'You'd be as well to head home, Ronnie. Nothing else is going to happen here tonight. We'll probably have to wait for the consultant in the morning, and from memory that's around eleven o'clock. Certainly no earlier.'

'You sure?'

'Yeah, I'm sure.'

'Right.' He kisses me on the head. 'Let me see if I can get you another blanket first. That one would barely cover a Tiny Tears.'

I manage a weak smile. 'Thanks.'

I'm checking through my work emails when he comes back a second later with a woolly blanket. 'Here you go. That'll keep you a bit cosier.'

I put the phone on the bedside locker. 'Thanks. Ronnie, can you stay a few minutes longer whilst I nip to the loo? I don't want to leave her on her own for even a minute.'

'Sure.'

I take my backpack and give myself a quick wash in the bathroom. It's amazing what freshening yourself up can do for morale.

'Right, all sorted. Ready for a sleep.'

'Yeah, see ya.' He heads towards the door. 'Let me know if anything changes.'

I frown. That was a bit abrupt. The stress of today must have finally got to him. No matter. He's going home to look after the kids, and I'm here to look after Aria. All that matters is that our girl heals, and quickly.

Chapter Twenty-six

Tuesday 17 August

To-do list

Can't even think of it with Aria in hospital.

I sleep fitfully, waking every time I hear Aria breathe differently, the clink of a trolley in the corridor, the whistle of a porter, the hushed murmur of nurses talking to each other, or the beep of Aria's bedside monitor. I hate hospitals. I hate them even more when one of my children is in them. Plus, the hourly checks the nurses make on Aria, though necessary, prevent me from falling into a deep sleep.

Aria is still asleep, her blonde curls falling haphazardly about her face. Apart from that, she doesn't look as if she has stirred all night. Certainly, I haven't noted any change in her position. I guess the painkillers they've given her have really knocked her out.

As dawn breaks, I take the opportunity to nip to the toilet, which is fortunately in the room, and wash my face and clean my teeth. As I return to Aria's bedside, a nurse, who looks to be in her sixties, comes in.

'Would you like some tea and toast?'

I could kiss her. 'That would be great, thanks.'

'She's a wee trooper, your girl. I was monitoring her

during the night. She's doing well so far.'

I give a faint smile. 'Thanks.'

I start going through my messages, replying to Sam, Nicky, Wendy and Jo, some of whom only heard late last night what had happened. As I'm replying to Wendy's, another message comes in. Caden.

Oh, for God's sake. That man's timing couldn't be more off if he tried. And anyway, what the hell does he want? I'm married, pregnant and he has a lovely girlfriend.

Hi, Lou, forgot to say in my earlier message, I really enjoyed seeing you again. C x

You have got to be kidding me. We're not going down that road again, and somehow, in hindsight, I realise what a mess me and Caden were. Me and Caden. Well, we weren't exactly a thing, but we had the potential to be a thing, and that is just as dangerous.

Wait a minute, what message? I got a lot of messages yesterday, but not one from Caden. I check, then double-check. Nope. Nada. He must have sent it to someone else or have it in his drafts. Or maybe I deleted it by mistake. Yeah, that's probably more like it. There's been so much going on, what with school starting and Aria ending up in hospital, then her op. I actually struggle to compute how much happened on the same day.

My fingers hover over the keys. Do I reply or not? It's quite clear he lied to me about having a long-term girlfriend, but hey, we weren't an item, although somehow that still seems duplicitous, and it definitely doesn't sit well with me.

Sod it! I bash out, *Didn't get a message from you*

yesterday. And I leave it at that. Surely that's stark enough for him to not want to reply.

Aria stirs, and I slide my phone into my bag and move over to her bedside. She's still pretty flushed and by the looks of it, still out of it. Poor baby.

My phone buzzes. Ronnie calling.

'Hi. How is she?'

'Yeah, she's had a good night, apparently. I didn't want to call you when it was the school run.'

'I was going to wait until after, but Gen doesn't know where Hugo's football boots are.'

'Oh crap, they're at Mum's. She was last to take him to a game. He can just wear his trainers today. Once won't kill him.'

'Fine. They've come home with all these forms from school to be filled in. There's pages and pages of them.' He's leafing through them as I can hear the rustling in the background. 'Internet security, school trip permission, social media permission, medication forms, Therapet form....'

'Yeah, we get them every year.'

'We do? What a load of–'

'I get it, Ronnie. Don't worry. They can wait a few days. I'll fill them in once we're home again.'

'I assume you haven't seen a consultant yet.'

I raise a hand up and outwards to stretch. I'm so stiff from lying in the chair all night. A passing cleaner raises her eyebrows and I smile. 'You assume right. I'll call you when there's any update.'

'Fine.' The line goes dead.

Someone's in a bad mood...

Wednesday 18 August

To-do list

Ask Mum to pick up a welcome home banner for Aria and give Ronnie Hugo's football boots for next time

Tell everyone that the consultant says Aria's op went OK and we're hoping to be home later

Update the school that she won't be in for around 2 weeks

'How's my favourite girl?' Ronnie comes into the room, which is now home to three other children and their families, and I'm even more glad Aria's getting home today.

'Really good, Daddy. Look at my cast. Remember Xander had one. We'll be twins.'

'Well, not exactly. Xander's cast came off last week. In fact–' he pretends to study her cast with great seriousness '–are you sure that's not Xander's cast you're wearing?'

'Ugh, no, it's not!' She bats him on the stomach with her good arm.

A glimmer of my feisty wee monkey returns, and I'm delighted to see it.

'Oh, I have something for you, from your teacher and your classmates.' Ronnie holds out a gift bag.

Aria's eyes go wide as I help her open the gift. First, a card, with everyone's names, or attempts at names – they are only four or five – on it, and then a lovely gift wrapped in pink tissue paper.

'Mummy, can you unwrap it, please? It's hard with only one arm.' Her eyes are shining. Whatever it is, I hope she likes it.

'It's a narwhal! Oh, I love it.' She picks it up with her left hand, nestles it in the crook of her elbow, then hugs it to her.

'She's lovely,' I say. 'What are you going to call her?'

Aria fixes me with her most scathing look and then rolls her eyes. 'Tell her, Daddy.'

Who's 'her', the cat's mother? I want to say, but refrain, in case I sound like my own mother.

'Its name?' Ronnie asks, looking like a sloth that's just noticed an oncoming truck and knows it won't get out of the way in time.

'Yes.'

'Oh, it's a very special thing, sharing a teddy's name for the first time. I think you should do it.'

Aria solemnly nods her head and says, 'You're right, Daddy. I can't believe Mummy didn't notice though.'

'Notice what?' I scrunch my eyebrows, and from the blank look on Ronnie's face, he has no idea what she's talking about either.

'Mummy, it's a boy narwhal, not a girl. And his name will be Wally, because he's a nar-wall.'

'Ah, apologies, I hadn't realised, sweetie. Makes perfect sense.' If you're four.

'Maybe Daddy can make Wally some breakfast, whilst I go and grab some downstairs at the canteen.'

Ronnie shoots me a 'help me' look as I pass, and I simply smile and keep walking.

Aria enjoys being waited upon by her siblings, although the novelty wears off fast for them, particularly when her demands include 'Bring me a fudge' and 'Cornie needs a bandage too.'

I'm in the middle of making some cannelloni when the

doorbell rings. I frown. I'm not expecting anyone.

I hear Gen open the door. Clearly, it's not someone selling something or asking if we need a new boiler as her voice sounds happy.

I'll pop this in the oven and then see who it is. But before I can do so, Nicky enters the kitchen, followed closely by Valentin and Xander.

'Nic!' I give her a hug and take in how well she's moving. She's considerably more mobile and steadier on her feet than she was a few weeks ago.

'Thought I'd come and see how the invalid is.'

'She's in the living room, holding court.'

Nicky grins. 'I've taught her well.' It strikes me that this is the first time Nicky has been to the new house. She's been decamped at Valentin's since she left hospital.

'Oh, Xander, is that for Aria?' I ask, taking the gift bag he has offered to me.

'Yes.' He smiles politely. 'Can I go play with Hugo? He's been wanting to show me his room for ages.'

'Of course. He's either in the playroom or upstairs. You'll find him, I'm sure.'

I turn to Nicky. 'Tea or something stronger?'

'I'm still on painkillers, so tea, please. In fact, no, I'll go all out and have real coffee, if that's OK.'

'No problem. Valentin? What would you like? Ronnie's in the garden. If you want, I'll bring you out some drinks. I think he's having a rare five minutes away from Aria's orders.'

Valentin gives a belly laugh. 'I can just imagine her ruling the roost. She needs to run for government.'

'Don't put ideas in her head. She'd be on the next train to London.'

269

Valentin leaves, I pop the pod machine on, then say, 'Let's give Madam this first, then we can have a chat.'

'Good plan.' Nicky smiles and it lights up the room and my heart. It's a relief to see her looking so well again.

'Hello, beautiful. I heard you'd been super brave,' Nicky says.

'Not as brave as you, but thank you,' she says with the sweetness of a Hollywood child star.

'Mummy told me you had a new narwhal from school, called Wally.'

'That's right. I named him myself.' She looks so pleased with herself, I have to turn away so she doesn't see me choke back a laugh.

'Well, I thought maybe Wally, since he's new to the family, he might like a new friend.'

Aria's nose rises in the air, curiosity piqued. She's squinting and trying to work out what's in the bag. Nicky takes it out of the bag for her and lays it on her lap. Aria doesn't need help unwrapping this one. There's paper flying in all directions. Subtle she's not, nor graceful.

'A dolphin!' she cries. Then she looks at it again and says in consternation. 'But dolphins are grey. Is this a special white dolphin?'

'No, this is a whale.'

'But whales are blue,' Aria says as if Nicky is dumb. I really must discuss with her how to mask her thoughts and feelings better. OK, she's four, I may have some wait.

'Blue whales are, but this is a special one called a Beluga whale, and he's my favourite. He's a big white whale who looks and feels a bit like a dolphin, but he's much bigger,'

Nicky says, clearly hoping her knowledge and personal connection will satisfy Aria.

Fortunately, it seems to. 'Hmm, OK. But Nicky, it's a girl, not a boy. Her name's Belle. And her last name's Uger.'

I can't help thinking that if we take Belle's first initial and add it to her surname and pronounce it slightly differently, we have what my daughter is a lot of the time, a wee b...ger.

'Lovely name,' Nicky says, the corners of her mouth twitching. 'Suits her.'

'Coffee?' I say, extending the metaphorical rescue pole to drag Nicky to safety.

She raises both eyebrows. 'Yes, please.'

Once we're in the relative safety and peace of the kitchen again, I make us coffee, and we settle down to chat. I love how there's a sofa at one end of this kitchen. It renders the space so casual and friendly.

'So, how are you really?' I ask.

She sighs. 'Getting there. Unsure when I'll have full mobility, but the physio's happy with my improvement. And as you can imagine, with money no object for Valentin, he's ensuring I see the best doctors. He wanted to move me to a private hospital when I was in originally, but I couldn't face moving. It was bad enough being there in the first place without having to be uprooted all over again.'

I give a sad smile.

'Plus, I'd built up a great rapport with one of the cleaners. She kept bringing me in Border biscuits.'

'I'd have brought you them in if you'd asked.'

271

Nicky clasps my hand. 'Oh, I know you would, but I've said I'll do the photos for her son's wedding. They're getting married next year and they've had such a terrible run of luck – kinda like ours.' She rolls her eyes. 'He lost his job, someone crashed into her car, the hotel they were meant to be getting married at went into liquidation and they lost their deposit.'

I go to interject, but Nicky stays me with a hand. 'And before you tell me, she's giving me a sob story, she didn't know what I did for a living at that point. So, they've finally got a date and a venue, although it's not as "luxurious" as the original one, she's paying for their honeymoon to Paris, and I said I'd happily turn up and do some photos, as they were just going to have friends film it on their phones.'

'You're too nice, you know that.' I nudge her with my shoulder.

'You'd have done the same. In fact, it's when stuff is taken away from you, like it was from me, you realise how much you still have and what's important.'

I know she's right. When the crash occurred, I didn't care about anything else, only the people in my life, those who were in that room. Nothing else mattered. And I'm just thankful that they're in my house again now, and that everyone is on the mend.

Chapter Twenty-seven

Monday 23 August

To-do list
Get Hugo's football boots back from Mum
Ask Wendy what to buy Logan for his birthday on Friday
Buy a 10 card for Logan
Reply to email re Patch's puppy training classes
Change Patch to different puppy food – research it – he seems
to have an intolerance
Dog chews and new dog toys
Worming tablets and flea tablets order for both dogs – call
vet – ask to send out

'Good luck. You'll be fine. See you Friday.' I kiss Ronnie
on the lips and expect him to linger a little, particularly
since I've made the effort to get up with him at five as he
has to go to Aberdeen for a nine o'clock start, but he stops
at a peck and heads out. He should have gone last night,
but he wanted to stay another night with Aria. Truth be
told, she asked him to stay, so he cancelled his Travelodge.

Once Ronnie has gone, it's almost like old times, when
it was just Bear and me, well, and now Patch, before the
rest of the house had stirred, except we're now in a different

house. Oh, fine, it's nothing like it at all. Bad analogy. Anyway, I'm enjoying my cup of coffee from the pod machine. It's not a Nespresso, it's a De Longhi or something. But the coffee it produces is lovely, and that's all I care about. Note to self: add pods to to-do list.

Bear and Patch are lying below my feet. I need to wake the kids soon for school, although Aria has another full week before she'll go back. The hospital suggested keeping her off as she's so little, she – and other kids – don't understand the concept of no-contact play.

I'm ordering some samples for Wedded Bliss and trying to catch up on the myriad of emails that have come in from Cerulean. I hope I haven't bitten off more than I can chew with this partnership. I was under the impression I could handle it, but I was basing that on living a normal life, not one constantly mired by chaos and disaster. Goodness knows how I forgot that was my day-to-day life and not an exception.

A message comes in from Caden. For the love of God. I'd ignored the last few messages. His *She wasn't the one. We were on a break* – channelling *Friends* with that one – and *Why are you so angry at me?*

I'm not angry, I'm disillusioned, and quite frankly at the moment, just pissed off, but I couldn't care less about Caden right now. I just want some luck. I'd simply like a chance to get back on my feet without the rug being pulled from under me every time. Is that too much to ask?

However, clearly not responding isn't having the desired effect.

Me: What do you want, Caden?

Caden: I miss you, I miss our chats. Our easy banter.

Me: *But you said you'd moved on. You know you need to move on. It can't be, between us. We can't be. I'm married. A mum. Pregnant with my fourth baby.*

I'm not sure I can be any clearer. Whilst, undoubtedly, I was in lust with Caden for a while, his fall from grace in my eyes was when I met his kind, gorgeous, funny Spanish girlfriend. And that only worsened when he texted me after he returned from Spain.

I mean, if I'm honest, he, and I, still flirted a little as we ate breakfast in Gatwick before taking our connecting flight to Madrid. And we got along so well, it was like chatting with a friend I'd known my whole life. It didn't even feel like flirting at the time, just indulging in some banter with a friend I was enjoying catching up with.

Caden replies again. *I just want us to be friends.*

Me: *I don't think that's possible for us.*

I drain my coffee and set my phone aside. Time to wake the kids.

Gen seems much more lethargic than usual. I hope she isn't getting her period. I mean, I know technically she should be getting it around now, but if the powers-that-be could give me a few more weeks, a couple of months even, to get back on my feet before springing that on me, I'd be eternally grateful.

'Hey, honey.' I slide my arm around her shoulders when she surfaces.

She gives me a wan smile. I frown. I hope she isn't coming down with something. That's all I need. The minute they return to school, everyone gets sick, and we all start falling over like dominoes. I place my hand against her head. No temperature.

'You feeling OK, hon? You're a bit pale.'

'Pale and boring,' says Hugo.

'Hey!' I bat him on the arm. 'Don't be mean to your sister. Apologise right now.'

'Sorry,' he says sulkily.

'Gen?'

'I'm OK,' she says, unconvincingly.

I decide to leave it for now, but I'm definitely keeping an eye on her.

'Bye, Hugo. Hey, where's my kiss?'

He rolls his eyes, comes up to the car door and fist-bumps me. Fist-bumps me. Oh, no, it's happened much more quickly than I expected. Second week of primary four and my kisses at school drop-off are no more. I thought I had at least another year.

The one positive I've managed out of our new school run is that we don't have three trips to make now, only one. Gen travels with her friends, and with Aria in primary one, albeit not attending school since her first day, I only have one drop-off and pickup to make. Result.

This morning, I have the follow-up meeting from my trip to Madrid with Charles Pickford. This time, it's just him and me, at the Glaston again. He made a follow-up appointment and Fabien has a conflict with his schedule, so he agreed that as long as we were both happy to hold the meeting without him, I could fill him in afterwards.

I arrive in plenty of time. He seemed happy with the work I did in Madrid. Now I want to be able to completely wipe out any reminder of the disaster that was our first meeting, by wowing him at this one. I got on well with his staff, so hopefully I can channel the same confidence as I found with them. It would help though if I could let go of the lingering vision of our previous meeting being me throwing up in the ladies.

When I return from my meeting, Aria is watching *Paw Patrol*. That girl has her nana twisted round her little finger. I decide to go easy on her. She has had a bit of an eventful start to her school life. And she'll return next week with everyone else knowing each other, since they've been in class for two weeks. Knowing Aria, that won't stop her becoming either teacher's pet, class clown or a mix of both by the end of the week. I smile at her resilience. She has an undeniable knack for being able to bounce back despite all odds.

I work near the living room bay windows as so much light streams in. It hasn't been as easy to accommodate both me and Mum in the same home office, but we're finding a workaround. Plus, currently, one of us has to spend time with Aria, whilst the other works. I don't want Aria sitting watching TV when she's supposed to be at school, much though she wouldn't complain at that.

All too soon, it's time to go pick up Hugo, and I haven't even done half of what I wanted to get through this afternoon. Mum offers to stay with Aria so I don't have to take her up to school with me. Once it's clear she's happy enough with that arrangement, I take the dogs' leads and walk up to school with Patch and Bear. It's a beautiful day, and usually I don't take the dogs, as I either have the car or have two hands to hold, Aria's and Hugo's, but since it'll only be me and Hugo, the dogs can come. And they're so well behaved. They're not likely to jump up and knock someone off their feet. Well, Patch could, if he was bigger, but he's still titchy. Bear is just an affable sort. He goes with the flow.

'Mum! You brought Patch and Bear!' Hugo's smile says it all as he allows me to kiss him on the cheek then takes Patch's lead from me as we walk back down to the house, via the park, and he tells me all about his day.

'I've got a few leaflets for you. We're having a health day next week, so no uniform that day because we'll be trying out different sports. And that's free, I think.' He frowns. 'And then we have a sponsored silence for the Beastie Cancer Care unit in Glasgow.'

'Beatson,' I correct softly.

'But you have to pay me for that.'

'Hugo, I'd pay handsomely to see you be quiet.' I laugh when he elbows me in the ribs.

'And you have to ask other people to sponsor me too. Like Aunt Wendy, Sam, Nicky, Uncle Rhys…'

'OK, although I think you'll find you need to ask them, not me. It's you who's doing the sponsored silence.'

He blows out a breath. 'Why do I have to do everything in this family?'

I try not to laugh. 'Hardly everything, Hugo. Now, quit whining, or I'll sign you up for sweeping chimneys.'

'Mu-u-um! You don't get chimneys any more.'

'Yes, you do. We have a chimney in our new house.'

He thinks this over for a minute, realising I'm right.

'Well, you don't get many chimneys.' He thrusts one hand in his pocket. 'No, Patch, no!' as Patch decides to do a wee right on the pavement.

'Let's hope it's just a wee he needs,' I say, sloshing some of the water from my bottle over it. That's the best I can do at short notice.

We walk through the park and sit on the bandstand steps, the dogs at our feet.

'I like the new house, Mummy,' Hugo says, peering through the trees in its direction.

'Me too.' I tilt my face to the sun, hoping it can instil me with some energy. We have homework to do next. That's always a joy. He's fine once he starts, but it's always a saga getting Hugo to cooperate once he's home, when all he wants to do is go out and play.

By the time Hugo and I make it back, it's twenty to four. Gen should be home any minute.

'Come and get a snack, Hugo. What would you like?'

'Ham sandwich, please, and strawberry milk.'

'OK, go wash your hands and go say hi to Nana, and then it should be ready.'

I'm placing the strawberry milk back in the fridge when the front door goes. Must be Gen. I walk into the hall, but no one is there. I frown. Strange.

I stand at the bottom of the stairs and see faint signs of shoes tracking up them. 'Gen,' I call up the stairs. No answer. 'Gen.' Still no answer. I take Hugo's snack through to him and shrug when Mum raises an eyebrow, then I pad upstairs to Gen's room. The door's closed. It wasn't, mid-morning.

I ease the door open. Gen is lying on the bed, a box of tissues beside her. A snuffling sound comes from under her pillow, which her head is beneath.

'Gen, what's wrong, honey?' I sit on the edge of the bed and stroke her back, willing her to turn over and come out from under the pillow.

Terrifying thoughts race through my head about the reason for her crying. I need to know my fears are unfounded. Finally, she lets me lift the pillow from on top of her head, and turns and flings herself into my chest, where she continues to sob.

'Hey, it's OK, it's going to be OK, whatever it is,' I say, hoping that's true.

When she finally calms down, I look into her eyes and say, 'Tell me what's wrong.'

She starts to tell me, but dissolves into more sobs. Then between breaths, she says, 'Rain broke up with me. He says he just wants to be friends, but some of the girls are saying he met someone in Switzerland, that they've seen photos of them together on Facebook. I just want to die.' And she bursts into tears again.

Well, she is almost a teenager, I suppose. Her hormones will be all over the place, and her teenage angst is commencing its upward trajectory. I should have seen this coming, particularly with me being hormonal too at the moment.

'Gen, I know it's hard at the moment, but believe me, throughout your life you'll meet lots of boys. Rain is a lovely young man–' God, I feel old saying that '–but you'll meet lots of equally lovely boys in the future. By Christmas, I promise you, you'll barely remember you were upset.'

'Christmas!' she shrieks and falls forward onto her

pillow again.

OK, that was clearly the wrong thing to say. Well, I'm new at this 'teenage management' thing.

'Hey, Gen.' I stroke her back again and her hair, trying to calm her down. 'He still wants to be friends. It's not that he doesn't like you, he does. He just met someone else who he likes too.'

'But I don't want to share him!' she squeals, going for a full-blown snot-fest now.

'No, no, you won't be sharing him.' Crikey, I had better get better at managing this stuff and soon. 'But you'll still see him, just as friends.' I've obviously forgotten the angst teenagers suffer when someone breaks up with them, and how it really does feel like the end of the world. Like there's no point living. Until the following week when they meet the new boy in town, or their big brother's new friend, or their sister's geeky schoolfriend who has suddenly become super-hot.

'Hey, I know it's tough, but how about we get some hot chocolate and churros and put on *Kung Fu Panda*. It's her favourite animated movie. The original one, although the second is a close-run thing.

'I have homework,' she says, between sobs.

'We'll do it later.' I want to see a smile on my beautiful girl's face, and I know Master Shifu and the gang is the way to do it.

Chapter Twenty-eight

Monday 30 August

To-do list
Remember Aria's appointment card
Money for meter at hospital for parking
Start looking for something to get Jo
Bedtime pants for Aria – has started wetting again – probably all the upset

'Right, Aria, time to go.'

'Do you think they'll let me keep my cast, Mummy? I thought maybe I could put it on my wall.'

I look at the cast. It's dirty, tatty and I'd like to consign it to the bin right now, but I realise the physician has to OK it first. 'How about we get you a nice poster, Shimmer and Shine maybe, to decorate your room with instead?'

'Ooh, good idea, Mummy. I love Shimmer and Shine.'

I'd never have noticed. I refrain from rolling my eyes.

The doctor had us in and out of Orthopaedics in ten minutes and, yes, Aria asked to keep her manky cast. Wee minx. She was trying to have the best of both worlds. My vigorous headshake to the doctor ensured the filthy thing met a grisly end in the hospital incinerator.

'So, you can go straight to school, now, poppet,' I say as we drive out of the hospital car park.

'Oh, I'm not going back there, Mummy.'

'No, I know, the doctor said you don't need to.'

'Not the hospital, Mummy. School. I'm not going back to school.'

OK, this is new, and rather unexpected. I thought she'd be dying to go back to school and affirm her position of head of whatever, probably head prefect at four, or possibly head girl. This girl doesn't consider anything out of reach.

'Aria, you have to go to school, five days a week, like Hugo. It's the law.'

In the rear-view mirror, I see her fold her arms. She's so authoritative, even in a high-backed car seat.

'Well, it's a silly law, and I'm not going, so that's that.'

I do hate when my children parrot some of my own phrases back at me. 'So that's that', 'and that's the end of it', 'because I said so'. God, I really am turning into my mother, and whilst I appreciate there are worse mothers I could imitate, or be compared to – Ronnie's, for example – I'd rather not be compared to my mother. Makes me feel ancient.

'But all of your new friends will be missing you.' She was only there just over an hour, but knowing Aria she spoke to at least twenty people in her class during that time, and she already knew most of them from nursery and the village anyway.

'Humph.' She's not to be mollified, is she?

'And what's that game they play at playtime? Corners? That sounds really fun. Hugo loves that.' She's always wanted to play Corners, but there are rarely enough children around to make it worth it.

'Fine! I'll try it. But if I don't like it, I'm coming home.'

Over my dead body. I'll have a word with Mrs McMaster, the headmistress, and the janitor. I'll ask him to check there are no gaps in the fences or hedges she can escape through, as once Aria has her mind set on something, it's very hard to change it.

I drop her at school, explain the situation to the staff, and am about to head home to do some work in what's left of the day prior to the school run at three when a message pops in from Ronnie.

Hi, Lou. I've booked something for our anniversary. Wendy's babysitting. Pack an overnight bag for Friday. Ronnie x

Friday? What's today's date? Thirtieth of August. Oh crap, he's right. It's our anniversary in a few days. I hadn't even remembered. Note to self: buy Ronnie anniversary card and present.

Me: *Sounds fab. Where we going?*

Ronnie: *A-ha, that would be telling. It's a surprise.*

Me: *Oh good, you know me, I love surprises.*

Ronnie: *Oh, you'll love this one x*

Me: *Can't wait x*

Friday 3 September

To-do list

Pack sexy underwear – by that I mean something that isn't

grey or Mummy pants. I won't be able to fit into them for much longer

Leave updated instructions for Wendy
Buy Nutella and honey nut flakes
Conditioner
Waxing

Ronnie has been incredibly mysterious about where we're going. He hasn't even told Wendy. And those two get on really well. Usually, he divulges things to her that he doesn't even tell me. He did, however, give me a beautiful Salvatore Ferragamo forest green scarf as an anniversary present. Not sure what I've done to deserve it, but check me, I'm wearing Ferragamo, darling!

No, kidding aside, I don't care about labels, but I love the scarf. It's gorgeous, just like my lovely husband, who, for once, bought me an extremely thoughtful gift. It makes the Hugo Boss shirt I bought for him seem paltry somehow, but it was one of the few things I could order and be sure it would arrive in time. I didn't have time to go into Glasgow for a browse, so online shopping was my go-to solution this time.

Since it's a mystery location, and I don't even know whether it's a lodge, or a hotel, or a yurt, I've opted for palazzo pants – really hoping it's not a tent, as they won't be the warmest. Also hoping it's not a campsite, as the heels I've worn are completely impractical for a field. Fortunately, my chiffon tunic will pass muster wherever we go, and I've teamed that with a slightly more substantial yet still dressy long cardigan so that I'm not absolutely freezing. Still worried about the tent possibility. Ronnie has a funny sense of humour. But if he does try to get me to eat beans out of a camping stove on our anniversary, I'll brain him with the bloody thing.

'You guys ready to go?' Wendy asks, once she has all three kids' bags packed and set to leave for hers for the night.

'Think so. Difficult to be sure when you don't know where you're going,' I say pointedly, inclining my head towards Ronnie, who is watching the exchange with interest, and dare I say, a slight smirk.

'See you tomorrow, Mummy.' Aria hugs me round my tummy. 'Bye, baby,' she whispers.

'Love you, darling. Be good for Aunt Wendy.'

'Mummy,' she deadpans. 'I'm always good,' she says in that self-assured and annoying way Hermione from Harry Potter has.

'So, we shouldn't have a problem then, should we?'

'Bye, Mummy. I'll look after Gen and Aria, for you,' Hugo says. 'Just you go with Daddy and have a good time.'

I glance over at Ronnie, but he's staring into the distance, his eyes unfocused.

'Thank you, little man.' I adopt Ronnie's phrase for Hugo, in light of Ronnie being on another planet at the moment. 'Be kind to Gen. She's having a rough time.'

'I will. You can count on me.'

'Oh, I know.' I ruffle his hair and turn at the sound of Gen talking to Ronnie. He pulls her in for a hug, and she buries her face into his shoulder and hugs him round the middle.

It's lovely to see them like that. He's her rock as well as mine.

'Right, everyone, time to go. I need to lock up,' I say

eventually, aware of the time. I'm hoping Ronnie has arranged dinner somewhere for later, as I'm starving. I also hope it's not too far away. Same reason.

The radio is playing a mix of hits from the eighties and nineties as we head up the A9. I wonder where we're going: Dunkeld, Pitlochry, Blair Atholl. They're all lovely little towns, in the heart of Perthshire, one of the most beautiful areas in Scotland. My mind roams to the luxury lodges I've coveted in the past, too expensive to justify splurging on. And at only just over an hour away, totally doable for a romantic weekend break away.

I have to say, I'm touched, and impressed. Ronnie isn't often one for making grand gestures, and I couldn't tell you when we last celebrated our anniversary away, but whether it's because we're expecting another baby, or because we've had a terrible time of it lately, he seems to have stepped up and taken matters into his own hands. He never books anything. I book all the holidays, check out hotels, lodges, everything. I pack almost everything. I buy almost everything, including the majority of the clothes he wears. So, for him to make an effort to treat us for our anniversary is special, and I appreciate it. Now I just need to know where we're going.

Jokingly harnessing Hugo, I say, 'Are we nearly there yet?'

He glances across at me and smiles. 'Not yet.'

'Will a Twix spoil my appetite?'

His eyes crinkle in amusement. 'Since when has anything spoiled your appetite?'

'You know what I mean. Have you planned dinner for

us?'

He frowns and shakes his head in a 'seriously?' fashion.

'Is it more than baked beans on a primus stove?'

He laughs out loud at that. 'Yes, it has a very nice restaurant. Satisfied?'

Ooh, so it's a hotel, or at least, unlikely to be a lodge. A snippet revealed.

'Are we far away?'

'What do you think this is? A séance?' Ronnie raises an eyebrow.

I burst out laughing.

We settle back into silence for a time then one or other or both of us sing along to the hits we know.

All the lovely towns I had considered earlier whizz past, then I see a sign for Aviemore. That'll be it. He'll have booked us somewhere there, or on the outskirts. I remember him saying the village of Boat of Garten was nice, but I've never been.

Aviemore comes and goes, and my eyes start to drift closed. Well, I am pregnant, I'll just have a little doze until we get there. That way I'll be refreshed.

'Here we are.'

I sit bolt upright. My mouth feels furry. I'll be brushing my teeth once I check in. I look around me. Outside looms the King's Compton Hotel. Looks rather nice, if a little like it plays host to coach trips, if the car park is anything to go by. As long as there's no tartan carpet, we'll be fine.

I yawn and unfold myself from the seat. Standing on the gravel and embracing the sky, I stretch as if I'm worshipping a god. Or maybe it's a yoga pose. Or maybe I just need to stretch.

Ronnie is all smiles. He's clearly pleased with himself.

'What time is it?' I ask.

'Eight o'clock. We just have time to check in and freshen up before dinner at half past.'

'Sounds good,' I say as my stomach betrays the fact I haven't eaten in far too long.

'Evening,' the receptionist says. 'Have you stayed with us before?'

Ronnie tells her we haven't whilst I realise I'm not actually sure where we are. I must ask him in a minute. I'd look an idiot asking in front of the woman. Maybe they'll have some literature on the hotel with the address on. I cast around the reception area, but it's all leaflets for whisky tours and castle trails and nothing remotely useful at all.

She hands us an old-fashioned key with number seven on it. Good. That's my lucky number. If she'd given me thirteen, I'd have had to hand it back. OK, maybe I am a little superstitious, but I don't avoid walking under ladders, as long as it's safe to do so.

Our room is lovely, understated, nothing like the Madrid room overlooking the Retiro, not like the suite we'd been staying in at Garfield Grange, but it's a big room, lovely bay windows, an armoire – no, this is definitely a wardrobe – a king-sized canopy bed with voile curtains over it, and the room smells nice. Molton Brown toiletries. Very swish.

But now I'm hungry, so a quick wash and I'm good to go for dinner.

'The soup today is lentil and chickpea, and the specials are on the separate sheet at the back of the main menu.' Our server pulls my chair out for me, and I thank him and sit.

'Would you like to see a wine list?'

Ronnie shakes his head. 'I'll have a lager shandy. Lou?'

'A sparkling water, please.'

The server smiles and says, 'I'll be right back.'

'This looks really nice,' I say, taking in my surroundings. Open fire over on the right, in a kind of snug area, stone fireplace, comfortable leather bucket chairs, pristine tablecloths, mood lighting, ambient music. It gets my vote.

'Monkfish…' I say.

Ronnie grins. 'Do you remember that year that every restaurant we went to, all their high-end dishes were monkfish and Parma ham?'

'How could I forget? We must have eaten it about twenty times that year.'

'What do you fancy?'

'Wouldn't you like to know?'

'Check you, getting fruity,' he says.

'It's being pregnant that does it.' I smile.

'Anyway, I think I'll have the scallops to start, then the halibut.'

'Good choice, I'm having the king prawns then the roe deer.'

'I don't like rowing,' I deadpan.

'Lou, that was absolutely rubbish. I should divorce you for that.'

'You know you love my jokes, really.' I lean over to kiss him on the lips, but jump backwards as if stung by a hornet. Caden is standing four feet away from me, chef whites on, his mouth agape, as if he can't quite believe his eyes. I know how that feels. He's so wrong-footed, he almost drops the platter he was carrying. Ronnie, oblivious, to all this, has suddenly realised I'm not listening to him and turns around to see what has captured my attention.

'Caden, fancy seeing you here. I didn't realise you'd started up here yet. When I spoke to Travis last week, he said you'd been away seeing family.'

Seeing family, my eye. Seeing Dolores, and lots of her, I'll bet.

Caden transforms immediately into Ronnie's best mate. 'Yeah, I've been coming back and forth a few times in the past month or so. Sorry to hear what happened with your house, by the way.'

Ronnie sighs. 'Yes, it was a nightmare, but we've moved into a house not too far away from ours for the foreseeable. Hopefully, we'll have an answer soon about whether ours can be rebuilt.'

'Yeah, that would be good if it could. A lot of upheaval otherwise.'

'It would indeed, and not the easiest thing to deal with when you have three kids, and another one on the way, eh, Lou?'

I think I'm going to be sick. At least Caden knew about the baby, but it feels as if Ronnie's laying it on a bit thick. And why are we here? Surely Travis wouldn't have suggested this? As I look around, I see all the references to seafood, Salty Squid lettering discreetly positioned above the servers' area. Oh my God, I can't believe I didn't realise we were here. I didn't know the name of the hotel, only the restaurant. That's all Travis told us, I'm sure of it. Not even Caden mentioned the hotel's name when we went to Madrid.

Caden has turned the same colour as his chef's whites. Finally, he says, 'Sorry, I'll catch up with you guys later, but I better go, or no one will be eating tonight.'

'See you,' Ronnie says, and I give him a tight smile, and whilst Ronnie's back is to me, my eyes widen at Caden, and I shrug. Hopefully, he interprets that as 'I had no idea we were coming here.'

My heart's racing, and I can't think why we've driven all the way here, for hours, to stay at the hotel Caden is chef at. Coincidence? I don't believe in coincidences. But if Ronnie knew about what happened between Caden and me at Ayren and Eloise's wedding, why only act upon it now?

No, I've got to be overthinking things. He probably fancied doing something nice for our anniversary, remembered Travis had this venture in the Highlands and decided to check it out. That'll be it. I need to chill and breathe and actually eat my food, as otherwise that will be a giveaway, especially after saying how starving I was.

When my food arrives, it looks gorgeous and smells delicious, to begin with, then my stomach churns, and I have to rush to the toilet.

The server returns shortly after I return to the table to ensure everything is OK as he sees I haven't touched my food.

Ronnie gives a wry smile and says, 'She's pregnant. Nothing wrong with the food. Just certain things set her off.'

Like that. Like him answering for me. Oh God, I dry heave again. I'm going to have to walk through this restaurant again and suffer the indignity of throwing up again. I think when I go back to the table, I'll tell Ronnie I need to go to bed. I feel terrible after all the effort he's made for us to come here, but it's all too much, and the smell of the seafood was the final straw. My poor stomach couldn't cope.

I'm standing at the sink, staring at my bedraggled, now greasy-looking hair, sunken eyes, and I wash my mouth out and swirl water around it and dig in my bag for a mint. I wonder if I can even keep that down. I breathe in and out, in and out, in and out. I feel as if I'm going to faint. I lean heavily on the sinks for support as my vision starts to swim.

I look up, about to try to lever myself up and away, to return to the dining area and tell Ronnie I'm going back to the room, when Caden fills the doorway.

'Caden, what are you doing in here?' My voice is shrill.

His eyes are full of concern. 'I'll apologise if anyone comes in. You look terrible. I saw you come in and knew something wasn't right.'

'Thanks.' I aim for a smile.

'Sorry, I didn't mean it like that. Here, wait a minute.' He disappears and returns a second later with a chair. 'Sit down. I don't think you'd make it to the dining room in the state you are at the moment.'

I don't even have the energy to resist. I do as bid and sit. I try to control my breathing, but it's not easy, particularly not with Caden standing right beside me.

After a few minutes, I have my breathing back under control. I raise my head to see Caden looking at me with a mix of concern and something else.

'You OK?'

I nod, although that wasn't the best thing to do as I sway a little again. He holds out a hand to steady me. 'OK, on the count of three, we're going to stand you up. Got it?'

'Yes.'

'One, two, three.' Caden supports me as I stand, but I wobble and cling to him as spots dance in front of my eyes. I'm just about managing to focus again when Ronnie bursts in and says, 'What the hell is going on? Get your hands off my wife.'

'She's feeling faint, Ronnie. I'm trying to help her up.'

'Yeah? What were you even doing in the Ladies' toilets in the first place?'

Caden doesn't have an answer to this and can't come up with an excuse quickly enough. He moves away from me as Ronnie supports me instead, his hand on my back, his arm round my shoulders.

'Lou, let's get you to the room if you're not feeling well.'

Back in the room, I change into my pyjamas and lie on the bed, a bowl strategically positioned below it.

'I'm sorry I ruined our dinner, Ronnie, especially after you went to so much trouble.'

Ronnie's face scrunches up in frustration. 'To hell with the dinner, Lou. I don't care about the dinner!'

His tone startles me, and I try to sit up, my eyes wide.

'I care about you and me, and our family, our growing family.'

'So do I,' I say.

'Do you?' He paces the room. 'Because it seems to me that you and Caden are a little bit closer than you should be.'

'He was just helping me because I felt unwell.'

'Don't lie to me, Lou. I know something's going on between you, or went on between you. I know it.'

My mouth falls open before I can stop it.

'See, your own body betrays you. So, did you sleep with him?'

I'm about to say 'I'm not going to dignify that with an answer,' but then realise how guilty that makes me look so I don't, but by that time, Ronnie has taken my hesitation as a yes.

'I knew it. How many times? Where? In our home?'

'No! Of course not.'

But Ronnie assumes that's my answer to his final question and says, 'So where did you sleep with him? When? Easy enough, I suppose, when I was away from home so often. Mug that I am, working away on an oil rig for a decade, trying to make enough money for my family, but all the time you've been shagging the chef, and God knows who else!'

His voice has risen several octaves, and I'm sure people in other rooms will be able to hear.

'Ronnie, keep your voice down, you'll disturb–'

'Keep my voice down? I've just found proof that my wife has been shagging another man and you want me to keep my voice down? Is that all you care about? Appearances?'

'I have not been "shagging another man".'

But Ronnie won't stop. He points to me. 'Is that baby, that baby you're carrying now, even mine? How could you do this to me, Louisa?'

'Of course it's your baby. Our baby. How could you even suggest that? How could you even think I would do that to you?' I say hotly.

Tears are running down his face now. 'I love you, I've always loved you, but I know something happened between

SUSAN BUCHANAN

you two. I could see it in your eyes, both of you. And the way he held you and was so gentle with you, you don't behave that way with someone you don't know intimately.'

He runs out of steam and sits on the end of the bed with his head in his hands and cries.

'Ronnie, you're partly right. Caden and I had "a moment", for want of a better word. A kiss. But that's all it was.'

He looks up from beneath his hands. 'And that's all it was, a kiss? You didn't sleep with him? Nothing else happened?'

I mentally cross my fingers, trying to blot Ayren and Eloise's wedding out of my mind. 'Yes, a kiss, and no, nothing else happened.'

'Where?'

'Does it matter?'

'It does to me.' Ronnie's staring at me intently now.

I sigh. 'OK, it's when we were away for my birthday in the Lake District.'

Ronnie's eyes darken. 'In the Lake District, with the kids and your sisters.'

I wince at the implication that the act took place whilst our children were around.

'Yes. Everyone had gone to bed. Caden had forgotten his mobile phone. Left it in the kitchen and came back for it just as I was going to bed.'

'How convenient.'

I let that comment pass.

'I'm really sorry, Ronnie. It was a moment of madness. It has never happened with anyone else, before you ask, and it won't happen again.'

He remains silent, so I continue. 'I'm sorry I hurt you. We'd been arguing a lot, and–'

Ronnie's chin juts upwards. 'What? So now it's my fault?'

'No, it's not your fault, but things hadn't been going so well with us, and I felt…I felt invisible.'

'Oh, here we go. Let's assess our feelings. Anything to get out of actually facing the fact that you, perfect Louisa, have screwed up.'

'Perfect Louisa? Are you out of your mind? When have I ever been perfect?' Now I'm getting pissed off. 'Ronnie, I'm so far from perfect, my life is so far from perfect, I don't even know where to start, but you and I haven't been communicating for a long time, so, yes, in the heat of the moment, I kissed someone, once, and no, I'm not proud of it, but not all of the blame lies with me.'

There, I'd said it. The ball was in his court now.

Silence reigns for a moment, then slowly and very softly Ronnie says, 'There's only one problem with that, Louisa. I know you're lying.'

I look at him, my eyes wide with shock, and I see that he does know. What he knows, exactly, I'm not sure, but he knows more than I've told him. How?

'You and I are done, Louisa. I can't be with someone who sits there and tells me a bare-faced lie, not when I caught you out in it.'

I wait to see if he'll elaborate. 'He texted you a few weeks ago, one night. You'd gone up to bed to settle Aria, left your phone downstairs. He mentioned how it was good to see you in Madrid. Madrid! Did you even go to Madrid for work? Have you been planning this all this time?'

It dawns on me now. The missing text message. Ronnie must have deleted it. 'Madrid? He was on my flight. His girlfriend was there. Dolores. She was lovely. We went for a drink. That was all. And I didn't mention seeing him in

Madrid, because, as you now know, I'd kissed him at my birthday weekend.'

'That's not all. The text was just the confirmation, the icing on the cake. I saw you at the wedding, the way you were with each other, I saw the way Travis cold-shouldered you the next day, but worst of all, Louisa, I saw you and Caden in the gardens. You thought I was sleeping, didn't you? Well, I wasn't. After you left the room and didn't come back, I came looking for you, and I saw you kissing Caden.'

I feel sick. Why didn't he say anything back then? Why didn't he intervene?

'I was about to punch his lights out, but then Travis came along with a couple of friends, and I ducked behind the hedge. I didn't want everyone knowing, or seeing my humiliation. Plus, I was drunk, so it probably wouldn't have been the best thing to do.'

'I'm glad you didn't, but only because that's not you, and I haven't been "shagging another man". I came out to the gardens that night because you told me you were going to Azerbaijan, and I was gutted. I couldn't believe we were so far apart, our communication had broken down so badly that you didn't think you even needed to discuss that with me before taking the job.'

'Yes, that was a mistake, and I felt guilty about that for a long time afterwards. It's one of the reasons I didn't challenge you and Caden there and then,' Ronnie admits. 'But I saw the way you were with him. And it wasn't just a peck. And it wasn't just once as you told me. And honestly, I think if you hadn't been interrupted, you would have had sex with him.'

Evidence of my guilt creeps up my neck like molten lava.

'See, you can't deny it.'

My voice is almost a whisper. 'No, Ronnie. I can't deny it,' I say softly. 'You're right. I was really upset, I was attracted to Caden and he was attracted to me. And I was happy to accept the comfort he was giving me, and respond in kind.'

His eyes flash with anger.

'But all I've ever wanted is that with you. That's why I've fought for you to get an onshore job again. I miss you, so much. Is it any wonder that occasionally, or in my case twice, I might have felt attracted to someone else?'

'And again, we come back to this being my fault. Louisa, I have never ever been unfaithful to you. Sure, I might indulge in a little banter at the bar occasionally when I'm out with the guys, but I have never laid a finger on another woman since the day we met.'

'Well, until Caden, I could say the same. And just so you know, it was only those two times.'

Ronnie scoffs. 'That's what you say. Earlier, it was "just once". Well, I didn't believe you then, and I don't believe you now. I'll leave you the car. I'm going to go stay in Aberdeen over the weekend. I'll get another room for tonight. I need some time to think about what we're going to do.' He looks pointedly at my stomach. 'And the baby's definitely mine?'

Now I'm riled. 'Ronnie, yes, I told you already. Yes, I screwed up, but I did not, I repeat, did not, screw Caden. Got it. So fine, take the moral high ground, bugger off to Aberdeen for the weekend. I'll drive back tomorrow. Happy anniversary.' I turn away from him and bury myself in the duvet and the pillow until I hear the door click.

After a few moments, I raise my head from the pillow. He's gone. He's really gone. What am I going to do now?

Chapter Twenty-nine

Friday 3 September

So, I do what I always do when I'm in a jam. I call Wendy.

'What a bloody mess. Are you going to be OK up there? Do you need me to come get you?'

'No, he left me the car.'

'Jo and I could come up, and one of us could drive it back, or Brandon could come.'

'No.' The last thing I need is my other brother-in-law finding out all the ins and outs of my marriage. I have a horrible feeling he'd be gloating.

'I can't believe he's just leaving you up there.'

Neither can I, especially when I'm pregnant and upset. Honestly, I don't trust me to drive, but maybe it'll be better tomorrow.

'Look, I'm going to call Jo. She can take the train to Inverness and come get you, and you can travel back together.'

'Who'll watch Jackson and Aurora?'

'Leave that to me. Right, try to get some sleep. We'll have a bit more perspective on things in the morning.'

'OK. I love you, Wendy,' I half sob.

'I love you too.'

Half an hour later, I'm nodding off, when I hear a noise at the door. Has Ronnie come back? I jump out of bed, open the door to see if he's there but not sure whether to knock or not, and I find Caden standing there. 'Caden! What are you doing here?'

'I came to check you were all right. Ronnie looked really angry. And I saw he'd checked into another room.'

'He was more than really angry. He knows. He saw us at the wedding.'

Caden's jaw drops. 'But how?'

I wave away his question. 'It's immaterial how, the important thing is, he did.'

'Oh, no. Oh, Louisa. I'm so sorry. But why didn't he…stop us?'

'He saw Travis and the others and realised we'd hear them, I guess.'

A couple walk towards us, eyeing us strangely, probably taking in my blotchy face.

'You'd better come in or we'll be the talk of the hotel.'

Silently, he follows me back inside.

'You can sit on the chair.' I sit on the edge of the bed, my legs dangling over the side.

'So, what now? Will he just need time to cool off?'

I look at Caden as if he has just landed in a UFO. 'Are you serious? Caden, Ronnie's left me. Left me! And our kids. And this one.' I point to my stomach then burst out into noisy sobs.

'Louisa, he'll calm down. He loves you, how could he not, and you have three children together, soon to be four. He's not going to throw that away.'

'Why not?' I mutter through my tears. 'People do it all the time.'

He doesn't seem to have a comeback to that.

'Do you want me to talk to him? We didn't sleep together, if that's what he's worried about.'

I lift my head. 'We may as well have done. We wanted to.'

Caden nods slowly. 'Yes, that's true, we did want to, and I must admit, if Travis hadn't appeared in the gardens at the wedding that night, I certainly wouldn't have had any qualms about taking it further.'

My eyes widen. 'And I know you wanted to, too, Louisa, but you're married to Ronnie, and what we did was wrong. I know it felt right, and in a different time, a different life, we could maybe have had a future, but I know your future is with Ronnie, and your four kids.' He tilts his head towards my stomach.

'You know that, and I know that, but Ronnie doesn't know that.'

'Ronnie doesn't know what?' Ronnie closes the door behind him. 'You have got to be kidding me. You! In my wife's bedroom. Well, the last time you may have got away with it, but not this time.' Ronnie lunges for Caden, but he's too quick, and he makes for the door but doesn't quite open it in time.

Ronnie slams him up against the door. 'You slept with my wife.' Slam. 'My wife!' Slam. 'You ruined my marriage.' Slam. 'And we have a baby on the way!' Slam. 'A baby I'm not even sure isn't yours!' Slam. 'You've ruined everything!'

The fight seems to go out of Ronnie then, and with one final slam of Caden against the door, he lets go of him, saying, 'You're not worth it!' Then he punches the wall, three times, and my heart feels like it has been sliced into a thousand pieces.

Caden looks at me and mouths, 'Will you be OK?'

I nod and indicate that he should leave.

He reaches the door, then turns and says to Ronnie, who is nursing his damaged hand. 'I'm so sorry, Ronnie, for all the damage I've done. But know this, that baby's yours. Never have any doubt over that. We never slept together.'

Then he gives me a tight smile, opens the door and is gone.

Friday 10 September

To-do list

Figure out what to do to make my husband come back

Buy tissues – man-sized, multiple boxes and packets – I've used them all up this week

Be kind to self – right now I'm not happy with who I am

Work on poker face with regards to what to tell the kids about Ronnie's absence

Pray

I haven't seen Ronnie since last Friday, and I wonder if he'll be home tonight. I haven't heard from him either, although I know he FaceTimed Gen and spoke to the other two. It's been a tough week since Jo drove up to collect me and drive my car back.

For a split second after Caden left the hotel room, I thought maybe Ronnie and I could patch it up there and then. But when he finally got himself together again, it became obvious that wasn't going to happen. He said he now believed we didn't sleep together, but also believed we wanted to, so it was almost as bad. I can't win. I have to agree with him though. If the roles were reversed, I would feel that way too. So, I know I only have myself to blame.

The kids, fortunately, are used to Ronnie being away, so they think he's just doing more training up in Aberdeen. Mum and Dad, however, have been asking questions, as they know what his new remit was, and that he was meant to be home a few days a week.

I'm sure Mum had also noticed the state of me. I seem to wander around with a tissue permanently tucked up my sleeve, my eyes streaming and puffy. I've claimed hay fever, but since I don't actually have hay fever, I don't know if this is the time of year when it's prevalent and so I'm not sure if anyone believes me, well, if Mum believes me. She can sniff out a lie at forty paces.

I'm prepping a lasagne for dinner, all three kids now back at school, and Mum has a book club lunch date, so I'm on my own, except for Patch and Bear. I don't know what I'd do without them. I may need them more than ever soon. Oh, and Baby. Baby seems, fortunately, unruffled by the events of the past week.

I've done virtually zero housework for a week and decide with the sun shining through the bay windows that I should spruce the place up a bit. A house like this needs to be cared for, and deserves it too.

I'm just dragging the hoover out from the cupboard in the hall when a shadow falls over the glass in the front door. Postman? I frown. Bit early. Then the sound of a key in the lock. Ronnie?

The door opens and I stand there, frozen in place, hoover in hand. All I'm missing is a fetching pair of Marigolds to top off this image of domestic bliss.

'Hi,' he says, unsmiling.

He's come for his things, hasn't he? My heart drops. No, no, no, it can't end like this. Not a word for a week and then he comes home, and finds me, not shagging anyone else, but hoovering. Surely that should go in my favour.

'Hi. I stand like the proverbial rabbit caught in the headlights, unsure which way to move. Put the hoover back in the cupboard? Drop the hoover and run into his arms and beg forgiveness? Play it cool and see what he says and does next.

I notice he has his bag with him. Is that good? Will I be happy for once to do his washing, or is the bag just to put more stuff in?

'How are the kids?' he asks.

'Good.' When he raises an eyebrow, I say, 'They're used to you being away.'

He murmurs an agreement, but he doesn't move from the entrance way. I'm tempted to hoover round him for one crazy moment, just to see if he'll move. I hate this statue that is my husband at the moment.

Although it's excruciating for me, I try not to speak next, instead waiting for him to make the first move. It almost kills me. I don't like silences, especially uncomfortable ones.

'Have you seen Caden?' he finally says, his eyes on me as he walks past me into the kitchen.

'No.'

He turns back and scrutinises me with those unfathomable chocolate eyes of his. 'Are you going to?'

'No,' I say emphatically.

I feel sick and a little dizzy. Not again. For God's sake,

give me a break, world. I have no idea if Ronnie is back to talk custody of the kids, how to divide up our assets, if he wants to go to counselling…no idea. He's not an easy man to read.

He studies me again then says, 'Do you love him?'

Poor Ronnie. I wish he wouldn't torture himself like this. 'No, Ronnie, I don't love him, and I didn't. I liked him, he was kind to me, funny, and we were attracted to each other. But I love you, I always have, since the first time I met you.'

His eyes don't waver, searching mine, perhaps trying to work out if I'm telling him everything.

'Do you love me?' I ask, afraid to ask, but needing to know.

He sighs a few times and then says, 'Yes, I do. We've had a lot of shit thrown at us, Louisa, and we've weathered those storms well, but this is different. This is fidelity. I thought we had the same moral compass.'

'We do, Ronnie. I honestly didn't plan for it to happen, either time we kissed. And it's not an excuse, but the second time I was low and lonely, and the first time I felt desired, something I hadn't felt with you in a while. And, OK, I'd had a few drinks, too. Not that that excuses it.'

'No, it doesn't.' He holds onto the top of a kitchen chair. He waits a few moments and then is about to say something, but I beat him by a millisecond. 'Where does this leave us?'

'Good question. I want what's best for our kids. All of them.' He glances down my body. 'And I don't think that's me being apart from them. How ironic would it be if I left an offshore job to spend more time with the whole family and then moved out?'

I nod, agreeing that would be sod's law. 'I want us all together too.'

'And I think you're going to need more support, with a new baby. And a new business. Plus, we still have to return to the house eventually.'

'Yep.'

'Louisa, I'm not saying I can forgive you, and I definitely can't forget. And I can't say I won't ever cast it up, because I might. What I'm saying is, if you promise me there will be no more secrets, no more "mistakes", then I'd like us to try again, initially for our family's sake, and in time, hopefully we can rebuild trust again.'

My heart doesn't quite soar, but the weight that's been sitting on it for the past week lifts considerably. I think in the circumstances, it's the best I could hope for. Ronnie isn't one for speeches, so I know it will have cost him a lot to make this one. He probably rehearsed it fifty times, and my heart aches that little bit more.

I move towards him and take his hands in mine. 'No more secrets, Ronnie. And I do want us to try again, you have no idea how much, and hopefully, one day you'll be able to trust me again as much as I trust you.'

He nods and brings my fingers up to his mouth and kisses them. 'Let's hope so.' Then he wraps his arms around me, and I reciprocate. We stand in that embrace for I don't know how long, but it feels right, and for the first time in a week I'm hopeful for the future.

We have a long road ahead of us, it's uncertain, but now at least I know we're prepared to travel it together.

Chapter Thirty

Friday 1 October

To-do list
Ensure have everything for the party tonight
Reply to all the Whatsapps regarding tonight's party
Double-check party to-do lists – food, drink, miscellaneous
Clean downstairs bathroom
Buy toilet duck x 3
Pick up cake from Icing on the Cake
Book aquanatal class for next week – check with Sam if need to book for her too

This time we go to the correct hospital first time, and not only because Ronnie checks the letter before we head off. I want there to be absolutely no error this time. I'm really excited. For some reason even more so than I was last time. I don't recall being more or less excited at my other scans with the other three kids, but today, maybe because I know this will definitely be my last twenty-week scan, I'm fizzing as if someone has just dropped a bath bomb into my bloodstream.

We arrive in plenty of time, but my heart sinks when I see the full waiting room, and I hope we're not in for a repeat performance of the previous scan, although I suppose that time the delay was my fault.

I'm carrying the prerequisite bottle of water, and I take little sips of it as we wait to see the sonographer. Doesn't seem like eight weeks since last time. That said, I do look a lot more pregnant. I'm noticeably showing now, and I've already had the old lady next door comment on my bump and how it will be a girl given my shape. Why do people always do that? And a woman in the shop the other day actually touched my bump, without asking me. I didn't know her. That's verging on physical abuse. I wanted to say 'Paws off!' but was so shocked, I couldn't even form the words.

It's been nice having Ronnie around the past few days. He was only in Aberdeen at the beginning of the week, as he settles into his new role. And with our housewarming party taking place tonight, and the whole family coming, there's a real sense of occasion in the air. We haven't all been together since, well, New Year when Sandra went into labour, and even then, Sam and Nicky and their offspring weren't there. Tonight will be special. It's a lovely big house, perfect for entertaining, and plenty of space, both inside and out where the kids can play. Plus, although technically we said goodbye to summer yesterday, we appear to be having something of an Indian summer. Who expected we could have seventeen degrees in Scotland in October?

It should be the perfect end to the perfect day. See baby on monitor, chill whilst kids are at school, prepare for party, collect kids, guests arrive.

'Louisa Halliday?'

The sonographer recognises me, and says, 'Did you

come here first this time?'

I grin, although that was a bit cheeky of her.

'Let's have a look at the baby. Pop up on the couch for me, please.'

Easier said than done. Popping anywhere apart from out of my trousers and jeans has become a no-no lately. Everything is an effort. I feel shattered all the time as if the baby is sapping my energy. I find myself drifting off early in the evening, even if someone is talking to me. Sometimes, especially if someone is talking to me, depending on who it is.

'Sorry, this will be a bit cold,' she says as she spreads the gel over my bump.

Yikes. It's freezing. I wonder if, just for kicks, sonographers put the gel in a special fridge before patients come in, and then they try to pass it off as room temperature. It certainly feels that way.

'There we go. Nice strong heartbeat.' She clicks her mouse a few times. 'There's the baby's head.' She draws her finger down the screen. 'Spine, legs, arms. Everything seems…'

I look at Ronnie. He shrugs, and we both look at the sonographer, but her head is bent over her keyboard, and she's studying her other monitor, which appears to have my medical notes on it. She glances between the screen and the ultrasound monitor again, then types something into her notes.

Thoughts of birth defects and dangers to the baby are swirling through my head. Hurry up. Why isn't she telling us anything?

'Sorry about that,' she finally says. 'Just an anomaly.'

'The baby's an anomaly?' I say, trying to keep my anger

in check. Hormones.

'No, your baby's not an anomaly, or rather the baby is, but not in a negative way. I can see there are no defects or any cause for concern.'

'Thank God,' I mumble.

We wait to see if she'll elaborate on what had her stumped.

She turns to us and says, 'Congratulations. It's twins!'

'Twins?' I squeak.

'Twins?' Ronnie looks like he's about to collapse.

'Yes, twins.' She beams at us both. 'Double trouble.'

She's not kidding. Wait a minute. So, we're going to have five children, not four? If it was six months earlier, I'd have thought it was April Fool's Day. Twins!

'But my sister's the one who has twins,' I blurt out.

'Well, now you do too.' She smiles at us. 'I know it's a lot to take in. Sometimes the smaller twin tucks itself in behind the bigger one in the twelve-week scan, and they can be so close to each other, that we can't see them, and it only becomes apparent on a later scan.'

Ronnie's eyes are wide in disbelief, and I get the impression mine resemble those of a startled rabbit.

'But, two babies…'

I can't work out if that's fear or awe in Ronnie's voice. All I can hear for sure is my heartbeat accelerating and the thud of 'two babies, two babies, two babies' going through my mind.

'But wouldn't they have had two heartbeats the last scan?' I'm clutching at straws here.

'Yes,' the sonographer goes on. 'Sometimes the babies' heartbeats are so in synch, it's hard to make out more than one. It's rare, but it happens.'

She then proceeds to show us both babies on the monitor. I sniff, and she passes me a tissue. Then I realise it's my eyes that are wet mainly. I'm crying, but I still haven't worked out if from happiness or terror. Two more children. I'm nearly forty. A geriatric mother, remember? Would a non-geriatric mother have taken this in their stride? Or would they too have been flabbergasted?

The sonographer talks away to us, assuring us the babies are healthy and that there is nothing to worry about, and tells me that I should make an appointment for the midwife again as pregnancies with twins are monitored more closely than with single babies.

'Did you want to know the sex of the babies?'

'No!' That comes out more emphatically than I meant it to, but I think I've had enough revelations for now. Plus, I've always enjoyed that surprise when the baby arrives. For tradition's sake, I think we'll keep it the same.

'You sure, Lou? Now there are two.'

'I'm sure, as long as you're OK with that.'

He holds up his hands. 'That's fine with me. Your prerogative. You get to carry our two babies.'

'OK, let me see if I can get some images where we're not revealing their gender.' A few minutes pass, then she says, 'There we go.' The sonographer prints off our scan pictures and hands them to us.

I hand one to Ronnie, and I look at mine. I trace the delicate curve of the back of the first baby, and the head of the other baby, who looks as if they're sucking their thumb.

And suddenly, with a clarity that's difficult to explain, the immense privilege this is hits me. Sure, it'll be scary, God, I have no idea how I'll cope, but will it be fun? Definitely.

A giggle bursts forth from my lips. 'Just think what the kids will say!'

Ronnie holds my hand as we walk back to the car. Now I know what people mean when they say they've had an out-of-body experience where they feel as if they're above events, looking down. We're having twins. Two babies. Two lots of nappies to change, two babies to feed. I look up at Ronnie. 'Just as well we didn't buy a buggy already, we're going to need a double.'

Ronnie squeezes my hand and says, 'We can do this, Lou. Think of everything else we've managed, everything else we've handled, all the crap that has been thrown at us. We can do this, you, me, the kids, and, well, the newcomers.'

Once we're seated in the car, Ronnie slides his hand across my stomach.

'Guys, or girls, this is your daddy speaking. We love you and we can't wait to meet you. Until then, be good for Mummy.' He leans over and kisses me full on the lips, and then it becomes a little more of a passionate snog, until two teenagers on BMXs go past shouting, 'Get a room, you pair!'

We laugh and head for home. Time to prepare for our housewarming party. We have all the more reason to celebrate now. What was it the sonographer said? Double trouble.

Everyone is finally here. It has almost killed me not telling anyone before now. And Jo was late, and my in-laws were stuck in traffic, so the passing time became unbearable as if someone was enjoying playing a trick on me. But now, all of our family, our extended family, is here for our housewarming. Mum, Dad, Jo, Travis, Wendy, Brandon, Ronnie, my monster-in-law Annabelle, Phillip. Rhys, Sandra and baby Isabella have travelled up from Dumfries. We haven't seen them since she was born. I can't believe it. She's so big already, and I try not to be annoyed that life has got in the way and robbed us of the possibility of seeing her grow up the first nine months. That'll need to change, especially with a cousin, sorry, two cousins, on the way for Isabella, of approximately the same age.

And our friends are here. The other people who matter to us most. Nicky and Valentin are talking to a heavily pregnant Sam, who is flanked by Emily and Ava as Erik, her husband, tells jokes and Xander shows the girls something on his phone.

Ronnie is circulating with drinks. Our eyes meet, and he winks. He knows I'm dying for us to make this announcement. I honestly may spontaneously combust if I need to keep it inside for a second longer.

Almost done, almost done. He passes a glass of fizz to Brandon, then Phillip, until finally he reaches his brother, Rhys. Then he comes towards me and puts his arm around me. I call our children by name then crook my finger, beckoning them over, where I encircle them in my arms and Ronnie follows suit.

Ronnie takes his glass and taps a teaspoon against it. Makes me feel as if I'm at a society wedding, not that I go to many, or any, of those. 'Ladies and gentlemen–' he begins.

'Where?' shouts Travis, and the adults laugh.

'And ne'er-do-wells.' Ronnie looks pointedly at Travis,

who raises his glass and says, 'Touché.'

'We have a bit of an announcement to make.' Ronnie makes eye contact with me, then everyone in the room, then me again, passing me the mantle.

I shake my head, and he raises his eyebrows, then turns to the assembled room and says, 'So, with no further ado, since my lady wife has delegated this to me, I am proud to say that next year we will welcome not one addition to the family, but two.'

A hush falls over the room. Eyes are out on stalks, jaws have dropped, a pin could be heard. Finally, Hugo says, 'So, we are getting a hamster. Yay!'

Happiness shines from Gen's eyes as she turns towards me, I nod, then she turns back to her brother. 'No, you dummy, Mum's having twins!'

'Twins! No way!' Hugo says. He stares at me then at my stomach as if he can't quite believe it. He's not the only one, and I've had all day to get used to the idea.

I hardly dare check out Aria's expression, but when I do, she is wearing a huge smile. She slides her hand onto my stomach and says, 'So, if you're boys, I think we should call you Henry and Ollie, and if you're girls, Rosie and Jess.'

'Hey,' Hugo says. 'Those are the names you chose for kittens.' He folds his arms and stares mutinously at his sister. 'We're not calling our brothers or sisters after cats.'

'Well, they're better than Mr Whiskers or Titan, or whatever other stupid name you were going to call the hamsters,' she says, then sticks out her tongue at him.

'Right,' I say. 'Just to be clear, Daddy and I will be choosing the babies' names.' That plural still feels weird. 'So, don't let's get into a fight about it, OK? We're here to celebrate tonight that next year, there will be two more members of our family.'

'That's right,' says Ronnie. 'And three more people in our lives.' He raises his glass in toast to Sam and Erik, just as Rhys butts in and says, 'Let's have a pic of you all together then, whilst there's still only five of you.'

We oblige, and for once I don't mind having my photo taken, not caring if my make-up has slid off my face, or my hair is in disarray. I revel in the moment, holding to me all that is precious: Ronnie, Gen, Hugo and Aria, as we pose together.

When Rhys pronounces he has the shots he needs, Brandon has the bright idea of putting an actual camera, imagine, on a tripod and setting the timer so we can all get in the shot, all...nope, I can't figure out how many of us there are. We all say cheese at the appropriate moment, and then we're done, having captured the moment for posterity.

It's only then that it truly dawns on me how much has changed, how much will change next year, and how very much I am looking forward to it. The Halliday family is growing, prospering, and I couldn't be happier if I tried.

Did you get your free short stories yet?

TWO UNPUBLISHED EXCLUSIVE SHORT STORIES.

Interacting with my readers is one of the most fun parts of being a writer. I'll be sending out a monthly newsletter with new release information, competitions, special offers and basically a bit about what I've been up to, writing and otherwise.

You can get the previously unseen short stories, **Mixed Messages** and **Time Is of the Essence**, FREE when you sign up to my mailing list at www.susanbuchananauthor.com.

Did you enjoy *Just One Day – Summer*?

I'd really appreciate if you could leave a review on Amazon or Goodreads. It doesn't need to be much, just a couple of lines. I love reading customer reviews. Seeing what readers think of my books spurs me on to write more. Sometimes I've even written more about characters or created a series because of reader comments. Plus, reviews are SO important to authors. They help raise the profile of the author and make it more likely that the book will be visible to more readers. Every author wants their book to be read by more people, and I am no exception!

Have you read them all?

Sign of the Times

Sagittarius – Travel writer Holly heads to Tuscany to research her next book, but when she meets Dario, she knows she's in trouble. Can she resist temptation? And what do her mixed feelings mean for her future with her fiancé?

Gemini – Player Lucy likes to keep things interesting and has no qualms about being unfaithful to her long-term boyfriend. A cardiology conference to Switzerland changes Lucy, perhaps forever. Has she met her match, and is this feeling love?

Holly is the one who links the twelve signs. Are you ready to meet them all?

A tale of love, family, friendship and the lengths we go to in pursuit of our dreams.

The Dating Game

Work, work, work. That's all recruitment consultant Gill does. Her friends fix her up with numerous blind dates, none suitable, until one day Gill decides enough is enough.

Seeing an ad on a bus billboard for Happy Ever After dating agency 'for the busy professional', on impulse, she signs up. Soon she has problems juggling her social life as well as her work diary.

Before long, she's experiencing laughs, lust and … could it be love? But just when things are looking up for Gill, an unexpected reunion forces her to make an impossible choice.

Will she get her happy ever after, or is she destined to be married to her job forever?

The Christmas Spirit

Natalie Hope takes over the reins of the Sugar and Spice bakery and café with the intention of injecting some Christmas spirit. Something her regulars badly need.

Newly dumped Rebecca is stuck in a job with no prospects, has lost her home and is struggling to see a way forward.

Pensioner Stanley is dreading his first Christmas alone without his beloved wife, who passed away earlier this year. How will he ever feel whole again?

Graduate Jacob is still out of work despite making hundreds of applications. Will he be forced to go against his instincts and ask his unsympathetic parents for help?

Spiky workaholic Meredith hates the jollity of family gatherings and would rather stay home with a box set and a posh ready meal. Will she finally realise what's important in life?

Natalie sprinkles a little magic to try to spread some festive cheer and restore Christmas spirit, but will she succeed?

Return of the Christmas Spirit

Christmas is just around the corner when the enigmatic Star begins working at Butterburn library, but not everyone is embracing the spirit of the season.

Arianna is anxious about her mock exams. With her father living abroad and her mother working three jobs to keep them afloat, she doesn't have much support at home.

The bank is threatening to repossess Evan's house, and he has no idea how he will get through Christmas with two children who are used to getting everything they want.

After 23 years of marriage, Patricia's husband

announces he's moving out of the family home, and moving in with his secretary. Patricia puts a brave face on things, but inside, she's devastated and lost.

Stressed-out Daniel is doing the work of three people in his sales job, plus looking after his kids and his sick wife. Pulled in too many different directions, he hasn't even had a chance to think about Christmas.

Can Star, the library's Good Samaritan, help set them on the path to happiness this Christmas?

Just One Day – Winter

Thirty-eight-year-old Louisa has a loving husband, three wonderful kids, a faithful dog, a supportive family and a gorgeous house near Glasgow. What more could she want?

TIME.

Louisa would like, just once, to get to the end of her never-ending to-do list. With her husband Ronnie working offshore, she is demented trying to cope with everything on her own: the after-school clubs, the homework, the appointments … the constant disasters. And if he dismisses her workload one more time, she may well throttle him.

Juggling running her own wedding stationery business with family life is taking its toll, and the only reason Louisa is still sane is because of her best friends and her sisters.

Fed up with only talking to Ronnie about household bills and incompetent tradesmen, when a handsome stranger pays her some attention on her birthday weekend away, she is flattered, but will she give in to temptation? And will she ever get to the end of her to-do list?

Just One Day – Spring

Mum-of-three Louisa thought she only had her never-ending to-do list to worry about, but the arrival of a ghost from the recent past puts her in an untenable position. Can she navigate the difficult situation she's in without their friendship becoming common knowledge or will it cause long-term damage to her marriage?

When a family member begins to suspect there's more to her relationship with the new sous-chef than meets the eye, Louisa needs to think on her feet or she'll dig herself into a deeper hole. But the cost of keeping her secret, not only from her husband, comes at a high price, one which tugs at her conscience.

With everyday niggles already causing a further rift between Louisa and husband Ronnie, will she manage to keep her family on track whilst her life spirals out of control? And when tragedy strikes, will Ronnie step up when she needs him most?

Printed in Great Britain
by Amazon

83779233R00189